Crossed Fingers

MARIANNE GUTTERIDGE

ELTON-WOLF PUBLISHING

Seattle • Los Angeles

Cover design: David Marty
Text design: Paulette Eickman

01 02 03 04 05 1 2 3 4 5

ISBN: 1-58619-026-1
Library of Congress Catalog Card Number: 2001086249

First Printing March 2001
Printed in Canada

Published by Elton-Wolf Publishing
Seattle, Washington

2505 Second Avenue Suite 515 Seattle Washington 98121 (206) 748-0345
e-mail: info@elton-wolf.com Internet: http://www.elton-wolf.com
Seattle • Los Angeles

To Gordon, My Husband

Acknowledgments

My thanks to Florence Ekstrand of Seattle and Howard Carlen of Dassel, Minnesota for their help in recreating the era in which this book takes place.

Chapter One

Anna Swenson shivered as she stood on the station platform with her Uncle Lars. It was Monday, January 1, 1923, in Fort Dodge, Iowa. She would soon be on her way back to the rural community of Grabney, where she was engaged in her first year of teaching. The wind howled around the corner of the building and hurled stinging snow on the few people who waited for the train, which was now screeching as it slowed down. With a crashing jolt it stopped, and a porter opened one of the doors and let down the steps.

The station platform that at one time had been cleared was encrusted in ice. Uncle Lars grabbed Anna's arm as they made their way to the coach. "Be careful you don't fall, Anna," he warned. "Here! Keep hold of my arm."

"I will. Yes, it's terribly slippery. Oh I'm so glad you could take me to the station."

"Well, it's certainly no weather for your mother and Elsa to be out in," he replied. "Besides they got the New Year's dinner, and I'm sure they'll have plenty of work to do cleaning up. And they still have enough to talk about with your Aunt Hazel. The boys probably left soon after we did; some movie on that they wanted to see. You get inside that train, now," he intoned in fatherly fashion. "This weather isn't fit for man nor beast."

She carefully reached for the handrail and stepped up the first two steps. "Good-bye, Uncle Lars," she said as she grabbed her valise that he hoisted up to her. He held out his hand, and she shook it warmly. "Thank you again for taking me to the station."

"Not at all. It was my pleasure. And give my regards to the folks in Grabney. And I think they've got a first class teacher," he said as he winked at her.

She smiled with surprise at this last remark. Dear Uncle Lars, her father's brother. It was through him that she had obtained her teaching position. There was no more time for conversation, so she followed the other passengers into the coach. It was only half full, and she took a seat on the station side. Looking out the window, she saw her uncle watching for her. She hardly had time to acknowledge his wave when the car suddenly jerked, and then it was moving. He slowly disappeared into the blur of snow, and she was left to make herself comfortable for the next two and a half hours.

She took off her bearskin coat and put it on the seat next to her. Of course it wasn't real bearskin, but it was a curly brown fur, and everyone called them bearskin coats. Her mother had insisted that she buy it to keep warm while walking to school in the winter. It reached nearly to her ankles. She stroked the soft fur, grateful that she had taken her mother's advice.

Anna wished her father were alive to see her now. He would have been so proud of her. She thought of her mother and sister Elsa, living above Uncle Lars' dry goods store, and how hard they worked tending the store and sewing dresses for the customers. Anna had done this also, continuing for two years after her high school graduation until they had saved enough money to send her to normal school in Cedar Falls. And now Elsa, two years younger than Anna, wanted to be a nurse. She was almost nineteen. Since her high school graduation, she had stayed home to help their mother by sewing and working in the store, but with Anna sending home money, she could probably begin training next fall at the Mercy Hospital. As it was in Fort Dodge, she still would be near their mother. So many things had changed.

What a wonderful Christmas they had had. She never thought that it would be fun to see Uncle Lars' boys, Arthur and Raymond. Art was sixteen and quite a show-off, with Ray, twelve, trying hard to keep up with him. They seemed to have the latest in everything, while she always felt the poor relation. Uncle Lars provided her family with their living quarters in exchange for the time they spent helping in the store. He had a lovely home, where they had Christmas dinner with the usual exchange of presents. Now that Anna was working and had money of her own at last, she could buy gifts instead of trying to make them. It was a wonderful feeling.

Crossed Fingers

She glanced out of the window at the white landscape, and as she saw an occasional farmhouse it reminded her of Grabney. How fortunate she was to be able to live with the Jensen family. Peter and Milly were so kind, and she loved their three children: Davey, a six-year-old first grader; Sarah, who was four; and the baby Lucy, just one year old.

And then there were the Parkers. Inger Parker was Milly's sister and the one who brought Milly over from Sweden, but they were definitely opposites. Inger, so pragmatic with hardly a trace of a Swedish accent, but Milly, well you would never mistake her for anyone but a Swede. Floyd, Inger's husband, he was something else, but Inger was the one to tone him down. Their three children were Walter, sixteen and working on the farm; Mabel, fourteen and in the eighth grade; and George, going on twelve. George, a sixth grader, was the brightest of the lot. Anna hoped that he could attend college, and she felt that he would if Inger had her way.

Her next thoughts went to the house across the road from the Jensens. Grace Kloster, who left so suddenly with her two children Joshua and Elaine after she buried her husband and father. Anna thought that some day she would like to visit them in the county seat where they lived with Grace's aunt. She supposed their house was empty, even though Jonah Larson was planning to make arrangements to buy the place and any livestock that was left. He was attending Ames Agricultural School and should graduate this spring. His parents owned the next farm.

"Tickets, please! Tickets, please!" came the call from the conductor as he entered the car.

Anna gave a slight jump at the sound, remembering the grouchy conductor who had made her feel so embarrassed last fall when she asked if they would stop at Grabney. She reached in her purse and pulled out her ticket. When he came up to her she handed it to him with apprehension, but felt relieved as she realized it was not the same man. "Be in Grabney just about on time, if this snow lets up a little," he stated, and he was off to the next passenger. With a sigh she put the stub back into her pocketbook. At least she now knew that he would have them stop in Grabney, which was not a regular stop on all runs.

She glanced out of the window. The screech of brakes let her know that they were coming to a small town. The wind seemed to have died down a little, and now it was snowing only slightly. A couple who had gotten on at Fort Dodge was getting off. They were greeted warmly by a man who was bundled up to his ears. As the train chugged away from the station, she could see them laughing. Perhaps they had been to the city to celebrate the new year and were home again. They seemed so happy, and she was happy for them. Holidays were a wonderful time.

She thought about reading one of the books she had brought along, but she discarded that idea as she settled back in the seat to continue looking out of the window. A few farmhouses were visible, with a light shining out of a window here and there. How different the landscape was from when she arrived last August and the fields were green with corn. Now snow was everywhere. She stood to see the river out of the window opposite her and saw that it was partly frozen over. Perhaps before too long Peter could get blocks of ice for the icehouse.

Settling back again in her seat, she thought about what she would do the next day in school, then mentally made plans for the entire week. She had been gone about nine days, and so much had happened during that time. She wanted to hear about what each of the students had done, and she had plenty to tell them.

Another short stop and the train was on its way again. She continued to pass the time in a dreamy fashion when suddenly the sharp whistle of the train jolted her. "Grabney!" called the conductor as he hurried through the aisle. Anna quickly reached for her coat and put it on, since she could see the station. Yes, she could see people on the platform. Matt the stationmaster was hurrying out of the depot, looking around, checking to see if he were needed. A young couple stood shivering waiting to get on the train. And then she saw Peter, and oh yes, beside him, Davey and Sarah. As the train screeched to a halt, she grabbed the back of the seat so she wouldn't fall. Then she took her valise and made for the door.

Peter was at the bottom of the steps as she disembarked and took her luggage. "Good to see you, Anna," he said with a welcoming smile, giving her a hand to assist her down the steps.

"Thank you, Peter. It's so good to be back. Oh hello, Bertha," she greeted a young woman getting on the train. Bertha responded in like fashion. Turning to the children Anna said, "And look who else came to meet me."

"Oh Miss Swenson," said an excited Davey. "We already got the icebox for Christmas, so we don't have to use the money you pay Mother to buy one. Wait'll you see it. It's white and just fits on the back porch."

"Now son, just calm down," laughed a bemused Peter as he gave Davey a pat on the shoulder. "Well Anna, I guess you've heard all the big news from him."

"That's wonderful Davey," she replied. "I can hardly wait to see it."

"But we don't have any ice for it now," said Sarah solemnly. "But it's already cold on the porch so we can keep our milk in it, and other things too."

"Come on now," said her father. "Let's not stand here all night. Hurry up! It's freezing! Let's get home, where we can have some supper. Your mother will think we got lost." He led the way to the side of the station, where Ginger and the sleigh were waiting. "Here! Let me help you up, Anna," and he gave her a hand, then lifted Sarah and Davey who sat one on each side of her. He quickly jumped in on the other side. "Put the blanket over your knees and tuck it in around you. Come on, Davey. You're on the outside, so tuck it in good so we won't all get cold."

"Hello, Peter. Hello, Anna. Happy New Year," greeted Ed Marson as he walked by their sleigh on his way to the family store across the street.

"I see you had company over the holiday," said Peter. "Suppose Bertha's going back to the county seat to work tomorrow."

"Yeah. I wish she could've stayed longer. If it weren't for this snow, she wouldn't've had to leave so soon. I could've taken her back in the car. But I'm glad the trains are gettin' through. Anyway, Happy New Year! Guess I better get goin'," and with a wave he walked quickly home.

"I'm sure Vi and Elmer are happy," said Anna.

"You can bet your bottom dollar they are," replied Peter. "To think that their boy Ed has a girl as nice as Bertha is just about as much as they could ask for." After that remark he sang out, "Giddap, Ginger!" and they were off across the bridge.

As they passed the church, Davey suddenly cried out, "And you know what, Miss Swenson? Reverend Blakeley gave everyone a candy cane for Christmas."

"And I'm going to save mine," said Sarah. "It's wrapped up, and I have it in my drawer in my bedroom."

"When are you going to eat it?" asked Anna.

"Maybe sometime, but Davey ate his, so he doesn't have one any more, and I do."

"Did Lucy eat hers?" asked Anna.

"I don't know," the little girl replied. "Daddy, did Lucy eat her candy cane?"

"Well now, I just don't know. Maybe it got shared with the grownups," and he laughed as they turned up the next road. "Did you have a nice Christmas, Anna? We were all thinking about you."

"Yes. It was good to see my family again, but I missed everyone here."

"Did Santa Claus come to your house?" asked Davey.

"I'll bet he did," answered their father, "because I see she is wearing a nice bearskin coat that probably came from the North Pole."

"Ohhhh," exclaimed both children as they touched the fur with their mittened hands.

"And now we're turning down our road, so we're almost home," Davey announced.

"I see Grace's house is dark," Anna said. "Is Jonah still planning to buy the place?"

"Yes I think they're going to work out all the details this coming week," Peter answered. "You know that Jonah's dad Olle owns his place free and clear. He got it from his folks who homesteaded. I think he's planning to do the buying at this point. Jonah doesn't have any money, anyway, and Olle's had his eye on that land for some time. He can just about manage the increased acreage with both William and Jonah at home, but he'll probably have to keep a fair amount in grass. He and Floyd'll be the big landowners around here. I can hardly manage with half a section, and they'll have twice as much."

"A square mile is a lot of land," Anna commented thoughtfully. "But you do fine with what you have."

"Half a square mile is enough for me," he added, "and really too much for one person to handle. I'll be glad when Davey gets a little older so he can help out. Anyway, to get back to the Larsons, Grace wants to sell it on contract so she has a monthly income, and that suits Olle just fine. That way he won't have to borrow from the bank. Land has gotten pretty expensive around here. I was lucky to get mine when it was a little cheaper before the war."

"Isn't Jonah planning to continue with his schooling?" Anna asked. "I remember that he was taking some courses with the Iowa Agricultural School in Ames."

"Oh yes, he's determined to finish his courses, and that's where the rub comes in. His dad thinks that it's not necessary to go to college."

"It sounds like Floyd and Walter," she replied.

"Plenty of farmers are like that. They've made it on their own and think the young ones can do the same. Now I won't say that Floyd isn't one of the best farmers around here, and you can't beat him for getting good prices at the market, but still so much research is going on, I'm sure there are some new ideas we could use. Anyway, Jonah's mother Sylvia thinks he should continue his schooling, so I think that there's a chance he will."

"It sounds as if Olle Larson may keep Grace's farm for himself and not let Jonah buy it," Anna commented.

"Well, that's what concerns me, but they'll have to work that out for themselves. All right, Ginger! Into the yard you go!" They turned into the farmyard, and Peter pulled up next to the house. "Here, I'll help you folks out and then put this rig in the barn and get Ginger rubbed down." He quickly alighted from the sleigh, helping each one on to solid ground before leaving for the barn.

"Miss Swenson, we're going to have a big supper for you, and Uncle Floyd and Aunt Inger an' Walter an' George an' Mabel are coming too."

"My goodness! That sounds like a real celebration. I thought you would have your New Year's dinner at noon," Anna commented.

"Not today, 'cause Aunt Inger was busy, and they couldn't come at noon," Sarah added.

Quickly the door was opened, and Milly's rosy cheeks and welcoming smile were seen in the doorway. "Oh, Anna! Yust look at you! Oh, to have you back again. Come in! Come in! Oh, it's so cold out here."

In the entryway Anna paused to look at the new icebox. "Oh, Milly! I see that Santa Claus was good to you. It looks wonderful!"

"Oh yes, and we keep things in it now, yust the same as when we get ice. It's so cold on the porch. The porch is yust like an ice-box," and she laughed as she ushered them into the warm kitchen.

"What's this?" asked Anna as she saw the table was set for a big dinner. "Davey said you were having your dinner at this time of day. I thought you would have it at noon."

"Oh, didn't Peter tell you?" asked Milly as she shook her head.

"Tell me what?" Anna asked with alarm.

"Oh it's terrible. Yust let me sit down," said Milly as she eased herself into a chair. "Sarah, you take care of Lucy. Take her upstairs to play."

Anna was so concerned that she forgot to take off her coat. She stood there holding her valise, waiting for Milly's explanation, fearing the worst but hoping for the best.

"Well you see, it's old lady Wheeler."

At that Anna sighed with relief. She feared it was one of Inger's family.

"Last night she went out to use the outhouse, and finally Charley and Bill realized that she hadn't come back. They didn't know how long she had been gone, but when they found her she was lying in the snow. She had a terrible gash on her head, and she was, oh yes, what is that word?"

"You mean unconscious," added Anna.

"Yes, that's it. And they don't know what happened to her, but Inger has been there all day helping. Oh, I hear Floyd's team coming in now. Yust you wait, Anna. Floyd will tell you all about it."

Chapter Two

Anna quickly took off her coat and hat. She was headed toward the entryway door when Milly jumped up. "Here, let me show you your new coat hook. With the icebox I had to change everything around, but there's plenty of room." With her usual efficiency she showed Anna the new location of the hooks.

"Thanks, Milly," Anna replied while she hung up her things. "I think it all fits in perfectly." As they went back into the kitchen she continued, "I'm going to take my valise upstairs to my room and tidy up a bit before everyone comes in. I can hear the Parkers coming, so I'll hurry so I can get back in time to hear what Floyd has to say about Mrs. Wheeler."

"You go right ahead. Don't rush. Floyd will want to get his horses in the barn."

Anna walked around the dining table to the stairs that led up from the corner of the kitchen. At the top of the steps she opened the door to her room. Yes, it was her room, just the same as she left it a little over a week ago. The pink-rose-flowered wallpaper, the birdseye maple dresser, and the brass bed with the double wedding ring quilt. Davey and Sarah had rooms on the west side of the house, and she could hear Sarah telling Lucy all about going to the station in the sleigh. She put her valise down next to her trunk and felt the warm air coming through the floor register from the kitchen. How thoughtful it was of Milly to remember to open it up. Looking in the mirror she realized she looked fine, and hearing the others coming in from the outside she turned and went down the steps. The first voice she heard, naturally, was Floyd's, but he wasn't talking about Mrs. Wheeler.

"I tell you, with that newfangled contrapshun there just ain't enough room for a body to move in your entryway. Had a heck of a time findin' a place fer my coat."

Milly's laughter rang out as she answered him. "There are plenty of hooks; you yust have to look. In fact I even put up two more. And in the summer you will be very happy to drink cold sweet milk, or iced lemonade, not lukewarm."

"That's what you say. And now Mother wants one. Where we're gonna put it I don't know."

"You know good and well where it's going," Inger retorted. "It'll go in the entryway opposite the summer kitchen." Inger was one of the fortunate women who had a screened room built on the back of the house so that in the summer her cookstove could be moved out there. Now that Floyd was getting tired of moving the heavy stove each summer, she knew that before too long she would have a second stove permanently situated in the summer kitchen.

By this time the Parker family had all entered the kitchen, and they were finding places at the table. Walter and George sat at the back against the wall, with Mabel at the end next to them where she could jump up to help when needed. Davey and Peter were the last to come in, with Peter lugging a pail of water. There were always two pails in the kitchen, one on the stove to heat and the other by the sink for drinking and cooking.

"Sarah and Lucy! Come down to supper!" Milly called from the bottom of the steps. "And bring your coat and hat, Sarah. You forgot to hang them up. Davey, did you wash your hands? Now Floyd, we want to hear what happened to Mrs. Wheeler, so sit down everyone and listen." Sarah came down the stairs, nearly dragging one-year-old Lucy. Chairs scraped against the floor as each person pulled up to the table. Milly lifted Lucy into her high chair. "Now Floyd, I think we are ready. Tell us what happened."

"Well, Mother here knows pretty much the same as I do."

"But you were there before me," answered Inger as she walked over to help Milly bring the food to the table. "You tell them what happened last night."

"Well, I'll start talkin' if you 'n Milly'll hurry up with the food. Had hardly a bite to eat all day, what with Mother dashin' back 'n forth across the road over to the Wheelers. What with this bein' New Year's Day an' all, it just ain't hardly fair." There was a general groan from the others, as they knew that Floyd would never let himself go hungry.

"Get on with it, Floyd," Peter called out.

"Well, lemme see. Say, them spuds sure look good, Milly, an' that ham. I smelled it when we was drivin' up. I s'pose we can't put on the feed bag until someone says grace."

Peter quickly obliged, as by this time Inger and Milly were seated. Food was passed around as Floyd began.

"Well, you see, it was like this. About eleven o'clock last night the phone rang. Well, I knowed it was too early for someone to wish me a happy new year, and anyways, who would? So I answers the phone, and it was Charley. He was all excited. I couldn't make head nor tail of what he was sayin', so I puts on my clothes. Mother 'n me was already in bed. An' I get the lantern an' trot over to his place, well, I wouldn't 'xactly say 'trot,' 'cause it was mighty slippery.

"When I got there, I could see that the snow in the back yard was all messed up, like someone had had a fight or somethin', an' there's Charley at the door lookin' pretty awful. 'What's up, Charley?' I says, an' he just mumbles somethin', an' so I follows him in the house. We go through the kitchen into the bedroom, an' I see the ol' lady lyin' on her bed, lookin' for all the world like she's dead. So I call Mother to come over right away, an' in the meantime I heerd what happened. Justa minute, I want a couple bites a supper."

"Inger, did you go over then?" asked Milly. "In the snow? In the dark?"

"Yes, but it was a while before I got over. Go on, Floyd, tell them what happened."

"Well, you folks is hardly givin' me a chance ta eat. Anyways, it seems that the ol' lady wanted to use the outhouse. Charley 'n Bill tried to get her to use the chamber pot, but she's a stubborn ol' biddy, an' once she makes up her mind there ain't no one stoppin' her."

"You mean she went outside in this weather at night?" asked Anna. "Isn't she about eighty years old?"

"Prob'ly, or a little older'n that," answered Floyd. "Anyways, they let her go 'cause there wasn't nothin' they could do to stop her, an' then they fergot about her an' went to bed. Charley says he was jus' ready to get into bed hisself when he sees the lamp in the kitchen still lit an' thought that was mighty pecul'ar. He doesn't see nobody in the kitchen so he goes in to ask his mother why she didn't blow out the lamp, an' he finds that she ain't in bed. Then he remembers that the last he knew was when he was talkin' to her just before she went out to the outhouse. Now he gets really scared. He gets Bill up an' they go to the back door, but they don't see nothin' at first. Then they thought maybe she was still in the privy, so they start to walk out there an' on the way they find her lyin' in the snow."

"By gosh, she could have frozen," Peter interrupted.

"By gum, she nearly did. Anyways they had a terrible time gettin' her up. That's why the snow was so messed up. An' they carried her into the house an' then they called us. She was white as a sheet an' cold as ice. Looked deader'n a doornail. Well, I knew this was no job for me, so I calls Mother an' she come in an' took over, an' me 'n the boys was mighty glad."

Inger continued the story. "I took one look at her and thought she was dead, too, but I could see she was breathing. She had a bad gash on her head, and bleeding, so I tell Bill to get me some water and some cloths so I can take care of that. Then I get the boys and Floyd to start rubbin' her down on her arms an' legs to bring back the circulation, an' to get a good fire goin' so the place can get warm. We got plenty of blankets, too, and a hot water bottle. Well, after awhile, and I don't know how long it was, but plenty long, she started to groan, and that was a welcome sound."

"But what happened to her?" asked Milly. "Why was she lying in the snow?"

"We don't really know the answer to that one," Inger answered. "At first I thought she had had a stroke. But she could have slipped and fallen and hit her head. There was plenty of ice out there where she fell."

"Did someone call the doctor?" asked Anna.

"Well we couldn't phone him that late at night, or rather it was early in the morning," Inger replied. "So after it looked as if she was warmed up an' that she was going to live, Floyd and I go on home. But I gave the boys, if you can call men in their forties 'boys', a good talking to and told them to stay with her all night, and I would be back in the morning."

"An' then Mother'n I went home to get a little shut eye. An' I guess you know the rest. Mother called Doc Bailey, an' he's comin' out tomorrow. Mother was there most of the day."

"How is she now?" asked Milly. "Is she, well you know, a...a...conscious?"

"She seems to be coming out of it a little. She's sort of trying to talk, but what she says doesn't make much sense. Anyway, the doctor can tell us more tomorrow."

"It sounds like she won't be out of bed for some time," said Anna. "And who's going to take care of her?"

"Well it ain't gonna be Mother," Floyd replied, shaking his head. "Them boys can jus' learn to manage on their own."

"And it won't be Mabel," Inger chimed in. "Mabel has school tomorrow."

"I yust can't see Charley or Bill being a nursemaid and taking care of anyone!" laughed Milly as she thought of those two middle-aged farmers.

"They're good at takin' care of newborn pigs and calves," added Walter. "They're real good at that. They're gentle as can be. I've watched 'em."

"Well, you're right there, Walter," said his father. "But takin' care of a sick person is real different. An' I don't think the ol' lady would let 'em take care of her anyway. What do you think, Inger?"

"I think they're going to have to hire a girl to come in, but I don't know who that would be. It depends on what the doc thinks. When I left there it looked as if she would be laid up for some time. And remember, she's probably over eighty years old."

"Is there someone around here that they could get?" asked Anna. "Has she ever had anyone in to help her?"

"Huh!" exclaimed Floyd, with a sound of exasperation in his voice. "She ain't never had no one to help out at all, 'cept maybe Jimmy Burns. An' that's only with the farm work when they're in a pinch. She likes Jimmy, an' he's jus' a kid an' they can get by without payin' him much, but I've never seen anyone else aroun' there workin'."

"And don't forget," added Peter. "She's about the most parsimonious person around here."

"What does that mean, Dad?" asked Davey.

"It's a nice word for stingy," he answered with a twinkle in his eye. "That means she doesn't spend any money she doesn't have to."

"I'll bet they'll never have an icebox like ours," Davey continued. "Is that why you don't have an icebox, Uncle Floyd?"

As Milly uttered a hush to Davey, Inger burst out laughing. "You've got a point there. all right."

"Don't you worry, Davey, I know that Aunt Inger will get her icebox," Milly said as she glanced at Floyd.

"Well now, I thought we was a talkin' about them Wheeler boys," Floyd put in. "Beats the heck out of me how we got from them to iceboxes."

"I think the real problem might be that with Mrs. Wheeler laid up, Charley and Bill will have a hard time running the farm," Peter said thoughtfully. "You know she bosses the heck out of them, practically runs the place herself, tells them when to do this and that. Not that there's a lot of work to do in the winter, and they can take care of the everyday chores easy enough, but if she's sick for a long time…."

"I think it's not that they can't do it, it's just that they are so used to her being the boss," Inger added. "What's more, they're both a little scared of her. She's a mighty domineering woman when she's not sick, and being sick is not going to make life any easier for any of them."

"Well, I say let's fergit this whole problem fer now," Floyd said as he cleaned up his plate. "An' what about them pies, Milly? I don't want them to go to waste."

"And we can't decide anything sitting here, anyway," Inger replied. "So let's just wait until Doc Bailey comes tomorrow and see what he says. That way we'll know for sure what the next step will be."

Chapter Three

Anna awoke sleepily. The air in the bedroom was cold, and she longed to crawl deeper into the covers. For an instant she almost forgot where she was. The clang of a stove lid suddenly brought her to reality. No, she was not in her home in Fort Dodge. She was in her bedroom at the Jensens', and Milly was up and making breakfast.

She threw off the blankets and leaped out of bed, shuddering as her feet hit the ice-cold floor. Quickly she stepped on the small rug by the bedside. It was not much warmer. Seeing the floor register from the kitchen open, she walked over to it and stood on the metal grate. The warm air coming from the kitchen stove swirled around her legs and puffed out her nightgown. What a luxury.

She glanced to look out of the window, but it was frosted over from the cold. She heard Milly putting more coal into the stove and knew that she must get going, but she still felt sleepy. There was only one thing to do. She walked to the dresser, took the pitcher and poured some water into the wash basin. With her hands she splashed the ice-cold water on her face. It was a quick way to wake up.

She dressed hurriedly and combed her hair. Before leaving the room she closed the register. No need to waste the heat during the day. As she left she heard Davey getting ready for school. Sarah was probably still asleep.

"Good morning, Anna," said Milly cheerily as Anna came down the steps into the kitchen. "I hope you had a good sleep."

"Yes, I did. It was nice to get back in my room here again," she replied. "Oh Milly, how long have you been up? I see you've even set the table."

"Oh yes, I did that while the porridge was cooking. I have

your lunch pails all ready too. Here, pour yourself a cup of coffee. Peter will be in soon, and we can have breakfast. Did you hear if Davey is up?"

"Yes," said Anna as she reached for the coffeepot and poured herself a cup. "I think he was probably getting dressed." She carefully sipped the hot beverage. "Sarah may still be asleep, though."

"Yust as well," Milly replied. "It's so cold this morning. What time did you want to leave for school?"

"I thought about eight o'clock." Anna glanced at her watch. "It's 7:30 now. Oh, good morning, Davey. I see you're all dressed and ready for school."

"I'm still a little sleepy," he answered. "When we didn't have school we didn't have to get up so early. And it's dark outside. I thought in the new year it would get lighter."

"You'll have to wait awhile for that, I'm afraid," said his mother.

Anna heard Peter coming up the basement stairs, where he had been separating the milk. She jumped up to open the door for him. "What is it we have to wait for?" he asked. "I hope we don't have to wait for breakfast. I'm starving."

"No, no of course not," answered Milly. "Here, give me the cream. We'll use the fresh cream this morning for our cereal. It's warmer than the cream from yesterday."

"Now that we've got the icebox, the stuff in there is too cold!" laughed Peter. "At least I don't have to put ice in it yet."

"When do you plan to get the ice?" asked Anna.

"Well, it just depends," he replied. "I'll have to wait to be sure it's thick enough, and then hope the snow lasts so I can haul it up here. Lucky we live next to the river. Anyway, it looks pretty good now. Floyd and I were thinking of perhaps this next week."

"Can I help you, Dad?" Davey asked.

"No time to think of that now," admonished his mother. "Hurry and eat your porridge. It's almost time to leave for school."

"I've eaten it all gone!" he said with exuberance.

"You've no such thing," said Milly as she turned from the stove and looked at his bowl that was only half empty.

"Ha! Ha! I crossed my fingers," Davey yelled out gleefully, as he raised his right hand to show that indeed his fingers were crossed.

Crossed Fingers

"Not that again," Milly sighed as she sat at the table. "Oh, Anna! This has been going on for the past week. I am so sick and tired of all this nonsense. I wish I knew who started it."

"Carl Anderson told us," Davey replied with a grin. "He said that if you crossed your fingers you could say anything that was not true and it was all right. Do you know about that game, Miss Swenson?"

"Oh yes, I do," she answered. She continued eating her oatmeal porridge which was covered with the thick fresh cream and thought of eight-year-old Carl Anderson, the only student in the school who could be a troublemaker.

Sensing that this could cause a disruption in the school, Peter spoke up. "Davey, let's have no more of that, and remember you are never to cross your fingers in school. I think we've had enough of this for one week, anyway."

"You are right!" added Milly firmly.

"If Carl Anderson starts this game, I know how I can stop it," Anna said. "After all, if the students think that they can do it, I can do it, too." At this remark, Davey gasped.

"Speaking of the Anderson family," Peter recalled, "Anders said he'd start the fire in the stove during January, so the place should be plenty warm when you get there."

"That's good news," Anna said as she got up from the table. "And now I think it's about time to get going. What about you, Davey? Are you coming with me this morning?"

"Sure am," he quickly replied, as he downed the last of his porridge and drained his glass of milk. He then scrambled to put on his coat and knitted cap. Milly wrapped a scarf around his neck and tucked the ends in firmly so that he would not get chilled. His gloves were in his pocket, and after he put them on he grabbed his school tablet, pencils and lunch pail.

By this time Anna had been upstairs and had collected her school supplies. She went to the back porch to get her outdoor clothes and felt as if she were in the icebox instead of looking at it. Quickly she came back into the kitchen and sat on a kitchen chair to tug on her galoshes over her shoes. It took several hefty pulls before they were on. The metal buckles felt as cold as ice as she grabbed them with her fingers and snapped them shut. In a few minutes, both were ready to walk the cold mile to school.

As they opened the door from the porch, an icy stillness greeted them. There was no wind, but a very light snow was falling. It was eerily quiet. Not even a sound came from the barn. They crept down the icy back steps. The dimness of the early morning hovered over them. The snow on their clothes looked like a light sprinkling of sugar.

As they reached the road between the houses, Davey remarked, "I wish Joshua was going with us. After his grandpa died, I thought they would come back here and live and we could be friends."

Remembering the tragedy that happened in the fall when Joshua's father was killed gave Anna a start. She felt goose bumps run up her back as she recalled being the first one to find his grandfather's body in the snow, and then Jonah Larson finding her after she fainted and carrying her into the barn. She quickly tried to get this out of her mind and said, "Well, I think Joshua and his mother and little sister are happy living in the county seat. And he never did get to walk to school with us very much, anyway."

"I know, but now I don't have anyone around here to play with."

As they came to the corner after the first half mile, Anna glanced up toward the Wheeler place and saw Mabel walking toward them. "Morning, Mabel," she called. "I'm surprised to see you here so early. Have you heard anything more about Mrs. Wheeler?"

"Mother was over there this morning," she answered. "She said it was a real mess and could hardly wait until Dr. Bailey came. You go on ahead. I'm going to the Larsons' to see if Erica is ready," and she hunched her shoulders against the wind that had suddenly sprung up.

The next half mile to the school was even colder as the wind was beginning to bite into them, so it was a welcome relief when they pushed open the schoolroom door and felt the benefit of Anders Anderson's warm fire.

At nine o'clock she rang the school bell, although all the students were present. Yet it was the custom to ring the bell to let the folks know that she was there and school was about to begin. Many people listened for it as a means of telling time. To others it brought back memories of youth. And still others considered it a reminder that there was work to be done and time to get at it.

She saw that all the lunch pails were on the side table and the coats and hats properly hung on hooks. There was one empty hook, with the name Joshua Kloster over it, so she removed his name, as he would no longer be one of her pupils.

At the front of the room she wrote on the blackboard, *Tuesday, January 2, 1923,* and then called the attendance. She now had only one first grader, David Jensen. She smiled at him as she checked off his name. No second graders, so she continued with calling those in third grade, "Annie Lindquist, Victoria Pearson, Carl Anderson." At least Carl answered and did not have his fingers crossed. She smiled to herself as she recalled Mr. Anderson's visit in the fall when Carl had misbehaved. After that, there had been no more mischief. "Philip Reed, Edwin Lindquist." They were fourth graders. No one in fifth grade. "George Parker." Mabel's brother was in sixth, even though he did nearly all seventh-grade work. "Lars Anderson, Edna Reed," seventh graders and "Mabel Parker and Erica Larson." They were in the eighth grade. That made eleven students.

A light snowfall continued during the day, but it was nothing that would alarm anyone. After all, these Iowa students were used to snow in the winter and came well prepared for it.

The day went well, but by afternoon Anna was tired. Suddenly the door opened while she was sitting at her desk correcting papers. It was Walter, Floyd and Inger's oldest. Eleven pairs of eyes in turning heads followed him as he walked up to Anna's desk. "It must be some emergency," she surmised.

"Excuse me, Miss Swenson. Doc Bailey is over at the Wheeler's, and he wondered it you could come over. He'd like to talk to you as soon as you can get away from school."

"Of course, Walter," she answered, wondering how she could possibly help Dr. Bailey.

"He's gonna be there a while. He was late 'cause he had some other people to see. He took his sled and didn't get here until about an hour ago."

"But how is Mrs. Wheeler?" Anna asked, knowing that all the pupils would be as interested as she was.

"I don't know. It was Ma who sent me to tell you. Can you come right after school?"

"Oh, yes. I'll leave right after three o'clock. Tell him I'll be there as soon as I can."

Walter left the room and waved good-bye as he went out the door. Anna tried to settle the pupils down, but could see that it would not do much good. "I'm sure you all heard that Mrs. Wheeler fell a couple of nights ago and hurt herself quite badly."

""Yeah, she fell in the ice goin' to the privy," Carl called out. "We knowed all about that."

"Yes, Carl, that is exactly what happened." This was no time to correct grammar.

"Anyway, Dr. Bailey is there now and asked me to meet him. Since it is nearly three o'clock, I think you can put your work away and go home a little early today." Immediately the desks were cleared, and the students sat ready to be dismissed.

Anna left Davey at the crossroads and walked up toward the Wheeler's. She had never been in their house before, and she hardly knew Charley and Bill. As she walked around to the back, she saw the doctor's sleigh in the yard and hoped that Inger would be there too. Two knocks on the door brought Charley to open it.

"Howdy, Miss Swenson. Come in. The doc wants to talk ta you."

"How is your mother, Charley? Is she all right?"

"I dunno. We had a terrible time last night. She talks, but she don't even know what she's sayin'. Can't even understand her much anyways."

At this point Dr. Bailey came out of the bedroom. "Well, Anna. I'm glad you could come so quickly."

"I came as soon as I could," she replied, still wondering what he could possibly want of her. "How is Mrs. Wheeler?"

"I left Inger in there with her. I think it's likely she had a slight stroke. That's probably what made her fall. She's used to walking in the snow, having lived in these parts all her life, and she may have slipped and fallen, but it seems more like a stroke. The bump on her head is most likely where she hit it as she fell. Lucky she didn't break any bones."

"Will she be all right?" Anna asked.

"No one can ever be sure about that, but from what I've seen she may be up and around before we know it. She's strong as a horse, even though she's not so young anymore. Anyway I wanted to see if you could do us all a favor. Inger!" he called. "Why don't you come on out here a minute."

Inger quickly came through the door, glad to be free from this added responsibility for even a few minutes.

"What I think we need is to get someone to help out until she's better," he added.

"I didn't think there was anyone around here who could do that," Anna said, hoping that he wasn't thinking of her.

"And Edna won't be none too happy having any other woman in her house," Inger reminded them, "much less be willing to pay someone to come."

"Well, you can't look after her," the doctor told Inger. "And it's for sure the boys can't. Anyway, I have an idea. There's a girl lives near the county seat just lost her mother. It's a possibility she could come and help out. She's not a young one, about thirty-five. Yes, just about that. I remember delivering her, yup, just about thirty-five years ago. Her mother was one of my first patients."

"If she's thirty-five, how can she leave?" asked Inger. "Doesn't she have a job?"

"Well, you see, her mother's been sick a long time. This girl's a real gem, just stayed with her mother all the time. Name's Sally Griswold. Ever heard of her?"

"Never heard of her," said Inger somewhat astonished.

"Probably the reason is that Sally's mother is deaf. They never went out anywhere. Her father works on the railroad and is gone quite a bit. He's not deaf, but doesn't hear too well. I guess you'd say he was hard of hearing. The way I got to know them is that I delivered Sally. The father came and got me in a panic when his wife was about to give birth. They hadn't lived in the area very long and didn't know anyone, but he had seen the sign on my door. One night I heard a frantic knocking, and when I opened the door there he was, so out of breath and scared he could hardly speak. He must have run the two miles from their place. Well, I grabbed my bag, hitched up the gray, and out we went. That's how I got to know the family. Sally has a younger brother Richard born, oh, I'd say about eight years later. Yes, it would be just about that. Sally turned out to be not only a big sister to Richard, but almost a second mother to him."

This story fascinated Anna, but she was still wondering how she could be involved.

"Anyway, to come to the point," continued the doctor. "Sally is real shy. She's a wonder of a worker, but she never learned to talk, that is, I mean to speak words, until she was in school. They used sign language at home. The father wasn't home much, works for the railroad, and probably didn't take a great deal of interest in the little girl, from what I gather, so she mainly talked with her mother. They made her quit school after the eighth grade and stay home, probably mostly to keep the mother company. I've asked around, but it seems she never did get out much. Richard got to go to high school and was well known in town. He even played on the basketball team. I s'pose I shouldn't say this, but he was the typical spoiled little brother. Anyway, I haven't seen him for quite a long time, and he may have turned out all right."

"And I s'pose that means that Sally and her mother did all the work for the men folks," Inger uttered all-knowingly. "Well, it's for sure not that way around our place."

"I do think you run things differently," commented the doctor, slowly nodding at Inger. "Anyway, one reason I'd like to get Sally away from her home is mostly because she's alone and needs something to do. She needs to get out and see things."

"Being at the Wheeler's is not exactly my idea of seeing things," Inger said, shaking her head.

"Well, I guess you're right," and he laughed. "But there are you five across the road and plenty of other nice folks around here. If she would come, and I think maybe I could talk her into it, she would do the Wheelers a favor, and just being here might do her a world of good. And don't forget, Inger, you can't be running across the road a dozen times a day."

"You're right there," Inger answered.

"What about her brother?" Anna asked. "And her father?"

"Her brother comes back home now and then. He's been working away most of the time since he graduated from high school. He's probably a nice enough fellow, but he got so used to a handout that whenever he was broke he came home. His mother was always a soft touch so would give him money, and before they knew it he was gone again. With the mother gone, he may not come back very often. But then again, with Sally all alone, he might surprise us."

"What about the father?" Anna asked.

"Of course he's gone a lot. As I said before, Sally is there mostly by herself."

"I can see that she might be very lonely," Anna commented thoughtfully. "She must miss her mother terribly."

"That's why I think it would do her good to get out and meet some people. As I said, she's a worker, all right. And she's been used to caring for her mother, so she'd be a good one to help out with Mrs. Wheeler. She knows the routine of a sickroom."

"Well," Inger said thoughtfully. "This isn't exactly the easiest place to work in. I can't see a young girl coming here. That old lady would give anyone a hard time. I'd feel sorry for the girl. And where would she sleep?"

"Sally is so quiet and sweet that I think even Mrs. Wheeler would get to like her," the doctor added. "And as far as sleeping, the boys each have a room. Guess they'll have to bunk together. Charley's room is closest to his mother's, so I'd suggest that he move out into Bill's room."

"But what do you want me for?" asked Anna, hoping that it was not to get the room ready for Sally.

"Oh, yes, I almost forgot about you. Anyway, I think I can talk Sally into coming out here, and if I can, I would like you to meet her at the depot. I thought that a young girl like you would be the best one to be the first person she would get to know."

Anna thought of her own introduction to the community last fall when Floyd met her and joked around so much at her expense that she realized that this idea of the doctor's was perhaps right. However, at the moment, no one knew if the girl would accept the job. She answered him by saying that of course she would be glad to do this if it would help any.

"Thanks, Anna. Well, I'll be on my way," he said as he grabbed his bag and noticed that Charley and Bill were standing in the doorway to the parlor. "Anyway, I'll let you know about Sally, and in the meantime you boys get this place cleaned up, whether she comes or not." He went out, leaving the four of them too astonished at this development to say much of anything.

Chapter Four

Wednesday morning was clear and cold. The air was still. Occasionally the sound of a cow mooing could be heard. Otherwise it was quiet except for the steady crunch, crunch, crunch sound as each footstep rhythmically pushed through the crust of snow. Anna left earlier than Davey so was the first to enter the school. She quickly made her way to her desk and lit the coal oil lamp. At least, today being clear, she could blow it out as soon as the sun was fully up.

Anna thought about her visit with Dr. Bailey and Inger the day before. She smiled to herself when she remembered the conversation that evening at supper. Milly's first remark was, "You yust can't send a poor girl like that to take care of Edna Wheeler. And those boys! Why, I've never heard of such a thing."

"Now Mother," Peter said calmly. "I think the doc knows what he's doing, and what's more, those boys can't manage to take care of her themselves. Let 's hope that this girl can be persuaded to come out here. If she doesn't come, Inger'll have to bear the brunt of the burden, and you don't want that."

"Oh no! Of course not!" She shook her head. "But I still think it's a terrible thing for that poor girl."

Anna was lost in thought and looked up quickly as the door to the school opened and George and Lars came in. "Has your mother heard anything from Dr. Bailey, George?" she asked.

"No. He hasn't called yet," he answered. She realized, of course, that he couldn't possibly have gone to talk to Sally yesterday, as it was late when he left the Wheeler's, and he had a long drive ahead of him to get home. She was surprised that he came in his sleigh instead of the quick trip on the 11:15 train, but then he no doubt had other calls to make in the country. If he came on the train he would have to make sure he caught the 5:10 back to the county seat. Perhaps they would hear from him this afternoon

"I'll fill the coal scuttle, Miss Swenson," George volunteered.

"And I'll fill the water bucket," Lars said energetically.

She had no sooner said, "Thank you boys," than they were out of the room going about their chores.

By mid-morning Anna had blown out the lamp. She looked out of the windows to see the sun glare on the snow. The room was brighter than usual because of this. It was much more pleasant than the gray day they had yesterday.

After school she didn't bother to stay to correct papers, but stuffed them in her satchel. She walked home as quickly as she could and opened the back door with anticipation, hoping that Inger would be there and that there would be some news from Dr. Bailey. However, the only sound she heard was that of the children playing in the kitchen. She leaned up against the wall and pulled off her overshoes, then hung up her coat and hat, and gratefully entered the warm room.

"Come in! Come in!" called Milly. "I hope you are not frozen. Here, sit down and have some coffee. I even have some pepparkakor left over from Christmas. You must have some of that." She bustled to open the tin of cookies.

"Have you heard from Inger or Dr. Bailey?" Anna asked anxiously.

"No, not a word," she answered. "But it's really too early yet. He's probably busy with patients in town."

"Haven't you heard from Inger?"

"Oh, ya! She has been there most of the day. She phoned this afternoon. I yust don't know what she will do if they can't get someone to help out at the Wheeler's," and Milly shook her head with worry. "Inger is so good to help everyone, but this is too much."

A stomping was heard coming from the back porch. Undoubtedly it was Peter kicking the snow off his boots. The outside door opened and banged shut. Everyone listened as they knew he was now taking off his mackinaw and hat, and putting them in the entryway. Soon the kitchen door opened. "Well, tarnation if I didn't smell the coffee way out in the shed. Just knew it was time to come in. Besides it's gettin' so dark I can't see to work any more."

"You were working in the shed?" Anna asked. "Is something wrong with the pigs?"

"Oh, no! This was the corn shed, where I store the corn seed. You remember last fall how I sorted out the ears of corn?"

"Yes. You picked out the best ears for seed. I always thought farmers fed the best ears to the stock."

"Not if you want to avoid buying seed, you don't. Anyway, most of the ears are about the same, but you do find really good big ears sometimes, I mean where the kernels are big. Those I save for seed, and I store them in the little shed next to the barn."

"It isn't dry enough to shell now, is it?" asked Milly.

"Oh sure. It was almost dry enough last fall, but the drier it gets, the easier it is to shell. Anyway, I'll do it in my spare time. But I hope the weather warms up a little. It's darn cold turning that crank all day. I'm going to make myself a little stove for that room. That's what Anders did. That way I can burn the cobs." He put his hands around the cup of coffee that Milly gave him, and felt the welcome warmth before taking a drink.

"What will you make it out of?" asked Milly. "You can't make a stove out of yust anything."

"I'll make it out of a five gallon can. It doesn't have to be big. And I can put up a little chimney. It'll be cozier than all get-out."

"Here, have some pepparkakor. You're sure getting fancy ideas," said Milly as she passed the tin to him. They spent the rest of the afternoon joking about Peter and his newfangled stove.

There was still no word on Thursday as Anna came home from school. She was somewhat worried, not because she was concerned about meeting Sally, but because Inger was having to spend all her time at the Wheeler's.

When there was still no news from the doctor by Friday afternoon, Milly and Anna had almost given up hope. "I yust think it is impossible for a young girl to come to that place," said Milly. "No wonder the doctor can't get her. And we don't even know what kind of girl she is."

"I don't think the doctor would have recommended her unless he felt she was all right," added Anna.

"And is she strong enough to take care of Mrs. Wheeler?" Milly continued while pouring herself another cup of coffee. "That lady is pretty big. Sally's mother may have been yust a skinny little thing."

"Well, we can only hope for the best," Anna replied as she left for her room. "I'll be down in a few minutes to help you with supper, Milly."

Anna climbed the stairs wearily, hoping the coffee she drank would give her renewed energy. Thank goodness it was Friday.

She had no sooner put her things on her bed than she heard the phone ring three long rings. That was Inger's ring. She knew that Milly would pick up the receiver, cover the mouthpiece and listen to the conversation. Probably everyone else on the party line would do the same. Perhaps this was Liza Crawford in the post office, relaying a message from Dr. Bailey in the county seat. She was the main one in the community who had a phone line out of the area.

Quickly Anna returned to the kitchen and anxiously waited for Milly to hang up. Milly noticed her and kept nodding trying to convey the message while still listening, but Anna had no idea what was actually being said. At last she hung up.

"Was that a message from Dr. Bailey?" Anna asked.

"Yes, Liza called Inger to tell her that Sally would be on the noon train tomorrow. Oh, Anna! Isn't it wonderful! He was able to get her, after all. I was so worried about Inger. She was working so hard over there. I'm going to phone her now and see if they can come down after supper. I want to hear all about it."

"Didn't you hear all about it on the phone?" Anna said with a smile, knowing that anything this momentous would need an evening visit.

"Well, but there is so much to talk about," replied Milly. "And well, let me call Inger now and see if they can come down," and she turned to the phone and turned the crank for three long rings.

The supper dishes were being cleared when they heard the jingle of bells, which meant that a sleigh had come into the yard. "That can only be Floyd and Inger," said Peter. "It's a wonder they finished supper this soon, what with Inger so busy."

"Mabel can cook a good supper," Milly stated firmly. "And oh, I am so anxious to see them."

"I'll go out and help Floyd put his horse in the barn." Peter shoved himself away from the table, grabbed his mac and dashed outside to give his brother-in-law a hand. "Come on in, Inger," he was heard to say.

"I'm a comin'," she replied with a big sigh. "I'm just waitin' to give these weary ol' bones of mine a chance to rest."

"Here, I'll take your coat, Inger," said Milly as she hurried out through the back entry.

"Give me a chance to get up the steps first." Inger puffed as she took them one by one, gave her coat to Milly and heaved a big sigh as she plopped herself down on a kitchen chair.

"Let me give you some coffee," Anna offered.

"Maybe later. We've just had supper. Thanks, anyway."

"Tell us what happened," Milly pleaded. "I couldn't hear it all on the phone. I think too many people were listening in."

"You've got it right there, all right," Inger laughed. "Just let my phone ring and the whole neighborhood listens in. When they call it a party line, they mean it. It beats all, really."

"Is this woman, I mean Sally, really going to be able come?" Anna asked.

"Be in on the noon train tomorrow," came Inger's straightforward reply. "And as far as I'm concerned, it can't be too soon."

The kitchen door opened bringing in a gust of cold air, and along with it Floyd and Peter. "Well Mother, I see you've got yourself a place to roost," Floyd surmised. "An' you better get mighty comfortable, 'cause it looks like we'll be stayin' the night." The three women quickly turned in his direction. "You see, Peter put so many blankets on ol' Clementine that she's as good as bedded down until mornin'. Just as cozy as can be. Yup!"

"Well Dad, I'd just as soon stay in this chair. I don't feel like moving one bit, so that suits me fine."

"Oh Inger, you are so funny, you make me laugh," Milly giggled.

"I'm glad someone's laughing, 'cause it sure isn't me," she said, rolling her eyes.

"You said Sally was coming in on the noon train tomorrow," said Anna, anxious to get back to the main subject. "Whew," she sighed. "Do you think you could take me to the depot, Peter?"

"Now I was a thinkin' of takin' you myself," Floyd chimed in. "After all, how many chances does a fella get to ride with a purty young schoolmarm?" It was hard to tell if he were serious or not.

"You'd scare her to death, and you know it, Floyd," Inger retorted. "And this is one girl that I want handled with kid gloves. If you scare her off, you'll be the one who'll be taking care of Edna. And I mean it!"

"Well Mother, if you mean it, then I guess you mean it and Anna'll have to ride with Peter. I was really jus' tryin' to do you a favor, Peter, but you see, the missus.... "

"That's enough, Floyd! I'm ready for that coffee now, Milly."

"I'll be glad to take you to the depot," said Peter with his usual generosity. "If I go out a little after eleven to get Ginger hitched up, does that sound about right, Anna?"

"Yes," Anna said thoughtfully. "We probably want to get there a little early."

"Well the train ain't gonna be early," Floyd advised. "Trains just don't come early. An' at least I won't be stuck with tryin' to haul off all her baggage. An' you don't even know what she looks like. You don't know nothin' about her. You might get the wrong person."

"Well," mused Peter. "Guess with all the crowd getting off at Grabney on a snowy Saturday morning, we'll just have to take our chances."

Chapter Five

Peter helped Anna into the sleigh and tucked some blankets around her, then jumped in on his side and put a robe over his lap. With a slap of the reins on the front of the sleigh and a "Giddap, Ginger!" they were off.

Milly waved to them from the back porch, and they returned the wave. "Hurry back!" she called. They laughed at this, hoping to hurry back, but she knew as well as they that it might take a little time to get Sally settled into the Wheeler place.

It had clouded over again, but the clouds weren't the dark clouds of a heavy snowfall. As they moved along, the wind had a bite to it and stung their faces. Anna pulled her scarf up over her nose, which she was sure had turned a bright red.

As they passed the parsonage next to the church, she remembered that she would be playing the piano for Sunday School in the morning. The downstairs room would be terribly cold. She sighed.

"What's the matter, Anna," asked Peter. "Are you sure you're warm enough?"

"Oh yes," she laughed. "I'm plenty warm. I was thinking about having to play the piano in Sunday School tomorrow. The keys will be like ice. Guess it will be another Sunday when I play with my gloves on."

"Oh, I'm sure you'll do all right," he answered. "Anyway, they're lucky to have you."

They crossed the bridge and pulled up at the depot. "Let's go inside," suggested Peter as he jumped out of the sleigh and tied the reins to the hitching post. "No point in waiting out here." He helped her down, and together they entered the small waiting room.

"Morning, Peter," called Matt Crawford, the stationmaster.

"Morning, Miss Swenson. Guess you're here to meet the new gal's goin' ta help out at the Wheeler's. Matt knew all the news, as his wife Liza was the postmistress and managed the phone line to the county seat. She wasn't above listening to other conversations.

"That's right," Peter answered.

"Well the train's on time, so you won't have long to wait." He paused as if stalling for time, then looked at the clock. "Yup! Well, it won't be long now."

Peter and Anna both glanced around at the clock. Trying to keep occupied, Anna walked over to the timetable posted on the wall.

"Well I guess there won't be many people gettin' off this mornin', so's I s'pose you'll...a...well...know who she is," Matt queried.

"Yes, I suppose so," answered Peter. "I don't think we'll have any problem there."

"Well, Miss Swenson, I guess a young girl like you could be a good friend to this young lady, a...a...whatever her name is," Matt continued.

"Her name is Sally Griswold," Anna answered.

"Oh!" Matt cogitated before continuing. "Comes from the county seat, don't she?"

"She lives about a couple of miles from the town," said Anna.

"Oh! That's probably why we never heard of her."

"Yes, that's probably right."

The sound of the whistle brought a halt to this inane conversation, much to the relief of Anna. The three of them went out to meet the train that had slowed as the wheels screeched to a stop. They looked around to see which door would be opened. "It's gotta be that car up there," said Matt as he jerked his head toward a coach about fifty feet down the track. "I seen the conductor goin' that way. C'mon!"

Anna followed the men, keeping her eyes glued to the ground as she carefully picked her way through the ice and snow. She heard the door bang open and then looked up to see a rather pale young woman standing inside the car. "Here lemme put the step down for you," the conductor's voice boomed out as he pushed her aside and jumped down with the portable step that he placed on the platform. The woman hesitated, looking at the three of them with a forlorn expression.

"Here, lemme help ya," Matt offered, and extended his hand to assist her.

She had two pieces of luggage, a sturdy canvas bag and a well-worn suitcase. She gripped them tightly, one in each hand, and tried to maneuver her way down the steps, but the space was narrow and her luggage cumbersome. She struggled with first one piece and then the other.

Matt jumped up the first couple of steps. "Here! I'll take those," and he grabbed both pieces, quickly depositing them in the snow.

The woman hesitated slightly as she stepped down to the portable step, but Peter held out his hand and helped her to the ground.

"You must be Sally Griswold," Anna said as she stepped forward to meet the woman. The stranger nodded. "I'm Anna Swenson. We came to meet you."

The moment of self-conscious silence was broken by the conductor grabbing the step, and banging shut the door. The train slowly got up steam and soon was chugging away from them.

Sally said nothing but glanced at the station and then back to Anna. Her heavy, brown wool coat was well worn and something that might have been in fashion fifteen or twenty years ago. Her hair was dark blonde. She shivered in the cold and struggled to put her heavy scarf around her head. With wool gloves and a black pocketbook over her arm, it was awkward.

"Here, let me help you," Anna volunteered. She quickly had the middle of the scarf over Sally's hair, and then wrapped it around her neck.

"Thank you," was her only reply as she looked shyly at Anna, then quickly lowered her head.

Anna guessed that she was frightened. It must all be so strange to her. She had been protected at home and now was out with strangers. Peter and Matt had gone ahead with Sally's luggage, so they were left alone. She struggled to think of something to say and then blurted out, "Let's hurry and catch up with Peter and get into the sleigh." They began to walk quickly. "I see you have warm overshoes. With this snow you need them." Soon they were at the sleigh where Peter and Matt were waiting. Sally noticed that her luggage had been put in a box-like platform behind the seat, and smiled at the men as if to acknowledge her thanks.

"This is Peter Jensen, and this is Matt Crawford," Anna said as she introduced them. "Matt is the stationmaster, and I live with the Jensen family. I teach school here."

"Oh, you're the school teacher. Dr. Bailey told me that the school teacher lived near when I'd be staying."

"Yes, I live just down the road," Anna answered.

"Let's not spend all day talking," Peter said with some admonishment in his voice. "It's cold out here, and the sooner we get going the better. Come on now ladies, hop up into the sleigh."

"I'll give them a hand," Matt offered. "You get yerself up, and you'll be gone in no time." He grabbed Sally's hand, much to her surprise, and soon she was sitting next to Peter with Anna on the outside. They tucked the blankets around them, and with a crack of the reins they were off.

The chill wind grabbed at them as they rounded the corner of the station. "That's the store over there across the road," said Anna, trying to give Sally an outline of the town. "They have a gas pump now." Sally nodded her head as she pulled the blanket up over her hands and arms. They crossed the bridge and Anna pointed out the church and parsonage. "Oh, and there's a path next to the river that we walk on when we come to town. It's only about a mile from where we live, but we don't use it much in this weather."

They turned to go east after the first mile, then soon came to the intersection which led south to the Jensens' and north to the Parkers' and also the Wheeler's. "You'll live just up the road a bit, on the left side," said Anna. "See, that's the Wheeler place straight ahead. The Parkers live across the road from them. Inger Parker has been taking care of Mrs. Wheeler. She'll probably be there when we arrive."

"Whoa!" called Peter as they pulled up next to the house. "Here, you ladies get out now, and I'll put Ginger in the barn. I'd let her stay outside, but I think we'll be here awhile."

"Oh, no! You go on home, Peter," suggested Anna. "I can walk home. And I think you're right. It may be a while before I can leave."

"Well, if you say so," said Peter with a welcome sigh. "I'll get the bags and bring them in." With that he jumped out of the sleigh and came around to help Anna and Sally down.

Anna led the way up the porch with Sally following and Peter close behind. The door was quickly opened by Inger who had heard them coming. "Come in! Come in! Well now, you must be Sally. I'm Inger Parker, your neighbor across the road. Here, let me help you with your things. Peter, you take her bags into her room. That'll be Charley's old room, the one next to Edna's. Here, let's have your coat. Anna, why don't you come with us and help Sally get settled." Yes, Inger was her usual efficient self.

The kitchen was warm and inviting. A pot of stew bubbled on the stove giving off a delicious smell. The door to Mrs. Wheeler's room on one side of the kitchen was closed. Next to it was the room where Inger led them. Anna was surprised at the spotless kitchen and knew it was Inger's doing. The heavy round oak table looked as if it had been scrubbed. There was no cloth on it as there would have been at Milly's, but of course not everyone had Milly's standard of housekeeping.

"Well, I'll be going now," said Peter after he put Sally's luggage inside the bedroom door. "Anna, you're sure you can make it home all right?"

"Of course," she laughed. "After all, I walk through the snow every day to school and back."

"She'll be fine," Inger called from the bedroom. "You just get on home and get to your own chores." With that remark, he was out of the door and soon on his way.

"Here, Sally, you make yourself to home," Inger said with her usual air of authority. "Anna, put your coat on the bed in there, and then come on out and help me set the table. Sally, get your boots off. Leave them by your coat that I hung on the hook. You can get your things unpacked later."

"Where are the boys?" Anna asked as she entered the kitchen.

"They're in the barn. And I told them to stay there until they were called," she confided in a rather hushed tone. "Let's have first things first. Let the poor girl get settled in a little. Lucky for us that Edna's asleep. I thought that if you stayed here awhile it might help break the ice."

"Oh, I'm happy to do that," Anna answered as she set the table. "Are there going to be five of us?"

"Yes," she answered.

Sally appeared in the doorway. She was slim, but not thin,

and dressed in a warm wool skirt, a white blouse and dark sweater. She wore tan-colored cotton lisle stockings and sturdy brown shoes. She was fussing with her hair, that had come loose but managed to get it pinned in place. The most noticeable thing about her was her face, which had the look of an innocent child. Her wide eyes wandered around the room.

"Sally, you come and help Anna set the table while I get the food on," Inger continued as if she had known Sally all her life. "I'll stay and have a bite to eat with you, and be around when Edna wakes up. By the way, Charley and Bill are out in the barn. They're the two men on the place, Mrs. Wheeler's sons. And we've always called them 'the boys'," she explained as she laughed. "Everyone knows them as 'the Wheeler boys.' Anyway, Anna, give them a shout, will you? It's time they got in and washed up."

Anna dutifully went out the back door and realized she did not have to shout too loudly, as Charley and Bill were standing just inside the barn door. With the first call, they started plodding their way to the house. The sound of their stomping up the back steps signaled their arrival. They could be heard to stop in the entryway to remove their coats. Soon the door opened, and the men stepped inside. They stood there, stock still. This was the first time they had had a hired girl, and neither one knew what was expected of them. They looked around the room as if they were the newcomers.

"Sally I want you to meet Bill and Charley," announced Inger. "This here's Bill, and this here's Charley. Say hello to Sally, boys."

A faint "Hullo" was uttered simultaneously.

"They have the bedroom off the parlor. They've been runnin' this place pretty much on their own since their mother's took sick, so if you have any questions, ask them. And then I'm just across the road. My phone is three long rings. You boys'll help Sally out, won't you."

"That's right," Bill answered solemnly. "We'll help all we can. Charley's a better help in the house than I am, 'cause he's been doin' most of the things in here."

"I've been tryin' to help Inger take care of Ma," Charley said. "I hope she don't give you no trouble."

"I hope she don't, neither," echoed Bill.

"All right then. That's enough of this talk. You two get washed up and we'll have dinner. Sally, you can sit here next to me, and then Anna, and Charley and Bill can take the other two places."

Dinner started out a rather silent meal, except for Inger's chatter. Charley and Bill said next to nothing, and Sally was busy listening to Inger explain the household routine. "I guess you know how to cook?" she asked Sally.

"Oh yes," Sally quickly replied. "I did all the cookin' at home after Ma got sick." Anna could see that she was becoming more at ease.

"If you need any help to find out where things are, just ask Charley. He's the one been doing a lot of the cooking."

With this remark, Charley smiled self-consciously and nodded his head. "I'm not such a good cook."

"Bill here spends most of his time outside working," Inger explained. "Not that Charley doesn't work outside, too, but it's just that when someone's needed in the house, it's been Charley that's helped out. Isn't that right, Charley?"

"That's right," he nodded.

At that point, dinner was almost finished and a sound could be heard from the other room. "Well, it sounds like your mother's waking up," Inger surmised. "I'll go see how things are with her, and you folks finish your meal."

"I'm finished," said Sally somewhat apprehensively. "Let me help you."

Inger was pleasantly surprised at this remark and replied, "That would be just dandy. No time like the present to get started on your new job. And I can get you acquainted with Mrs. Wheeler."

"I'll do the dishes while you're in there," Anna volunteered.

"No, you go on home, Anna. The boys can help with the dishes."

"Sure! We're used to doin' the dishes," Charley remarked. "You go on home like Inger says."

"Well, if it's all right, I will," she answered. And then Anna turned to Sally. "It's been good to meet you, Sally. I hope we see a lot of each other. Charley or Bill can walk you down to our place sometime, or I can stop in on my way home from school."

"That would be nice," Sally answered. "But I might not be able to get away much, so maybe you could come here." Anna put on her coat and the good-byes were said. As she went out of the kitchen she could hear Mrs. Wheeler calling again and saw Inger and Sally enter her room. I hope that everything will go all right, she thought as she went down the back steps and started home.

Chapter Six

Supper over, Anna was sitting at the kitchen table working on school lessons. She glanced up at the coal oil lamp that stood in the center of the table. The light that emanated from it cast a bright circular spot on the table, and this became dimmer as the distance from the lamp increased. Shadows were elongated and then blended into the semi-darkness. She thought of the light it gave, compared to the electric lights in Fort Dodge. When she arrived last fall there was sunlight into the evening, and little need for lamplight. As daylight decreased during the fall, she became used to working by the light of the lamp. When she was home at Christmas she was suddenly aware of how bright electric lights were, and on returning to Grabney it was almost a shock to find herself trying to work with not much more than candlelight.

She pushed her papers closer to the center of the table and glanced at Peter who was sitting across from her reading the newspaper. He looked up, asking, "How are the lessons going?"

"Not bad. I think I'll be finished soon. I want to make sure I finish everything tonight, since tomorrow's Sunday. But I'm having a hard time concentrating as I can't get the Wheelers off my mind."

"I wish Inger and Floyd would hurry up," Milly said anxiously. She was getting the children ready for their Saturday night baths. There was a second lamp on the kitchen counter that gave off just enough illumination to enable Anna to see that part of the room. "They said they would be here right after supper, and it's after seven o'clock."

"I hope everything went all right," Anna commented. "Sally seems like such a nice person, and capable too, but I think she'll have a hard time with Mrs. Wheeler."

"The woman was difficult enough to handle when she was fully competent," Peter added, "but to have her in this condition will be a tough job."

"I'm yust glad I don't have to take care of her," said Milly, shuddering as she poured a panful of hot water into the washtub, followed by another and then some cold water from the bucket on the kitchen counter. "Here Peter, you hold Lucy while I get Sarah bathed. Hurry, Sarah! Get your clothes off. The water will get cold."

"I hope you have enough water, Peter commented as he took the child. "I'd hate to think of going out tonight to get more. It's so cold that I'd have to lower the bucket on a rope into the well, as the pump's froze for sure."

"I have plenty," said Milly. "I yust wish we had enough cistern water for baths. Hard water always gets so scummy from the soap. And you're next, Davey, so you can start getting your clothes off now. It won't take me long with Sarah. Your clean pajamas are on our bed."

Anna thought back to last fall when she had her first bath in the washtub and smiled.

"A penny for your thoughts, Anna," Peter said as he looked across the table.

"Well, I was thinking of my first bath in the washtub last fall in the entryway. I was so afraid that someone would try to come in."

"At least now you're used to bathing in the kitchen. It's too blamed cold to take a bath out there now. You'd have icicles on you before you finished. With Milly and me in the bedroom, at least we can give you a little privacy. And we did offer you the parlor, if you remember," he said grinning.

"That's almost as cold as the porch. Fine choice you gave me," she said as she smiled. "This way it works out fine, and it's better than trying to take sponge baths in the bedroom. I've heard that a lot of teachers have to do that."

"In the tub with you, Davey," said Milly as she added more hot water. "And Sarah, put on your nightgown and crawl in our bed until I'm finished with Davey."

Anna kept on with her schoolwork as the Saturday night ritual continued, ending with Lucy. The three children were packed into their parent's bed, and happy giggles of laughter could be heard coming from the room.

Milly emptied the water from the tub into the sink that drained outside.

"You're lucky that drain isn't frozen solid," Peter told her. "And it's sure making a lake of ice where it empties. Maybe you should let me toss the dirty water out the back door."

"And have someone slip on it," Milly responded with indignation. "We're managing yust fine."

"Whatever you say, Milly," Peter said shaking his head and smiling.

The sound of a sleigh was heard entering the yard. "Oh, that must be Inger and Floyd," she said as she rushed to open the kitchen door, which ushered in a blast of cold air.

"Let's get this door shut," called Peter as he jumped up from the table. "Milly! Get inside here! It's freezing out there, and you'll catch your death of cold." He shook his head as he heard Milly dash down the back steps. "Well, there's no stopping her, that's for sure," and he closed the door.

"I'm as anxious as she is to learn what's happened," said Anna.

"I sure hope it all works out," Peter replied. "By the way, it's time for you children to be in bed. All right, Davey and Sarah, up you go. Your mother will put Lucy down in a few minutes, so let's have no arguments." They slowly came out of the bedroom and wistfully climbed the stairs, knowing that they would be left out of any further conversation.

The scraping and stamping of boots could be heard, which indicated that the new arrivals would soon be in the room. "Well, I'll be jiggered," said Floyd as he flung open the door. "Looks like Milly's got us all set up for a Saturday night bath."

"Sit down and take a load off your feet," laughed Peter. "You can have your bath later, providing you go out and haul in some more water."

"Now that just ain't fair," Floyd complained. "Anyway I see you got coffee, so where's them cookies?"

"I'll get them," Anna said as she went over to the cookie jar.

"I just fed that man," remarked Inger as she entered the kitchen, followed by Milly. "And here he is, at it again."

"Sit down! Sit down!" Milly said with some exasperation.

"Tell us what happened at the Wheeler's."

"Well it's kinda funny, in a way," mused Inger. I never thought I'd see the day when things at that place were in such a state."

"But what happened?" Milly asked in an urgent plea.

"Go on, Mother," Floyd said. "Tell them about the money. That's one for the books."

"You mean that Sally was wanting her money now?" asked Milly.

"No! No! Nothing like that," and Inger waved her hands as if to quiet them. "Well I think I better start at the beginning. You see when Anna left, Sally and I went into the bedroom. I could hear Edna calling, well not calling really, but making some sort of noise that I knew she wanted someone. So I go in first, and then Sally follows. Edna takes one look at her and starts to gabble, making all sorts of strange noises, shaking her head and waving her arms. The next thing I know, Sally has left and gone to her own room. Well, I know a sick room is not too pleasant, and Edna didn't exactly put out the welcome mat, but I didn't think Sally'd chicken out on me like that. Next thing I know, I can hear her opening her suitcase and for sure I thought I was up the creek without a paddle."

"Oh my goodness! Was she leaving?" Milly exclaimed.

Inger continued. "I turn around and there is Sally holding a bed pan. She said it was the one she used with her mother, and she thought we might need it."

"That's wonderful," commented Anna. "It sounds like she's taking the job seriously."

"You bet she is. We've sorta had to make do so far. I did the best I could, but being stuck out here in the country, with it being winter and all, well I just didn't have the right equipment. I'm sure Edna felt as frustrated as I did, but that's the way it was."

"Of course," nodded Milly. "And I don't know what they would have done without you."

"When Edna saw the bedpan, she looked puzzled at first. Then Sally talked to her and showed her what it was for, and I thought I saw some sign of recognition on her face. I think Edna can understand a lot of what we say. Anyways, she looked at Sally and I'll swear I saw her smile. For Edna that's something. Then Sally took a good look at the room and said that we should clean it up. That meant also changing the sheets. I know they hadn't been changed since she fell, and that was nearly a week ago. Goodness knows when they were changed before that."

"Guess it's sorta like bein' sewed in yer winter underwear in the fall and not takin' it off until spring," Floyd added.

"Even Bill and Charley aren't that bad," Inger said with a wry grin, "but I must admit that it looked as if the bedding had been on for longer than I care to think."

"Oh Inger, you have had a terrible yob," Milly commiserated.

"Well you do what you have to do, so I go out and ask Charley to get me some clean sheets, and he said we can't change his mother's bed because she doesn't let anyone change it but herself. Well, now what'm I to do? It's obvious the old lady can't change it, so we've got to. He brings in the sheets, and I strip off the top sheet. Edna flails her arms this way and that, kicks her legs, and I think she is havin' some sort of fit. Then Charley appears at the door. 'Ya can't change Ma's bed. I tol' ya that before. She won't let no one change her bed.' Then he gets rather conspiratorial and beckons me into the kitchen. 'Come here an' I'll tell ya.' So I go out into the kitchen, leaving poor Sally with this ravin' maniac."

"Wait'll you hear what he told her," laughs Floyd. "If it don't beat all. Just guess what Charley said."

"You've sure got me stumped," answered Peter. "So what was it?"

"Well," Inger continued, "Charley tells me very quietly that his mother keeps money hidden under her mattress. She never trusted banks, and from the sounds of it the boys don't, either. They didn't know how much she had, because they never went into her bedroom before, much less try to change her bed. So I look back into the room and see that Sally has put the covers back over Edna and is stroking her forehead and getting her calmed down. Well, nothing to do but to take the bull by the horns and get the bed changed. I tell Sally. But she suggests that we wait a little, get Edna some coffee and see if that will help. It does help. Sally sits by the bed and in her calm way she helps Edna drink the coffee, and gets her to eat a little besides. She doesn't even say anything, just sits there reassuringly, smiling and helping her.

"To make a long story short, Sally asks me to get her a clean nightie, and before I know it she has her bathed and changed."

"What about changing the sheets? She can't stay in those dirty sheets after she's all clean," Milly surmised with a critical frown.

"We both did that. This time when it came to changing the bottom sheet Edna was getting a little sleepy again and pretty soon she was out. Sally tucked the bottom sheet next to Edna, put the clean sheet where that one had been and carefully rolled her on her side so she was off the dirty sheet and on to the clean one."

"That's the way they do it in the hospital," Milly asserted.

Inger nodded an assent, but not wanting to be interrupted she continued with, "Then I grabbed it and jerked it out from between the mattress and springs. It was sorta stuck on the springs. What happened next you'll never believe."

Everyone looked at Inger with some puzzlement.

"Well out flew an old flour sack full of money. In fact some of the bills had fallen out and were stuck in the springs."

"Money in a flour sack?" asked Milly.

"This beat all," said Peter shaking his head. Anna was about to add her comments but was stopped by Inger's next remark.

"Now just calm down, and I'll tell you what happened after that. I called the boys in there, and they helped lift up the mattress, and we got it all. We counted it at the kitchen table. And this is something I don't want repeated."

"The children are upstairs," Peter reassured her. "They can't hear."

"Well that old lady had stashed away close to five thousand dollars."

"What!" everyone exclaimed in unison.

"You mean lots of bills, like twenty dollar bills?" asked Milly.

"That's right! We counted it twice. Almost five thousand dollars! Goodness know how long she's been saving it."

"All that money just stuffed in loose in an old flour sack?" asked Peter as wide-eyed as the rest of them.

"Not all of it was," Inger continued. "Now be quiet while I finish. There were several bundles of twenty-dollar bills, each one tied with some old string. There were also some bundles of ten and five-dollar bills. One had a rubber band around it. There wasn't any change, so I guess she used all the change she got or kept it is a separate place."

"Like the sugar bowl," said Peter winking at Milly.

"We haven't looked into that yet. But anyway, at the top of the bag were a bunch of one dollar bills, I mean around a hundred or so, and these were just loosely stuffed in, along with some larger bills. It looked like she would take time out every now and then to sort them, but the one dollar bills she kept at the top and who knows, she might have used them for shopping at the store."

"I can see her now reachin' in, grabbin' a handful of bills an' trottin' down to the store," joked Floyd.

"That I would like to see," said Peter. "Anyway, what did you do with it? It's sure not safe under a mattress."

"Well, it's been safe there for nigh onto how many years, so we got a new sack, put most of the money into it, and shoved it back under the mattress. There's no point in trying to get it into a bank now, and we put it in the same spot where it was so the old lady can feel it under her. I wondered why that mattress was so lumpy in that place. I kept out plenty to cover any expenses they might have, like going to the store and paying Sally. I gave it to Bill and told him to put it in some safe place, and guess where he puts it, in another flour sack under his mattress.

"Charley always said that when they needed money their mother went into her bedroom and brought out what they had to have. The boys knew she kept it there, they just didn't know how much she had. Whenever they were paid for something, she always kept the money. She probably isn't the only one around here who keeps money hidden around the place."

"Like Milly and her sugar bowl," said Peter.

"Oh Peter!" Milly admonished him. "I yust keep a little money in there, not thousands. I don't have thousands," and she laughed. "But what about Sally. She could steal it and run off."

"Well, if I'm any judge of character, and I think I am," Inger replied. "I think Sally is very trustworthy. She was most insistent that we put the money back under the mattress in the very place where we had found it. She said she knew that Edna would expect to feel it where it had always been."

"And if the old lady'd wake up, they'd have a right hard time gettin' to the money again," Floyd added.

"What a revelation," exclaimed Peter. "We always knew she was tight fisted but never imagined she had that much money. I really think they should put it in a bank sometime."

"At this juncture, I'd leave it up to them," counseled Floyd. "The ol' lady may get better faster'n we imagine, and I wouldn't want to be around if she found it was missin'. It's been safe this long, and no one else knows about it. Anyway those fellas haven't even been to a bank. They wouldn't know what to do with a bank account."

"Well, maybe you're right, Floyd," added Peter. "But sometime they should bank the money."

"That's for them to decide," Inger advised. "Anyway, I've had enough to do with that family for awhile, and I know how difficult Edna can be. We're the only ones outside the family who know about the money, so if we keep our mouths shut, there'll be no problem.

"Getting back to Sally, " she continued. "When I left, she was giving instructions to Charley to build his mother a commode that she could use in the bedroom. It could sit next to the bed, and before too long she might be able to use it. It would be a lot easier than a bedpan, and Charley was pleased to be asked to help. He's always liked to build things, so I think this is right up his alley. It won't be a really good job like Anders would do, but it'll do.

"It sounds to me as it you still have plenty to do over there, Inger," said Peter. "I think we'd better all keep our fingers crossed to see if this works out."

"You're right, Peter," added Milly as she held up her right hand with her fingers crossed.

"Well this is enough of that," Floyd cut in, shaking his head. "Come on, Mother, it's time we got goin'. Five-thirty comes pretty early in the mornin', an' we gotta let these folks get their baths. Couldn't have them goin' to church dirty now, could we?"

"How come you're gettin' up so early, Floyd?" joked Peter. "Planning to get the chores done before you go to church? Be a nice treat to see you there."

"That's enough outta you," came the jocund answer. "Someone's gotta stay home to look after all the farms of you guys who go off tryin' to make a good impression." As they made their way down the back steps Floyd could be heard to say, "Judas Priest, it's cold. C'mon, Mother! Get a move on! Well, toodleoo, everyone."

Chapter Seven

Peter drove them to church. They were all well bundled up in the sleigh. "I'll pick you folks up after the service," he remarked as they climbed down to the well-trodden path of snow that led to the building. "Hope you don't mind my not going to church."

"Of course not," remarked Milly. "It's the only thing to do. I don't want Lucy playing on the basement floor. It's yust too cold. I don't think they'll even have a nursery today."

"Then can I go home with George?" begged Davey.

"Can I go home with Mabel?" Sarah seconded.

"Well, we'll have to see if Mabel will have a nursery," Milly replied. "Oh, there's Inger coming in with George. I guess Walter's staying home. "Oh, Inger," she called waving to her sister and scurrying toward their sled to make the suggested arrangements.

Anna grabbed Sarah's hand as she and the children climbed the heavily salted wooden steps. "I can feel the little bumps of salt under my shoes," exclaimed the child. "I think they put too much salt on the steps."

"That's to make sure no one slips and falls," Anna replied as she opened the door. "Here, hurry inside."

Reverend Blakeley was there to greet them. "I started the fire early, but you'll probably have to play with your gloves on this morning," he said to Anna. "Anyway you'll do fine," he added with his usual warm smile. "The church should be heated up by eleven o'clock, but I'm afraid that downstairs it's more than a little chilly."

They made their way to the clammy basement, where Sunday School was held, and found that he was right. The whitewashed concrete walls were as cold as the snow outside. A chilly draft emanated from them, and people huddled together on the benches in the center of the room. Everyone left on his wraps. With her fingers still feeling icy, even wearing her gloves, Anna successfully got through the morning's songs. She felt far more confident now than when she had arrived in Grabney last fall and found herself volunteered to play for the Sunday School. She had replaced Mrs. Simms, who still played the pump organ for the main service. Anna smiled to herself, recalling the new Ford Mr. Simms had bought and how he showed it off. Well, now they were obliged to use their sleigh the same as everyone else. With the new gas pump at the store, she wondered how long it would be before other farmers had cars. No doubt this spring would see more shiny Chevrolets and Fords, probably bought on the same "easy little payment plan" at $35.00 a month that Mr. Simms had used.

Sunday School over, the children went home with George and Mabel. They would take Inger back after the service when Peter picked them up. She was quite indispensable in the community, the mainstay of both the Sunday School and the School Board.

Church was a little shorter than usual, so Peter was not in sight when they left the building.

"Well, I've never heard of such a thing." It was the voice of the self-righteous Mrs. Simms. "A young girl working at the Wheeler's!"

"She's just like a hired girl," Inger quickly retorted. "Plenty of people have hired girls."

"But with a hired girl, there's a woman to…well…supervise. With them two men, I just don't think it's right. From what I've heard, Edna don't know up from down."

"Sally's got a good head on her shoulders," Inger continued. "Anyway, those two men wouldn't hurt a fly."

"Just the same, it's not decent, that's what."

"Well, Florence, if you want to take over the job, it's fine with me. I've done several days over there, so I've had my turn." Dismissing the woman with a turn of the head, she called, "Here comes Peter, Milly."

"You'll be sorry," Mrs. Simms blurted out peevishly as she climbed into the sleigh that her husband had brought out of the church barn. "Just remember I told you so."

By the middle of the week, Anna thought that she should pay Sally a visit. She could do this on the way home from school, so on Wednesday morning at breakfast she suggested it to Milly.

"Ya, that is a good idea," she nodded. "But I'll call Inger so that she can let Sally know. You know she goes over there every morning. I'm sure Sally might want to have the coffeepot on and a few cookies made."

"I don't want to put her to any trouble. I just want to say hello," said Anna. "I feel rather awkward about going. I don't even know her. It was only because of Dr. Bailey that I got involved in the first place. And what if Sally isn't ready for company?"

"Inger will see to it that she is ready," added Milly with a knowing nod. "You can depend on that. And you're the only young person around here. Goodness knows, the poor girl needs a friend. Charley and Bill aren't exactly what you would call good company."

So that day Anna left school a little early. It had snowed during the night, adding a few inches to that which had fallen before. She stopped on the porch to gaze at the scene. The white, fluffy blanket covered the landscape, obliterating sharp edges into undulating curves, piling tent-like against the fences and concealing all signs of life that remained dormant under its blanket. The children had tramped down a good path. She could see where they had scrambled into the road to make snowballs. This was such a change from Fort Dodge, where the snow quickly became black with soot and dirt.

When she came to the crossroads she gave a sigh as she looked south toward the Jensen farm. This morning it seemed like such a good idea to visit Sally, but now doubts assailed her. Racing through her mind were thoughts of what would she talk about. She felt very uncomfortable about this visit, but knew she had committed herself and so turned and walked slowly toward the Wheeler's. Once or twice she looked back toward the Jensens' but then plodded on, knowing that Inger would have told Sally that she was coming, and that meant she had to go.

She turned into the Wheeler yard. The bleakness of winter gave the farm a gloomy atmosphere, and this place held not a vestige of charm. The entire farmyard was in various shades of gray. Most of the snow had been well tramped down during the day, so it lacked any sense of whiteness. The beauty of the fresh snowfall was gone. Even the few trees that remained were bare of leaves and looked forlorn and forgotten. She realized that when she was here the past Saturday she hadn't noticed the gloominess of the place because she had been with Peter and Sally. There were many more things to think about then, but now she was alone and her aloneness made her more aware of her physical surroundings.

There was the house, a rectangle sitting amidst this gray. It had once been painted white, as Anna could see from the area under the roof of the front porch where flakes of paint still clung precariously to the old wood. The sides were a weather-beaten gray, with boards that curled at the edges, showing the effects of winter storms and summer heat. There were no footprints in the snow leading to the front door, which was not unusual in farmhouses, as everyone generally entered through the kitchen, the front door being reserved for important occasions. However, with the Wheeler home it gave the place an uninhabited look, especially as no lights in the house were visible from where she stood. Slowly she made her way around to the back.

There was no one in sight, but she could hear activity in the barn, another gray building. She took a deep breath, climbed the well-worn back steps, grooved with the indentations of many a footstep, and firmly knocked on the outside door. After a brief pause it was opened by Sally.

"Come in, Anna. Come in," Sally said, as she escorted Anna through the porch into the kitchen, which was warm and inviting. The smell of coffee and fresh baking permeated the room. It had a cared-for appearance, even though the furniture had seen better days. The oilcloth on the table had been well scrubbed, its age showing in several places where the printed pattern was worn off. In some spots, the top layer had even peeled off, showing the thin woven threads underneath. The stove had been blackened. Everything looked tidy. Even though Inger had done a remarkable job getting things in order, it was obvious that Sally had taken over the place. She was a hard worker and evidently took pride in what she did.

From Sally's greeting, Anna knew that she was expected and welcomed. There was a short silence as the two women stood there awkwardly looking at each other. Sally seemed apprehensive, as if she didn't know what she should do next.

The silence was broken by Anna. "How are you doing, Sally? I hope I haven't come at an inconvenient time."

"Oh no!" was the sudden answer. "I'm so happy to have you." Then there was another awkward, short silence, as if she forgot what she was to do next.

"You certainly have made the place look nice," Anna said as she admired the room. "You must have been working day and night."

"Oh no," she commented shyly. "I've tried to get things nice, but there is still so much to do. Look at the congoleum rug. It's all wore through. And we need new curtains." She pointed to where two ragged pieces of fabric hung above the sink.

"Oh that will come in time. You can't do everything at once," Anna said with a reassuring smile.

"Let me take your things," Sally suddenly offered, realizing that Anna still was dressed for the outside, and she hurried to help her take off her coat.

"I'll put them over this chair if that's all right," Anna suggested. "You're sure you have time to visit? Is Mrs. Wheeler asleep?"

"Yeah. She sleeps a lot, but I never know when she's gonna wake up." Sally smiled a little self-consciously. "Would you like some coffee? I made some fresh a little while ago. I thought you'd be comin' about this time. Inger said it would be after school." As an afterthought she added, "An' I made some cookies, too."

"I'd love some coffee," Anna said as she watched the young woman go over to the stove and pour two mugs full. Trying to think of something else to say, she looked around the room again and remarked, "The kitchen looks so nice, Sally. You must be keeping yourself very busy."

"Oh, Inger has helped me. But I like to have things clean." She gave one mug to Anna and put one on the table for herself. "The cream 'n sugar are there. Oh, sit down, Anna. Let me get the cookies." She quickly headed for the cupboard and returned proudly carrying a plate full of cookies and set it carefully down on the table. "I hope you like oatmeal cookies."

"Oh yes," replied Anna, helping herself to a cookie and pouring some of the thick cream into her coffee. There was a prolonged silence during this procedure.

Anna wondered how she would break it when suddenly Sally asked, "How is school? The schoolhouse isn't too far from here, is it?"

"No, it's just up from the crossroads. Did you go to a one-room country school?"

"Oh no! Our school was big, two floors and brick. The grade school an' the high school was in the same building. It was in the county seat. I walked to school every day. I really liked school, but I didn't get to go to high school."

"That's too bad. I'm sorry."

"Oh, it's all right. Ma needed me at home to keep her company. Ma taught me how to sew, and we sewed for other people in town and earned money that way. Richard needed extra money 'cause he was on the basketball team and goin' around with all the boys."

Anna had had experience herself in sewing and earning money from her mother's dressmaking business. "Richard is your brother."

"Yes. Richard is a lot younger than me. An' he got to go to high school. Ma and Pa both said that a girl don't need to go to high school if she can sew an' cook." By this time Sally was beginning to warm up to the visit and lost herself in the conversation. She also was starting to make configurations with her hands.

Anna was fascinated and found herself staring. Suddenly Sally became very self-conscious. "Oh, I forgot. I'm signing," and she quickly put her hands in her lap.

"You don't have to quit. I think that's very interesting," Anna remarked. "I've never seen anyone do that before. Dr. Bailey said that your mother was deaf and that you used sign language."

"I just forget myself sometimes," Sally admitted. "When I take care of Mrs. Wheeler I often forget and use sign language, 'cause it's almost like my mother bein' sick. I don't think she minds."

"I'm sure she doesn't, said Anna. "But tell me more about your brother."

"Oh Richard is so great. He was the star of the basketball team, and they went to lotsa places to play games. That's one reason he needed more money. I got to see him play a coupla times, when they played in our high school gym. Dad was home, so he took me. We were so proud of him."

"I understand your father works for the railroad. Does he know where you are?"

"I wrote him a letter 'n told him. He'll get the letter when he gets home again. I thought maybe sometime he could stop off in Grabney, so I told him how to get here. I mean how to get to the farm here. He can ride free on the train. Isn't he lucky? Maybe he'll come sometime."

"That would be nice. Is your brother around?"

"No he ain't. He said he don't want to be stuck in some small town, so he left to get a job somewheres. Richard is so smart. Ma said that she never saw anyone smarter than Richard. He's workin' in some city, I guess. He said he might go out west." She suddenly looked forlorn. "We didn't even know where he was so he could come to Ma's funeral."

Anna could see that a change of subject was needed so asked, "How are you getting along with Charley and Bill?"

Sally's face brightened. "Oh they're no trouble at all. They're up before I am and get their own breakfast, always oatmeal 'n eggs 'n bacon 'n fried bread 'n coffee." She laughed. "Then they go out and do the chores. They come in for dinner and sometimes sit around in the kitchen where it's warm, but they're no bother. Charley often helps with the dishes. I'd never heard of a man doin' woman's work before, but he said Inger tol' him to. Bill most always goes back to the barn. They stay in here after supper, though, an' they like to play cards. They play gin rummy a lot and sometimes hearts. Even playin' cards they don't talk much."

"I know they're pretty quiet fellas," Anna added.

"That's right. They're pretty quiet. But I don't mind. I'm not used to a lot of noise. Ma and I always signed, and Pa too."

"How are you managing with the food? Do you get things from the store?" Anna asked.

Sally looked serious for a moment, undoubtedly remembering the money hidden under the mattress. "Oh, Bill keeps the money mostly, an' they said if I needed anythin' they'd git it for me. I do all the bakin', so until I run out of flour or sugar or somethin' like that I don't need nothin'. We got lotsa potatoes an' carrots and stuff like that in the root cellar."

They heard Mrs. Wheeler stirring in her bedroom.

"Oh Sally, I think it's time for me to go. I hear Mrs. Wheeler, and I think she needs you."

"I'll jus' be a minute," Sally said as she hurried into the bedroom. “Don’t go yet.”

Anna rose to put on her coat, and as she did so she could hear the heavy clump of boots on the back steps. Turning around, she saw Charley and Bill entering the room.

“Hello Charley. Hello Bill,” she greeted them.

“’Lo,” came the response from each of them.

“I see ya had some coffee,” said Charley.

“An’ them cookies,” added Bill. “We stayed out so’s you could visit.”

“That was nice of you,” Anna said smiling at the two self-conscious men, who stood side by side. “Anyway I think it’s time for your coffee and cookies now.”

“Yes’m,” Charley nodded. “Then we’ll go do the milkin’.”

Sally reappeared. “Oh, I see the fellas are in. An’ you got your coat on, Anna.”

“Thanks for having me in, Sally. I’ll come back again sometime.”

“Oh yes! Please do. I’ve gotta go back in there,” and she pointed to the bedroom. “You guys help yourself to coffee.”

As Anna made her way out the back door the last thing she heard was, “An’ don’t you eat all them cookies.”

Chapter Eight

The third Wednesday of the month was Club day for the ladies of Grabney. During the coldest months of the year meetings were sometimes canceled, but with Mrs. Wheeler's accident and the coming of Sally Griswold the ladies couldn't wait another month to hear the latest news, even though the party line usually gave them most of the information they wanted. Mrs. Blakeley, as the minister's wife, always had the first meeting of the year, since the Club was technically an organization sponsored by the church and was officially the Ladies Aid. It was through the efforts of this group that the field next to the church was turned into the picnic ground with plenty of space for annual picnics as Fourth of July and Labor Day and the accompanying baseball games.

Anna hurried home from school, anxious to hear about the local goings-on. She found Peter stoking the wood range and Lucy and Sarah playing on the kitchen floor. "Guess you beat Milly home," he said as he glanced at her. "Is Davey with you?"

"He'll be along soon," she answered. "The last I saw of him he and George were busy throwing snowballs at the fence posts. I guess they never get tired of doing that."

"Yes, and in the summer they throw rocks at the posts," Peter added, smiling at the thought. "Milly should be along soon. She rode over with Inger and'll probably be let off at the corner. Sorry I don't have any news or gossip to relate. Sarah and Lucy have been my only companions, and they don't go in for such."

"There's no use my hanging around here then," Anna laughed. "I'll bring my things upstairs."

"By the time you get back to the kitchen, Milly's bound to be home, and she'll probably drag Davey in with her," he called to her as she went up the flight of steps.

Crossed Fingers

In her room Anna looked out of the window. It was so different from when she arrived last fall and the view was of acres of green cornstalks. Now it was all white, except for the tracks of Peter and the animals around the barn and the pens and the sheds. There was the silo near the barn, standing round and gray with small doors leading up to the top, and a ladder next to them. Through these, Peter would get the silage for his stock. He had to start with the top door first, and as he used up the silage he would work his way down. In the fall the chopped cornstalks were blown into it. It was packed tight as the air had to be kept out. Peter had explained that they couldn't let it ferment enough to make alcohol but it did ferment enough to make it change chemically. He called it the animals' sauerkraut. The windmill was constantly going on these windy days. It pumped water to the trough for the animals. There were many sheds, and one of the largest was for the farm machinery. Anna realized what a huge investment a farm like this was and what a huge job for Peter and Milly.

She heard Milly's and Davey's voices and peered closer to the window to get a glance of them coming around the corner of the house, then hurried down the stairs.

"Oi, yoi, yoi, but it is so cold," exclaimed Milly as she came in from the back porch. "Davey, come in and shut the door. Quick, I must have some coffee. I want to get warm again." Peter obliged by handing her a cup.

"How was club?" asked Anna.

"It was yust fine until Florence Simms came," she answered with a frown. "You know that woman. She has to have something to criticize, and now it is poor Sally. She hasn't even met the girl, but that doesn't stop her from going on and on."

"I suppose it's the same as it was in church," Anna remarked.

"That's right. Only now she says that since we don't know Sally's family, we really don't know what she's like. Why hasn't any of her family come to check up on her? On my goodness, it was yust too much," and Milly waved her hands in exasperation.

"The woman is thirty-five years old. She doesn't need a nursemaid," commented Peter.

"Oh! I haven't told you the really exciting news," and Milly's hands were waving again. "Esther Pearson is expecting in April. You know Anna, she's lost two babies from miscarriage. If they had lived in town, one of them might have made it. You see Esther was helping Joe with the harvest when she felt the pains come on. It was yust too much heavy work."

"And Joe has never forgiven himself for it, either," added Peter. "It was a sad time for them, especially since she had already lost one."

"Now I know why they needed the hired hand last fall," Milly said excitedly. "Anna, you remember Harley Cobb. He's the one who helped Jim Wilson, the sheriff. He said Harley gave a... what was it?"

"An alibi," said Peter.

"That's right. But now I know why they needed a hired hand," Milly continued. "I guess Esther didn't do any of the harvest work. I wondered how they could afford to pay someone."

"They couldn't afford not to," commented Peter. "I guess Joe must be pretty excited about this. He sure wants a boy."

"And Victoria will be a wonderful older sister," Anna added.

"What a sweet child she is. Don't you think so, Anna?" Milly asked.

Anna nodded as she knew Esther from teaching Sunday School with her, and she had Victoria in the third grade. They were indeed a very nice family.

Milly continued with hardly a pause to catch her breath. "Dr. Bailey had been to see her when he was at the Wheeler's, and he said she's doing fine. Inger knew that the doctor was over there, but she kept it to herself because she thought if Esther were expecting it would be best not to say anything. And then it was possible that she had lost another one. And Inger didn't even tell me."

"You ladies carry on," Peter said as he pushed himself away from the table. "And if you'll excuse me, I'm on my way to do the milking. Davey! You coming with me?"

The cold weather continued with a light snow now and then. On Friday Anna visited Sally again, and the evening conversation at the Jensens' was centered around Edna Wheeler's progress. "She was sitting up in bed," Anna reported. "And she could even say a few words. Sally said that Charley had to explain to his mother who she was. From what I saw, Mrs. Wheeler seemed to take to Sally."

"I wonder if she thinks one of the boys has gone and got married," Peter commented.

"I yust can't imagine that," said Milly. "Those men are too old to get married. And who would want to marry them?"

"There's always someone," he replied.

"Well, don't start talking like that, or Florence Simms will hear you and then we'll never hear the end of it," Milly scolded. "Anyway, it's nice of you to stop by so often, Anna. I'm sure that she appreciates it. It isn't too much fun being tied to a place like that."

It was Thursday the 24th. The school day was progressing quite well. Anna had just given the instructions for the next afternoon's craft session when she heard a knock at the door. All the students looked up. It was unusual for someone to knock at the door. Most everyone simply entered. The knock was repeated. All heads swiveled to a stop with eyes on the door. "George, will you see who it is?" she asked. He quickly left his seat and opened it. There stood Charley Wheeler, looking quite apprehensive and uncomfortable.

"Come in, Charley," she called, feeling a chill go up her spine, thinking that something terrible must have happened to bring Charley to the schoolhouse. "Is something wrong?"

"Oh no, ma'am," he said self-consciously. "Sally sent me," and he stood looking straight ahead, fussing with his hands in his gloves and the whole room looking at him.

Anna heaved a sigh of relief and waited for Charley to continue, but he remained silent. He watched George retain his seat, then slowly looked from one student to another. She finally broke the awkward silence. "What does Sally want you to tell me?"

"Can you come over after school today? Yup. That's what she wants me ta ask ya."

"Continue with your work, everyone," she instructed as she walked from the front of the room to the door where he stood. "Yes, I think I could manage that. And she sent you to invite me?"

"Yup! Well, you see we have comp'ny. Her brother Richard come to visit, an' Sally's all excited. An' that's all. Guess I'll go now."

"Tell Sally I'll be delighted to come." As he turned and exited quickly Anna could almost feel the relief he must have felt on leaving the school. And she could feel some excitement, too, partly for Sally and partly for getting to meet this brother of hers.

"Davey, tell your mother that I'll be visiting at the Wheeler's," she called to him from the schoolhouse door as he ran to catch up with George.

"I know all about it," he shouted over his shoulder. "You wanna get ta see her brother, an' his name's Richard."

Anna was a bit taken aback with his answer and guessed that during afternoon recess the entire student body must have spent the time discussing Charley and his trip to school. "Oh well," she thought as she smiled to herself. "It would be interesting to meet Richard, after all." She quickly tidied up her things and soon was on her way to the Wheeler farm. Her thoughts were on this very subject when she climbed the back steps.

"Hello! You must be Anna the school teacher." Anna looked up and saw the back door had been opened by a very pleasant-looking young man. "Come in. We've been waiting for you."

"Oh Anna, come in," said Sally as she hurried to the door. "This is my brother Richard."

"Yes, I guessed who he was," she laughed.

"Well now, don't just stand there," Richard said with mocking friendliness. "I'll take your coat, and you can put your books on the table." Anna noticed that there was very little resemblance between Sally and her brother. He was fairly tall and slim with blond hair and moved with ease. His face still carried traces of a summer tan, and from her first introduction to him she realized he was outgoing, whereas Sally was shy. Perhaps his time on the basketball team helped give him an air of self-confidence. He was wearing what looked like a fairly expensive wool shirt. He is definitely no farm boy, she thought.

"What a surprise this is," Sally said as she beamed. "Imagine, Richard coming here! I thought maybe my dad would, but never Richard."

"And why not?" he asked. "Wait'll you hear why I came. Anyway, let's sit down." He pulled out a chair for Anna and then sat across the table from her, with a chair for Sally in between.

Sally quickly arrived with the coffeepot.

"You'll never believe this, Anna," Sally said as she poured the strong coffee into their cups. "He even brought my sewing basket."

"And you can imagine how I felt, comin' on the train, carryin' a ladies sewin' basket. Anyway, I knew she had a bunch of quilt pieces in an old flour sack, and I knew if I didn't bring them it'd mean another trip here and back. So I put it in the sack, too. Here I was sittin' on the train, and next to me a half-filled flour sack, sort of like I was carryin' my provisions." He laughed and winked at Sally.

"How did you know that Sally wanted her sewing basket?" asked Anna.

"I wrote a letter to Dad," Sally chimed in. "An' in it I said that I had forgot my sewin' basket. I guess I had so many other things to think about, I never thought to bring it. And what's more I prob'ly didn't think I'd have enough time to sew."

"Well now, big sister, now that I brought it, do you think you'll have enough time to sew? I don't want to have to bring it back again."

"Oh Richard! You're just teasin' me. Of course I'll have enough time to sew. An' I'm so glad you brought it."

Before long Charley and Bill were heard in the entryway, stomping the snow off their boots. Richard was up in a second, opening the door for them. "Hey! Come on in!" he said jovially. "We've eaten almost all the cookies."

"Hello Charley, hello Bill," said Anna.

They greeted her with their usual monosyllables and seemed awed with the presence of this stranger. They shuffled self-consciously to their seats at the table, not knowing what to expect.

"How long can you stay, Richard?" asked Anna. "I think it's wonderful that you came. Sally has told me so much about you."

"Now just what have you been sayin' about me? Nothin' bad, I hope."

"Oh of course not," and Sally blushed. "An' Anna, I wanted Richard to stay at least until the Saturday train so he could see Floyd an' Peter gettin' ice for their icehouses, but he says he has to leave tomorrow. He was gonna go back today on the 5:10, but I begged him to stay all night."

"I guess I can manage one night here," Richard admitted. "But I really have to get back home by tomorrow, 'cause I'm meetin' a fella the next day or so. We're goin' to work together."

Charley looked puzzled. "If he's gonna stay all night, where'll he sleep?"

"Don't worry about me. I can sleep anywhere, on the floor if necessary. Just give me a blanket, and I'll be all right."

"Oh no! You can't sleep on the floor," Sally said. "We'll figure out something," thinking as she spoke. "Bill an' Charley have their bedroom, their ma has one room off the kitchen, an' I have the other. We could make you a bed in the parlor."

"The sofa's sorta small for him to sleep on," Bill said, looking at how tall Richard seemed even when sitting down. "What about the bunkhouse? That has a bed, an' we got plenty a blankets, an' there's a stove in there too. Nobody's usin' it now."

"Yeah. Jimmy won't be comin' aroun' till next summer," Charley added.

"Well, who's Jimmy?" asked Richard.

"He's a kid who helps us out when we got too much work to do," Bill answered. "But he don't come in the winter time."

"An' the bunkhouse has a stove, so it can get plenty warm in there," Charley explained with enthusiasm. "An' there's still a little coal in there too and plenty of cobs."

"Sounds like just the ticket," Richard said.

"I've been out there, an' it's plenty clean," Sally added. "That way you can have a place of your own. But are you sure you can't stay one more night? We're all goin' down to the river Saturday mornin'. It'll be such fun."

"I'm not goin' down," Bill said. "I'm stayin' home to look after things. Anyways, I'm not too int'rested in gettin' ice, so I said Charley'n Sally could go an' I'd stay home."

"And are you going too, Anna?" Richard asked.

"Of course! I wouldn't miss it for anything. We've been thinking about this for so long that it doesn't seem possible that the time has finally come to get the ice."

"You mean really everyone's goin'?" he continued.

"Well, not everyone in Grabney," Anna laughed. "But the Parkers across the road will be there, and the Jensens, that's where I live, just down the road toward the river. They're the ones getting the ice for their icehouses."

"See, Richard!" Sally scolded. "I tol' ya it would be fun, that everyone would be there. Can't you really stay? An' you could sleep in the bunkhouse."

"Really I would love to, but Frank an' I are gettin' ready to go out west. Guess there's plenty of good jobs there. Why we may even get to Califor-ni-a."

"Gee! That's really far," Bill exclaimed. "Why are you goin' so far? Ain't there no work aroun' here?"

"There's not much work here, not in the winter anyway. An' there's too much snow. I'm getting pretty tired of traipsing aroun' in the cold. Nope! California has not a bit of snow. Jus' like summer, almost. An' it's the place for me."

"How could they have winter with no snow?" asked Charley.

"Here's your school teacher," and he nodded at Anna. "You explain why they don't have snow."

"Well," she began, "the sunniest part of California is farther south than we are, and they get more sun. They also don't get the cold winds from Canada. Does that explain it?"

Bill seemed deep in thought and then said, "They couldn't make icehouses out there, then."

"You're right Bill, an' where I'm goin' they couldn't even make a snowball."

Anna looked at her watch. "Dear me! It's after four o'clock. I must be getting home."

"Do you really have to go, Anna?" Sally asked.

"Tomorrow's Friday, and I have a lot of papers to correct tonight."

"Oh, that's right," Sally said. "I forgot that you usually stay later at school. So Charley, as long as Anna's goin', why don't you take Richard out an' show him the bunkhouse? I'll get some extra blankets. Get the fire goin' so that it won't be bone chillin' cold when he goes out there tonight."

"I'm sure glad to have met you, Anna. Sure you can't stay for supper?" Richard asked as he pushed himself away from the table.

"Oh yes! Can't you stay for supper?" Sally asked.

"No, but thanks, anyway. I really do have to get back home. Milly will wonder what happened to me, although I'm sure Davey told here where I was."

"Well, if that's the way it's gonna be, let me help you on with your coat anyway," and Richard held out her warm bearskin coat. "This sure is a beaut," he commented, "but where I'm goin' we won't need nothin' like it. An' I can't wait to get out there."

They climbed down the back steps together, followed by Charley carrying the blankets.

"Come back soon, Anna," Sally called.

"Thanks Sally, I'll see you Saturday morning."

There was a light snow on Friday, just enough to give the landscape a clean, fresh look. The afternoon craft session went fairly smoothly. Since snow was not a novelty anymore, few students bothered to glance out of the window. They were more interested in the sled that Lars Anderson and George were building. Mabel and Erica Larson were knitting mittens, and trying to finish them before winter ended. The younger girls were working on scarves, many of them in various colors from yarn donated by the ladies of the community.

Anna glanced at them now and then as she tried to finish correcting the morning tests. Today she had determined to stay at school until they were all graded and Monday's lessons prepared. This weekend was bound to be busy, and she didn't want to spoil the fun by thinking about schoolwork.

At last it was 2:45. Lars had finished his sled, and they were anxious to try it out. She stood at her desk. "It's a quarter to three," she announced, "so let's clean up before we leave for the weekend." George got out the sweeping compound, and Lars the broom. Students cleaned off their desks and moved them out of the way so the floor could be swept. The oily smell of the compound filled the room. That very odor alone brought a sense of cleanliness. In fifteen minutes the room was tidy, desks were back in place and the students were sitting ready to be dismissed.

It was after four o'clock when Anna finished grading her last paper. She gave a sigh of relief and arranged the corrected papers and Monday's lessons on her desk, ready to distribute on Monday morning. It was getting dark a little early as it had clouded over. A light snow had started falling. She put on her galoshes and bundled herself up for the outdoors before blowing out the lamp. As she stood on the porch she thought she saw someone walking up the road. She concentrated on the image and recognized Richard as he came into the schoolyard.

"Well school teacher, I think you're stayin' a little late," he called to her.

Trying to not show her surprise she answered, "Well, Friday tests mean lots of correcting, and then there're Monday's assignments to get ready. How did you know I was still here?"

"Saw the light from the windows. I'm on my way to the station."

"Aren't you going the wrong way?"

"Well, I thought since I had a little extra time I'd see if you were still here. You don't mind if I walk you to the corner, do you?"

"Oh no. Just a minute while I tug on this door to get it shut. In the winter with all the snow it sometimes swells a little," she said as she slammed it shut, and came down the steps.

"Aren't you gonna lock it?" he asked.

"We don't lock the school doors here. What if people got caught in a blizzard? They just might find a schoolhouse and could go in and save themselves. There're cobs for fire starters and coal."

"It'd be better to paint the schoolhouses red instead of white then. How can you see a white schoolhouse in the snow?"

"I suppose you're right," she answered as they walked down the road. "I know that some schoolhouses are painted red, but I'm not about to get a paintbrush out tonight and start. Anyway, you're getting the 5:10, aren't you? I hope you told the stationmaster to have it stop in Grabney. It doesn't always, you know."

"Yes, I asked about that when I came, and they said that on Friday and Saturday it would stop. Guess with the snow there's extra mail or somethin' that'll be comin' in on the train."

"How're you going to get to California? Are you going on the train?"

"What we do is what we've done before."

"This is you and your friend Frank?"

"I'm surprised you remembered his name. Yeah, it's Frank Wiggins. He an' I've been goin' around for some time. We get to a town, an' if we need money we get some kind of job, then when we have enough we move on. We've sort of drifted before, but now we have plans to land ourselves somethin' real good. Sometimes we can hitch a ride, but in this weather it's not so easy."

"Why don't you wait until spring?" Anna advised. "Everything's going to be snowed in now, except maybe Florida."

"Or California," he answered. "And California's the place we wanna go to. There's more jobs out there. Frank's got an uncle lives in South Dakota. He's been around a lot so we're gonna go there first. We can bunk in with him for a while too if there's too much snow around."

"Here I am at the corner," Anna said. "Sure you won't stay an extra day to see the men get the ice?"

"No thanks! I think I've seen enough ice to last me a lifetime. Anyway I just wanted to ask you if it's okay if I write you, maybe send you a postcard."

"Oh yes," she answered, surprised at his request. She'd never before had a fellow ask if he could write to her.

"But I didn't even get your last name."

"It's Swenson, S-W-E-N-S-O-N. And you can mail it to Grabney."

"Okay. That is what I'll do, Miss Anna Swenson."

"It's beginning to snow a little harder and getting dark. And you have two miles to go, so you'll have to hurry to catch the train," she said with some concern.

"I'll make it fine," he laughed with carefree abandon. "So when I get to California I'll send you a postcard. And this time I'm gonna strike it rich, like in the gold rush."

"Good luck then," she said as she turned down the road.

"With you wishin' it for me, I'm bound to have it," he answered and waved to her as he headed on a run toward Grabney and disappeared into the falling snow.

Chapter Nine

Saturday, January 27, dawned clear and cold. The ice on the river was as thick as it was going to get. Today was the day they had been looking for.

"Come here, Sarah, and let me tuck your dress into your leggings," Anna called to the child who was struggling with her apparel. She knelt down beside her. "Here you've got it all bunched up. Now that's better. Now, let's get your suspenders over your shoulders. Good!" she smiled. "Here, sit up on the chair and I'll help you with your galoshes." Anna stood and lifted the four-year-old, putting her on one of the wooden kitchen chairs. "If you're going to go down to the river and watch your daddy get the ice, you'd better be dressed warmly. Here's the right one. Let's do that first."

"Davey, you'll have to wear your muffler," Milly reminded him. "And be sure to pull your cap over your ears. It's cold outside. How're you coming with Sarah, Anna?"

"Fine. We have the galoshes on so we're ready for the sweater and coat."

"The mittens have a string on them, so put them on first so they go into the sleeves of her coat," reminded Milly. "That way she'll never lose them."

"I think we're about ready then," Anna answered. I'll put on my things and we'll be off."

"Don't let them stay out too long, Anna. It's so cold."

"I'm used to the cold," Davey said. "Don't forget I walk to school every day."

"Yes, I know," said his mother. "But walking to school is different from standing in the cold and watching your father and Uncle Floyd."

"They've been working about an hour, haven't they?" asked Anna.

"Yes, I think it's about time that they were coming back with a load," Milly replied as she checked Sarah to make sure she was bundled up.

"Let's hurry then," Davey said anxiously. "I don't want to miss anything."

"All right then, I'm ready. Let's go," said Anna.

"Now you keep ahold of Miss Swenson's hand, Sarah. It's dangerous down near the river."

"But it's all frozen over, Mama," Davey added. "The kids have been skating on it all the time. You can't fall into the water. I wish I was old enough to have ice skates." He came over to his sister and leaned over to talk to her. "Do you want to see the kids go ice skating, Sarah? They always skate on Saturday. Carl Anderson says he gets to go out on the ice and slide around without skates, just on his shoes." He straightened up and asked, "Can I do that, Mama?"

"I don't know about that," she answered. "It depends on your father. Keep an eye on him, Anna. Oh dear, I'm not sure about this at all. And you stay out of the way, Davey. Don't bother the men."

"Are you sure you don't want to go with the children, Milly?" Anna asked. "I could stay with Lucy."

"Oh, no thanks, Anna. I have seen enough ice cut up. This way I'll have some time to myself to do a little work around here. I yust don't want the children to be a bother to you."

The cold air rushed in from the outside as they opened the entryway door. "I'm sure I won't want to stay too long," Anna remarked as she shivered. "So don't worry. And I'll watch them."

"Good-bye! And children, you behave yourselves," Milly called to them as she shut the door.

As they were carefully making their way down the porch steps they heard Peter's voice. "That's Daddy!" Davey yelled as he ran toward the sound. He stopped at the corner of the house and called back to them. "I see him. He's almost here. Hi Daddy! Wait for me!" And Davey was off at a run.

"Wait for me too, Daddy," called Sarah as she tugged on Anna's hand, pulling her toward the icehouse where her father had stopped to unload.

"Oh, you tied the ice to the stone boat," Davey remarked with some surprise. "How much ice did you get?"

"Hold on there a minute son," his father answered. "You can see for yourself how much I got. Now I have to get it off and get it into the icehouse."

"I'll help you with that Peter," came the voice of a young man who hurried up to where they were."

"Well I'll be darned. Is that you, Jonah?" Peter said with surprise. "Where in the heck did you come from?"

"I got in on the 5:10 yesterday. I've a week off from school to do some reports. Let me give you a hand. I've heard about your icehouse. Now I see it's time to fill it up."

"You're right. This is the ice for Milly's icehouse," said Peter as he shoved the first block off the stone boat, which looked more like a sled and consisted of a large piece of wood attached to two wooden runners. It was also used during other seasons to haul loads. Running over the stones and dirt, it gave a very bumpy ride. "You probably know that it all started when Milly got the idea of having an icebox. Well, we got the icebox all right, so now we need the ice to go in it."

"I see you cut the pieces just the right size too," Jonah remarked.

"Well, you can't have them so big they won't fit into the icebox," Peter continued. "And what's more, it's easier for me to cut them to size now than to have to saw them up later."

"So that's how the sides got so smooth," Anna remarked. "How on earth can you saw ice?"

"Well, it's a lot like sawing wood, but goes faster," Peter explained. "You'll see when you come down to the river."

"Looks like you did a great job on the icehouse," Jonah commented as he stepped inside and admired the structure. "Here, you shove the ice to the doorway and I'll heave it inside. I see you've laid a nice bed of straw on the ground. I'll put it on the far side so you'll have room near the door for more."

"Thanks. Yeah just shove it over as far as you can. Be sure and pack some straw around each piece. I don't want them to freeze together. I've got plenty of straw in there and a stack of it outside here, so it should be insulated pretty good."

"I can't believe that it will stay frozen all through the hot summer," Anna said with some doubt.

"Oh, it'll stay frozen all right," Peter replied, nodding his head. "Just as long as folks don't think they can come and sit in the ice-house on a hot day to cool off. That wouldn't do. It has to stay shut up."

"When I first saw it, I thought it was a little hill, but I knew you didn't have a hill like this on your place." Jonah continued looking around as he shoved the blocks inside. "I can see that after you dug it out you built a framework, and then put the dirt and sod on top. This is really clever. I suppose you're the only one around here with one."

Peter laughed. "Well, that's a long story, but after Milly got me to build her one, Inger wouldn't take no for an answer until Floyd had one built for her."

I guess my ma will be next," Jonah laughed. "But in the summer a cold drink will taste mighty nice. Oh hello, Anna," he said as he came out of the icehouse. "I see you're all ready to go down and watch the proceedings."

"That's right," she smiled. "And I have two helpers here who are very anxious to get involved."

"Let's go, Daddy," said Sarah. "Can I ride on the stone boat? Oh, please!"

"You'd fall right off, Sarah," her father answered. "Then I'd be in hot water with your mother for letting you get banged up and cold. Let me get Ginger turned around now, and we can all go back down to the river."

"How are things going at school, Jonah?" Anna asked. "Here Sarah, you keep hold of my hand, and let Davey walk with your father."

"Better yet, let me put her up on my shoulders," Jonah offered, and lifted her up with a hefty swing, sitting her securely on his shoulders. "Put your hands around my head, and I'll keep hold of your feet. That's the way. We'll follow your dad and Davey."

"And Ginger, too," the child corrected.

"Yes, that's right. And Ginger too."

The snow had been tramped down in the yard and was a bit slick. "Careful, Anna," Jonah warned. "There's a lot of ice here. Don't fall."

"Oh, I won't. I'll be careful."

"I didn't get to answer your question about school. Well, it's going pretty good. I think I can finish this year."

"That's wonderful. You mean you'll be going full time?"

"I can get some time off to help with the spring planting, but other than that I'll be away most of the spring."

"I guess your dad and William have taken Grace's animals then," said Anna, referring to the livestock on the farm across the road, when Grace Kloster left it after her husband's and father's deaths. "I hadn't seen the animals in the Kloster barn, so I assumed that they were on your folks' place."

"Yes, we were able to make room for them, and it was much easier than traipsing over to their place twice a day and hauling feed besides. Dad paid her outright for them, and so that part of the deal is closed."

This perked up Anna's interest. "I understand that your father has signed the papers to pay for the place on contract."

"That's right. And he did say that when I'm able, I can buy it from him. That'll be a while, though. But since it's next to ours, it works out real well. That way William can buy dad's place and we'll be next to each other."

"I think your father must have had all this in mind for some time," Anna commented.

"Maybe so. I'm not sure that he's too happy about my spending all my time in school, but it's just that he has no idea how much I'm learning. At least I have a job where I can pay my room and board, and I also have almost enough for tuition. Mother saved some money which she lent me, and while she pretends Dad doesn't know about it, I'm sure he does."

"I think he's really proud of you for doing this," Anna said, "but at this point he doesn't want to admit it."

"Maybe you're right," and he laughed.

As they turned to go on the road between the farms, Anna glanced at the Kloster house.

Jonah noticed this. "I suppose you're wondering what I'm going to do with that place. I was talking to Ed Marson. Did you know that he and Bertha were going to get married in June?"

"Yes, I'd heard that," she answered.

"Well, Ed said he and Bertha were looking for a house they could move to the land across from the parsonage. Sigurd Torgerson owns it, and he said he'd sell him a couple of acres, and that's all that Ed wants."

"That's wonderful," Anna commented. "That way they can work in the store and still have a place of their own, with enough land for a little garden."

"I was hoping maybe Ed would buy the Kloster house from me, but he didn't want it. Besides, it's pretty run down. I would've given it to him if he'd taken it."

"Has he found something else then?" she asked.

"He was lucky. There's a school a couple of miles from here that hasn't had any pupils in it for half a dozen years or so and the district decided to put it up for sale, so Ed bid on it and got it. This is a perfect time of year to buy a place like that, because with all the snow he can move it on skids."

"When's he going to do that?"

"When I got off the train yesterday I stopped by the store and offered to help him if he could move it this week. He had planned to do it soon anyway. It's almost February, and the cold weather might not last. So guess I'll have another project besides studying."

"I've never heard of farmers moving a building as big as a school," Anna said. "How on earth do they do it?"

"It's not such a big job. They move schoolhouses all the time. When the children in one area grow up and they know it will be years before another generation comes along, they just relocate the school where the children are."

"It sounds simple," she replied, "but I don't think it's that easy. You make it sound like it's an everyday affair," and she laughed.

"There they are! There they are!" Sarah yelled, as they approached the riverbank. "Look at all those guys ice skating. I want to get down and play on the ice."

"Just a minute, young lady," cautioned Jonah. "We have to get down this bank first. Now hold on tight, and Anna, you grab my arm, and let's hope I don't fall." In this fashion they carefully made their way down the hill to the river.

"Now I see how they do it," said Anna. "Until now I couldn't imagine sawing ice."

There was quite a group chopping and sawing up the blocks.

Floyd and Walter had one load on their stone boat and were slowly coming up the riverbank. As they passed, Floyd called out to Sarah, "What're you doin' up there so high? You better get down and work. I could use a little extry help."

"I can't do that," she reminded him. "I'm too little."

"Well hurry up and grow then, 'cause I'm gettin' mighty tired of doin' so much. Say Jonah, your dad tol' me you was plannin' to help Ed move the West Schoolhouse. Some time this week, I s'pose."

"Probably toward the middle of the week, after he gets things ready," Jonah replied.

"Well if it don't take all week to get this durn ice, Walter an' me'll be glad to help. Imagine, the whole place's froze over an' we have to come down to the river to collect blocks of ice. I ain't never seen the likes of it. Come on, Clementine! Giddap!" And he waved as they made one more trip up the hill.

"How're you doing, Peter?" Jonah called as they approached the river.

"Not too bad. George and Lars are helping me. By golly, they nearly got another load ready for me by the time I got back."

"I see you've gone out a ways from the bank," Anna remarked. "How do you know where's the best place to get the ice?"

"First we chop it into a couple of places to see how thick it is," Peter explained, "and when we find some that is about eighteen inches thick, then we chop enough out so that we can start sawing. Next to the bank it's frozen with grass and brush and we don't want that. Anyway it was a little too thick there, so we went out a ways where you see the boys working."

"I hope they don't fall in," Anna said with some alarm.

"I hope so, too," Peter agreed. "But I've told them to be careful, and they seem to be heeding my advice."

"Let me help," Jonah offered, and he took another block of ice from George and heaved it on the stone boat.

"Davey, you stay close to shore," called his father. "I know those kids are skating way out in the middle, but you stay where I can see you."

"Can I go out on the ice?" Sarah asked. "Davey's out there, and I want to go, too."

"I'll take her out a ways," volunteered Anna. "I think it would be rather fun to go out there myself," and she took Sarah's hand and they pretended to skate on the slippery surface. "I'll keep an eye on Davey, too, so you can get on with your work."

"Thanks, Anna. Much obliged. If he gives you any trouble, send him home."

"Oh, he'll be all right," she answered. "Davey, you remember to stay close to us," she called to him.

"Say Charley, is that you?" Anna heard Jonah call out. She turned and saw Charley and Sally coming down the riverbank.

"'Lo, Jonah," Charley gleefully called out. "Whatcha doin'?"

"I'm helping Peter get ice for his icehouse. C'mon. Give us a hand."

"Hi, Sally," Anna called as she and Sarah made their way toward the shore. Sally waved a greeting. "Jonah, have you met Sally?"

"Don't believe I have."

"This is Sally Griswold. She's taking care of Charley's mother. I'm so glad you came down here, Sally. I didn't know if you'd be able to make it."

"Mrs. Wheeler's sleepin' now. She usually sleeps 'bout this time of the mornin'. I figger she won't wake up for another coupla hours or so. Anyway, Bill's home, an' he said he'd look in on her."

"Come on out on the ice with us. Sarah and I were having fun slipping and sliding around."

"Are all those people out there from Grabney?" Sally asked as she looked at the crowd horsing around on the ice.

"You mean the ones up there?" Anna asked as she pointed in the direction of the bridge. "I don't know but I think I've seen a couple of them in the store. They may live across the river."

"You would have seen more of them if they were younger and the school was closer to town," Peter said as he passed by them to get more ice. "You remember Mrs. Downey from church, don't you, Anna? Well some of those are her boys. They're in high school."

"That's right," Jonah added. "As I recall there aren't any real young children just across the river. The Webster School was moved farther south about five years ago. Most of the children south of us go there. I suppose some day the Grabney School will be moved closer to town when the children in school now are grown."

"That'll be a while," Peter said as he heaved a hunk of ice out of the river and skidded it along to the bank.

"I know some of them guys. Don't go near 'em," Charley uttered vehemently as he screwed his face up, showing his anger. "They can be real mean."

"You're right, Charley," Jonah acknowledged. "I recall a couple of them were pretty mean to you one time. They can be pretty rough, and I don't think you ladies would want to play any of their games."

"We'll stay around here," Anna explained. "I remember at home the gangs that congregated on the ice. Sometimes it got a little rough, especially when they played hockey. Mother wouldn't let us go down there. She said 'Boys will be boys, so you stay away from them,' and of course we did. So come on Sally, let's go out on the ice. We'll stay down here with the Grabney kids."

"Okay," Sally smiled. "I've never done this before. It looks like fun. So Charley, I'm goin' out with Anna. An' we'll stay close. So you help the men get the ice."

"I have to keep an eye on Davey, too," Anna said. "Let's skate over to where he is, that is if you could call this skating." The three of them caught up with Davey and many of the other rosy-faced children who were out for fun this particular Saturday.

Soon Jonah's dad Olle and brother Will were there to help. Mabel and Erica came with their ice skates and squealed as they sat down in the snow to attach them to their shoes. There was so much help that Peter and Floyd were kept busy loading up and taking off.

After an hour or so Anna felt quite chilled and knew that they should be heading for home. She could see that Peter was about ready to leave. "Davey, I think it's time we went home. Why don't you go with your dad?" she called to him. "Come on, Sarah. Aren't you getting cold?" Anna could tell that the child was slowing down.

"A little," she replied between chattering teeth.

"Sally, come on up to the house with us. I know Milly will have some coffee on, and you've never met her."

"That'd be nice, Anna. I am gettin' a little cold," she shuddered.

"You come with me, Davey," Peter called.

"I'm coming," he answered. He was moving a little more slowly than he had been when they arrived.

The three of them followed Peter and Davey up the hill. Anna and Sally each took one of Sarah's hands as they walked up the road, and on the count of "three" they lifted her up and jumped her a distance of three to four feet. "Do it again," she cried, and the three laughed as she was jumped again and again. Soon they were at the Jensens'.

"Oh, this feels so good," Anna exclaimed as the warm air enveloped them as they entered the kitchen. "Milly, this is Sally Griswold. I thought we would come in and get warm."

"Oh yes," she answered cheerfully. "I'm so happy to meet you. Yust sit down. Oh yes, take off your wraps and put them over a chair. Here, I'll get the coffee," and she hurried to make her guest welcome.

Anna returned from hanging up her coat in the entryway, followed by Davey who was ready to get inside. They sat down and told Milly all about the morning's events. Soon it was nearly noon, and Sally realized that she should be getting back to the Wheelers so that she could have dinner on time.

"I'll walk back with you, Sally," Anna said. I'm so glad you were able to get out. It'll only take me a minute or two to get bundled up again."

"That would be nice, Anna. I haven't had such a nice day in a long time."

"Careful of these steps," Anna warned as they left the back porch. "Oh I hear Peter coming again. He must be ready for dinner by now. They gave him a hearty greeting as they turned to go into the road.

"By the way, how is Mrs. Wheeler doing now?" Anna asked.

"Oh she's a different person," Sally answered. "She's even beginnin' to talk."

"That's good news. The last time I was up I thought she was doing better. She seemed to be aware of what was going on."

"I think she always understands what people are sayin' to her, but she just can't talk back very well."

"I know you've been a great help to her. I don't know what they would have done without you."

"Oh I dunno. Anyone could do what I've done. But it's

like a real home to me. The men're real nice. Charley's a good help, and neither one is no bother at all. An' they seem to like my cookin', too."

"They're lucky to have a good cook like you."

"I hope I'm not too good. I think I'm gettin' a little fat."

"You could use a little weight," Anna surmised good-naturedly. "Is Mrs. Wheeler eating all right?"

"She sometimes gives a bit of trouble, but I don't mind. I'm used to that."

"I'm sure you'll have to stay around a good long time before she's really well," Anna added.

"Well, I'll stay as long as they want me. I really don't have nothin' to go home to, now that Ma's gone."

They turned into the yard and made their way up the back steps and into the kitchen. Sally glanced into the bedroom. "I guess she's sleepin'. Bill must still be out in the yard. I would've thought he'd be in the house by this time. I thought Mrs. Wheeler'd be awake too. Guess I'm lucky. This'll give me time to get dinner. I'll just take off my boots and stick them in the entryway. Why don't you put your coat over a chair, Anna. It'll stay warmer that way. That's why I keep mine in the bedroom."

"Thanks Sally, but I think you have too much to do to bother with me," Anna replied.

"Oh no! I hope you'll stay awhile." She bustled into her bedroom and could be heard taking off her wraps and humming to herself.

Anna walked over to Mrs. Wheeler's bedroom door and looked in at the sleeping figure. The woman was lying very still. Too still, Anna thought. She also looked very pale. Yes, she must be sleeping very soundly. Anna took a closer look and felt a chill of fear. There was no sign that she was breathing. Anna waited and watched.

"Oh, you haven't even taken off your coat yet," Sally said as she came out of her room. Anna didn't answer, which puzzled Sally. "What's the matter? Is something wrong?"

"It's Mrs. Wheeler. Sally, is she usually so quiet when she sleeps?"

"Oh no! She snores. She must be snoring." Sally pondered an instant, then walked over to the door where Anna stood and looked at her patient. “Oh Anna! She don’t look right at all.” She rushed over to feel Mrs. Wheeler’s chest. There was no movement. Sally stood there as if transfixed, shaking her head, and then let out an agonized cry. “Oh no! It’s just like with my Ma. I think she’s dead.”

Anna began to shake and leaned against the doorjamb to steady herself. As Sally desperately tried to feel for some sign of life in the woman, Anna could see Mrs. Wheeler’s right arm hanging over the side of the bed. And stranger yet, looking at her hand she could see that she had her fingers crossed.

Chapter Ten

"Listen Charley! What'd you do this morning after you slopped them pigs?" Bill shouted across the yard to his brother.

"I didn't do nothin', Bill," he answered defensively. "I jus' slopped the pigs an' that was all."

"Well, I'll tell ya what ya fergot ta do," Bill retorted with some anger. "Ya fergot ta shut the pen, an' they got out, an I been chasin' pigs all over this place fer darn near two hours."

Anna could hear two sets of sturdy footsteps coming up the back steps, but Bill was still out in the yard, so there must be someone with Charley. She could feel herself shaking. Now they were in the entryway.

"Gosh durn," Charley moaned. "That's the second time I done that. Bill is madder'n hops. An' I promised him I'd be careful and never do it agin."

"Well he's got the pigs in now," Jonah said. "Let's go in and sort this thing out. Come on, Charley." He opened the kitchen door. "Oh, Anna. Hello again. Come on in, Charley. Anna's here. Let's get a cup of coffee."

They were followed by Bill, who stormed into the entryway. He ripped off his coat and jammed it up on a hook with a vengeance. "By gosh Charley, I'll have yer hide if you ever do that agin." He entered the kitchen and slammed the door shut. "Oh, hello Jonah."

"Afternoon, Bill," Jonah said. "Sounds like you've had real trouble this morning."

"You bet I have. An' it's all on account of that fool brother a mine."

"I didn't mean to do it," Charley pleaded. "I was jus' so excited 'bout goin' down to the river that I guess I was in too much of a hurry. I never thought I left it open, but I guess I did."

The men were making so much noise that no one could hear Sally moaning. Suddenly, as Jonah looked at Anna, he was aware that all was not well. He walked over to her to escape the argument going on between the brothers. "What's the matter? Where's Sally?"

"In the bedroom," Anna said as she turned to look in that direction.

"You're upset. What happened? Did Mrs. Wheeler take a turn for the worse?"

"Yes," she answered, slowly looking over at Charley and Bill, who were still engaged in the argument. "Oh, I've got to help Sally. Here will you take my coat?" She handed him her wraps and went into the bedroom.

"Oh Sally," said Anna as she put her arms around the weeping woman. They stood there comforting each other for a minute or so, not realizing that Jonah was now standing in the doorway.

Sally cried out between sobs, "Oh, Anna, this is so terrible. What'm I gonna do?"

Jonah walked over to the bed and soon realized that Mrs. Wheeler might not be alive. He picked up her right wrist to feel for a pulse. After a moment he shook his head and then pressed one of his fingers to the side of her neck to see if he could feel one there. Shaking his head again he felt her chest to learn if there were a heartbeat, no matter how weak. He stood up and thought for a moment. "Well, first thing, I'm going to get you two ladies out of here and sit you down in the kitchen."

"But what happened?" moaned Sally still standing by the bed. "She was fine this mornin'. I can't believe she's lyin there lookin' like that. Is she really...dead?"

"It looks that way, Sally, answered Jonah. "As to the reason, I'm not sure why. Only the doctor can tell us that, but it looks to me like she had a stroke. You know she had one before, and when a person has one stroke they are likely to have another."

"But she was so fine this mornin'," Sally repeated.

"This can happen at any time," Jonah said, trying to comfort the young woman. "Why don't you two come out into the kitchen and sit down? You both look a little pale."

"And what'll we tell the fellas?" she added, as Jonah ushered them gently into the kitchen and into chairs.

"What's goin' on?" Bill asked. "What were you all doin' in Ma's room?"

"But it wasn't my fault, Bill," Charley continued pleading. "I didn't mean ta do it." He then looked at Sally. "An why's Sally cryin'? Is it 'cause I fergot ta shut the pig pen?"

"It's not that at all," Jonah said in as calm a voice as possible. "Your mother has had a bit of bad luck." He paused to give them a little time for this to sink in. "I think she had another stroke."

Everyone was silent until Bill looked up and said slowly, "But she'll be all right, won't she? She was gettin' all right after the other one."

"I'm afraid not, Bill," Jonah answered. "This time she didn't make it."

"Whatya mean she didn't make it?" Charley asked plaintively. "Oh no! You mean Ma's dead? What'll we do without Ma?"

"You've gotten along fine without her for nearly a month." Jonah was trying to keep the situation calm. "I think maybe she realized that you two can manage by yourselves now."

Bill sat down in a chair at the table shaking his head looking rather dazed. "I dunno. I guess we can."

"There are some things that need to be taken care of fairly soon," said Jonah. "Why don't we get Inger over here. I think she'd be a big help."

"I'll get her," and Charley dashed out the door and down the steps.

Bill stared after him, then slowly spoke. "We could've phoned her. It would've been quicker."

Sally sat up and looked at the group. "It's best to let Charley go over there. It'll give him somethin' to do. I remember when my ma died I wanted to run over and get someone to help me, but there was no one to go to."

No one answered her as they stared at the table or looked around at the walls of the room. Anna started to say something but changed her mind and looked at Jonah with the hope that he would break the silence.

He looked back at her, then abruptly got up and announced, "Well, I can smell coffee, so I'm going to pour everyone a cup. Is that all right with you, Sally?"

She looked up at him, still bewildered by the recent turn of events and answered mechanically. "Sure. That's fine."

"What'll we do about Ma?" Bill asked. "What'll we do now?"

"Inger will know what to do," Anna said comfortingly.

"That's right," he said. "Inger always knows what to do."

"Let me get the cups, Jonah," Anna volunteered. She rose slowly from her chair and tried not to look into the bedroom as she took down four cups from the cupboard. "Oh, I guess I'd better get five. Charley will want a cup too."

"Wait'll he gets back, Anna," Bill advised. "Coffee'll jus' get cold."

Yes," she agreed, as she gave the cups to Jonah for him to fill.

"Sugar'n milk are on the counter," Sally said listlessly.

"Oh yes," Anna replied. "I'll put them on the table."

"When did she die?" asked Bill, who still seemed dazed. "It musta been when I was out with them pigs."

"I should nevera gone to the river this mornin'," Sally wailed. "I shoulda been here when she needed me."

"There was nothing you could do," Jonah said to console her. "If you had been here, she could have slipped off in her sleep without you even knowing it."

"But still, I feel so bad," and she started crying again.

"You drink this coffee, Sally, and you, too, Bill," Jonah suggested. "Here, let's all sit down at the table and wait for Inger to come."

They didn't have to wait long, as voices could soon be heard in the yard, and shortly thereafter Inger and Charley came through the kitchen door to find four solemn faces looking up at them.

"I got Inger, all right," Charley announced. "She was jus' gettin' ready ta eat dinner, but she come over, anyway."

"Don't bother about all that, Charley," Inger commented in her usual pragmatic fashion. "I'm sure sorry to hear about your Ma, Bill, but guess it was bound to happen. She was a tough old lady, but there are some things that you just can't avoid. Let me go and have a look at her." Inger went into the bedroom.

Everyone was quiet as they waited for her to reappear. After a couple of minutes she came to the door of the room and they turned in unison to hear her verdict. "You're right...She's gone...Too bad...She was a great old lady." She paused to look at the group. "Well, I guess I'll let someone pour me a cup of coffee." Inger slowly walked to the table and took a seat.

"I just knowed I should'na gone to the river this mornin'," Sally wailed.

Inger quickly tried to stem her tears of regret. "No, no. Don't blame yourself. There was nothing you could do. She would've died even if you were here. When it's time to go, it's time to go. And she'd had a hard time of it lately. Sally you gave her the best care possible this past month. We'll always remember that."

"I'm sorry about Ma," Charley said soberly, nearly close to tears. "But Sally took real good care of her."

"I think she took good care of all of you, if you ask me," Inger commented.

"Yup, she did," Bill agreed. "Sally's sure a good cook, an' Ma liked her too. I could tell that Ma liked her."

"I thought she was gettin' so much better," Sally said. "I didn't think she would die. I thought she would get well."

"All of us were hoping for that, but it's as I said before, we never know," Inger added. "Anyway, I'm going to phone Floyd and get him over here. He can help us make some arrangements." She got up from the table, went to the wall phone and cranked three long rings. Everyone was completely silent as they listened to her conversation.

"Floyd!———You better come over here.———That's right.———Bye." She hung up. "He'll be over in a jiffy. Just about time to let us finish this coffee. The next thing I'll do is phone Doc Bailey. Once I call Liza, everyone will know what happened. Let me finish my coffee first."

"You wanna cuppa coffee, Charley?" Sally asked.

"Nope!" Charley muttered. "Jus' don't feel like nothin' now."

"To think we was havin' so much fun today, an' then this had to happen," and Sally burst into tears again.

"I know how awful you must feel, Sally," Inger consoled, "but you can't let this get you down. You've done the best you could."

She continued through sobs, "But I liked livin' here an' helpin an' doin' the work. An' havin' people to talk to. It was so nice, like a dream, an' now it's over."

"Don't go jumping to conclusions now, Sally," advised Inger. "Let's take this one step at a time. And you don't have to leave right away. Goodness knows, the men will need you to help them get through this." The clomp of footsteps was heard coming up the back steps, then into the entryway. "If I'm not mistaken, that's Floyd." Jonah opened the door. "Well, sure enough."

Floyd stepped into the kitchen and closed the door. "I'm real sorry to hear about your Ma, Charley 'n Bill. I know this is a pretty hard thing to take." He continued to stand by the door.

"Yup! Shore is," Bill said. "But I guess like Inger said, it was bound ta happen. Jus' hard when it comes, that's all."

"Well the first thing we must do is get ahold of Dr. Bailey," Inger said. "I'm going to phone Liza and see if she can get through to the county seat to locate him. She went to the phone and rang the post office. "Hello Liza.———This is Inger.———Had a spot of trouble out our way. Seems Mrs. Wheeler had another stroke and it looks like she didn't make it.———Yeah, that's right.———Well, we need to get ahold of Dr. Bailey to sign the death certificate. Think you could reach him?———He is!———You say at Devons'?———Could you give them a call? Our line doesn't go out that far.———Tell them I can have Walter come and pick him up. It shouldn't take too long here and he can still get the 5:10 back to the county seat.———Good! Thanks Liza. I'm at the Wheeler's now so ring me here.———That's right. Bye."

Inger hung up the phone. "Well, that's a bit of luck, for us at least. The Devon boy was ice skating yesterday and broke his leg. Probably horsing around too much. They always were a wild bunch. Anyway the doc's there now. Came out on the noon train. Liza will call back if she can reach him."

"Walter can make it there in no time," suggested Floyd. "They live just a coupla miles across the river."

"Exactly," answered Inger. "And as for what we should do next, we'll wait for Liza's phone call, and then Sally and Charley and Bill you're coming to our place for dinner. It's all cooked, and we've plenty of food, providing Floyd didn't eat it all while I was over here."

"I jus' hardly had time to set myself down before you called me over. An' you know, Mother, I wouldn't eat without you."

"I don't feel right about leavin' her here alone," said Sally.

"Nonsense! Your staying here won't do her any good, and you'll sure be a lot better off with a good meal inside you. That goes for Bill and Charley, too."

The phone interrupted the conversation. Inger quickly answered it and learned that the doctor would be finished in about an hour. "Well, that settles it. Walter will have time to eat before he leaves. Anna and Jonah, you're welcome to come, too. I didn't mean to ignore you."

"Thanks, Inger," Anna replied, "but I should be getting home. I never intended to stay so long."

"I've got to be running along too," Jonah added. "I'm sure that my mother is wondering where I am."

"Come on, now! Get your things on and let's be off," Inger directed.

"That's sure nice of you to have us," Bill said. "We 'preciate it."

Charley looked wistful. "I don't wanna leave Ma here all alone. I'll stay with her an' then come on over when Bill'n Sally get back."

"That's nice of you, Charley," Sally said.

"Well, let's the rest of us go then," Inger continued. "Floyd has to eat and get back to the river to get more ice before it gets dark."

"You sure know how to spoil a man's dinner," he answered.

"As if anything would ever spoil your dinner," she said, raising her eyebrows.

Chapter Eleven

The afternoon sun shone brightly in the clear blue sky. "Not a cloud. It'll be another cold night," said Jonah as he and Anna left the others and started down the road. He glanced over at the silent figure walking slowly beside him. "I'm real sorry you had to run into a situation like this. It's a shame, because it's the second time you've been the one to find someone who died."

"Well, it's not nearly so bad as last fall when I found Mr. Evans frozen to death," Anna replied. "And at least this time I didn't faint." They both recalled that event when Jonah carried her into the Kloster barn and laid her down in the hay.

"Maybe I'm bad luck for you," Jonah said, trying to be jocular. "Both times when I've come home I've found you having to cope with something awful like this."

"It does seem strange that in just a few months there are two persons who have died. Well, three, counting Roger Kloster."

"From the time when I was a kid, whenever something like this happened, I used to worry about what was going to happen next," Jonah continued. "But my mother kept reminding me that when you have a community this large and people getting older, there's bound to be a death every few months. It happens everywhere."

"I guess you're right," Anna agreed. "I know it's the same in Fort Dodge. It's just that there I'm apt to read about a death in the paper or hear about it from someone, and I don't really know the person. Here in Grabney I seem to know more people."

Jonah continued thoughtfully. "In cities there are so many people that a person never ever meets. You have your own group, and that's about it. All the services are provided for you. You may know who the mailman is, but he isn't a part of your life. I guarantee that here Liza Crawford is definitely a part of everyone's life."

"And if she's not a part of it, she'll make herself a part of it," Anna laughed.

"That's for sure," he added. "Here in the country everyone knows each other, and we depend on each other. In the winter we're snowed in, so when something goes wrong we all have to help. The rest of the year we're working so hard there isn't time to go anywhere outside of Grabney. Our social life is pretty close to home with church and picnics. And I guess you could call meeting at the store a social activity." He laughed at this last remark.

"Then there's always the party line," Anna added with a smile.

"You're right about that. But I think one reason people listen in is that they feel isolated here. It's also not just that they don't want to miss out on anything, but that they're really interested in what's going on. In many ways we're like a great big family."

"A family that doesn't always get along," Anna said with a smile as she related how Mrs. Simms felt about Sally coming to work at the Wheeler's.

"Oh, yes, there's always the cantankerous ones. You haven't heard half the squabbles. We'd hear them when my mother came home from the club." Anna laughed as she tried to imagine what the meetings were like.

"And then we have people like Inger," Jonah continued. "Every town needs an Inger."

"She really is wonderful," Anna admitted. "No matter what happens, everyone can rely on her. And they don't hesitate to call on her, either."

"She's the backbone of the community," Jonah said. "For example, she'll get Floyd to get ahold of Anders to build a coffin, and Anders will be more than happy to oblige. She'll talk to Reverend Blakeley, and he'll take care of the service and the burial."

"And of course, she was the one to get Dr. Bailey out here," Anna said. I guess what's getting me down is that I feel so bad for Sally. We were having such a wonderful time this morning. It was the first time Sally has been out to have any fun. And Charley, too. They were both having such a good time."

"Say, I've noticed a real change in Charley since she arrived, "Jonah said. "I've never heard him say so much before. It's amazing. I remember him from when I was a kid. He was always shy, but most of the time no one saw him. He was in school before I was, so I don't know much about that, but all the time I knew him his mother kept him at home, just working around the place. This morning he was carrying on a decent conversation. One reason I came back with him is that we were talking, and I could see that he was enjoying himself."

"I think his mother must have been so bossy that he was afraid to open his mouth. Floyd was about the only one who could get anything out of him. After his mother's stroke, he probably had to start thinking for himself." Anna looked up and saw they were passing the Larson home. "We've come to your place already."

"Oh, I'll walk you home." Jonah said as he smiled at her. "It's such a nice day that I hate to go inside. Anyway, I'd give Sally a lot of the credit. She probably listened to him and didn't shut him up. Bill has always been the strong one of the two of them, although he never said much, either. But he was the one his mother gave the orders to, and Charley had to take them from Bill. The few times I was there, Mrs. Wheeler would listen to Bill, but she'd never let Charley open his mouth."

"Charley seemed to enjoy helping Sally, too," Anna recalled. "I know that Sally was really surprised that Charley was such a good help in the kitchen."

"I'm sure he enjoyed helping Sally a lot more than he did his mother," Jonah said with a smile. "I imagine with Bill out tending the livestock, Charley was stuck with a lot of the household chores. I recall that Mrs. Wheeler always preferred to be outside working, too."

"That's what Peter has told me. Anyway, it's sad to think that Sally was so happy there, and now this happened. Well, I guess I'm home," she said almost regretfully.

"So you are," he added.

"Oh, Jonah!"

"Yes."

"I've been thinking about something else that's been bothering me."

"What is it?"

"You know when you went into Mrs. Wheeler's room to see if she was alive. I saw that you picked up her right arm and felt for a pulse. Did you happen to notice that the fingers on her right hand were crossed?"

"Let's see," he continued thoughtfully. "I remember her hand was hanging over the side of the bed, and I lifted it up a little at the wrist when I tried to feel for a pulse. Yes, come to think of it, I did notice that her fingers were crossed. I remember that they stayed crossed as I carefully lowered her hand back to where it was, and I thought that was interesting, although I was more concerned about her pulse than the crossed fingers."

"But why would she have crossed her fingers?" Anna asked rhetorically.

"I'm sure I don't know," he answered. "It probably doesn't mean anything. They just happened to be crossed, that's all."

"I guess you're right," she replied. "But it still seems strange to me. Anyway, I'd better be getting in. Milly will no doubt have heard the news and want all the details. Can you come in?"

"Oh, thanks, but my mother'll be waiting just the same as Milly, and wondering where I've been all this time. By the way, tell Peter I'll try to hurry with dinner so I can get back and help him. Tell him I'll bring one of dad's saws too. I could see that he could use another one." He waved to her as he turned up the road, calling back as an afterthought. "Will you be out again this afternoon?"

"I don't think so," she laughed as she waved back. "I've had enough cold weather for one day."

As Anna started up the back steps, Peter was leaving the entryway. She gave him Jonah's message.

"Well, I could use some extra hands, and Jonah is a good one. You better get in and get some grub, Anna, and from the looks of things Milly's not going to let you out of her sight until she hears all about what happened."

Chapter Twelve

The next morning Anna and Milly were a little late for church, as they had stayed downstairs in the Sunday School room to help clean up. As they entered, the congregation was standing and singing the last verse of the opening hymn, so the two of them quietly slipped into the back row of wooden folding chairs. The church had never been able to afford proper pews, and this way the chairs could be brought to the basement to be used for church suppers. The children sat on benches for Sunday School, but the adults preferred chairs. Hymnals were placed on every other seat, and Milly surreptitiously picked up the one on her chair and held it open as if she had been there the entire time.

As they sat down, Milly looked across the aisle to see Sally and Charley. She elbowed Anna and nodded her head toward the newcomers. Anna glanced over and gave Milly a surprised look. "This'll set the tongues awagging," Milly whispered to her, then realized that Reverend Blakeley was speaking, so quickly paid attention to the service. They weren't the only ones to be aware of the couple in the back row. While people tried to conceal their curiosity, it was obvious that word was spreading. This was especially noticeable when the congregation stood to sing or read a response, or when they were seated again. Heads swiveled slightly to the rear, and smiles were given to the person in the row behind as if this were the original intent; however, eyes went to the back of the room.

Anna and Milly were aware of this and were somewhat amused at first, then became slightly irritated as the movement of heads seemed to sweep like a wave until it reached the front of the room. "You'd think they'd never seen a newcomer to church," Milly whispered to Anna during the second hymn. "I hope Sally and

Charley don't notice it. I suppose they're here because of what happened yesterday." Anna nodded, hoping that Milly would keep the rest of her comments to herself until after the service.

Before the last hymn, Reverend Blakeley announced the passing of Mrs. Wheeler. This was followed by a chorus of low murmured voices. He mentioned that the funeral service would be held on Wednesday afternoon at three o'clock, with burial in the cemetery immediately following. He then nodded to Mrs. Simms, who began playing the final hymn. As it was concluding, he walked down the aisle to take his usual place at the front door. He stopped when he came to Sally and Charley, shook hands with them and continued talking to them until the music ended.

As the congregation started to exit, Milly grabbed Anna's arm and pulled her across the aisle to where Sally and Charley stood. Her sudden movement was intended to keep the gawkers at bay. "I'm so sorry about your mother, Charley," Milly said sympathetically. "Anna told me all about it, didn't you, Anna?"

"Yes," she replied and quickly tried to think of something else to say to ease the awkwardness of the situation. "I'm so glad to see you both here. I guess this is the first time you've been able to get away for church," she said, speaking directly to Sally.

"I didn't know much about the church here," Sally answered, "but the Reverend was over last night, and he was so nice that I knew I'd like to come. I never got to go to church much at home."

"An' she was plannin' to walk here by herself, an' I tol' her she couldn't. I tol' her I'd hitch up one of the horses an' take her in the sleigh," Charley said emphatically. "That's how I come to bein' here. But I'm glad I come. An' Sally's right. The Reverend is real nice. He's plannin' a nice service for Ma."

"I'm sure it will be nice," Anna added, unable to think of much else to say. She was wondering where Mrs. Wheeler's body was, but of course could not ask.

"How're ya doin', Charley?" asked Ed Marson, who came to stand in the row in front of them. His lady friend Bertha Clemson was with him. "I'm real sorry about your ma."

"We're doin' okay, I guess," Charley answered.

"Have you folks met Sally Griswold?" Anna interjected, and then continued with the introduction. "Ed's family runs the store, and Bertha and Ed are getting married in June."

"I've never been to the store," Sally said. "Maybe I can go there now, but then maybe I won't be here," and her voice trailed off.

"Bertha, you've cut your hair!" Anna exclaimed with surprise in an attempt to change the subject. "You look like some of the pictures in *The Ladies Home Journal.*"

"I don't think I look that good," said Bertha, as she blushed a pleasing shade of pink.

"Milly and I've often talked about cutting our hair, but we just haven't had the nerve," Anna continued. "Where did you get it cut?"

Bertha laughed. "I just took out the scissors and cut it myself. And I did it without telling anyone." She glanced at Ed, who smiled proudly at her. "I was real worried that Ed wouldn't like it. But he says he likes it fine."

"I sure do," Ed replied. "Bertha's real clever."

"The only offer we've had to cut our hair," Milly said, "was from Floyd. And I wouldn't trust him with a pair of scissors." At this they all laughed.

"If you'd trust me, I'd be happy to cut your hair," Bertha offered. "I've been comin' here almost every weekend. I offered to cut Ed's ma's hair, but you know Vi. She wouldn't have any part of it. Oh, I guess we'd better be off," she said looking around. "Vi said dinner would be at noon, and we're about the last ones out of church."

"I'll see you at the service Wednesday, Charley," Ed said as they left. "Bertha won't be able to make it. She has to work. So long."

"I guess we'd better be going, too," Milly realized as she looked around to see the nearly empty room. "But Sally, how are you making out? Is there anything we can do for you?"

"We're doin' fine, I guess," Sally answered. "Jonah came over last night and said his ma wanted us to come to dinner at their place today. That was real nice of her."

"Sylvia Larson is a good person," Milly added. "I'm glad that you don't have to eat at home today."

"An' we better get goin'," Charley remarked. "I don't wanna be late." Milly and Anna moved aside so they could leave.

"Goodbye," Sally said as they made their way toward the door. "Don't forget to come and see me, Anna."

Anna gave her a promise to do so, and they followed the couple to the door where the two women stopped to chat with the minister. "It's sad about Mrs. Wheeler," Reverend Blakeley said as his eyes followed Sally and Charley as they walked to the barn. "By the way, Anna, I set the service for three o'clock, hoping that you and some of the older pupils could come, but it would mean that you would have to let school out a little early. If I leave it any later than that, we'll run into trouble with it getting dark for the burial."

"I can do that. No one will mind getting out a little early."

"Oh, there's Peter waiting for us," called Milly. "We'll have to hurry. Inger's family is coming over for dinner, and there are so many things to do."

"I'm sure you'll manage fine. You always do," the minister said as he stepped out on the porch and pulled the door tightly shut.

The Parker family arrived promptly at two o'clock, sitting down immediately to dinner, which was devoured with gusto. "I've never seen such hungry beings," Inger commented. You'd think Milly and I never fed you. We just barely sat down, and now it's gone. Milly'n I've been jumping up and down so much that we haven't had a chance to finish."

"It's haulin' all that ice yesterday did it," Floyd commented. "If you'd been out workin' with us, you'd a sat down ta eat an' not been dashin' around the kitchen so."

"That's my pie!" Milly shouted as she saw Floyd stick his fork into it and try to exchange his empty plate for her full one.

"Jus' checkin' ta see if you was alert," came his sardonic comment.

"What I want to know is, what's happening about the funeral?" Milly asked as she grabbed her plate firmly and sat back down. "Has Anders made the coffin? Who's going to dig the grave? Where's Edna now?"

"Whoa! Hold yer horses, Milly!" Floyd rebounded with his answer. "Jus' one thing at a time. Well, since you asked, first I got ahold of Anders, an' he had enough lumber to make a coffin, so he went ahead an' got it done yesterday. Glad I caught him early so's he could do most of it before it got dark. He sure does a first class job with the scraps of lumber he has. Tomorrow he's goin' to rub it down with linseed oil and turpentine."

Milly hesitated, "A...well, what I mean is, well, is Edna in it now?"

"Why don't you take over, Mother," Floyd said. "You sure you goin' to finish that pie, Milly? I'd be happy to take it off your hands."

"You keep your hands off my pie," Milly retorted as she pulled her plate closer to her.

"I'll get him another piece of pie," Mabel offered.

"You do that, Mabel, and I'd be much obliged," her father answered. "All right, Mother, you tell them what happened next."

"All right, Dad. Just you settle down now. Anyway, Walter got Dr. Bailey there by the middle of the afternoon. He took care of a few things that have to be done with the deceased, so I was glad we could reach him when we did. He'll have to send the death certificate out later, but he wrote down all the facts. He said it looked to him like it must have been a stroke. Of course you can't always tell for sure, but it must have been something like that or a heart attack." She shook her head in thinking about it, then continued. "After he left, we shut the door to her bedroom, and everyone came back to our place. He said that as soon as the coffin was finished we should put her in it and put the body in their shed. The weather's so cold that it'll be fine."

"Has Anders finished it?" Peter asked.

"I guess it was gettin' on pretty late," Floyd added. "Maybe ten o'clock. It was after the Reverend come by to make the arrangements for the funeral. Anders phoned us an' said it was ready, so's we told him to come on. He brought Lars with him. They stopped at our place first, so I told Lars to stay home with George, an' Walter'n Mother'n I went over with him. We got the coffin in an' set it on a coupla kitchen chairs in the bedroom."

Inger continued. "Sally, bless her heart, lined it with a clean sheet and put a fresh pillow case on one of the pillows. I helped her dress Edna in clean clothes. She was getting pretty stiff by this time, so we had to cut off her nightgown. I think the only dress the woman ever owned was the wedding dress she was married in. We found it and cut it down the back and tucked it under her. It looked real nice. It wouldn't have fit her anyway. By this time things were getting too much for Bill and Charley, so I told them to go into the parlor and take Sally with them. Well, to make a long story short, Anders, Floyd and Walter lifted up the body and put it in the coffin. I fussed with her hair a bit, and plumped up the pillow under her head. Then Bill, Charley and Sally came out to see her, and they were pleased she looked so nice.

"Anders put the lid on and nailed it in only a couple of places, as they will want it open for the funeral. After that, they carried it out and put it in the shed. Anders'll be back tomorrow to rub it down. He couldn't do it on Sunday."

"It sure beats me, this not workin' on Sunday business," Floyd commented. "The cows don't give me any rest on Sunday. The animals have to be fed. Mother has to feed us. But we're jus' s'posed to sit around when there's plenty of things we could be doin'. Here's Anders, havin' to come over on a Monday ta finish what he could have done today."

"The Bible says we are to rest on Sunday," Milly stated piously. "That's what we were always taught."

"My Mother always told me that every stitch I sewed on Sunday had to be taken out by my nose on Monday," Anna said as she grinned. "But I noticed that sometimes my mother would sew on Sundays after we were in bed, and she never took out the stitches, and certainly not with her nose."

"I've never heard about that," Mabel said as she laughed to herself. "How could you ever take out stitches with your nose?"

"Well anyway," Inger added. "The job will be done, and Edna will have a nice final resting place. "

"Inger," said Anna. "I was wondering if you noticed something about Mrs. Wheeler."

"What's that, Anna?"

"When I saw her—that is, when Sally and I found her—I saw her right arm was hanging over the side of the bed."

"Nothing unusual in that, is there?" Inger asked.

"No, it's not that. But I noticed that the fingers on her right hand were crossed. Did you see that, also?"

"Yes, I did notice that," Inger replied. "In fact I noticed that when I first looked at her. I don't know why I did it, but I uncrossed the fingers. I suppose it was because I knew that the body would begin to get stiff, rigor mortis, I guess they call it. It just seemed best to me to put the fingers in a more natural position. What makes you ask?"

"I don't know, except that it seemed strange to me that she would have crossed her fingers," Anna replied. "Why would someone cross their fingers in a situation like that?"

"Maybe she was hoping not to die," Mabel said. "Sometimes I cross my fingers when I worry about something, like crossing my fingers before a test at school, and hoping that I know all the right answers."

"Somehow that jus' don't make sense to me," Floyd commented. "I jus' can't see Edna crossin' her fingers for any reason."

"Well, we don't know why she did it, but it's probably not important," Inger added. "And it is important that she look nice at her funeral. Goodness knows, the people around here think she was odd enough, and if they ever saw her in her coffin with crossed fingers they'd probably think she was putting a hex on someone."

"You're right about that," Milly added as she gave a shiver.

"I still think she knew she was going to die and didn't want to, so she crossed her fingers hoping not to die," Mabel said with firm resolution. "That's what I would do, anyway."

"We should probably forget it," Anna said. "I don't know why I brought it up, except that it seemed odd. But if people around here would get the wrong idea, it's best not to say anything about it."

Chapter Thirteen

It was Wednesday, January 31st. The students were delighted that school would be dismissed one hour early. Most of them would not be attending the funeral, but many would have to arrive home early enough to take care of younger brothers and sisters so that their parents could go.

Anna and Davey hurried home, accompanied by Mabel and Erica Larson. The girls had volunteered to take care of the Jensen children.

"It's nice of you girls to stay with the children," Anna said.

"It's just too cold to have a funeral," Mabel replied. "I'm sure the church will be cold, and then standing in the graveyard for that ceremony will be awful. I'm glad I don't have to go."

"Well, you didn't really know Mrs. Wheeler, anyway," Anna added. "There'll be plenty of time for you to attend funerals. And I agree with you about the cold. I don't see how they managed to get the grave dug. I thought that they'd have to wait until the ground thawed."

"But what would they do with Mrs. Wheeler then? I mean, well you know, the dead body," Mabel asked, looking as if she had seen a ghost.

" I was wondering about that," Anna replied. "I don't know much about it."

"I know," Erica piped up. "Well, I don't know anything about where they'd put the...the coffin until the ground warmed up, but I do know Reverend Blakeley had a terrible time getting someone to dig the grave. Most of the time there's someone who comes in on the train looking for work, but not in the winter. Matt said a couple of fellas were around sometime last week, but they must have had a job lined up, because he didn't see them again."

"Who did he get, then?" asked Anna.

"Jonah would have helped, but he was busy with his school work, and he promised to take a day off to help Ed move the school-house on Friday. William and Walter got stuck with the job, but it turned out better than they thought. Charley and Bill said they wanted to help, too, because it was their ma."

"When Walter came home Monday night, he was so tired," said Mabel. "They had to use pickaxes to get down to where the dirt wasn't frozen. Reverend Blakeley came out to tell them how to do it and how deep to go."

"But they did get to go to the Blakeleys' for coffee and pie and to get warmed up," added Erica. "And they got to come home for dinner. But still they didn't finish until suppertime. And now the dirt that they shoveled out is so frozen they don't know if they can shovel it back."

"I guess that means a few more people will be using pick-axes," Anna added. "No wonder Reverend Blakeley wanted to have the service a little early."

"That's right," Mabel laughed. "Come to the funeral, but bring your pickaxe and shovel."

"I guess we shouldn't laugh, but that is a funny idea, Mabel," said Anna.

The girls were right. The church had been heated only enough to bring it slightly above the temperature outside. There was a fairly good turnout. After all Mrs. Wheeler had been a long-time resident and people wanted to pay their respects. Florence Simms played the pump organ with gloves on, and fortunately the service was brief. At the end everyone filed by the coffin, which was then nailed shut and carried to the cemetery. Charley, Bill and Sally had sat in the front row and were the first to leave, accompanied by Reverend Blakeley.

The graveyard was indeed freezing. Anna, Milly, Peter and Inger's family had sat fairly near the front of the church, and were among the first to leave. It was a cold walk through the crunchy snow to the gravesite. As they stood around in the icy chill waiting for everyone to gather, most of them stamped their feet and rubbed gloved hands together, speaking in hushed tones.

Anna noticed that Sally was tearful, so she walked over and

put her arm around her. "I know this is hard on you, Sally, but you're bearing up so bravely."

"It's just like losin' my ma all over again," the woman said, sobbing quietly. "An' Charley an' Bill are sad, too. They're not cryin', but I know they feel awful."

There was some movement in the crowd as the coffin arrived, carried by Peter, Floyd, Olle Larson and Anders Anderson. They set it on the ground over the heavy straps that Reverend Blakeley had placed there for the purpose of lowering it into the grave. The minister then said a few final words, concluding by asking everyone to support the family of the deceased. He also mentioned that the Parkers would be having a gathering at their house directly following the burial. The pallbearers carefully picked up the straps and the coffin was gently lowered into the grave.

As the crowd dispersed for the barn and their sleighs, Jonah came forward with Walter and William ready to fill in the grave. Pickaxes and shovels had been concealed nearby. It would not be an easy job they had before they could go home.

Floyd had Clementine and the sleigh nearby so he could bring Inger home to get ready for the guests. "Jump in, Milly," he called out to her. "Let's get goin' so we can beat the crowd. Peter said he would stay and help the boys fill in the grave."

"But he has his good clothes on," exclaimed Milly. "He didn't tell me he was going to do that."

"He's probably not stayin' long, an' I wouldn't worry about his clothes. That dirt's so hard it wouldn't make a spot on anythin'. Come on! Get in!"

"Where's Anna?" Milly asked as she scoured the grounds. "We can't leave her here."

"She's over there with Sally and the boys," Inger indicated with a nod. She'll come home with them."

"If she don't get goin' soon, Peter'll have her workin' with a pickaxe," Floyd added. "Come on, Milly! Get in!"

Milly jumped in beside Inger, and they were off. "I wonder who's coming." She turned to glance at the sleigh behind them. "Hello, Florence!" she waved.

"Milly! What are you doing?" Inger admonished. "Turn around and sit still."

"I was yust checking to see who was coming, and you might

know that the Simms would be one of the first."

"I didn't know you were all that friendly with that nosey old biddy," Floyd remarked.

"Oh, I'm not," she answered. "But when I turned around to check on who was behind us, she saw me, and I had to have a reason for looking, so I waved."

"Beats me!" Floyd continued. "It's real amusin' that they have to use their sleigh same as us poor folk who can't afford to have a shiny new Ford. No doubt he'll be showin' off again soon as the snow's gone."

"The only reason they came to the funeral was to get a good look at Sally," Milly said.

"But she had to play the organ," Inger reminded her.

"Anna played the organ at the other funerals we had this winter."

"Well, I wish they would've drove their car so we could all see it dumped in some ditch," Floyd said with a chuckle.

"They wouldn't have made it out of their yard, so you wouldn't have seen a thing," Inger told him.

"Guess you're right. Okay Clementine, whoa there! Let's let these ladies off here so's they can hurry inside, an' you an' me can head for the barn. Off you go ladies, and get a move on. I can't wait to get out of this bone chillin' cold. I'm just hankerin' for a cuppa hot coffee. Bless me if I'm not."

Other sleighs were close behind so Inger and Milly hurried up the steps and into the kitchen. "That's so nice of you to have the farewell party at your house," Milly said as she took off her wraps.

"Well, Sally and the boys couldn't do it. I don't suppose they even know that it's customary. Anyway they've been our neighbors ever since we came, and it's the least I can do. I'd feel guilty if I let this slip by."

"It's something that should be done," Milly agreed. "I know they will appreciate it. I wonder how many people will come."

"Looks like quite a few, if the sleighs following us are any indication," Inger added, "but we're ready for them. Yup, here comes someone now." The back door was thrown open, and first to enter was Florence Simms. "Come in, Florence. Coats go in the bedroom. You know the way."

"Joe'll be in as soon as he tends to our horse," Florence informed them. "It seems so strange to us to have to go back to a sleigh when we have that lovely car. But of course we wouldn't want to get it out in this dreadful weather. Oh! What a wonderful spread you have," cooed the uppity lady as she eyed the table. It was laden with a mouth-watering assortment of cookies and cakes. "And you are using your lovely silver coffeepot. Wasn't that a wedding present?"

"That's right," Inger answered as civilly as possible as she turned to the door. "Here, you folks come on in. Take off your things and put them in the bedroom. Help yourselves to whatever you want. Oh! Mr. and Mrs. Blakeley. Here Milly, take Mrs. Blakeley's coat."

"We can take care of ourselves, Inger," the Reverend said. "You ladies get on with your work. Looks like you'll have enough to do with this crowd. The men'll be in soon after they get their horses put up. Floyd took care of ours. Guess being a minister has some advantages."

"I hope that helps make up for all the disadvantages," Inger said jokingly. "By the way, ladies, you might as well go in the parlor now so you can get a seat before the men come in."

"I don't see Anna and Sally and the boys," Milly said with some concern. "I thought they would've come by this time."

"We saw them turn into their place," Mr. Blakeley informed her. "No doubt they'll be coming soon. Anna will hurry them along."

The heavy tramp of men's boots accompanied by hearty conversation could be heard coming up the back steps. The door opened. "Come in! Come in!" Inger said brusquely. "Hurry up now! That cold air is making quite a draft." Half a dozen men tromped through to the kitchen. As each one came through the door he stopped talking, took off his hat and immediately put on company behavior. "Let's get the door shut. Coats in the bedroom." Several ambled over to the bedroom door taking off their coats on the way while the rest stood rather self-consciously, hat in hand, waiting to get into the bedroom.

"Nice of you to have us, Inger," said Anders Anderson. "Everyone appreciates the trouble you've gone to, to do this."

"Anyone can make cookies and cakes, Anders," Inger replied,

"but there's not a one of us who could do the job you've done. That was a beautiful casket, and on such short notice."

"Just sorry I didn't have better wood to make it look real nice."

"It was yust grand, Anders," Milly said with a far-away look in her eyes. "You are so good at making things out of wood, and so kind to do it."

"It's the least I can do, Milly. Everyone around here tries to do their share."

"Well, not everyone," Inger remarked.

"I think most everyone, Inger," Milly added. "And Anna says that Lars is talented, too. She said the chest that he made in school last fall was really nice. But where is Anna? Listen! Is that them coming?"

"I'm surprised you can hear anything outside with all the racket going on in here," Inger said. "Oh, wait! I think I hear someone coming up the back steps. Yes. I'll bet it's them."

Anna opened the door and ushered Sally, Charley and Bill inside. "Here Sally, let me take your coat," she offered. "Bill you and Charley come with me and I'll show you where to put yours in the bedroom."

"I'll come with you Anna," Sally said as she looked apprehensively at all the strangers, who had become very quiet at the arrival of the newcomers.

Suddenly Inger spoke up. "Come on, everyone! Take a plate and fill it up and get some coffee. I guess the ladies were the first to get to the parlor, so you men will have to make do with the kitchen."

Just then, Floyd and Peter strolled into the room after having removed their wraps and leaving them on the porch. Milly gave Peter the once-over to make sure he hadn't soiled his clothes. Apparently satisfied, she returned to filling the plates with cookies, while Inger continued giving orders. "Floyd, you see that everyone gets plenty. Milly and I are going in the parlor. Come on, Anna and Sally. Fill up your plates. Anna, will you grab the coffeepot? Milly and I'll take a plate of cookies."

"Now Mother," complained Floyd. "Leave some for us."

"There's plenty for you. You men can get your coffee from the pot on the stove. And I want you to all see that Bill and

Charley get taken care of. Floyd! Get them a couple of chairs."

"We'll do fine, Inger," Peter said. "You and the ladies go in the parlor. We can take care of ourselves."

Anna carried the coffeepot, with Sally following close at her heels. "We may have to sit on the steps going to the upstairs, Sally," she said. "It looks a little crowded."

"That's all right with me," she answered. "I can hear the men folk already starting to talk about farm stuff. I wanna stay with you."

"I'll set the coffeepot on this table. Come on. I see a place on the steps where we can be by ourselves. I'll point out the people to you." Sally followed Anna up a couple of steps and they sat where they could see and not be seen too well.

"This parlor is really grand," Sally said as she looked awe-struck around the room. "And the stairs go up from the parlor and not the kitchen. It looks just like I've seen in some magazines. And I've never seen such a beautiful rug, except maybe at the Larsons', and oh, the davenport and chairs. Oh, but Anna, I don't know anyone," and she looked from one face to another.

"You know Inger and Milly, and there's Sylvia Larson," Anna explained. "Are you getting enough to eat?"

"Yes, I got plenty." She quietly looked again over the group of ladies. "This is sorta nice. I was scared to come, 'cause I thought they would be talkin' about Mrs. Wheeler the whole time, an' askin' me questions. But I see it's not like that. It's just like a family get-together. Bill 'n Charley didn't wanna come neither, but I tol' them that their ma would want them to, 'cause it was a party for their ma. Guess she never had nothin' like this before. Too bad it had to wait until she died."

"Well Mrs. Wheeler wasn't really sociable with the people around here. She pretty much stayed at home, from what I've heard."

"An' I s'pose Charley 'n Bill had to stay home, too," Sally said thoughtfully. "I had to stay at home, 'cause my ma didn't wanna go out. That's prob'ly why I get along with them so good. We were all stay-at-homes. Oh, I hope they're gettin' along okay in the kitchen."

"I'm sure they are. Peter and Floyd will make sure of that."

"I wish we had had a party like this after my ma died. We didn't do nothin', just got her buried. Most folks didn't even know she died. Sometimes when I went to the store, people'd ask me how she was, and I'd have to tell 'em. I could see they felt awful for askin' me."

Anna could see that Sally was becoming upset, so she changed the subject. "Sally, how are you getting along at the Wheeler's?"

"Oh, we're doin' fine. But there is one thing Anna. When they took Mrs. Wheeler out of her bedroom, we shut the door. The boys'n I didn't want to go in there. I know that we should go in there and clean it up. Guess we'll have to do it sooner or later."

"I hope you're going to stay there awhile. I think the boys need you. They're going to be completely lost if they lose both their mother and you."

"Dr. Bailey said I should stay, too. I'd like to stay 'cause over there I have somethin' to do. If I went home there'd be nothin' for me. An' the boys said they want me to stay. Bill says he's never had such good food," and she laughed. "It's fun to cook for them, 'cause they really eat good."

"I'm glad you're going to stay. Then it is important that Mrs. Wheeler's room get cleaned up. Maybe Charley would move in there."

"I dunno. I know I've got Charley's room, but I don't wanna move into Mrs. Wheeler's room. Maybe Charley wouldn't mind goin' into his ma's room. We could fix it up so's he wouldn't see any of her things. But I dunno when to do it. It's really hard. But we gotta do it, I know. I'd ask Inger to help, but she's done enough."

"Maybe I could help," Anna said with all the enthusiasm she could muster. She wasn't sure she really wanted to do this, but she realized that Sally needed some moral support.

"But that's too much trouble for you," Sally added quickly.

"It's not at all. And I'm sure Inger wouldn't mind. She would know more about where to put Mrs. Wheeler's things, you know, store them some place."

"You mean, make the room over so maybe Charley would like to have it for his room," Sally said.

"That's right," Anna continued.

"But when can you do it? You're busy teachin'."

Anna thought awhile. "Tomorrow's no good, because I don't have enough time. And Friday I want to get away from school as fast as possible to see them move the schoolhouse for Ed. You'd like to see that too, wouldn't you, Sally?"

"Yeah. I heard about it, but I didn't think much about it, with so much goin' on. I've never heard of anythin' like that."

"Meet me at the corner after school, and we'll go together," Anna continued. "Oh, but first I'll probably have to go home and drop off my things. And I want to get my Brownie Kodak camera. Anyway, keep an eye out for me. I may even let school out a little early. I know all the kids will want to see it. By the time school is out they should have it pretty much moved."

"I heard someone say it'd take all day," Sally said.

"It will, but Floyd said by the time school is out they should be almost finished. They only have to move it a couple of miles. Oh, I see people are starting to leave." Anna stood up. "Anyway let's clean up Mrs. Wheeler's room on Saturday. I'd have time then, and I'm sure Inger could spare a couple of hours to help. We can make plans on Friday. Okay with you?"

"That's fine with me," said Sally as she got up from the steps.

"Come on, then. It's time I introduced you to the ladies before they all go," and Anna and Sally came down into the parlor, where Sally acknowledged the introductions.

Chapter Fourteen

Anna fumbled as she opened the schoolhouse door Thursday morning. "Davey! Give me a hand," she called. "I can't manage with all these books and my lunch pail."

"Sure, Miss Swenson," he called back as he bounded up the steps, grabbed the door handle and with a mighty shove pushed the door open.

"Thanks, Davey. Oh no, I don't need any more help. You leave your lunch pail here and go back outside and play." She looked at the five-pound peanut butter pail with the wire handle as she carried her things to her desk. Her mother would be shocked to see such a thing, but it was a good lunch pail, and all the students had either a peanut butter pail or a honey pail. No doubt her mother would have made her one out of linen lined with matching fabric, and of course embroidered. She laughed to think of it. One good thing her mother did give her, though, was the bell on her desk. When she tapped it and heard the "ding-ding," it gave her a proud feeling. She knew then that she was a real teacher in a real schoolroom with real students.

As usual, she opened the day with the students standing, giving the pledge of allegiance and singing "America." Last fall, after Anders Anderson had refinished the pump organ, she was able to play it, which was a great help to the singing. Mr. Anderson mentioned that it would be better for the organ if it were not against the wall, as the cold or heat from the outside could damage it. Thus he placed it near her desk facing the students so she could play and see them sing. He had even polished the back so it was not unsightly.

"You may be seated," she said as she took her place behind her desk. "I have something in mind which might interest you.

You all know that tomorrow Ed Marson is going to move the vacant schoolhouse that's a couple of miles west of town on to a place that he bought."

"You mean the Torgerson place," Carl corrected her.

"Raise your hand if you wish to speak, Carl," she admonished him. "Yes, that's right. He was lucky that Mr. Torgerson would sell him a couple of acres right next to the bridge, across from the church. I understand Ed's been spending the past month jacking up the school and putting runners, or I guess you call them skids, under it so they can move it. Mabel?"

"They're getting married in June. How can he fix up a schoolhouse and make it into a house by then?"

"Well, I don't have the answer to that question," Anna replied. I'm sure it'll take a lot of work. Just imagine making a house out of this school." At that idea everyone looked around the small building. There was a general murmur of voices as they shook their heads. "To get back to the reason I'm discussing this: it is because I know that all of you would like to watch the school being moved. Am I right?" The answer was decidedly in the affirmative. "I had thought that if we take a short lunch period tomorrow and cut short our recesses we could leave here about 2:15 instead of three o'clock." Comments were again very positive about this idea. "I'm telling you now so that you can inform your parents tonight. That way they'll know where you are when you don't show up at home. Yes, Edwin?"

"I thought all the dads would be helpin' the move. My dad said he was gonna be there." There was an immediate chorus of answers, "Mine, too!"

"I'm sure that the fathers will be there, but it's the mothers that should know where you are. Philip?"

"My dad said he was gonna bring his team. How many dads are bringin' teams?"

"I don't know," Anna answered. "Who knows how many teams will be used? Lars, do you know?"

"George knows more about it than I do, 'cause his dad's gonna drive the teams, but I think it's gonna be four teams."

"Can you answer that for us, George?"

"Philip's dad'll have his team, and Uncle Peter'll bring his, and the Larsons'll bring theirs. Then Joe Simms'll bring his team.

Dad said we could probably do with the four teams, but if we need more, there's the Torgersons and the Swangs. They're right close."

"How come ol' man Simms isn't usin' his car to pull the schoolhouse?" Carl spoke up loudly. "How come we just use horses when cars are better?"

"How can you be so dumb, Carl?" Mabel yelled at him. "Even I know the answer to that."

"If you're so smart, then tell why. I'll bet you don't even know."

"I do so know," she answered haughtily.

"Now, now!" Anna said to calm them down. "Mabel, why don't you explain to Carl the reason we don't use Mr. Simms' car."

In a firm and positive tone, Mabel gave her answer. "In the first place cars can't be driven in snow. They just slip and slide around. That's why Joe Simms hasn't driven his car to church. And then it isn't strong enough to pull something as big as a schoolhouse." With this she gave a smug shake of her head.

"You mean horses are stronger than a car?" Carl shot back.

"Yes, I do!" she retorted. "My dad said so."

"Yes, you're right, Mabel," Anna said. "Several teams are stronger than a car. But what I want to know is, just how are they going to do it? I heard they were going to pull it down the road. George, you have your hand up. Can you answer that?"

"Well, they talked about it yesterday at our place and I heard all about it. You see the road is too full of drifts and wouldn't be level enough to pull anything as big as a schoolhouse. And it might not be wide enough in some places. Anyway, they're going to pull it across the fields. There's nothing planted now, and the fields are pretty flat. They'd have to cross one road, but there'd be enough men to level that much out."

"What about the fences?" Davey called out.

"That's why they need so many men. Dad'll drive the teams, but they have to get hitched up special. There'll be eight horses, two in a row. Our team'll go first 'cause Dad'll be drivin', and he's used to our team. Then the men who have their teams will walk along beside them. But Lars' dad'll go first with a bunch of men to make sure there are no big rocks or hunks of ice in the way. And also they have to take down the fence posts and cut the wire so dad can drive the teams through. Then they have to put back the posts and splice the wire together again."

"That was a very good explanation, George. I can see you paid close attention to everything that the men discussed. Yes, Lars?"

"Dad told me they're lucky the ground is pretty flat, 'cause if it wasn't, and with this much snow the schoolhouse could start runnin' downhill and run away with them, or maybe tip over if the hill was steep enough, and even kill some of the horses."

"But I thought that the winter time was the best time to do this," Anna questioned.

"Not really," Lars continued. "Most things get moved after the snow is gone."

"How can you pull anything with skids on dry ground?" Anna asked.

"Well, you can't," George answered. "But then you'd be lucky if you had teams of mules, Dad said. They're stronger than horses. The way it's usually done is to put wheels under the house or the barn or whatever you're moving. Then the house gets pulled just like it was a wagon. Dad said that once in the Dakotas he saw a fella movin' a two story house."

"I guess moving this schoolhouse is enough for me," Anna said with a smile. "Anyway, this has been a most interesting discussion, and tomorrow I'm so anxious to see them do it. Mr. Parker told me that by the middle of the afternoon they still wouldn't have it all the way to where it will be moved, so if we leave school early we'll be in time to see it. But remember, no one is to get is the way."

"If George's dad is boss, nobody'll get in the way," Carl added.

"That's for sure," said a rather shy Edwin Lindquist.

"I'm glad George's dad is so strict, because with kids in the way accidents can happen," Anna warned. "Tell your parents what we have planned. And be sure to remember what you saw, because on Monday each of you will be writing about this experience."

"Oh no!" Carl groaned.

"Oh yes, Carl," Anna said. "And now it's time to get on to our regular work."

Friday at 2:15 the children fled the schoolroom as if it were on fire, and Anna was close behind them. She hurried home to drop off her things and get her camera. As she was rushing back up the road, she waved to Sally, who was hurrying down from the Wheeler place.

"I heard the kids yellin' and screamin' as they was comin' from school," she said when they met at the corner. "So I knowed it was time to come,"

"How are you doing today?" Anna asked. "I hope the funeral and the party Wednesday weren't too much for you and the boys."

"Oh, no," she answered. "The boys was really happy about the party, an' they thought the funeral was real nice. They was still sad, a course, but they'd never been to a party like that. They thought their ma would have liked it too. Too bad she couldn't a come. Why do they have parties after a funeral?"

"I think it's to get all the persons together to remember the person who died. I've always felt that it's to help the people who are left, to show them that they aren't alone. Oh look! They're just about halfway across the Torgerson field. Let's hurry, Sally. I want to get a picture of this."

"I see some of them puttin' back the fence posts," Sally said excitedly. "Oh, there's Charley helpin'. Bill said he'd stay home. He said someone had to stay home, an' he's not much for goin' out anyways."

"Here Sally, I'll hold up the barbed wire while you go through," Anna suggested while she put her foot on the lowest wire to push it down, and carefully held up the middle wire. "Careful now or you'll get caught on one of the barbs." With Sally safely through, she did the same for Anna and then they hurried to where Floyd was urging on the teams. There was no joking with Floyd. He was all business, and she could see why he was selected to be the leader. Everything was going smoothly. The horses were doing a steady, slow pull, and the schoolhouse was moving.

"Hello Anna," Peter called. "Get back a bit and you can get a picture of the whole operation. We're going great now. You should have been here a few hours ago when we had to cross the road. That was really something. And be sure to get one of Anders and his gang putting back the fence posts," he called after her.

"I've never seen a house moved," Sally said as her eyes opened wide with amazement. "This is really somethin', ain't it, Anna."

"It sure is," she answered. "Let's go over there so I can get a few good pictures. Maybe I can get a couple of the students." She carefully got the house and team in the viewfinder and clicked the shutter. She saw Charley standing over by the fence. "Hey Charley!" she yelled. "Come over here so I can get a picture of you and Sally."

"Oh Anna," Sally said. "You don't want a picture of me."

"Of course I do. Come on, Charley! Get over here!" He came with a self-conscious stride, stood beside Sally, and Anna got her photo. Next she walked over to the fence. "Mr. Anderson, look this way, and get the rest of your gang to look this way too. I want to get a picture. Lean on your shovels or something."

"Don't know what you want a picture of us for," he joked. "If we stop work for a picture then no one'll believe we did anything." She got her picture and then walked back to Sally and Charley who were following the schoolhouse as it moved.

"Where're they gonna put it?" Charley asked. "I don't see no place for it."

"Way over there," Anna pointed. Can you see the place that Ed has flattened out? That's where it's going. I can see Ed and Jonah working on it now."

"I don't see how it's gonna work out at all," Sally questioned. "From the looks of it, the way it's shakin' so much as they move it, well it's jus' gonna be like a rockin' chair house."

"I'm sure it will be all right," Anna answered. "You can see that none of the windows are broken. Anyway, they'll get it moved tonight. And then tomorrow a lot of the men are planning to come and help Ed build a foundation for it. Peter was telling me about it. What they will do is have the house sit on posts of wood. You know, the way the Wheeler house is."

"I'd sure like to see that," Charley said. "It must be a lotta work."

"I'm sure it is," Anna answered. "Why don't you come over tomorrow and watch? Anyway, I have to go to the store and see if Vi has some things I can use to make valentines. In less than two weeks it's going to be Valentine's Day. Want to come with me, Sally?"

"Sure, Anna. I've never been to the store before. If I'd known we was comin' to the store I'd of asked Bill for some money. We're gettin' low on a coupla things."

"Don't worry. Vi will let you have them on credit."

"My dad said never to buy on credit."

" Vi and Elmer always let folks take home things from the store when they don't have the cash on them. They know that they'll always get paid the next time they come in." The two women were fascinated with how the team pulled the schoolhouse and continued to glance at the progress being made as they crossed the bridge.

"It says **GRABNEY GENERAL STORE**," Sally said. "I guess a general store means that they sell almost everything. Is that what it means?"

"Yes. This store has a little bit of everything. Ed even brings coal from the store to school for us. What the children like most is the big jars of candy."

Sally's eyes were wide as they entered. "Oh look, Anna, they even have dishes and lots of things for the kitchen. How come they have all those chairs around the stove?"

Elmer heard the question. "That's what all the wives want to know. If it weren't for Ed movin' the schoolhouse, those chairs would prob'ly be full."

"Oh Elmer, this is Sally Griswold, and Sally, this is Elmer Marson. He and his wife Vi run the store."

"Pleestameetcha, Sally," Elmer said in his folksy manner. "I saw ya at the service an' at the Parkers'. I've knowed Charley n' Bill since they was little shavers. My dad and mother started this store, an' as a kid I worked here too. Then when my folks got old, Vi an' me took over, an' now Ed's gettin' married, so we'll have another family to work here."

"I thought you'd be out with the others watching all the excitement," Anna said.

"Well, I was there for a while, but Vi has to get the supper, so I had to come back in. Now, what is it that I can do for you ladies? Just give me a list an' I'll write it down an' get all the things lickety-split. What about you, Sally?"

"I dunno, but we're outta a coupla things, oatmeal 'n bread. You see I didn't get to bake for a coupla days. But then I got a problem," Sally blushed as she spoke.

Anna intervened. "Sally didn't know that I was coming to

the store, so she has no money with her."

"Well now, that's no problem," Elmer answered. "Sally, you can have all the oatmeal n' bread you can carry. I guess you're walkin' home. That right?"

"Yeah, that's right."

"The smallest oatmeal I have is a ten pound sack, but I'm sure you can manage that. An' choose whatever bread you want. We still have several loaves. Now what about you, Anna?"

"You know, Valentine's Day is in less than two weeks and I thought I'd stop by to see what you'd have so we could make valentines at school."

"That's really Vi's department," Elmer answered as he walked over to the stairs. "Mother! Come on down. There's someone here I want you to meet, and Anna needs some things for school."

No doubt Vi had been listening to the conversation, as she came down the steps immediately. Elmer started to introduce her, but Vi interrupted. "Well now, Elmer. I met Sally at Inger's on Wednesday. How're you doin', Sally? Nice to see you gettin' out a little."

"Oh, I'm fine," Sally replied.

"Are you gettin' everything you want?"

"Oh yes. Jus' some oatmeal n' bread." She gave the loaf she had chosen to Elmer.

"Now I'll jus' write down the things you bought, Sally, an' I'm gonna keep this list. The next time you or Charley or Bill come into the store, you can pay for them."

In the meantime, Anna had explained to Vi what she needed and was assured that red paper, doilies and valentine pictures would be in by next week. "Thanks, Vi. Why don't you phone Milly when they come in, and I'll be down that day or the next."

"That'll be fine Anna," Vi answered. "And it's good to see you, Sally. I heard you were plannin' to stay on at the Wheeler's, an' I'm glad of that. Once the snow's gone, it'll be much easier for you to get to the store, but don't hesitate to call if you need anything. Floyd comes down all the time, and he can bring it home for you."

"He always checks to see if we have any mail," Sally added. "We almost never have any, but the lady at the post office gives it to him if we do."

"That'll be Liza," Vi said. "You'll have to get out and meet all the folks around here."

"Now that she doesn't have to be so tied down to the house, I'm sure she'll get out more," Anna said. "Anyway, we better get going. I want to get one more picture of the moving. When I get the pictures developed, I'll show them to you."

"That'd be nice, Anna," Vi answered. "Elmer got a few this mornin' but they prob'ly won't be as good as yours."

"I'm not so sure of that," Anna called back as they went out the door.

"I've got to get home to get supper," Sally said. "I didn't know it was gettin' so late. Maybe I'll get Charley to carry this oatmeal, then you don't have to carry the bread for me."

"Oh, I can carry the bread easily."

The two hurried across the bridge in time to see the teams pulling close to the house site.

"I see Charley over there, Anna. I'll take the bread." She did so and hurried to Charley to unload the heavier half of her load.

"Come over here, Jonah and Ed," Anna called. "Let me get another picture before it gets too dark."

The two men willingly obliged, and the picture was taken. "Why don't you go on home, Jonah," Ed suggested. "There's nothin' more for you to do today. You better get back to your schoolwork. Thanks for all your help."

"Okay then, Ed, I'll be off," Jonah replied. "I'll walk you back, Anna, if that's all right with you. Say, where did Sally go?"

"Oh, she went over to get Charley. It's time she was getting home to supper."

"I'm glad you could make it to see the schoolhouse get moved," Jonah said as they headed up the road. "Did you get several pictures?"

"I got all I could. That last one was number eight, so I'll be able to send the film in on Monday. Did you get finished with your report?"

"I can finish tomorrow. Ed'll have enough help to get the foundation built. But I must say it was fun getting out in the open today. And how often does a person get the chance to move a schoolhouse?"

"Not very often, I guess," Anna replied. "By the way, when

do you have to leave?"

"Not tomorrow, anyway. I'll leave on the noon train Sunday."

"I'm sure your mother is glad to have you an extra day," Anna said.

"I'm glad to have it, too. But speaking of my mother, she asked me to ask you if you would like to come to supper tomorrow night. When Erica heard this she got really excited. Having a schoolteacher to supper is quite something. We'd all be happy to have you come. Do you think you can make it?"

"Oh," said Anna, surprised at the invitation. "That would be very nice. Are you sure it's not too much bother?"

"Not too much bother at all. I hope you don't have any other plans."

"No, I don't. The only thing I'll be doing tomorrow is helping Sally clean out Mrs. Wheeler's room. I'm not really looking forward to that, but she does need help. They haven't touched it since they took the body out. I'm going over in the morning. Inger said she would come over, too."

"That's thoughtful of you to do that. I hope that supper at our place will take your mind off the Wheelers for a while. Kirsten is home too. It's sort of a going-away supper for me."

"How nice. I'm really looking forward to it. Thanks for inviting me."

As they continued walking home they talked of school and Grabney and Ed and Bertha, and as they walked they both were thinking of supper the next night.

Chapter Fifteen

The wind was blowing in cold gusts as Anna walked toward the Wheeler's Saturday morning. She wrapped her muffler once again around her neck and hunched her shoulders to keep warm. She was glad she owned a fur hat that was pulled down over her ears. She folded her arms over her chest and shivered as she hurried up the road. The snow had hardened to ice, and walking became treacherous. She slowed down so she wouldn't fall and was glad when she reached the Wheeler's back steps.

The door was opened as she carefully went up the first step. "I saw you from the bedroom window, Anna," Sally said as she greeted her. "It's awful cold today. You should've stayed home, but I'm awful glad you came. Don't take your coat off in the entry. Come in the kitchen where it's warm. Just put your things over a chair."

"I had no idea it was so cold when I left the Jensens'," Anna said. "I hope the wind dies down, so the men don't have too hard a time working on Ed's house."

"Has Peter left yet?" Sally asked.

"He was having another cup of coffee when I left," and she laughed. "I think he's trying to postpone it as long as possible."

"Charley'll be glad ta hear that. He wants ta go, but he's still helpin' Bill out at the pens. They was a bit slow gettin' the milkin' done today, an' so they're slow in sloppin' the pigs. How about a cuppa coffee?"

"No thanks, Sally. I've had enough coffee for now. I think we should get right to work. The sooner we get in there, the sooner we'll finish."

Sally sighed. "You're right Anna. It's a job I don't wanna do, so we better get it done. I wonder when Inger's comin'."

"Probably before too long. It's not even nine o'clock, and she has her own chores to do. Inger will be the best help in sorting out Mrs. Wheeler's things, but we can do things like change the bed and tidy up a little."

Sally opened the bedroom door. A musty sickroom smell greeted them. "I should've opened the window," Sally said as she backed out of the room. "But it's been so cold, I didn't want to. Anyway, I didn't even wanna go in the room. Guess I was sorta chicken."

"You weren't at all," Anna smiled at her, and then became serious. "This room has some unpleasant memories. Anyway, we're here to change all that." She strode firmly through the doorway and stopped suddenly as she looked at the bed. It was obvious that it had not been touched since Edna Wheeler had been lifted out into the coffin. "Sally, I think I know where we can start. Do you have any clean sheets?"

"Sure. They're in my room. Just a minute. I'll get them."

"While you're doing that, I'll start pulling the old sheets off. But Sally," she called as Sally went through the kitchen and into her bedroom. "I think first we better take care of that flour sack under the mattress." Anna bent down to reach for it. "Can you help me lift the mattress? I can't find it on this side. It must have slid to the other side."

"Here, I'll help you," Sally said as she reentered the room with the clean sheets and pillowcase. "Let me lift up the mattress, an' you can pull it out." She grabbed hold of it and held it up, balancing it on her waist.

"Sally!" Anna said with alarm. "I can't find it. Here, let's lift it up all the way. I'll help you, and you can look. I can see through the springs to the floor, and it hasn't fallen down there." The two of them held on to one side of the mattress, lifting it up completely, but it was obvious there was no flour sack of money.

"Oh, them boys!" Sally said disgustedly as they flopped the mattress down. "They prob'ly was worried about it an' took it out. But they should've tol' me. Wait 'till I get ahold of them." She went to the back door and called out, "Charley! Bill! Get in here! You're through sloppin' the pigs anyway, an' I'm not comin' out ta get you. An' make it fast."

Anna could see who was running this household. She smiled

to herself that Sally had changed so, since she first came to work on the place. Soon she could see both men walking across the yard, and then heard their clump, clump as they climbed the back steps. They filed into the kitchen, Bill first. Charley shut the door. They stood there like two schoolboys who were being blamed for something they knew nothing about.

"Whatsa matter, Sally?" Charley asked. "Gosh durn, but you seem mad or somethin'. I've never seen you get mad before."

"I've every right to be. Now just tell me what you did with that flour sack that was under your ma's mattress."

"We didn't do nothin' with it," Bill said. "Whatsa matter, anyway?"

"Well it just ain't there," she continued. "Anna'n I've been lookin' for it, an' it just ain't there."

"Well, where is it then?" Bill asked, irritated that Sally had called them in.

"That's what I wanna know," Sally retorted. "Where did you guys hide it?" I s'pose you thought you could keep it a secret from me."

"We didn't hide nothin'," Charley said. He looked very confused.

"Well, if you didn't, who did?" Sally was obviously very upset.

"What's going on?" Inger entered the kitchen and banged shut the door. "You were making so much noise you didn't even hear me come up the steps. I've never heard the likes of it over here."

"Sally can't find the flour sack with Ma's money," Bill said.

"What do you mean, she can't find it?" Inger looked puzzled. "It should be right under the mattress where we left it."

"But it's not, Inger," Anna said, feeling that it was time that she entered the conversation. "Sally and I heaved the mattress up way off the bed, and it's not there at all."

"Let me see," Inger said as she walked into the room. "Phew! I can see what you mean when you said it needed cleaning out. Come on, Bill, lift up the mattress. Maybe it got stuck in the bottom sheet or something."

Bill came into the room, followed by Charley. Together they lifted the mattress while Inger searched all around it. "Okay boys, put it back. It sure isn't here. On second thought, let's look through the drawers in her dresser to make sure it didn't get there by mistake."

"We ain't even touched the sack," Bill said. "We wouldn't put it in a drawer. Ma never would've liked that."

"Just to make sure, let's check the floor and everything." Inger opened the drawers and made a quick search as the boys looked around the floor. Sally and Anna stood observing from the doorway, hoping that someone would find it.

"All right, it's not here," Inger concluded as she went into the kitchen. "Bill, have you checked to see if the sack I gave you is still where you put it?"

Bill was out the kitchen door and into the parlor in a flash. Anna didn't know he could move so fast. Quickly he returned with his flour sack. "It's here," he said with relief as he held it up for all to see. "I've got it, an' it's still fulla money."

"Well, that's something," Inger remarked. "Bill, dump the money out on the table, and let's count it. Let's make sure it's all there." They counted it carefully and found that he still had his original amount, a little less than one thousand dollars. "You sure don't spend much money around here."

"I bought some oatmeal an' bread yesterday," Sally explained. "An' I didn't have any money, so we owe for that."

Inger was concentrating so hard she didn't hear her. "All right now. And don't get excited when I say this, but it looks to me like someone has come in here and taken your four thousand dollars."

"But we ain't never gone," Bill said. "An' no one knowed about it."

A silence followed, broken by Inger. "There's one time I can think of that you were all gone, and that was Wednesday at the funeral and at the gathering at our house. Someone could have come in then. Didn't you come home before you came over to our house?"

"I came with them," added Anna. "But we didn't go in the house."

"That's 'cause we wanted to hurry," Bill said. "So we put the sleigh away an' took care of the horse, an' then we come right over to your house."

"But nobody knowed about the money," Sally said, close to tears. "We never told no one."

"There's something I should have thought of," Inger said. "Everyone around here knew that Edna kept her money on the place and not in a bank. The point is, she was always here, so no one would try to find it. And if she was away from the house, Charley or Bill were always around."

"That's right," Charley agreed. "We was always around. Ma kept tellin' us to always keep an eye out for strangers."

"How could they have found it so fast?" Anna asked. "I would think it would take awhile, and then someone would have seen whoever did it walking away from the place."

"Let me tell you this, Anna," Inger said forthrightly. "The two places where money is hidden that people always joke about are the spare sugar bowl and under the mattress. And it's where they really do hide it. I don't think it took anyone too long to figure that one out. And if the folks here were gone to the funeral and to our place, someone who knew about that could figure how long that would take, get the money and skip out of here easily."

"I wonder how come they didn't get my money?" asked Bill.

"I couldn't really tell you the answer to that," Inger answered. "It could be that they never guessed that there would be money in two places. Or it could also be that with finding this much money and wondering when someone would be coming back, they didn't want to take the chance of getting caught, so they high-tailed it out of here."

"Perhaps they were in here when we came back from the funeral," Anna added. "And they were just lucky we didn't come in the house."

"Well we really don't know the answers to any of these questions, and we also don't have any idea who took it," Inger surmised.

"I know who," Charley said with authority. "It's them Downey boys. They was always mean to me. I just know it was them."

"Let's not jump to conclusions," Inger said, trying to calm him down. "The person we do need to contact is the sheriff. Yes, I think we better phone Jim Wilson. Stealing this much money is a serious matter."

"Well, let's phone him, then!" Bill almost shouted.

"First, let's think about this a little," Inger cautioned. "If I phone the sheriff from this phone, everyone can listen in, and we really don't want people to know the money is missing."

"Why?" Bill asked. "Everyone's gotta know, so we can catch the person who did it."

"But if it's someone around here, then they'll be hard to catch, 'cause they'll know we are looking for them."

"We could go down to the post office," Sally said. "That lady has a line to the county seat."

"Yes, we could do that, but Lisa would soon have it broadcast all over the countryside, and then where would we be? No, what we should do is to phone from the store. Remember Vi and Elmer put in a line when they started selling shoes for Jack Jarvis, so they could phone him when they needed to? They don't usually let people use their phone. In fact, they had it put in upstairs. In this case, I know that we could use it."

"What about the other people in the store?" Anna reminded her. "As soon as we asked Vi if we could use the phone, they'd be sure to wonder why."

"I don't think you'll find many people in the store today," Inger reminded her. "The men are helping Ed with the house, and the women are busy getting ready for Sunday. The problem that I can see is, who'll go to the store? If I went, people would be sure to see me and wonder why I hadn't sent Mabel. Anyway, they would be curious. The quieter we keep this, the better."

"I have an idea," Anna suggested. "Sally bought some things at the store yesterday, and she owes Elmer for them. Charley could bring Sally and me in his sleigh, and she could pay them back. That way I could go upstairs and phone."

"It would be better if Sally bought some other things, also," Inger remarked. "Sally is there anything else you need at the store?"

"Well, we're almost out of flour and we'd need the sleigh to bring that back. We could use some sugar too, an' oh yes, coffee. They have so many things there that if I looked around I could prob'ly find other things we need."

"Jus' don't go spendin' too much money," Bill cut in. "We don't have so much money now. Ma never spent much money."

Inger looked disgusted as she replied, "Bill, you still have plenty of money. It's time you folks bought a few of the things that would make life a little more pleasant instead of scrimping and saving all the time. Your ma saved her money, but look what it got her. It's gone now. You and Charley haven't had any decent new clothes for years. And there's Sally. She didn't come here to live like some poor folks. The thousand dollars that you have is a lot of money, more than almost everyone around here has. With luck, you'll get back the money that was taken. Let Sally buy a few things that will make this place more comfortable. Well I guess that's enough of that."

"Awright Inger, if you say so," Bill said solemnly. "I guess you're right."

"Good!" Inger exclaimed. "All right now. Let's talk about the trip to town. Anna, you know the sheriff, and I think you know what to tell him. I'm sure he'll be discreet in coming here. Okay Charley, get one of your horses hitched up to the sleigh. Bill, give Sally enough money to buy what she needs. And the three of you get going. The sooner we get hold of the sheriff, the better."

Chapter Sixteen

The wind had died down considerably when the three of them set off for the store huddled together in the sled. As they left the yard, Inger was crossing the road to her house, and gave them a wave as if nothing was wrong.

"Sally! You sure you got the money?" Charley asked anxiously.

"It's right here in my pocketbook," she answered as she clutched the top of her purse tightly with both hands, pressing it against her lap.

At the mention of the money, Anna glanced at the hands tightly clasped around the pocketbook. "I like your mittens, Sally. Did you knit them yourself?"

"Sure did. I can't knit gloves; too many fingers. They're too much of a problem, but mittens, they're easy." She held up her hands for Anna to see. "My good gloves are storebought, but they're not as warm as my mittens."

"Don't let go of your pocketbook, Sally," Charley warned, looking at Sally as she showed Anna her mittens. "If you lose that, we won't have any money for the store."

"I won't lose it. I'm always careful with money," she answered as she gripped it tighter. "I always had to take care of the money for my ma when she got sick, an' I never lost any of it."

"I think you don't have to worry about Sally losing the money, Charley," Anna said. "She's holding her pocketbook so tight she's about to wear it out."

"I jus' wanna make sure, that's all." They turned the corner and Charley called out, "Hey! Look at all them men workin'. Inger was right. She said all the men'd be workin' on Ed's house. I wisht I was there." They waved as they passed the group, then crossed the bridge and stopped at the store.

"I'll hitch up Henrietta after you get out," Charley said.

"That's an interesting name for a horse," Anna remarked as she jumped down from the sleigh. "I've never heard of a horse named Henrietta before."

"My ma named her that. Said she didn't have no girls, an' she took a fancy to the name, so she gave it to a mare. You go on up the steps, I'll be right behind you."

"Kick the snow off your boots," Sally told Charley. "It won't do to make a mess inside. An' don't kick it off on the steps. They've been swept. Do it like we did."

The three paused at the top of the steps, standing on the wide porch. "Let me do the talking first," suggested Anna. "I saw Elmer over at Ed's new place, but we don't know who else might be in the store. And we want to keep this quiet." The two nodded assent. Charley opened the door, and they hurried in. There was no one behind the counter, and Anna assumed that Vi must be upstairs. "Hello, Vi." she called.

A head poked out from behind a stack of canned goods. It was Vi. "Hello, Anna. Oh hello, Charley n' Sally. S'pose you thought the place was deserted. Actually, I was tryin' to get caught up with some sorting since nobody's here. But now that you're here, what can I do for you?"

"Vi, are you sure no one else is here?" Anna asked.

"My goodness, why so secretive?" Vi answered with some curiosity. "I guess you can see that this place is pretty empty."

"It's just that I have a favor to ask of you, and I don't want it to go any farther."

"Speak up, Anna!" Vi looked at Charley and Sally who were standing quietly aside. "If there's something I can do for you, I will."

"I know you have a phone to the county seat," Anna continued. "Inger said that you did, and it was Inger who suggested that I ask you if I could use it."

"If Inger is behind something, then you can bank on me to help. Is that it? You want to use the phone?"

"That's right."

"Go on upstairs and help yourself, then. It's on the wall next to the parlor. This here phone's the local one," and she tilted her head toward the one on the wall behind the counter, looking at

Sally and Charley as if to explain.

"It's pretty serious, Vi," Anna explained. "Inger said I ought to tell you, but be sure to keep it to yourself."

"I know how to hold my tongue," Vi assured her.

"Well you can tell Elmer, of course." Anna hesitated, feeling rather uncomfortable. "I don't really know where to begin."

"Well, whatever it is it can't be that bad, so get on with it." By this time the situation had piqued her interest.

"You see, Charley's mother always kept the family money in her room, actually under her mattress."

"Well that don't surprise me one bit," Vi said and laughed at the thought. "She's not the only one to do that. I s'pose now that she's gone you want to make arrangements to put the money in the bank. The bank's closed on Saturday."

"Oh no. It's not that. I wish it were," Anna said wistfully. "The problem is that when she had her stroke we left the money under her mattress because we knew she would get upset if she didn't feel it there." She paused. "It was really lumpy, but she was used to it, I guess. We couldn't put it in the bank. That would have been too much trouble, and there was trouble enough with it being New Year's, and the snow and her getting injured. Since it had always been there, we thought it would be safe enough."

"Well, I should think it would be," Vi nodded.

"Don't fergit Bill's money," Charley said. "Oh sorry, Anna. I shouldna said nothin'."

"That's all right, Charley. Inger did give Bill some money for expenses. She thought that Mrs. Wheeler wouldn't feel it if some money was gone."

"The whole thing sounds reasonable to me," Vi concluded. "So now, what's the problem?"

"The problem is that the money's gone. We hunted and hunted. Inger even came over and hunted, too. We can't find it anywhere. Inger thought that while we were at the funeral, or maybe at her house after the funeral, someone came in and stole it."

"Oh no!" Vi exclaimed. "Who would ever have done a thing like that?"

"That's just it. We don't know."

"Well, are you sure it's missin'?" Vi asked. "I mean, have you looked everywhere?"

"We looked everywhere. It's not anywhere," Sally said, then quickly added, "But Bill gave me some money, so I can pay you for the things I got yesterday. And we need some more things, too."

"Now don't you worry none about that, Sally," Vi said. "I'm not worried about getting paid for the things you bought. Now Anna, I think you better hurry upstairs and phone Jim Wilson before anyone else comes in here. My land! I've never known anything like this to happen."

"Thanks, Vi. Maybe it will turn out all right, but calling the sheriff is the only thing we can think of to do."

"You're right there, Anna. And if it's not stolen, Jim won't mind being called. He hasn't been around here for some time, anyway. He usually tries to visit about every month or so. You go on upstairs now, and I'll take care of Sally and get the things she needs."

They watched as Anna quickly went up the steps to the living quarters. Vi shook her head, "I just can't believe it, but if Inger thinks that's what happened, the best thing is to call the sheriff. Now what can I do for you, Sally?"

"I bought bread and oatmeal yesterday."

"Elmer told me about that. Let's see, I'll just find where it's written down." She pulled out the drawer that held the receipt books and sorted through it. "Oh, here it is. That was a ten-pound sack of oatmeal and a loaf of bread."

"That's right," Sally answered.

"Now what else did you want?"

"We need flour," Sally added. "I couldn't even bake, 'cause we were almost out of it, an' I didn't have time to, anyway. An' then I could use about five pounds of sugar."

"How much flour do you want, Sally?" Vi asked, as she got a pencil and made sure the carbon paper was flipped from the bottom of the pad to between the yellow and white pages.

"Twenty five pounds, at least. Oh, I s'pose we should get fifty pounds." She looked around the counter. "I'm gonna need some yeast cakes, too, an' cheese. Could I get a coupla pounds a cheese?"

"Sure can," Vi answered. "I have a wheel of cheddar cheese right there on the other side of the cash register. Is that all right?"

"Sure is," Sally said as she glanced at it. "An' oh yes, we need coffee. Gimme one a those bags a coffee." Her eyes strayed to the shelves in back of the counter. "An I see you have nice calico prints. They're real pretty."

"Those are really pretty, Sally, some of the nicest we've gotten in," said Vi as she walked to where they were stacked.

"If I got two yards I could sew kitchen curtains. Oh, the curtains we have is all ragged. It would be so nice to have new ones."

"How're you gonna sew 'em, Sally?" Charley asked.

"Your ma has a sewin' machine. I saw it in her bedroom under a bunch of stuff. When we get the room cleaned out, I'll put it in my room."

"You're going to stay on then?" asked Vi.

Sally hesitated before she answered, "At least for a while."

"I hope you stay a long time," Charley said, and then looking at Vi he explained. "You see, I'm not so good a cook, an' when the spring comes, Bill'n I'll have to be out plantin' an' doin' all the farm work. We need Sally to keep house."

"That's a good idea," Vi acknowledged. "Yes, I remember before your pa died that your ma used to sew up things. Why, she bought material here. She probably was the one to make the curtains that are there now."

"She did a lot of work outside, too," Charley reminded Vi.

"Yes, that she did, even before your father died. But after he died she took over runnin' the place. Guess she had to. Anyway, which one do you want, Sally?"

"I like that one with the flowers," Sally said pointing to a bolt with lavender violets.

Vi got it down for her "You said two yards?"

"Yes, that'll be plenty. How much is it?"

"Twenty-nine cents a yard," Vi answered as she lay the fabric on the counter, measured it with a yardstick and cut it off. "Now, let's see if you need anything else. What about salt or baking powder? What about thread?"

"I saw a coupla spools a thread on the machine," Sally replied, "an' I can't think of anythin' else. I'll make a list, so next time we come I'll know for sure."

Anna was coming down the stairs when she heard Vi say, "All right then, I'll add it up. Charley, you get two sacks of flour and take them out to the sleigh. I'll get the sugar measured into a paper sack." She took the scoop from the sugar bin, put a sack on the scale and scooped out five pounds. Then she wrapped a string around it. "Give me a coupla minutes, and I'll get the rest of your order."

"Oh Anna," Sally said as she walked over to her. "I bought some calico for new kitchen curtains. I'm gonna sew 'em on Charley's mom's sewin' machine. Won't they look nice?"

"They will be a real improvement," Anna answered.

Vi looked up and asked, "Anna, did you get through to Jim?"

"Yes, I did. I explained everything to him, and he said he would do some scouting around and probably come over Monday."

"Monday!" exclaimed Vi. "Isn't that a long time to wait?"

"He said it would be better if he looked around first, to find out if anyone has had more money to spend than usual."

"That's a good idea," she agreed. "I'll keep my eyes and ears open here, too. I think I mentioned before that Jim usually comes by here every once in a while, and he hasn't been here for over a month, I'm sure. No one will think anything about it if they see him comin' around."

"He said the same to me, and tomorrow being Sunday, if he came, then people would wonder if something was up."

"I see Charley's gettin' the things in the sleigh," Vi said as she looked toward the door. "Let's see, Sally, here's how much you owe. Do you have that much money on you?"

"Sure!" she answered confidently. "Bill gave me twenty dollars." She took the twenty-dollar bill out of her pocketbook and handed it to Vi, receiving the change, which she carefully put back into the pocketbook. "I think we better get goin. It's almost time for dinner, an' I haven't even started cookin' it."

"If it's nearly that time, Elmer and Ed'll be comin' in, so I better get busy myself. You folks come back again. And Anna, tell Inger I'll keep this little matter to myself. I don't even need to tell Elmer. He'll find out soon enough."

As they came to the Wheeler yard, they saw Inger looking out her parlor window. Before they had finished unloading, Inger dashed across the road and followed them into the house. Anna explained her phone call to the sheriff, and Inger seemed satisfied. "Well, that takes care of that," she said. "Now we'll have to wait until he comes Monday. I can see you got more things from the store, Sally. That's good."

"Oh, Inger. I got such pretty material for new kitchen curtains. Just look and see." Sally held up the fabric. She had insisted on carrying it home herself.

"That looks mighty fine to me," Inger commented. "You are a wonder, Sally. You're worth a lot. And that reminds me, speaking of how much Sally is worth, Bill, have you paid Sally for the month of January?"

A shamefaced Bill answered that he had not.

"Well, we have to figure this out. Now the arrangement was that Sally was to get paid a dollar a day. Isn't that right?"

"That's right," Bill said, and Sally nodded her head.

"All right, now. Sally came on January 6th, so her pay starts then." Inger looked up on the wall where the calendar was hung. "Where's your 1923 calendar? The one you got on the wall says December 1922."

"Oh, I forgot all about that. You mean the one from Elmer's store?" Bill asked.

"That's the one," Inger said.

"I dunno where 'tis," Bill said as he looked around the room.

"It's under them papers on the sewin' machine in yer ma's room," Sally told him. "I know where it is. Okay if I get it, Inger?"

"Go ahead," Inger answered. "Just make sure you don't touch anything else, though." Sally quickly returned with the calendar. "Now boys, let's get this put up." With a determined stride she walked to the wall and exchanged the new for the old. "All right now, let's see how much you owe Sally. Bill, you count out the days, and remember: count only January."

He put a grimy finger on each date, counting out loud, and then replied, "It's twenty-six days."

"That's right, so you owe Sally twenty-six dollars. I'm sure Sally has some change from the store, so go get a twenty-dollar bill from your room, and I think we'll have enough," Inger directed. Soon the transaction was completed. It was decided that Sally would keep her money in her purse, and the household money would be kept in Bill's room until a coin purse could be located. "Now I'm glad that's settled, and Sally, don't let Bill forget to pay you again. I'm going home. What about you, Anna?"

"Oh yes, I'll go out with you."

As they left the kitchen, Inger turned around and said, "By the way, you folks. Remember you are to say nothing about this at all. If you go to church tomorrow, Sally and Charley, just keep this to yourselves."

Three heads bobbed a silent nod.

Inger grabbed Anna's arm as they went down the back steps. "Thought I was going to slip again for a minute. Anyway, paying Sally reminded me of something. I haven't given you your January paycheck."

"Don't worry about that, Inger. There's been too much going on."

"That's for sure, but it's no excuse. If I'm to be head of the school board, I have to do the job right." As they came to the road Inger looked up at the sky. "I'm sure glad the wind died down. Those clouds don't look so threatening, either. We may even get some sun."

Anna scanned the horizon from the schoolhouse to the church. "And maybe the snow will melt."

"I wouldn't count on it. Anyway, Floyd an' I'll be down after supper. I'll bring your paycheck then."

"Oh!" Anna hesitated. "I may not be home. I was invited to the Larsons' to supper."

Inger's eyebrows shot up; however, she managed to conceal her surprise before replying. "Well, isn't that nice. Sylvia keeps a good house and cooks a decent meal. I'm sure you'll enjoy going there. And about your paycheck, if I don't see you, I'll leave it with Milly."

Chapter Seventeen

It was impossible for Anna to get through the kitchen without confiding in Milly about the day's events. Fortunately, Davey was outside with Peter, and she spoke quietly enough so that Sarah and Lucy were out of earshot.

"Oh, yoi, yoi!" Milly exclaimed. "What goings on around here I never heard of. What will it be next?"

"I hope there won't be any 'next'," Anna said as she went upstairs. "Inger and Floyd will be down after supper. No doubt they'll fill you in on all the details. I'm going to see if I can get all my papers corrected before I go to the Larsons'."

The walnut clock on the kitchen wall had just struck six when Anna came back downstairs. Peter was coming into the kitchen from the basement where he had separated the milk. "I'll put the cream in the icebox, Milly. I saw that you didn't need any more whole milk. I'll be back as soon as I slop the pigs with the skim." He looked over at Anna, "Well! Aren't you all gussied up." She was wearing the rust-colored wool dress her mother had made her for Christmas. "Don't tell me it's Sunday already, or are we having company?"

Anna smiled, "Sylvia Larson invited me to come over for supper. Kirsten is home for the weekend, and I've never met her."

"Sounds like a good reason to me," Peter said without conviction.

"Also, she said Erica has wanted me to come over for a long time."

"I can understand that," he continued as he nodded. "And William will be home, of course. And Jonah, isn't he home for the week?" He looked at her with a twinkle in his eyes.

"Yes, I guess so." Anna was getting a bit fidgety. "Is there anything I can help you with, Milly?" She glanced at her watch. "I don't have to leave right now. Supper isn't until 6:30, and it won't take me five minutes or so to get up there."

"I wouldn't have you help, wearing your best dress," Milly said. There was the sound of footsteps on the porch followed by a rap on the door. "Go see who that is, Peter. My land, who could be coming this time of night?" She knew very well who it was.

"I wonder." Peter smiled to himself as he opened the kitchen door. "Well, Jonah! Come on in. Good to see you. How's the studying going? Take off your coat and sit down."

"No, thanks. I can't stay. But the studying is going fine. I'm nearly finished with the report. Only a few loose ends to tie up."

"Anna was just telling us that she was having supper at your place. Is that right?" At this remark Anna's face turned a delicate pink.

Jonah laughed. "And I'm here to fetch her. Guess I'm a little early. Are you about ready, Anna?"

"I'll get my galoshes and coat from the porch," she said, having partly regained her composure. She was glad to have the chance to escape for a few minutes, even though the porch was bone-chilling cold. This would get rid of any pink blush showing on her face. She shivered as she tugged on her galoshes, leaning against the other coats to do so. Her bearskin coat was like ice as she put her arms into the sleeves. She opened the door, returning to the kitchen and savoring its warmth. Her hat, muffler and gloves she had set on the steps to the upstairs, so she walked over to them and put them on. "Now I'm ready."

"All right, then. I guess we better get going," Jonah said as he opened the door.

"Have a good time, Anna," Milly called after her. "And be careful you don't slip in the snow."

"I'll see that she doesn't," Jonah called back. "And I'll bring her back safe and sound too. Watch these steps, Anna," he said as he took her arm. Anna wasn't going to remind him that she navigated these steps several times a day.

"Thank you, Jonah. Oh, I can see that there's a little bit of moonlight, so it's not so dark."

"I brought a flashlight, anyway," he said as he groped in his pocket, struggled a little to get it out and then turned it on. "Well, that helps, doesn't it?"

"Yes, it does."

They rounded the corner of the house and headed for the road. "Oh, by the way, did you finish cleaning up Edna Wheeler's room? I saw you coming home about dinnertime."

Anna thought a little and then decided that Jonah could be trusted with the latest developments. Besides, she also valued his judgment and wanted to confide in him. "Well Jonah, you see, it's like this. I don't know where to begin, but no, we didn't finish cleaning her room."

"It sure must have been a mess, then. I remember when we came back from the river last Saturday that it looked pretty good. I thought Sally must have had a hand in it. She looks like a good worker to me."

"Oh, it wasn't that. Sally had things pretty neat."

"What was the problem then, just too much stuffed in the dresser drawers? I suppose trying to clean out a person's life possessions is a pretty big job."

"No, it wasn't that. You see we found a problem. Inger said not to tell anyone, but I think you should know. I'm sure she wouldn't mind if I told you. She's coming after supper to tell Milly and Peter about it."

"Now you really have me in suspense. First we come home from the river and find that she has died, and now you tell me there's something else?"

"This is different from her dying," Anna continued with some hesitation. "You see, when Sally and I went into the room we first started changing the bed. You know she always kept her money under the mattress."

"Yes, I guess everyone knew that."

"Well, the money is gone."

"Gone! How do you mean the money's gone? It just can't have disappeared. Are you sure you looked everywhere for it?"

"Yes! We looked everywhere, all of us, even Inger."

"Do Charley and Bill know anything about it?"

"No! We all looked. The boys don't know anything about it. They were as shocked as we were."

Jonah thought a little. "I'm sure the boys would be very protective of the money. Well then, what could have happened to it?"

"The only thing we can think of is that someone came in when we were at the funeral, or at the gathering at the Parkers', and took it."

"Yes, I suppose that was about the only time when no one was at the place. So you're saying that you think someone stole it."

"Yes. It must have been stolen."

"What's being done now? I mean, how could this have happened? You said Inger was going to tell Peter and Milly about it, so she was there too."

"Not at first. Sally and I found it was missing. Then Sally thought that Charley or Bill might have taken it and put it some place else, but they said they never touched it. Inger walked in just as Sally was giving the boys a real scolding over it."

"I would've liked to have seen that!" and he laughed. "Sally must have changed since she came. But what are you going to do?"

"We've already done it. Inger said to phone Jim Wilson, and that's what I did."

"I hope you didn't use Liza's phone."

"Of course not!" She laughed at the thought. "What we did was, Charley drove Sally and me to the store. While Sally was buying more things from Vi, I went upstairs and phoned the sheriff. He'll do some scouting around before he comes out here Monday afternoon. He said the first thing to think of when money is stolen is to look around and see who's been spending more money than usual."

"That's a good idea. I never thought of that. Well, here we are."

Anna stopped and gazed at the house. "Your house has always looked to me like a house in town. It's not made like a farmhouse. It has a wide front porch and a door in the center, like you have stairs to the upstairs in a front hall."

"That's exactly what we do have. But it didn't happen by accident. Dad spent many years doing over the place. You see, mother came from the county seat. Her folks didn't want her to marry a farmer, and Dad wanted to show them that they could have things just as nice out here."

"When did he have time to do it all? I mean with the farming, that takes up so much time."

"He did most of it in the winter, at least the inside part, and he did that himself. Several years in a row he had good crops, and they went for a good price, so he had enough money to hire carpenters who could do the outside work when the weather was decent. Oh, don't go around back. Mother said to use the front door. It never gets used. It's supposed to be for company, and you are the company."

Anna smiled, "I never thought of myself as company." Her expression changed quickly as she asked, "Promise you won't tell anyone about the money?"

"Don't worry. Mum's the word, but it'll sure give me something to think about. Can you see the steps all right?"

"Oh, yes. I see you even cleaned them off."

"Well, couldn't have company going up steps with snow on them now, could we?"

Erica had been watching out for them through the beveled oval glass in the door and opened it as soon as they got on the porch. The delightful aroma of a roast filled the air. It always amazed Anna at the sumptuous meals that were prepared by farm wives. In town they had to buy every morsel they ate and were careful to keep down expenses. But on farms, most of the food was produced right on the place. What they bought were staples like flour and sugar, and of course coffee.

"Let me take off my galoshes," Anna said. "I don't want to track snow in the house."

"Here, you lean against the porch and I'll pull them off for you," Jonah suggested.

Anna laughed. "I haven't had anyone pull off my galoshes since I was a little girl." She did as she was told, and after a couple of firm tugs they were off.

"Bring them inside, Jonah," Erica said. "If you leave them out there, they'll get damp. Mother has a rug just inside the door for them."

"I guess your mother thinks of everything," Anna remarked. "Oh, let's hurry inside so we don't let all the warm air out." She looked around. It was just as she had imagined. There was a staircase that led upstairs a few feet inside the front door. On the left was a parlor, and on the right of the steps was the dining room. The heat was coming from a newly blackened potbellied stove, located in the parlor near the stairs. It was likely that this stove used the same chimney as the kitchen stove.

"I'll hang up your coat, Miss Swenson," Erica said. "I can put it in the coat closet under the stairs. Put your other things on this hall table."

"Thanks, Erica."

"Aren't you going to take my coat, too?" Jonah asked with a teasing smile.

"You're not company. You get to hang up your own," she replied smartly.

"Oh, Anna," said Sylvia Larson as she came from the kitchen wiping her hands on her apron. "We're so glad to have you here."

"Thank you. I'm happy to have been invited." Anna noticed the table had been beautifully set with their good china.

"We're almost ready for dinner. Olle! Anna's here!" she called looking toward the kitchen door. To Anna she said, "He always sits in his favorite chair in the kitchen. It's like pulling teeth to get him out of it. Kirsten's in the kitchen, too, helping with the dinner. William!" she called up the stairs. "Come down. It's time for supper. Oh Kirsten, come and meet Miss Swenson."

A slightly plump, smiling teenager poked her head around the kitchen door. "Hello, Miss Swenson. I don't even have my apron off, Mother. Give me a minute and I'll be in."

Anna returned the greeting, noticing the resemblance between Kirsten and Sylvia. They were nearly the same size, with blonde hair and blue eyes. Her glance then went to Erica, who had whitish blonde hair and was a slender little thing. Even at thirteen she was quite petite.

Olle hurried out of the kitchen to meet his guest. "Sorry I wasn't at the door when you arrived." He shook her hand. "I see someone's taken care of you." He smiled, "I'm assuming you didn't walk all the way up here without a coat."

"I took her coat, Daddy," Erica said with a firm nod. "Mother, may I sit next to Miss Swenson?"

"Of course you may. And here's William. William, you know Miss Swenson."

"How do you do, Miss Swenson." He walked over to her and shook her hand. William was a young image of his father, light brown hair and husky, firmly built, muscular and not fat. It was obvious they worked hard on the farm. Jonah and Erica resembled each other, slim, blonde, blue eyes.

Sylvia seated Anna between Erica and Jonah, opposite William and Kirsten. Kirsten helped her mother bring the food to the table. Olle said grace, and there was the usual light conversation while the food was passed.

Anna looked at Sylvia. "You have a beautiful dining set and buffet. It's walnut, isn't it?"

"Yes," she replied. "It belonged to my grandmother. My grandparents lived in Des Moines and were fairly well off. This is her china and silver, too. I was the only granddaughter, so she gave them to me."

"This is the nicest I have ever seen," Anna commented as she looked at the flowers painted on her plate. "You say your grandparents lived in Des Moines, but your folks live in the county seat?"

"Oh yes, and that is a long story. You see, my mother came to visit some of her relatives who lived in the country, where she met my father. He was working as a bookkeeper in the county courthouse. It seems Mother stayed longer than her parents had anticipated, and after she returned to Des Moines they kept up a correspondence. As you can guess, she married my father and they moved to the county seat. Well my grandparents were horrified that their daughter was living in 'the sticks'."

Jonah laughed, "That isn't all, Mother. Tell her the rest."

A slightly shy Sylvia continued. "Well, I don't know if I should."

"Oh, come on," came a chorus of voices.

"Well, I met Olle when we were in high school in the county seat. He could go only two years, because he had to get back to the farm and help his father. He was the only boy in the family."

Olle interrupted. "You see, Anna, my dad was trying to manage this whole place by himself. He had two homesteads, one for himself and one for my mother. That's half a section, and that's too much for one person. Of course, my mother worked it too. She had to. Anyway, I had to take time off from high school for farm work, and in town I had to pay room and board. Our kids are lucky they stay with Sylvia's parents when they go to high school. It was just not working out, so I quit high school. It didn't matter, anyway. I wasn't learning anything to do with farming. I learned far more working with my dad."

"Let me continue, Olle," Sylvia interrupted him. "Even though he didn't go the last two years, I still remembered him, and I would see him when he came to town."

"And there was my dad, wondering why I was so anxious to go on errands for him in the county seat," Olle laughed.

"You were pretty clever, Olle," Sylvia admitted. "Anyway, after high school, my parents sent me to stay with my grandparents, so then Olle and I corresponded. When we were married, my parents thought I was moving out to the sticks." Everyone laughed.

Olle looked up from his plate. "Yes, your mother really had her feathers ruffled."

"But she's not like that now," Kirsten said.

"No, of course not," Sylvia added. "She knows I found a good one when I found Olle. You see Olle's parents had farmed this place and with Olle's help were doing quite well. We moved in with them. Of course, the house was not like what it is now. Before we could build a place of our own, Olle's dad took sick with arthritis, and he knew he couldn't do the work any more, so they moved down south. Since Olle was the only boy they had and we wanted to buy the farm from them, that's what we did."

Anna looked from Sylvia to Olle. "And you've done a beautiful job. This is one of the nicest farms in the whole country, and this house is beautiful."

"It didn't happen by accident, let me tell you that," Olle said as he shook his head. "It was just plain hard work. But it's worth every bit of it. Sylvia doesn't have to be ashamed of where we live or what we do for a living."

"Oh Olle, I never would be," she quickly replied, and she beamed as she looked at her husband. "And I'm so proud of Olle. Now, what about you Anna? We've bored you enough with talk of our family."

The dinner continued with Anna filling them in about her life in Fort Dodge, going to normal school and getting the position in Grabney.

"So, what does your mother think about your coming to a little country school?" Olle asked.

"She was really pleased that I got the job. And I'm saving money so I can go back to school next summer."

"Well, I guess to be a teacher you need to go to school," Olle said thoughtfully. "But I wonder if it's really necessary. You already know more than any of your students. Now take William here. He went through high school, and I don't know as he learned much that would help him earn a living. Of course then we've got Jonah. All these reports! I just don't know what's the good of it all."

"I think it's time we cleared the table for dessert," Sylvia interrupted. "Pass your plates to Olle at the end. William, you and Kirsten can both help."

Dessert was peach cobbler, made with Sylvia's home canned peaches. It was accompanied by coffee served with the usual thick cream that floated on top of the coffee. It amazed Anna that she could hold another bite.

After the table was cleared, Kristin and Erica went to the kitchen to do the dishes, while the others visited in the parlor. A large grandfather clock stood against one wall. Anna guessed that it probably belonged to her grandparents, although some of it was obviously new. Heavy drapes were pulled over the glass curtains, the same as in the dining room. They helped keep in the heat. As the clock chimed nine, Anna rose to go. Thanks and good-byes were said. Jonah left with her to escort her home.

"You have a lovely family, Jonah," Anna said as they walked down the path to the road. "And what a beautiful home. The parlor and dining room are lovely."

"Well, we don't use them much in the winter," he commented. "We keep the kitchen door shut and mostly stay in there. And when we light the parlor stove, it really helps heat the upstairs bedrooms. We won't be cold tonight."

"I guess you'll be leaving on the noon train tomorrow," Anna said, thinking how nice it had been to have him home this past week.

"That's right," he answered, and hesitated a little before continuing. "But I'll be back sometime this spring. There'll be another dance in Brewster sometime in March. They have it when they can be sure there's no snow. I was wondering if you would go with me. Ed said we could go with him and Bertha in Elmer's car."

"Oh! That would be really nice." She realized that Ed and Jonah must have planned this during the week, perhaps yesterday when they were moving the schoolhouse. "Can you get time off from school to come?"

"They hold the dance around the time for spring planting, and we have time off for that."

"I'd like very much to go," Anna said. "And to go with Ed and Bertha would be a lot of fun."

Chapter Eighteen

Anna thought that Sunday would never end. First it was the looks she exchanged with Milly and Peter during breakfast, thinking about the missing money and not being able to discuss it with the children around.

Next was Sunday School, although this kept her busy enough to get her mind off the trouble at the Wheeler's. She was now the only teacher in the primary group. Anna had been an assistant to Esther Pearson, who was the main teacher, but since Esther was expecting in April and had a history of miscarriages, she was staying close to home. So Anna came prepared with a theme story and a craft. She followed the lessons suggested in the teacher's manual. Since this was the youngest group in the program, she had to make sure that the project for the morning was not too complicated. This morning there was the story of baby Moses, and she planned on each child making a folded paper boat. She often tried out her projects on Sarah, who was a member of the class. The child was delighted that on Sunday Miss Swenson was her teacher.

Then it was time to attend church. Sally and Charley came and sat in the back. Anna slid into the seat next to them. As usual, she was a little late for church as she had to clean up from Sunday School. They nodded to each other and smiled, but other than that there was no communication between them. She wondered if anyone else in the community knew about the money.

At the end of the service Sally whispered to Anna. "Can you come over right after school tomorrow, in case he comes then?" Anna nodded her head as Charley and Sally quickly left.

Florence Simms stood and stared at them as they hurried out the door after shaking hands with Reverend Blakeley. "You'd think they'd be a little more friendly," she said to no one in particular. "After all the fuss and bother we went to with the funeral and all." Much to her chagrin, no one paid the slightest bit of attention to her, and her monologue ended with a "Humph!"

After dinner Peter concentrated on his newspaper, and Milly read a story to the children. "I still have some papers to grade, Milly. I hope it's all right with you if I do schoolwork on Sunday?" Anna asked.

"Of course," she replied. "I'm glad we do things differently now, but sometimes I feel a little guilty about it. I know my mother would never let us do a thing but sit around and read the Bible. Sometimes we went visiting, or people came to visit us. But when we had visitors or if we visited another family, the children had to sit still in chairs and listen to the grownups talk. We usually kept our hands folded in our laps. I can't imagine doing that now."

Davey looked up. "Dad, did you have to do that, too?"

"That's right," Peter answered. "And most people didn't even cook on Sundays. Why they kept a pot of beans or stew or soup on the stove, and that's what they ate."

"I'm glad we don't do things that way," Davey concluded.

"Well, I try not to work on Sunday," Milly replied. "It's good to have a day of rest. There are many places now where it's a hard and fast rule not to work on Sunday, but I think you have to make allowances, so I'm not so strict. I wouldn't want to go back to eating beans or stew the whole day."

"I like a day off, too," Peter added. "And we do try to make Sundays more restful, but I'm going to have a couple of calves coming along, and also the pigs, and I'm not neglecting my animals for anything."

"We attend the Lutheran Church in Fort Dodge," Anna said. "They are very strict. Mother let us read books on Sunday, but I think I told you before that sometimes she would sew after Elsa and I were in bed. I'm sure she didn't want to set a bad example for us. And I didn't want to set a bad example for the children by correcting papers."

Peter shook his head. "You could never set a bad example for the children, so go ahead and correct your papers or whatever it is you have to do."

"Thanks. I'll wait until after supper anyway."

In the evening Anna looked up from her papers and said, "Oh, by the way I'll be going over to the Wheeler's after school tomorrow. Sally asked me if I would."

"I was wondering what she whispered to you after church," Milly said. "Is that when Jim Wilson's coming?"

"We don't know," Anna answered. "He said he would come sometime tomorrow. That's all we know."

Peter put down his paper. "Well, you can bet your bottom dollar that he'll have done a fairly good search of the countryside before he comes. He doesn't do things halfway."

"And he has a place to farm, too," Milly added.

"He may be a farmer, but he's one up on the rest of us. He certainly knows the sheriff business."

"I've never understood how he can farm and still have time to be sheriff?" Anna asked.

"That's because he has a full-time hired hand," Peter answered. "I'm not sure he really breaks even on that, because the salary for a sheriff isn't too much. But then, he probably does all right. Anyway, if you ladies want to stay up all night talking, that's fine, but for me I'm ready to hit the hay. What about you, Mother?"

"Oh, I guess I'll get to bed early, too. Stay up longer if you want, Anna. A light in the kitchen won't disturb us."

"Thanks, but I'm through with these papers. Oh, Peter! If you're going for the mail tomorrow, would you mail my roll of film to be developed? It's in the Kodak envelope, and the order's all made out."

"Be glad to. Just leave it on the table in the morning."

"Oh, and I have my deposit ready to mail to the bank. I'll leave that on the table, too."

At this remark, Milly perked up. "Peter, I forgot to cash the check Anna paid me. I'll give it to you tomorrow. Vi always cashes them for me."

"Well, another twenty five dollars to go into the sugar bowl," he surmised. "You sure that sugar bowl isn't getting too full?"

"I yust keep change in the sugar bowl, not bills."

"Say! Just happened to think. Thought our mattress was getting pretty lumpy," he said with a knowing nod.

"Oh, you know I would never keep it there."

"Where do you keep it, then?" he asked.

"I'm not telling," Milly answered. "And it's not under the mattress and not in the sugar bowl."

He turned to go into the bedroom. "Just don't forget where you put it, Milly. Anyway Anna, I'll be glad to mail those for you."

"Thanks." She picked up her papers and headed up the stairs. "Tomorrow's going to be a big day, and it's just as well I get to bed now myself. Goodnight. See you in the morning."

"Goodnight Anna," they called.

Anna was surprised to see Anders Anderson in the schoolhouse when she arrived. "Are you going to do the stove this month, also?"

"Well, it's not really my month, but Joe Pearson's so worried about Esther that I told him I'd do it for him. It's not much trouble. We get up early anyway, and the boys help with the chores."

"That's really nice of you," she said.

"I was also a bit curious. I stayed because I wanted to ask you somethin'. With all the commotion last week, I forgot. Did you use up all the coal a week ago Friday?"

"You mean from the coal shed?" she asked.

"Oh no, I mean from the scuttle."

"We may have used it up during the day, but we always see that the scuttle's full of coal before we leave. We leave plenty of cobs, too. Inger said to be sure and do that in case someone is stranded and has to use the schoolhouse for shelter in a storm."

"That's what I thought. I even asked Lars about it, and he remembered him and George goin' out and gettin' it filled. Oh well. Anyway, whoever was here didn't mess up the rest of the room."

"But why would someone stay in the schoolhouse when they could see farmhouses? They could easily have gone to one of them," Anna said in a curious tone of voice.

"Well, don't you worry about it," Anders said reassuringly. "It's probably some drifter. They're pretty independent. Whoever it was probably knew the schoolhouse was here and the next day hitched a ride on the train. Since we're close to the railroad, it's an easy stop. It happens almost every winter. At least the place didn't get messed up. I remember one time someone cooked on the stove. I think it was Floyd had to clean up that mess." He laughed at the thought. "Floyd'll never forget it. Oh, guess I better get goin'. I hear Lars and Carl comin'."

"Thanks, Anders," she called to him as he went out the door.

It was a little after three when she packed up her things. George had finished his project that she had gotten from the state agricultural extension agent so she would have that to read. And Lars was almost through with his. She was pleased with the progress of these boys. As she slammed shut the outside door, she thought of what Anders had mentioned. It gave her a creepy feeling to know that someone was actually in the schoolhouse without her knowledge. She hadn't given it a thought before today. Inger had mentioned that it happened sometimes, but it seemed so unlikely.

She squinted at the glare of the sun on the snow. The sun had been out for several hours, but the snow hadn't melted. The air was cold, and the snow was crisp. As she made her way to the Wheeler's, she walked at the edge of the road where the snow hadn't been trodden on, and she listened as each footstep made a crunching sound. It reminded her of when she was a child happily crunching her way to school after a fresh snowfall.

At the Wheeler's she could see no sign of company, but as she came up the back steps she heard voices in the kitchen. Undoubtedly Sally had been on the lookout for her, as the back door was opened before she could knock. "Come on in, Anna," she said quietly. "He's here."

"Hello, Anna," said Jim Wilson as he rose from his chair at the far end of the table to greet her. "Glad to see you. We're just getting underway with our discussion. Take off your wraps and sit down. I'm sure Sally'll give you a cup of coffee. That right, Sally?"

"Sure. Anna, you sit next to me. Just a minute, and I'll get you some coffee. Help yourself to cookies." Soon they were all sitting around the table. Bill and Charley, seated on the wall side, looked apprehensive. They had never had a sheriff come to their house before.

Jim took out a paper and pencil from the inside pocket of his jacket and began. "From what you have told me, the flour sack with the money had four thousand dollars in it." They all nodded. "And you first noticed it was missing on Saturday when you started to clean out her room." Again, nods from everyone. "And you've looked everywhere in the house to make sure it didn't get put someplace else?"

"It's not any place," Sally said. "No one would've put it any place else, an' anyways we looked all around for it, an' it's no place here."

"Now, you've said the only time you were all gone from here was when you went to the funeral and then to the Parker's," Jim continued. "Are you sure there was no other time?"

"We've thought about it so much," said Sally. "Well you know Inger come over on Saturday when she died, an' when she left she asked us to come to dinner. Bill an' I went, but Charley stayed home."

"I didn't wanna leave Ma here alone," Charley added. "It didn't seem right somehow." His face brightened. "But I went over an' got dinner after they come back."

"An' then on Sunday," Sally continued slowly. "After church Charley an' I had dinner at the Larsons'. "Bill coulda come, but he stayed home."

"I don't know them so good," Bill said. "I didn't go to church anyways."

"But Mrs. Larson sent home dinner for Bill," Sally added quickly. "But there just wasn't no other time 'cept at the funeral that the house was empty. When Charley an' I went down to watch the men gettin' ice for the icehouse, Bill was here. An' anyways, that was before the money was taken."

"What day was that? Jim asked.

Anna answered. "That was on Saturday morning, a week ago Saturday. That's when we came back from the river and found Mrs. Wheeler had had a stroke."

"An' if Charley'd never left the gate to the pigpen open, I mighta been in here with Ma," Bill interjected.

Charley looked downcast but said nothing.

"Why don't you tell me what happened, Anna," Jim asked. Anna carefully described their return, remembering to mention that Jonah had also been there, that Mrs. Wheeler had not been dead long as the body was still warm, and that Inger came over and called Dr. Bailey, who determined that Mrs. Wheeler had died of a stroke.

"All right, let's look at the bedroom," Jim said as he rose from his chair. "I understand that you're anxious to get it cleaned."

Sally opened the door and led them into the room, which still had the musty smell of a sickroom that had been closed for a week.

"Is this where the money was hidden?" the sheriff asked as he lifted up the mattress. "And is this the way the bed was? Didn't she have a pillow?"

"Oh, I took the pillow and put a clean case on it, for when we put her in the casket," Sally volunteered. "The ol' pillow case is there. I jus' left it when we fixed her up an' I forgot to get it washed."

Jim reached down and picked up the pillowcase. "From the looks of this, she must have been a restless sleeper. It sure looks mussed up, and soiled too."

"Sometimes she got really 'roused up," Sally admitted. "I thought maybe she was havin' bad dreams. But she usually calmed down right away when I came in to her. But I never noticed that it looked so bad before," she said as she looked at the pillowcase. "Anyway, that was still before the money was taken."

"You're right, Sally," Jim answered. "Well I think I've had a good enough look around the room. I don't see any telltale footprints or anything else that would give me a clue as to who stole the money, so feel free to clean it up now. But keep thinking about what happened, because you might just remember something important."

"Well, what about them Downey boys?" Charley asked. "I'll bet they took the money. They're mean ones."

"They may be mean, Charley," Jim said, "but I checked around, and as far as I can see they didn't have anything to do with it. Anyway, I've gotta get going, so I'll get my coat and be out of here. I'm staying at the Blakeleys' tonight, and I don't want to be late for supper."

"I'll get your horse," Bill said as he left to go to the barn.

"Oh, can't you stay a little?" Sally asked Anna as she was putting on her coat.

"I really have to go, Sally. It's getting late, but I'll try to stop in again sometime this week."

"Thanks again for the coffee and cookies, Sally," Jim said as he opened the door. "Come on, Anna. We don't want to freeze these people out."

As they walked down the steps they could see that Bill had

Jim's horse and was leading him from the barn. "By the way, Anna, is there something else you would like to tell me? I had the feeling that you were holding something back."

"There is one thing that's been puzzling me," she answered. "And that is that when we first found Mrs. Wheeler, she had the fingers on her right hand crossed."

"That does seem a bit odd," Jim acknowledged. "No one else mentioned it. I would think Tom Blakeley would have noticed it, since it is a bit unusual. Were they that way at the funeral?"

"No," Anna answered. "Inger straightened them out. She did it before Mrs. Wheeler got cold."

"What do you think it means?" he asked.

"I don't know," she answered.

"Did you notice that she did this often?"

"I never noticed it before, but then I didn't see her all that much," Anna said. "Oh we talked about it a little at the Jensens', and the best that we could come up with was that she could feel the stroke coming on and was hoping not to die."

"From what I've heard of her, it doesn't seem to fit with her personality," Jim said. "But then of course, you never can tell. If she thought she was going to die, then she might do just that."

"Yes, that's true," Anna said and became very serious. "I still can't help but think that she was trying to tell us something, and yet I can't imagine what it was."

Chapter Nineteen

Every day Anna hurried home from school, hoping that there would be some word from the sheriff, but every day she was disappointed. "I wish he would call and let us know what he's found," she said to Peter and Milly Friday afternoon as she came in from school.

"Well, he may not have found anything," Peter said. "I'm sure he'd call if he knew something. He may think he's off on a wild goose chase."

"But the money was not there," Anna reminded him. "And so someone must have taken it."

"I agree with you," he nodded. "But the person who took it must be lying low. Anyone with that kind of money around here would be suspect. Oh, by the way, Anna, Vi said that she had the makings for valentines that you wanted."

"Oh, good!" she replied, happy to get her mind off the Wheeler family for a while. "If the weather is nice tomorrow, I'll go and get them."

On Saturday the weather was nice, with no new snow and the temperature almost warm enough to start an early thaw. "I won't be long, Milly," Anna said as she left.

"Are you going on the path by the river?" Peter asked.

"Yes," Anna answered. "It's much shorter, and I'm sure it's tramped down by this time."

"Well, take your time," Milly advised. "You don't want to slip when there'd be no one around to help you."

"I'll be plenty careful," Anna called back to her as she went down the steps.

"And be sure to find out any news from town," Milly added

as a last- minute thought. "Peter always forgets."

As Anna walked toward the river she recalled the fun they had sliding on the ice only two weeks before. By now, it was quite chewed up from where the blocks were taken for the icehouses. To think that they had had so much fun and then to come back to find Mrs. Wheeler dead. She shuddered to think of it.

Looking at the landscape she realized that this was the time of year when it could appear quite dreary. There was no fresh snow to give that lovely white, sharp crispness. Instead there were sagging humps around the fence posts. The tops of dried, yellow cornstalks at the Kloster place where they hadn't been cut tipped at peculiar angles, poking through the snow. Limbs of trees were bare of snow where the wind had whipped it off, and they gyrated helplessly with each fresh breeze. The path was a grimy brown, colored by the trodding of boots and the oily coal smoke that belched from the train engines and traveled across the river.

The church was dark, but she could see a light in the kitchen of the parsonage. She imagined Mrs. Blakeley doing the Saturday baking. She had had some happy times in that kitchen, and she hadn't been there for some time. Quickly she headed across the picnic ground and soon was knocking at the parsonage back door.

"Oh Anna! It's you. How nice," was Mrs. Blakeley's warm greeting. "Do come in. I'm so glad to see you."

"Oh thanks," she replied. The smell of warm bread wafted out to meet her.

"Your cheeks are red as roses. What are you doing out this time of day? Here, let me call Tom." She went to the hall door. "Father! Guess who's here? It's Anna, come to visit us."

When he appeared, his wide smile indicated it was obvious that he was delighted to see her. He shook her hand warmly. "Well, take off your coat. Say, I'll bet you smelled Mother's apple pie."

Anna laughed at the thought. "I remember last fall when I came we had apple pie, but I don't know how you could make one this time of year." She glanced at the counter where a freshly baked pie was placed next to three loaves of bread. "Oh, I see there is one. I suppose you made it from dried apples."

"No, no!" he answered. "Mother uses fresh apples. Right after we pick them in the fall we carefully wrap each one in newspaper and put them in the pantry. Why they last all winter, even into springtime."

"Don't bother her with all that," Mrs. Blakeley scolded jokingly. "What I want to know is what brings Anna out on this cold morning."

"Give me your coat then, and sit down," he motioned to a chair at the table. "And I think Mother'll give us each a piece of pie. Probably spoil our dinner," he laughed, "but then ,that doesn't matter."

"I didn't intend to cause all this commotion," Anna remarked. "I just saw the light and remembered that I hadn't stopped by for a while, and I wanted to stop in and say hello."

"But you do look like you have something on your mind," he continued as he ushered her into a chair.

"Actually, I was going to the store to buy paper and doilies and other things to make valentines, but I have been worried about something. It's probably nothing, but still I can't get it off my mind."

"I knew it! All right! You start eating and then tell us," Reverend Blakeley said. "Now Mother, I think you gave Anna the biggest piece," as he looked across the table, "but I'll eat this one, anyway. Company comes first."

"She's not going to get a word in edgewise if you keep this up," advised his wife as she joined them and sat next to her husband.

"All right then, Anna," he said firmly. "Spill the beans."

"It's really no secret," she admitted.

"Are you worried about Sally staying with Charley and Bill?" he asked. You don't believe what Florence Simms has been saying, do you?"

"Goodness no," she laughed. "But it is about them, well, about their family. Well, actually it's about Mrs. Wheeler."

"You mean about the money?" Mrs. Blakeley asked.

"No, not that," she said. "It's what I saw when we first found her."

"I remember you were the first one to find her, isn't that right?" he asked. "So now, what's bothering you?"

"Well, it may be nothing at all. Maybe I'm foolish to let it worry me, but I just can't help but keep thinking about it."

"It sounds pretty important to me," he said. "I can't imagine your worrying about nothing. Come on! Out with it!"

She self-consciously pursed her lips and then began slowly. "Well, you see, when I saw her she was lying so still. I didn't know she was dead at first. I thought she was sleeping. Then I realized she wasn't breathing, or it looked like she wasn't breathing. And the next thing I saw was her right hand. It was hanging over the side of the bed, and her fingers were crossed. You know like playing a game and crossing your fingers. I can't get that picture out of my mind."

Reverend Blakeley nodded his head. "Yes, Jim told me about this. He didn't know what to make of it but said it was rather peculiar. Why would a person die crossing her fingers? Did anyone else notice it?"

"Yes," she answered. "Jonah did."

The reverend thought a while. "I didn't notice it when I saw her in the coffin. But then her hand was perhaps turned so I couldn't see it," he added.

Anna answered quickly. "Oh, Inger straightened them out before the body became rigid. It did look a little strange. It looked like she might be superstitious, and Inger said the people around here thought the Wheelers were peculiar enough and if they saw her with crossed fingers they'd have a heyday."

"The whole situation seems very strange," Mrs. Blakeley said. "To think that she died, and then the money was taken. Someone had to be very cunning to get away with the money." She glanced at Anna and then at her plate. "Why Anna, we've kept you so busy talking that you haven't had time to eat your pie. You go ahead and eat now, and let Tom and Jim worry about this."

"I'm glad you came to tell us," the reverend added. "I'm going to see Jim again this week. I'll mention that it still bothers you. It may mean nothing, but then you never know. Jim's a good sheriff. If there's a clue, he'll follow up on it. Right now he's at a dead end, because if someone had money they'd probably be spending it, and there's not a hint of that anywhere."

"You know, Tom gets over to Brewster and Langton when he does their services, and usually hears most of the gossip," Mrs. Blakeley said.

"And the news, too. Don't forget that, Mother. It's not all gossip."

"Speaking of news," Mrs. Blakeley added. "You do know,

Anna, that there's to be another dance in Brewster this spring."

As she lifted her fork with her last bite of pie Anna blushed slightly. "Yes, I know about the dance."

"I hope you're going," Reverend Blakeley said. "I had a mighty fine dance with you at the last one."

"Well," she hesitated, and looked down at the pie on her fork. "Jonah has asked me to go with him. He said we could go with Ed and Bertha in Elmer's car."

"That's the best news I've heard for a long time," Mrs. Blakeley said with a smile. "Jonah's a mighty nice young man. I'm glad he had the sense to ask you, but then, Jonah always did have a lot of good sense."

"I really must be going," Anna said as she got up and put on her coat. "Thanks for the pie. It was delicious. And I hope I didn't give you anything to worry about."

"You just quit worrying," said the minister as he opened the door for her. "Goodbye now. See you in church tomorrow."

Anna felt so fortunate to have such a marvelous couple for the minister and his wife. The Lutheran minister in Fort Dodge was a good man, but it was probably the country atmosphere that made this couple special, particularly the fact that they chose to be in a country church.

Vi spotted her as soon as she opened the door to the store. "I have so many things for you, Anna, that you'll have a hard time choosing. You should see all the cute things they have now'days. I have them hidden behind the counter. I said you could have first choice, and everyone else comes next.

"Hi Anna," said Bertha as she came down the stairs. "Vi wouldn't even let me buy some until you came," and she laughed.

Anna looked up at her. "Hello Bertha. I forgot that you might be here. I'm so glad to see you."

"And I'm glad to see you, too," Bertha answered. "'Cause Jonah told Ed that you'n he'd be goin' with us to the dance. After you're through buyin' the valentines, come on upstairs and we'll talk about it."

Anna stood admiring this friendly, rather plump, young lady. "Your hair looks so nice. I've thought about having short hair so many times, but I know it wouldn't look as nice as yours."

"Of course it would," Bertha answered. "Mine's nothing special. I just cut it, that's all. Say, I have an idea. After you choose the valentines, I'll cut your hair."

Anna gasped at the idea. "You mean today?"

"Of course."

"You let her do it, Anna," Vi commented. "She does a beautiful job. And you'd look so cute with bobbed hair."

"I don't know," Anna hesitated. "I never thought about doing it so soon. I mean I thought about it, but…."

"I know," Bertha said. "You just didn't have the nerve. Well it's all the latest style. Vi has some barber shears. I'll help you choose the valentine things, and then come upstairs and we'll cut it."

"What about you, Vi?" Anna asked.

"Oh, I'm too old to have my hair bobbed," she replied. "People would think I was puttin' on the dog."

"Maybe Mrs. Simms," Anna said laughing. "I can't wait to see her hair bobbed."

"That'll be the day," Vi chuckled.

"Come on, Anna," Bertha coaxed. "Let's choose your valentine things and then get upstairs and cut your hair. I know you really want it done. Together we'll be the belles of the ball, well, the dance at least."

"You sure will be," Vi added as she got out a box from under the counter. "Now you just get busy and look through this box and set aside the ones you want."

"Oh!" Bertha exclaimed. "There are hearts, and doilies, and look at these cute cupids."

"I have red paper, too," Vi added. "That's for those that want to cut out their own hearts, maybe make a really big one."

"I have eleven pupils," Anna said as she put some of the items aside. "So I'll need at least enough for eleven, and I'm not sure just what each one will want."

"What about the boys? Bertha asked.

"Oh, I don't know," she answered. "But I remember from my school days the boys made valentines that were as attractive as those made by the girls. But don't ask me who they'll give them to. Oh, and I'm going to get enough for my Sunday School class."

"What kind of a lesson can you have using valentines?" Vi asked.

"One from the New Testament," she answered. "You know

about being kind to one another, that sort of thing."

"I like that idea," Bertha said as she helped Anna choose. "How many paper doilies do you want?"

"At least one for each person. Everyone uses paper doilies on their valentines. Some even use two and crunch them up to look like they're gathered. I'd better get a lot of doilies." She sorted through the box again, and by the time she was finished she had quite a stack on the counter. "Oh, I think I have enough now, Vi."

"It's time to go upstairs then," Bertha said. "Vi, are your scissors still in that drawer?"

"That's right, next to the clippers I use on Elmer and Ed."

"Oh dear!" Anna exclaimed. "You really are serious about the haircut. What will Milly think?"

"Milly will love it," Vi encouraged. "Before too long she'll be down here for a bob herself."

"We've talked about it," Anna said. "Looking through all the magazines, that's all you see is bobbed hair."

"Come on then," Bertha coaxed as she started up the stairs. "And don't worry. We'll save your long hair. Before I make the first cut I'll divide it in two and braid each half. Vi has some ribbons we'll tie it with, and you can have two beautiful braids to save."

"All right," Anna said with some hesitation as she slowly climbed the stairs.

Chapter Twenty

Anna had two parcels to carry home. One was the package of materials for making valentines, and the other held her two long braids. Vi had carefully wrapped each in brown paper and tied them with a string.

She turned her head from side to side and felt the emptiness in her hat where her long hair had been pinned up in back. Her fur hat came well down over her ears and covered all but the very front part of her hair, so she knew that anyone she met would never guess that she had had her hair bobbed. But then, chances were not very likely that she would meet someone on the way home. She thought of how carefully she had brushed her hair every evening. It was so long it came down nearly to her waist, and so thick too. She was often complimented on what lovely thick, brown hair she had, and it did look nice pinned up in back. She could put a special twist in it that was very attractive. Now it was gone. What had she done? But she had thought about it for several months, and of course it was the latest style. What would the Jensens think? Would Milly really like it so much that she would get her hair bobbed?

She turned into the yard and walked toward the back porch. Slowly she climbed each step, then opened the back door. She would take her coat off in the entryway and leave her scarf and hat on until she got upstairs. Yes, that was the best idea. Then she could look at herself in the mirror in her room and see if it really looked as good as Bertha and Vi had said. Maybe her hat had messed it up. She took off her coat and hung it on the hook then braced herself to open the kitchen door when it flew open in front of her.

"Oh Anna!" exclaimed Milly. "Let me see your hair. Liza

saw you leaving the store and ran right over and heard all about it. Then she called me to see if I knew. Oh, take off your hat. I can't wait to see it."

Anna stood there for a moment, surprised. Apprehensively she slowly pulled off her scarf and then her hat. "I'm afraid my hat messed up my hair," she said. "I'll need to go upstairs and get it combed right."

"Oh, it looks beautiful," Milly said excitedly. "You look yust like the lady on the cover of the *Ladies Home Journal.* Turn around. Let me get a good look at you. Oh Peter! Doesn't it look nice?"

"Looks all right," echoed Peter as he glanced up from his newspaper. "You should've waited till spring, though. Your head'll get mighty cold. That's a lot of warm wool that got whacked off."

"Don't listen to him, Anna," Milly confided. "And yust think, you don't have to wash all that hair now. But, oh dear me! What did you do with your long hair? You didn't let them throw it away, did you?"

"That's in one of these parcels," Anna said as she gave a big sigh and opened up the smaller of the two. "Look at this." She held up the two braids and looked longingly at them. "This is what used to be my hair."

"It's yust beautiful. Oh you must save it. Oh I can hardly wait for church tomorrow. What will the ladies say?"

"Well, I can hardly wait for supper," Peter said.

"Oi yoi yoi I almost forgot." Milly dashed to the stove to dish up the meal. "Oh, Anna, when you go up, will you call the children? They're in Sarah's room, I think."

"I'll do that," Anna answered. "And it won't take me but a jiffy to put my things down and I'll be back to help you." It took her longer than she thought with the two older children questioning her about her hair and fascinated with the two long braids. However, they were soon seated at the table, with Lucy still in her high chair, but pushed up to the table now.

"It looks like it's going to thaw," Anna commented.

"I think you're right," Peter agreed. "And I've got to get going on my new hog pens. I have six sows going to farrow, and if I don't get those pens ready I'll be in real trouble. Got to start this afternoon. The lumber came in yesterday. Got it all sorted this morning."

"When will that happen? I mean with the sows?" Anna asked.

"Most likely about the first part of April. The weather should've warmed up by then, but spring may be late in coming. Easter isn't until the middle of the month, and that's the way I usually count on the change in seasons. Plowing has to start at least by then too, and then it's planting time."

"And I thought I had problems with Lincoln's birthday, Valentine's Day and George Washington's birthday," Anna said.

"Is that what you have in that other parcel, Miss Swenson?" Davey asked. "Is it things to make valentines?"

"That's right, Davey," she answered. "But first, Monday is Lincoln's birthday and we'll talk about him. I think I'll let the older students write about him, and those in the first three grades can copy something that I'll write on the blackboard. How does that sound?"

"Well," he hesitated. "I'd like to make the valentines first."

"Valentine's Day isn't until Wednesday, so you can make your valentines on Tuesday, and on Wednesday we'll have a little valentine party. I know somebody's mother who said she would be happy to bake valentine cookies."

"Do we each get to make just one valentine?" Davey asked.

"If you have time, you can make more."

"Well, who do we give them to?"

"That's up to you," Anna answered. "But I have plenty of materials, so you can make more at home."

"What about me?" Sarah asked.

"Don't worry. You'll get to make them in Sunday School."

That seemed to settle the matter. Peter was first to finish the meal. He excused himself and set out for the shed to get started on his pens.

On Wednesday, the day of the valentine party, Anna laughed to herself as she got ready to leave school. She tucked a valentine for Sally in her pocketbook, put three valentine cookies in her lunch pail, and was soon on her way. She was glad of the opportunity to visit with Sally, because she felt she had neglected her, having not returned to clean out Mrs. Wheeler's room.

She was happy that the day had been such a success. In fact, so far the entire week had been successful. It started with Sunday.

She always kept her hat on in Sunday School and Church, but there was so much talk about her short hair that she was obliged to take it off. To her surprise, even Florence Simms seemed to approve. And she much confess to herself that it did feel good to be rid of brushing it every night and pinning it up in the morning. Milly was right. It would be so much easier to wash. It also wouldn't use so much soft rainwater from the cistern. The time in September when the cistern went dry and she had to wash her hair in the hard water from the well was an experience. She remembered pouring vinegar over it to take away the stickiness and make it soft. Short hair also gave her a sense of freedom. She felt like a new person. By Monday all the children had heard about it, so she didn't have to go into long explanations at school. Mabel and Erica voiced strong approval, and while their hair was fairly short, Anna guessed that they would be the next ones to get a real bob. Maybe Sally would even have her hair cut, she thought as she turned into their road.

"Come in, Anna," Sally called from the back porch. "I was hoping you would come, so I kept an eye out for you."

"Thanks, Sally," she said as she entered the kitchen and put her things down on the table. "You know it's Valentine's Day, so I brought you a valentine," and she reached into her pocketbook and brought out one which she had made with doilies and cupids pasted on a large red heart.

"That's so nice, Anna. I can't remember when I got a valentine before." She held it in front of her. "I know. I'm going to put it on the wall in my room. That'll look real nice. But here, take off your coat an' sit down. Have some coffee. I'm sure you're tired with all the work you've been doin'."

"I am a little worn out," she admitted, "but the coffee will put the starch back in me," and she smiled. "And oh!" She reached into her lunch pail. "Here are three valentine cookies Milly made. We had them at school, and I saved some for you and Charley and Bill." She took them out of her lunch pail and gave them to Sally.

"They're real nice. You musta had lotsa fun this week. What've you been doin'?"

"Do you really want to hear?"

"I sure do. Things around here ain't too excitin' sometimes. Well, I mean nice and excitin'."

"All right! On Monday evening Milly and I got together and

decorated a box to be used for the valentine party. We covered it with red paper and pasted doilies on the sides. You know, for a valentine box."

"I remember my teacher used to do that, too," Sally said in dreamlike fashion.

"Then we cut a slit in the top so everyone could put in their valentines. I also made valentines for the students. I wanted them to be a little different, so I cut two slits in every one and stuck in a peppermint stick."

"Oh what a good idea," Sally said enthusiastically.

"Of course on Tuesday, after they made their valentines, there were giggles and whispers as the students came to the front of the room and put their valentines through the slit in the box. Then this afternoon I put the box on the center of my desk and opened it. You know how it's done. The teacher pulls out the valentines one by one and calls out the name of the person who gets it. That's exactly what I did. After Carl Anderson was given one, he looked at me and roared out, 'Who gave this to me?' Everyone laughed, especially Mabel and Erica who kept giggling to themselves."

"I guess I know who pulled that trick on him," Sally laughed.

"And then we had the valentine cookies that Milly made. It was lots of fun. You'll have to come to a party at school sometime, Sally. I know you'd enjoy it."

"And I could bake cookies for it, Anna. That'd be real fun. Oh, I'd love to come to a party at school. I've never even seen your schoolhouse."

"That's right. You'll have to come sometime then. Oh. But I feel I've let you down, Sally. I didn't get back to help you clean out Mrs. Wheeler's room."

"Oh, Charley 'n me figured out we could do it. In fact Charley's sleepin' in it now. We made it into his room."

"What did you do with all the things that were in there?" Anna asked.

"There wasn't too much, an' there was extra room in the shed, so we just bundled up the things and put them in there."

"Will they stay dry?" Anna asked.

"Oh sure! Bill 'n Charley both said it was fine. They don't keep nothin' much in that shed, anyways. All she had was mostly clothes, an' they weren't much good. She had some pictures, an' we put them in the parlor."

"I'll bet you had fun looking at the pictures," Anna remarked. She turned her head as she heard someone coming up the steps and entering the back porch. Charley soon came into the room.

"Oh hello, Charley."

"'Lo, Anna," he mumbled in his usual fashion.

"I'm sorry I didn't get up here again to help you and Sally clean out your mother's room," she apologized.

"Oh, we did it fine. I'm sleepin' there now. We got all of ma's stuff cleared out."

"I'm glad you got it done," Anna replied. She looked at Sally. "You mentioned the clothes and the pictures, but didn't she have anything valuable? Most people have something like rings or brooches."

"That was one thing I wanted to tell you about, Anna," Sally said as she frowned. "The only thing we found that was real nice of hers was her wedding ring. An' that was tucked in the bottom of one of the drawers under some clothes. We was lucky we found it."

"Well, at least you found it," Anna remarked. "I suppose she hadn't worn it for a long time. But you look worried, Sally. Is there something else that you haven't told me?"

"I'm sure that somethin' is missin'," Sally answered. "You see, Mrs. Wheeler always kept Mr. Wheeler's pocketwatch on top of her dresser. I seen it lotsa times."

"Wasn't it there?" Anna asked.

"No," Sally sighed. "Well, we didn't remember it until we had the room almost all cleaned. I guess it was when we found the wedding ring that we remembered the watch."

"Yup!" Charley said. "We couldn't find my dad's pocket watch. It was real purty too, gold."

"An' it always sat on her dresser. I remember seein' it. It was real nice and with a gold chain," Sally said.

"An it had my dad's initials on the back of it," Charley added.

"And it's really gone?" Anna asked.

"Yup! It is," Charley said firmly. "We looked all over the room."

"We didn't miss it at first," Sally added, "'cause we were gettin' the bed fixed up an' sweepin' up an' all that. Then we cleaned out the closet, 'n after that we started on the dresser, an' when we found the wedding ring I remembered the watch."

"Does Bill know anything about it?" Anna asked.

"Nope!" Charley answered. "An we all looked for it, all over the place."

"I thought it coulda fallen behind the dresser," Sally said. "But we looked there, too."

"I can't believe it," Anna said as she shook her head. "I suppose you don't remember when you last saw it."

Sally thought before she answered. "All I remember is that it was there when she was sick. After she died we didn't go in the room, 'cept like when the sheriff come. An' things was happenin' so fast that I jus' don't remember."

"I suppose the person who took the money also took the watch," Anna surmised. "After all, it was a good gold watch, and if it was in plain sight it would be a temptation to take it."

"Yup! He did," Charley stated. "But it won't do him no good if he don't have the same initials. R.B.W. That's what. R.B.W."

"It must have been quite a fancy watch to have initials on the back," Anna said. "I don't know what to make of this. Have you told Inger?"

"We was so worried that we didn't tell nobody." Sally looked downcast.

"Well!" Anna heaved a sigh. "It seems like trouble just won't go away from here. I don't know what to tell you, except that we must tell Inger."

"Yup," Charley said as he headed for the door. "We gotta tell Inger."

"Wait a minute, Charley," Anna called to him. "If you're going over to Inger's I'll go with you. I should be getting home, anyway."

"Thanks, Anna," Sally said. "I don't have the heart to talk about any more bad news."

"Don't you worry, Sally," Anna responded as she picked up her things and got ready to leave. "Inger will probably tell the sheriff, so let's let him handle it. There's nothing more that we can do."

Chapter Twenty-one

February was going quickly. The weather was getting slightly warmer, but not enough to melt the snow. It was gone from the roofs of the houses, but that was more from the heat inside than outside. Icicles hung from the eaves of barns where the sun had melted enough snow during the day to slowly drop water down the roofs. Before it could splash to the ground, the freezing cold formed glistening shards of ice. They were beautiful, but Peter warned the children not to stand beneath one, as it could break off and come down like a spear.

"How are you coming with your pens, Peter?" Anna asked as she sat at the kitchen table after supper correcting essays on George Washington.

"About halfway through, I guess," he answered as he continued glancing through the newspaper. Suddenly he stopped reading and looked up. "That's a sleigh I hear." He quickly folded the paper and set it on the table. "I'll bet it's Floyd and Inger with the mail. You know your pictures came today, Anna." Peter got up and went to the door.

"That's what Milly told me." She quickly stacked her papers and pushed them to one side.

"Davey and Sarah, you get yourselves off to bed now," their mother called from her bedroom.

"But I'm looking at my valentines," Davey whined.

"Listen to your mother," Peter scolded. "You've had the valentines for over a week. Take them upstairs with you. Now both of you. Scoot!" The two youngsters gathered up their things and slowly ascended the stairs.

"Come on in!" Peter called as he opened the kitchen door for Inger and Floyd, who had just come into the entryway.

"Don't mind if we do," came the answer from Floyd. "Hurry up, Mother! Let's not heat up the outside."

"Here, take off your things," Peter said. "Make yourselves at home."

"I'll take your coats," Milly offered as she hurried out of the bedroom. "I'll yust put them on this chair over here. That way they'll stay warm. Oh, I see you've got Anna's pictures."

"Here, Anna," Inger said as she gave the large envelope to her.

Anna quickly opened it and took out the glossy prints. "Oh, look! Here's one I took of the students. See Davey? He's in the front row. And there's Mabel in back. You can't really see much of them because they're all bundled up, but their faces show." Milly and Inger sat next to each other at the table. Anna passed the picture on to Milly, who in turn gave it to Inger. Peter and Floyd looked over their shoulders.

"You were lucky it wasn't snowing that day," Inger commented.

"Yes, I was. And here's another one I took of them, but I got back farther to get the schoolhouse so I could show my mother and Elsa what it looks like. Oh, and here's the one of your family, Milly."

"Oh my, don't we look like a bunch of ruffians," Milly laughed. "And the house! It looks like it should have a good going over. You'll have to get a picture of the place when my flowers are in bloom. Too bad you didn't have your camera last fall."

"Remember, I hadn't saved up enough green trading stamps then," Anna answered.

"Oh, it's so nice to have pictures," Milly said enviously. "I'm going to get a Brownie Kodak with my trading stamps. Oh, I can hardly wait."

"Here's one I took in Fort Dodge."

"That must be your mother," Milly said excitedly. "And is that your sister?"

"Yes, they're standing in front of the store with my Uncle Lars and Aunt Hazel. I was lucky to get this one because it started snowing. I would've taken more pictures there but it was usually snowing or it was too dark. Here are the three I took when they moved the house. Look, Floyd and Peter and the teams pulling the schoolhouse."

"We look mighty small," Floyd joked as he looked over Milly's shoulder. "I'd a thought that you'd tried to get us bigger and forget about the house."

I've got a new roll of film, and I can take one of you any time it's light enough," Anna replied. "So you better be ready."

"Watch out with him, Anna, he'd break the camera," Inger added.

"He'd better not do that," she laughed. "And here's one of Anders and some of the men working on the fence. I'm happy that these turned out. The next one is Sally and Charley."

"That's real nice," Milly said as she nodded her head and held the photo up so the men could see it.

"And the last one is Jonah and Ed. It was getting dark, so they aren't quite so clear as in the others."

"Well, you got them, and that's the main thing," Inger remarked. "I think it looks all right."

"Let me see the one with your mother again, Anna," Milly said. It was passed to her and she examined it carefully. "Oh, I think you look a little like your mother, but maybe more like your father."

"Yes, that's what most people say. Elsa looks more like my mother."

"If you show these pictures to her she'll think we live in the…in the…oh I can't think of the word."

"You mean boondocks, Milly," Floyd told her.

"That's too big a word for me," Milly answered. "I think it looks like, oh yes, the sticks. Anyway Anna, you have to invite your mother to come visit. Oh, yes. You must invite her to come. When do you think she can?"

"What about tomorrow, Milly?" Floyd joked. "Let's see, she could take the train and be here by supper time."

"Oh Floyd! You're always making fun." Milly got up from the table and went to the stove. "But I want her to come after the snow is gone." She brought the coffeepot to the table and started pouring coffee. "And I could bring her to the club meeting, and she could visit the school, and go to church, and oh so many things."

"Providing she wants to come," Inger added.

"Oh, I think my mother would like to come," Anna quickly put in. "I have always wanted her to, but I thought it might be too much trouble for Milly."

"Not too much trouble at all," Milly said. "I yust didn't know if she would want to come, or maybe she wouldn't have time with her working and all."

"I'm sure she could make the time," Anna added. "It's so nice of you to want her. I'll write her tonight and ask her, and I'll send her the picture of your family. Sit still, Inger. I'll get the cookies."

"Don't ask her to come before I get the house clean," Milly said and paused to think. "Yes, what about the end of next month? I'll be sure to have the cleaning done by then."

"What are you talking about, Milly?" Inger said sardonically. "Your house is always spotless. But in another month we'll have better weather. Yes, that's a good time. And speaking of cleaning house, Sally has done a mighty good job of the Wheeler place. She's even finished making the kitchen curtains."

"I'm so glad," Anna said. "I'm going up there tomorrow."

"Then you can show her the picture of her and Charley," Milly added. "I don't think she's had many pictures taken of her."

"Probably not," Anna said. "And this is a good one. Charley was so shy he almost didn't let me take it. I think he will be the most surprised."

"You know, Inger, I think Sally has really taken ahold of that place," Milly surmised. "I'm surprised she got the curtains made so quickly, what with that old sewing machine. Goodness knows how long it has sat there with no one using it."

"And that's another thing," Floyd remarked. "Something we never give a thought to. Sally tried the machine and it just wouldn't work right, so guess what? Bill takes it all apart, cleans and oils it and it works like new. I always knowed he was good with farm machinery. That guy can fix anything. But a sewing machine, well that's a different story, but not for Bill."

"It's yust like a real family then," Milly commented. "I can't believe how life is so good for them."

"Now if they could only get back the money that was taken, everything would be fine," Inger added.

"Have you heard anything more about the pocket watch of Mr. Wheeler's?" Anna asked Inger. "I know it always sat on the dresser, and I can't say for the life of me when I last saw it, but it's gone for sure. It was a darn nice watch too, and expensive, I think."

"Did you talk to Jim Wilson about it?" Peter asked.

Inger paused before she spoke. "I called him from Vi's phone and explained that it was missing. That's about all. He said he'd keep a lookout for it. Not many people around here have gold pocketwatches, and with the initials on the back it would be easy to identify. We don't seem to have had any tramps around here this winter, so where it's gone to stumps me."

"Oh, Inger!" Anna exclaimed. "I just thought of it. I think we may have had someone stay in the schoolhouse a night or two."

"When was this?" Inger asked. "I never heard about it."

"Let me think. Anders mentioned it one Monday morning about a week after it happened. It was about the time that Mrs. Wheeler died, and there were so many other things to think about. I guess I wasn't worried because Anders said the place was kept neat. It was just that the cobs and coal had run out, and he asked me if we had filled the bucket on Friday. We always get in coal and cobs on Friday. It's just part of our Friday chores."

"Well, he's lucky that whoever it was didn't make a mess," Floyd remarked. " I remember the time I came in on Monday and there was food burned on the top of the stove, and spilled on the floor and everywhere else. It sure was a mess, and it had to be my turn to start the fire. I'll tell ya, school started in a cold building that day, and that teacher, whatever her name was, was she ever uppity about it."

"Anders told me about that," Anna said with a smile. "Anyway he told me not to worry about it, because no damage was done, so I guess I put it out of my mind."

"Anyway, I doubt if a tramp or some hired hand wandering around would get in to steal a watch," Inger added. "They wouldn't know enough about the places around here to know where to look or what to look for."

"Jimmy Burns is the only one they've ever hired," Floyd said. "And he hasn't been around. And anyway, he isn't the kind to steal anything."

"Do you really think that stealing the money and the watch are related?" Peter asked.

"It's certainly possible," Inger said. "I'm sure Jim is working on all these ideas. But he thinks it most likely is someone who's living near enough to do it and then go home or go back to wherever he's working."

"I wonder if we'll ever find out," Anna pondered, more to herself than to the others. "I keep waiting to hear some good news." She brightened. "Anyway, when I go there tomorrow I'm planning to bring the Sears and Montgomery Ward catalogs. Then Sally can put in her first order."

"Your curtains are beautiful," Anna said as she entered the Wheeler kitchen. "Oh Sally, you've done so much to improve this place."

"Did you hear that Bill fixed the sewin' machine?" Sally asked.

"Yes, Inger and Floyd told me all about it. I had no idea Bill was so good with machines."

"Me, neither. I could'na done it without him. An' now I have the machine sittin' in my room. It's a Singer. Look, a real nice one. You can see it from here" and Sally pointed to where it stood. "My ma had one, so I know all about how to thread it 'n take care of it. It's just like it's too good to be true." She suddenly became downcast and heaved a sigh. "Now if we could only get back the money and the watch. That's a real piece of bad luck. Two pieces of bad luck."

"Don't you even think of that," Anna tried to be cheerful. "Here I brought two catalogs, so let's sit down at the table and choose something for you."

"I've never done this before," Sally said. "This is the first time I've had any money of my own. What do you think I could buy?"

Soon they were both seated at the table, huddled over the catalogs. "You know Sally, it's almost spring time, and I'll show you what I bought last fall. They're called farmerettes and they're like overalls, only for women. They look really nice. I'm sure you'll be planting a garden this spring, and you don't want to do it in a dress. Here they are. Look at them."

"Oh I've never seen anything like that," she said with an admiring gaze. "But how would I know what size to buy?"

"That's easy. I'll help you with that," Anna said. "They have a size chart in the back of the books. And here is the order form. We'll fill that out together, so I can show you how."

"I see there's a place to add up the money. I don't know if I have the right change."

"You don't send money in the mail anyway. I'll take you down to the post office and Liza will write out a money order. It's just like sending a check from a bank."

"I don't know anything about checks, either," Sally commented. "Oh Anna, I have so much to learn."

"You'll learn it fast enough," Anna assured her. "But aren't there some things for the house that you would like? Bill can give you the money for those things."

"The first thing is I want a new oilcloth for the table. Can we find one in the catalog?"

"Of course. Here. Let's look in the index." She ran her finger through the items in the "T" section and flipped to the correct page. "Okay. Here it is. Now look at the different kinds they have."

"I really like this red and white check one. That's my favorite."

"All right. For this first order we'll get two things, your farmerettes and the tablecloth." Anna wrote out the order, with Sally following every detail.

She went into the bedroom to get her purse and called out over her shoulder. "Oh Anna, I have the household money in a nice old leather coin purse that Inger found, so I don't have to even ask Bill for money. I have money left over from the twenty dollars Bill gave me before, and that's more than enough for the tablecloth."

"Let's get Charley to drive us to town," Anna said. "That way after we go to the post office you can stop at the store and see if there's anything else you need. Oh, and before we call Charley in, I brought some pictures for you to see. Remember when we watched them move the schoolhouse? I have those pictures now."

"Oh, I really want to see them." She hurried to the table again and they sat laughing at the photos and thinking of the good time they had that day.

Chapter Twenty-two

"Anna! Hop in," Inger called to Anna, as she reined in Clementine at the intersection of the crossroads near the school. "Liza phoned me and said there was some mail she wanted me to pick up. She also said there was a letter for you, probably from your mother. Glad I caught you."

"Oh thanks, Inger," said Anna as she climbed into the buggy. "I can tell it's really spring when the snow has melted enough to be able to take a buggy out again."

"Well this is the 7th of March, and if the roads haven't cleared by then, we're in real trouble. It's time we got to plowing. Easter's late this year, and that means we get a late start. Giddap, Clementine!" With a slap of the reins, they were off.

"How come Liza phoned you about the mail?" Anna asked. "She usually doesn't do that, does she? I thought she waited until someone came and got it."

"Usually she does," Inger answered. "But then again, she's pretty much stuck in that post office, and when there's not much doing on the party line, she just invents a reason to get people in to visit with her."

"Gossip, you mean, don't you?"

"I guess you could call it that. But then everyone around here uses her as a source of information. If you want to know something, then you call Liza. This time something came that even Liza didn't want to discuss over the phone. It's a postcard that came for Sally from her pa. When Liza won't discuss something over the phone, then it's important enough to make a trip to town."

As they came up to the post office Anna asked, "Did you hear that Matt and Liza are planning to buy a car?"

"I think everyone knows that by now, but it really surprises me," Inger remarked. "They don't go enough to use one, but I suppose they feel they have to keep up with Elmer and the Reverend, and maybe the Simms, too."

"I'm surprised they have enough money to buy one," Anna added. "From the way they live, I always thought they were a little hard up."

"Well they both have good jobs. And I'm sure they're getting it the same as everyone else, on the thirty-five dollar a month plan. They don't worry about keeping a horse 'cause they don't go anywhere, not even on the train, and they could do that for free. Goodness knows what they'll do with a car." She pulled up to the post office. "Here we are. Let's get out and see what this is all about."

Liza was waiting for them as they entered the small one-room post office that was next to the train depot. As they entered they stepped on to well-worn floors. In front of them was the counter space where Liza reigned supreme. Next to this in the other half of the room was a wall of post office boxes. Each had a shiny brass door. People seldom used the combination lock on their box as when Liza saw someone coming, she would rush to get their mail and hand it to them. By giving out the mail she could usually string out a bit of conversation.

Liza was as usual behind the counter. "Oh, Inger!" Her raspy voice was loud enough to be heard in the store across the street. "I see you've got Anna with you. Well, no matter. Come on over here, both of you." She reached into her apron pocket. "Take a look at this." She held up a penny postcard. "Now! Would you believe it? I just ask you. Would you believe it?" If Floyd had been there he would have raised a rumpus about her reading mail that didn't belong to her, but Inger was not about to cause any commotion. After all, she was going to read it, too.

"Quit waving it around and let me read it," Inger nearly shouted back at her. With an air of triumph, Liza handed over the grimy, pencil-written card. Anna came closer and they read it together.

Dear Sally,
You git on home now. The place is a mess and you gotta clean it up. You gotta cook my meals, too. That's yer job. If you don't git home soon I'm coming to git you.
Yer Pa

"Well, I'll be darned," Inger said. "If that doesn't beat all. I suspected her father would be something like this, but I never guessed he would go this far." She shook her head in disbelief.

Liza jumped in with her thoughts. "This is probably the first time in her life that Sally's had any independence, and he's hide bound to take it away from her."

"That's what it looks like," Inger said as she re-read the card.

"What he wants is pure slavery," Liza affirmed. "Now I must admit that when she first showed up I did have my doubts about her. None of us knowed her, an' she could have been the wrong type. Well, you know what I mean."

"Yes, we know what you mean, Liza," Inger remarked. "But Doc Bailey wouldn't have recommended her if he had had any doubts about her."

Liza had not had her say and interrupted Inger to continue. "When I heard she was doin' such a good job with old Edna, well, I changed my mind. Why, that lady was a handful before she took sick. I'm sure she was near impossible after the stroke."

"You don't have to tell me," Inger said.

"I know I don't," Liza continued with hardly taking a breath. "We all know the trouble you went to takin' care of her. Lucky to get Sally, an' her doin' such a good job. An' then cookin' and takin' care of them two men. I'm sure they never was fed so good. Even Vi said that she never sold them much but flour and oatmeal and coffee and stuff like that."

"Sally is a good cook and—" Inger tried to get a word in edgewise.

"Well, that showed she was really here to work. An' then to see her in church, an' to get Charley to come to church too, why that's almost a miracle. So I changed my mind, yes I certainly did, and I hope everybody else around here does, too. I see most everyone and I've been tryin' to let 'em know how I feel." Liza gave a big sigh.

"I'm glad you changed your mind," Inger added. "I doubt if everyone has, but I'm glad you did."

"And here's my two cents' worth," Liza continued, having gotten her breath. "Her pa can't take her away from here, not if she wants to stay. What's he intend to do, just come out here and drag her away?"

"I have no idea, Liza, but it looks that way. It all depends on how she feels about going back."

"Well, it was just a week or so ago that she put in an order to Sears. I filled out the money order for her myself. An' she told me about makin' new curtains for the kitchen. Why when she came, Matt said she was a scared chicken. Now look at her. She's changed, I tell you, she's sure changed. An' you can't tell me she wants to be dragged back by her pa. Anyway, she's old enough to do what she pleases."

Until this time, Anna had been listening first to one woman and then the other, too baffled by their conversation to say anything, but now she suddenly came to life. "I'm sure she wants to stay here. She said this was the first time in her life that she had any money to spend. She really is happy."

"Well, we'll just have to wait and see," Inger said with a sigh. "Anyway, Liza, give us the rest of the mail. I'll take anything else that the Wheelers have, too."

"They don't have nothin' else, but Anna, you have a letter from your mother." Liza disappeared behind the boxes to bring out the accumulated mail for the Jensens and the Parkers. "Here's the Jensen mail, and here's your letter." As she handed it to Anna she fully expected it to be read aloud to her and looked very disappointed as Anna tucked it in her pocketbook along with the rest of the mail.

Before heading for the door Inger said, "Thanks for the mail, Liza. I'm glad you let me know about the card from Sally's dad. It'll probably be best if we bring it to her. She might be quite upset, and then again she may feel it's her duty to go home and take care of her dad. I just hope she stays, though. She's made a remarkable change in that household."

"Well, I think it's been good for her to be here. Why as Matt said, 'It's made all the difference in the world to her.' Anyways, I just hope that things work out for the best."

Inger and Anna turned to leave.

"Oh, don't go yet," Liza called to them. I didn't get to tell you about the new car we're gettin'. It's gonna be a Ford."

"And we heard you're going to learn to drive it," Inger said.

"You bet I am," she replied.

As she opened the door Inger called back, "By the way, Liza. Let us know when you take to the road. And let us get to the house to tell Sally before you get on the party line." She shut the door behind her and didn't wait for a reply.

"I didn't know Liza liked Sally at all," Anna commented to Inger as they got into the buggy and headed for the Wheeler's.

"I'm not sure she does. But Liza goes with the flow. Now, if Florence Simms was to come in, the conversation might take a different turn."

"It must be awful for Sally to have a dad like that," Anna reflected. "You think her whole life she has been bossed around like that?"

"Oh, I'm sure of it," Inger answered. "And that's why we won't know how she's going to take this card until we get there. She's so used to doing what her folks told her that she's hardly had a thought to herself. Doc Bailey had a hard time persuading her to come here. That's for sure. He told me about it. It was only because her mother had died and her father and brother weren't home that she came. Otherwise she would be home alone most of the time."

"And she told me she never had any money to spend," Anna said. "If she bought anything, it was with her mother or father, and they told her what to buy, even her clothes. That's really sad."

"Well, there are lots of ways of raising kids," Inger commented. "At least I don't think she was beaten, but then with a father like that I wouldn't doubt but what she was. Well, we're close to home. I'm going to pull in at our place and let George take Clementine and the buggy." She drove a short distance into the yard. George was watching for her, so they greeted him and climbed down. "You can put these away. Tell Dad I'll be back as soon as I can. And will you call Milly? Just tell her Anna's at our place. On second thought, take Anna's school things and their mail and drive down with them yourself. No point in getting the party line too excited."

Anna gave him her school papers and the mail, and they waved him off to the Jensens'. They walked slowly up to the Wheeler back porch. "What are you going to say, Inger?" Anna asked.

"Not sure of that myself," she answered.

They went into the entry and knocked on the kitchen door. Sally opened it. They could see that she was startled to see them. "Inger! Anna! Oh, come in. What a nice surprise. I didn't know you was comin' today."

"We didn't either,until a short time ago," Inger said as casually as she could.

"Well,sit down. Want some coffee?"

"Oh, no thanks,Sally. We just stopped by to leave off the mail," Inger continued. "I happened to meet Anna coming home from school,and I knew there was a letter from her mother, so I took her with me."

"Can your mother come and visit?" Sally asked.

"I haven't read it yet," Anna said rather solemnly. "But Inger has a postcard for you."

"Oh a postcard!" Sally beamed. "It must be from Richard. Oh, Richard! Richard! I knew he would write me." She wriggled with excitement.

Anna's first thought was to feel sorry for Sally, who would undoubtedly be very disappointed when she learned the postcard was from her father. Then she found herself staring at the woman. "Why are you crossing your fingers, Sally?"

"Oh!" Sally laughed. "This is the name sign for Richard. I cross the fingers of my right hand and touch my left shoulder. See, like this." She repeated the movement. "When deaf people talk they use name signs like this," and she did the motion again.

Anna felt a creeping chill go all the way up her spine. She stood there almost frozen.

Chapter Twenty-three

"Is that Richard's card? Can I have it? Oh please, Inger," Sally pleaded. "I think you're just teasin' me."

The short conversation between Sally and Anna regarding Richard's name sign had bypassed Inger. She was more concerned with how Sally would react to reading the card from her father. "It's not from your brother. It's from your pa."

"From my pa!" Sally exclaimed. "My pa don't write much. He couldn'a written me."

"Here it is, Sally." Inger reluctantly handed the card over to her and they watched her as she read it.

"What does he mean I have to come home."

"I guess he's demanding that you come home and take care of him and the house," Inger explained.

"Oh no! That's awful! I know my pa. If I don't come home he'll be comin' to git me, jus' like he says," and she slowly sank down in the nearest chair. "Oh, I don't want no trouble aroun' here. My pa can git awful mad. I s'pose I have ta go. He says it's my duty."

"It is not your duty to keep house for a man like that, even if he is your pa," Inger stated emphatically. "You're not a child, Sally. You're thirty-five years old, and you have a life of your own to live. He can't make you come home."

"Oh, but you don't know my pa. He can. An' he will," she said, wide-eyed. "Oh Anna, what am I gonna do? I don't wanna go, but he can make me."

Anna was nearly oblivious to the conversation. Her mind was still fixed on the crossed fingers that meant Richard's sign. "Uh! What did you say, Sally?"

Two pairs of boots were heard tromping up the back steps

and into the entryway. Then Charley and Bill slowly trod into the kitchen. They looked at the women, surprised to see Inger and Anna. "What's goin' on?" Bill asked.

"I brought Sally a postcard from her pa," Inger answered matter-of-factly.

"Oh! That's all." He seemed satisfied with the answer. He and Charley helped themselves to a cup of coffee and sat down at the table. The eyes of the women watched them, but no one said anything.

Bill looked up," What'd he say?"

"He said he was comin' to git me 'cause I have ta come home," Sally answered, close to tears.

"Ya wanna go home then," Bill said dejectedly.

She slowly shook her head. "He said it was my duty. I gotta take care of him an' the house."

"If you go, then who's gonna take care of us an' our house?" Charley asked with alarm. "We can't do it by ourselves. I thought you liked it here. We was gettin' along so good."

"But when yer pa says it's yer duty—" Sally faltered.

"Forget the word duty," Inger said firmly. "Remember you're thirty-five years old. You can do what you like. If you want to go home, you can go home. But if you want to stay here, you can stay here. Do you want to stay here?" Sally looked at the floor, then at Charley and Bill. "Answer me!" shouted Inger. "Do you want to stay here?"

"Yes. A' course I wanna stay here. But you don't know my pa. He can make trouble. If I don't go home, he'll really make trouble."

"Forget about that, Sally. If you want to stay here, then stay here. He has no claim on you. I think your duty is here to help Charley and Bill. And if it's trouble your pa wants, he'll have to meet Floyd first."

"An' me too," Charley added suddenly filled with righteous indignation.

"Do you really think I can stay?" she asked.

"Of course you can stay," Inger said. "If you want to stay, you can stay. After all, you are working and earning your own living. By the way, Bill, did you pay Sally for February?"

"Yes'm," he answered. "I paid her twenty-eight dollars."

"Good!" Inger said. "I'm glad you remembered to settle that. Now Sally, have we decided that you want to stay?"

"Yes, I wanna stay. I don't wanna go back home. It's all work there, an' nobody around to talk to. An' when my pa's home he always goes into town an' I'm left alone an' well, he drinks a lot. But I don't want him to come and make trouble."

"You forget about that," Inger advised. "Now I suggest that you take that card and dump it in the stove. Just get rid of it."

"You mean burn it?" Sally asked.

"Of course I mean burn it. It's not going to make you happy with it sitting around here, so burn it and forget it. And if your pa comes out here, we'll know he's on his way long before he gets to the place. Matt'll see him get off the train, and you can be sure Liza will phone me right away."

Sally smiled as she got up, walked to the stove, lifted one of the lids and shoved the card inside. "You mean like sorta pretendin' I never got it."

"If that's the way you want to look at it, that's fine. Come on, Anna. I reckon it's time we got going," Inger said as she headed for the door. "And Sally, you have supper to put on the table."

"That's right. Okay, Charley an' Bill, you git washed up now. I gotta set the table. Bye Inger. Bye, Anna. Thanks fer comin'."

Anna was still in a partial daze as she and Inger walked toward the road. "Well at least that's settled for now," Inger said and heaved a sigh of relief. "I don't suppose her pa will come out here, anyway. Doc Bailey told me he was a weak specimen. Say, you were mighty quiet in there. I forgot. You have the letter from your mother, and you didn't even get to read it."

Anna tried to focus on Inger's conversation. "What was that, Inger?"

"My goodness but you seem preoccupied. I mentioned the letter from your mother. You haven't read it yet."

"Oh! Well, I'll read it when I get home," she answered.

"Is there something else on your mind?"

Anna thought before she answered. "No, just something that Sally said."

"Well you don't have to worry about that now. I think the whole matter is settled. She's happy living over there, and we probably won't hear any more about it."

"You're right." She sighed. "This is where I leave you. Thanks for picking me up and taking me with you."

"I'm glad I had your company. Tell the folks we'll be down in a coupla days."

All the way home Anna thought about the sign for Richard. It couldn't have been he, because he was gone before the money was taken, and yet it continued to bother her.

"George left your things on the table, Anna," Milly announced as Anna came through the door. "You sure were a long time delivering mail to the Wheeler's, but I'm sure Sally was glad to have the company."

"It wasn't so simple as that, Milly," she replied and then related the entire story before she went upstairs, leaving Milly shaking her head in disbelief.

Anna sat on her bed and took the letter from her mother out of her pocketbook. She opened it somewhat apprehensively as she was hoping that her mother hadn't planned to come the weekend of March 31st as that was the date of the dance. If her mother came then, she probably couldn't go, and it promised to be such fun going with Jonah and in Elmer's car with Ed and Bertha. She started reading. There were a few preliminary remarks hoping Anna was doing fine and that the weather wasn't too bad. She read on. Yes, her mother said she was happy to be invited and the best date would be to arrive Saturday March 24th. She'd take the 2:40 from Fort Dodge and arrive in Grabney at 5:10. Returning she would leave on the Monday noon train. She couldn't come later because she was busy sewing Easter outfits, and she could only stay the weekend because she had to get back to work. At least that was settled. Knowing her mother, perhaps it was best that she could stay only two days.

Anna hurried downstairs to tell the news to Milly. "Oh, I hope the snow is gone by then and that it warms up a little," was Milly's comment. "But never mind, we'll show her a good time anyway. We'll have Saturday night supper with just us. After church on Sunday, I'll plan a special dinner and invite Inger and her family. Oh, that will be wonderful." Milly continued to rhapsodize about the plans she had for that weekend, while Anna continued to brood about her visit with Sally.

"I'm going to the post office to mail a letter to my mother and tell her it's all right to come on the 24th," Anna announced to Milly after school the next day.

"Peter could take it in the morning, Anna," Milly replied.

"Oh thanks, but I thought I'd stop by the Blakeleys', that is, if I can get away from Liza and her talking about their new car."

She walked as fast as she could on the bumpy, slippery path to town. Knowing that Liza would be there ready with questions involving Sally and the postcard from her father, she thought up several excuses so she could make a quick exit.

"Hello Anna," Liza greeted her. "How did things go yesterday?"

"Just fine, Liza," Anna said as she handed her the letter to put in the outgoing mail.

"What happened?"

"Nothing much happened. Sally has decided to stay."

"What about her pa? It sounded as if he was real ornery."

"Sally decided to stay, and so we'll have to wait and see what happens," Anna explained. "Anyway, Inger thinks that his bark is worse than his bite."

"That's a good one. You're not leavin', are ya?"

"I have lots of school papers to correct. Tomorrow's Friday, you know."

"Is your mother gonna come?" Liza threw in a last desperate question.

Yes, she'll be here on the 24th. So long, Liza." With that, Anna shut the door and was on her way to the Blakeleys'.

She went around to the back, as she could see a light in the kitchen, and hoped that Mr. Blakeley would be there too. She knocked on the door and could hear heavy footsteps coming toward her. It must be the Reverend. The door opened. "Well, Anna. What brings you here? It's almost dark. Shouldn't you be home correcting papers? Come in."

"I'm saving those for this evening," she replied smiling.

"Take off your coat and sit down," Mrs. Blakeley said as she continued preparing supper.

"I don't really have time to sit down, and anyway, what I have to say may not be important, but it's nagging at me."

"It's about the stolen money and watch, isn't it?" he asked.

"I don't think so," she admitted. "It's about something else.

But first I'll tell you about what happened yesterday."

"If you're going to tell us about the postcard from Sally's pa, we know all about that. I stopped by the Wheeler's this morning just to see how things were going, and Sally told me the whole story. I'm glad she's staying. And if her pa comes here to bring her back, well, we'll just wait and see."

"Inger doesn't think he'll come. I hope that's true," Anna added. "But that's not why I'm here. It's what happened when we were talking to Sally."

"Go on."

"You remember that I thought that when Mrs. Wheeler had her fingers crossed it might be something important, like a clue about something."

"Yes, I remember."

"Well, yesterday when Inger went to give Sally the postcard, Sally thought it was from her brother Richard, so she excitedly said 'Richard, Richard.'"

"Yes."

"When she said Richard's name, she crossed her fingers and put them on her left shoulder. I asked her why she did that, and she said that that was Richard's name sign in sign language. So crossed fingers is another way of saying Richard."

"That's very interesting," Reverend Blakeley mused. "Was her brother here when Mrs. Wheeler died?"

"Not that we know. He was planning to take the train back on Friday. In fact, I saw him walk down to the station."

"Well then, the crossed fingers probably don't have anything to do with her brother," the minister concluded. "We'll probably never know what that means."

"But I still feel so uneasy about it," Anna persisted. "When you see Jim Wilson could you mention it to him?"

"I certainly will if you want me to," he replied. "But don't worry yourself about it. I'll tell Jim, and if he thinks it's important he'll get in touch with you. Now! I suppose you've heard the big news around here. Matt and Liza are getting a Ford."

"I was lucky to slip out of the post office, so I didn't have to hear the story again," Anna answered. "And I hear that Liza is going to learn to drive."

"That's right. That's what she's been telling everyone. And

she's proud as punch. Goodness knows that woman doesn't really have much to call her own. All I can say is that we'll have to put up a big dinner bell and ring it as an alarm when she hits the road."

"Who's going to teach her?" Anna asked. "And who's going to teach Matt? I don't think he knows how to drive."

"Matt said he'll pick up the car some day when Elmer has to go in to pick up an order of supplies for the store. They should have it before the end of the month. Ed'll go with them, and he'll be the one to drive the new car back."

"But Matt still has to learn to drive," Anna added. Then with a twinkle in her eye she said, "I know. Ed'll teach Matt, and you'll get to teach Liza."

"I've been a praying man for a long time, Anna, but I think it would be overdoing it to ask the Lord to keep me safe while teaching Liza to drive."

"And I'd have something to say about that, too," laughed Mrs. Blakeley.

"Anyway, Anna," the Reverend said, "Don't you worry about the crossed fingers being Richard's sign. We'll get the word to Jim Wilson and let him do the worrying."

Chapter Twenty-four

"This is the middle of March and what we need is a good old fashioned chinook to warm this place up," Peter pronounced at breakfast. "I've got six sows nearly ready to farrow, the pens all finished and I want to finish the plowing before all the little piglets come popping out."

"The ground's too hard to start plowing now, Peter," Milly cautioned.

"Don't I know it. The other day I took a pickaxe out, and it was like chopping solid rock. Another few days, though, might see a real thaw. I could feel the air was warmer this morning."

"I think it's warmer, too," Anna added. "We don't have that cold wind any more."

"This is such a busy time on a farm, Anna," Milly said as she sat down at the table. "It seems that once the weather gets warm it all has to be done at once."

"I'd like to get in some harrowing, too. That disk harrow is a dandy, and I need to get the plowing done and the ground broken up. That'll give Gus and Olle a real workout. They're two big workhorses who've been pretty much stuck in the barn all winter. Then of course there's the planting. And in the meantime we'll be getting all those little pigs."

"Can I have a little pig for my own, Daddy?" Sarah whined. "Oh, please."

"You can look at all the little pigs, but we're not having any pigs for pets around here," her father answered firmly. "And you know, Sarah, that little pigs grow up to be big pigs, and you're no match for a big pig."

"But why can't mine stay little?" she continued with her high-pitched voice.

"Just the same as you can't stay little," Peter answered.

They were interrupted by the phone, two long rings and a short. "Who can be calling this time of morning?" Milly asked as she walked over to pick up the receiver. "Hello.———Yes this is Milly.———Oh, Reverend Blakeley. Yes, Anna's here. She's eating breakfast. Yust a minute. Anna it's for you."

"For me?" Anna said with surprise as she got up to answer the phone. "Hello, Reverend Blakeley.———No, I'm still eating breakfast. We won't leave for school for another fifteen minutes.———Today after school?———Yes I could come.———A proposition?———No, that's fine.———I'll see you sometime between 3:30 and four o'clock, then.———Thanks.———Good-bye."

"Now I wonder what the Reverend wants?" Milly asked. "Did he tell you?"

"No, not a word," Anna replied. "In fact I could hear Mrs. Blakeley coaching him in the background, but I couldn't hear what she was saying."

"Guess we'll just have to wait until Anna gets back to find out what this is all about," Peter said as he got up from the table. "Well, I'm off to check on the stock."

"Tomorrow is Friday the 16th of March, so we'll have our weekly spelling test," Anna told her students before the close of school. "And remember to bring your craft materials for the afternoon. Are you ready to make your chest, Carl?"

"I am if Lars will help me," he answered.

"I'll help him Miss Swenson, and George can help, too. He's through with his chest now."

Anna saw that Mabel's hand was raised. "Mabel."

"Erica and I were wondering if we could make chests too?"

Carl quickly chimed in with, "Girls can't make chests."

Anna answered. "Oh yes, they can. Mabel, if you and Erica want to make a chest, you may. I think that would be a good idea. Do you have wood for one at home?"

"We can't get it for tomorrow, but we could have it by next Friday. But we'd need George and Lars to help us," Mabel explained.

"I'm sure the boys would be glad to assist. Isn't that right, boys?"

"Is it going to be a hope chest?" Edna whispered to Erica.

"Hopeless chest you mean," Carl said loudly, directing this comment to the girls. "Ha! Ha! You're going to make a hopeless chest."

"Carl! That's enough out of you," Anna admonished. "I think it's a nice idea to make a hope chest, and if that's what the girls are going to do that's fine. No doubt they've been making things already to put in it."

"I don't care what you say, anyway, Carl Anderson," Mabel shot back at him. Then she faced Anna. "Erica and I have been embroidering pillow cases. And our mothers give us a piece of silverware each birthday. And it's fun to collect things like that."

"Good. And George and Lars, will you help them?"

A nod in the affirmative from both boys was the answer that was needed.

"If you are ready then, you may be dismissed." Anna quickly tidied up her desk and hurried after the children so she could be at the Blakeley's by a little after 3:30. She made a quick stop at home to drop off her things and then walked down the well-trodden path next to the river to the Blakeley house. They were expecting her and had coffee and cookies ready.

After the usual friendly introductory remarks, Reverend Blakeley became very serious and said, "Now then Anna why do you think I asked you to come here?"

"I have no idea. In fact, I was wondering myself."

"Actually I wanted to discuss with you a little more about the crossed fingers being Richard's name. Now that I've thought about it, I'm not sure I understand. I remember you telling me that you thought the crossed fingers somehow tied in with Sally's brother Richard. Isn't that right?"

"Yes, of course," Anna answered. "I think I told you that Sally said that was his name sign. She told me that since her mother was deaf, they had to use a hand sign to indicate things. The letter 'R' in the deaf alphabet is crossed fingers. Since Richard's name begins with 'R' they use that sign to indicate him. I never knew much about it, and I think it's really interesting."

"Now I'm beginning to get the significance," the minister acknowledged.

"It's very interesting," said Mrs. Blakeley. "I've heard about sign language, but I was never sure just how it was done."

"I'd like to know more about it," Anna continued. "Sally was shy about signing when Richard was here, but when he comes back to visit I want to ask them to sign so I can see how they do it."

"Well now, that does explain it a little better," the minister said. "However, I wonder how Edna would have learned this, especially if Sally were shy about signing."

"Sally told me that she often signed around Mrs. Wheeler. It was sort of like taking care of her mother again. I'm sure she talked about Richard and probably explained the sign."

"Yes, I think you're right," Reverend Blakeley concluded. "Anyway, it may be just a hunch, but it's worth following up. Actually, I've talked to Jim. He was by this week. You know he comes around about once a month. He said he'd like to talk to you about it. So I thought that you could do this on Saturday."

"I'm not so sure you're going to go for this scheme of his," Mrs. Blakeley said.

"Of course she will, Mother. Now I'm not able to get into the county seat, but I found out that Elmer will be going. I thought you could go with him and meet with Jim."

"Oh, that would be fine," said Anna. "I guess Elmer wouldn't wonder why I'm going to the sheriff's office, because Vi probably told him a little about it."

"Now Tom, tell her the other part of the story," his wife urged with some apprehension.

"Well you see," he began, "this is the day that Matt's going to get his new car. Ed's going in with him and will bring the new car back. While you're in with Jim, they can be getting the car, and you can ride back with them."

"Couldn't I ride back with Elmer?" she asked.

"Elmer will have the car loaded up with supplies, and he'll want to get back right away."

Anna was apprehensive. "Is Matt going to want to drive the car?"

"I think he thinks he will, but I'm sure that Ed will do the driving," Reverend Blakeley answered.

"Oh, that would be all right," agreed Anna. "I am anxious to talk to him." She paused. "You're sure Liza isn't going along to pick it up. Doesn't Matt have to stay around when the trains come in?"

"No, he doesn't have to," Reverend Blakeley answered. "Besides, he'll probably be back before the noon train comes in."

Another thought struck Anna. "But won't Matt wonder why I'm going to talk to the sheriff?"

"I doubt it. Jim always checks with Matt about local things. Matt may know more than we do about it. And if you're wondering if he'll tell Liza, he won't do that, either. Matt is pretty closed-mouth. Now doesn't this sound like a good plan?"

Anna had to admit to herself that it was good planning, and she was anxious to talk to the sheriff. She was also anxious to get home in one piece, but after all, if Ed were with them, there'd be no problem; at least, there shouldn't be a problem. Hesitantly she said, "As long as Matt isn't going to do the driving, it sounds all right to me."

"Well then, it'll get all settled on Saturday. I already checked with Elmer, and he said he'll be leaving about nine o'clock."

"I told Tom not to make arrangements before he asked you," said Mrs. Blakeley.

"Now, Mother. I knew she'd be a sensible girl and go along with it. This is a much better idea than taking the afternoon train and having to spend the night there. Of course I'm sure Jim would let her have one of the beds in one of those nice cells he's got, so she wouldn't be without a place to stay."

"Oh Tom," laughed his wife. "I can just see Anna sleeping in a jail cell all night." Anna laughed with her.

"I'd be glad to take you myself, Anna, but I've got to get ready for Sunday, and with Elmer and Ed going in, there's no point in having all of us making the trip. By the way, can you be at the store by nine o'clock?"

"Oh yes," she said as she continued laughing. "I'll be there."

"You be sure and stop by here first, Anna," Mrs. Blakeley advised. "I have a good warm car robe that you can use. It gets mighty cold riding in the back of a car."

On Saturday morning there definitely was a thaw in the air. The river path was now more mud than ice and snow. Anna had to pick her way carefully, trying to step on the clumps of grass at the side of the path rather than the path itself. This was somewhat risky, as they could be icy. She slipped a couple of times but caught herself before she fell. As she neared the parsonage she heard Elmer starting up his car in front of the store.

Mrs. Blakeley had been watching for her and came down their back steps with her car robe. "Now you be sure and tuck it in good around you," she told Anna. "Put it over your knees and wrap your legs up well. A car ride in this weather can be mighty cold. You don't want to catch a chill. At least I see you're well bundled up."

"Yes, I hope I wore enough clothes," Anna remarked. "Thanks for the robe. It'll probably keep my teeth from chattering. I'll bring it back to you when we get back."

"I hope everything goes all right. I'll be waiting to hear." Mrs. Blakeley waved to her and went back into the kitchen.

Anna hurried over to the store. Her heart fell as she saw Liza standing next to Elmer's car. Then she realized that Liza wasn't wearing a coat, so she was staying home after all. Vi was standing on the store steps watching the proceedings.

"Morning, Anna," Elmer greeted her. "Well, I see you're all set to go, even brought your own blanket."

"Yes, Mrs. Blakeley lent it to me."

"I've never minded the cold in the car," Elmer called out. "Besides we've got blankets in the back seat just in case."

"But Anna will need something on the way home," Vi called out. "She'll be riding by herself in the back seat of Matt's car."

"Guess you're right there," Elmer said and then jokingly added, "And she won't have no one to warm her up."

"Let's you and me get in back, Anna," Ed said, pretending he didn't hear his father's remarks. He helped her in and shut the door. "That way Matt can watch what Dad does and maybe learn a few tricks. Driving a Ford's a bit different from a Chevy, but once you get going on the road it's mostly steering around the ruts and holes."

"I'll get in front," Matt said as he got in and slammed the door shut. "Let's go."

"Wait a minute, Dad," Ed called out. "I want to make sure all the side curtains are fastened right. In this weather you could have us frozen stiff." Ed promptly checked the snaps that fastened the curtains to the fabric of the roof. Anna looked out through the window on her side and found it was quite clear. She had heard that these windows were made of mica, a good substitute for glass.

They were strong and pliable. The windshield was made of glass.

Ed hopped in the back seat of the car and sat behind his father. "Here, help me with these," he said as he unfolded a heavy blanket from the back seat. "Let's tuck it around ourselves. I've never ridden in the back seat before, but Ma says it can get mighty cold."

"Mrs. Blakeley lent me one of her car robes, too, so we should be doubly warm."

Anna grabbed her half of Ed's blanket and made sure it was firmly tucked around her. Ed did the same and then called out, "All right, Dad! I guess we're ready."

Elmer drove onto the road that ran by the railroad tracks, next to the river. Even with the curtains snapped firmly in place, cold air seeped in around the sides, and Anna was glad that she had bundled up well for this outing. The road was full of ruts, and they bounced and laughed as the car jerked them toward town.

Main Street was the main thoroughfare. Elmer pulled up in front of the Café. "Why don't you get off here, Anna," he advised. "The courthouse is just down the next block. I'm goin' to turn around and park over at the dry goods store across the street."

Ed was quick to get out and come around to open Anna's door. "Here, let me help you." He held out his hand, and she climbed out as gracefully as she could. "Don't worry about that car robe of the Blakeleys. I'll take care of it. You know where you're goin' now?"

"Yes," she assured him. "It's in the next block."

"Let's get out here, too," Matt suggested as he climbed down from the front seat.

"You remember the sheriff's office is in back of the courthouse?" Ed asked Anna. She nodded, remembering when she visited him there last fall. "Then you get along, and we'll meet you there after we finish gettin' the car. I suppose it'll take us about an hour or so."

The county seat had about three or four hundred people. At the edge of town on Main Street stood two-story family houses. The street was lined with trees that would give shade in the summer, but now were bare and forlorn-looking. The business section, about two blocks long, was a hodgepodge of small stores. The one large building was the county courthouse. It was set back from the street with a lawn and trees lining the walkway to the front steps. Anna walked around the building to the rear and opened the door to the sheriff's office.

"Morning, Anna." Jim Wilson was there to meet her. "Thought you'd be here about this time." Anna looked around the room. "Oh, if you're looking for Bert, I gave him the day off." She remembered the deputy she had met on her last visit and was glad she wouldn't have to explain things to him, too. "No one's in jail, either. Come on in and sit down. Here, take off your coat."

The room was pleasantly warm, a change from the car. She sat in the wooden chair opposite the sheriff's desk with her coat draped over the back.

"Hope you're comfortable there, Anna?" She nodded. "Then we might as well get down to business. Is that all right with you?"

"Yes," she nodded again.

"When I was out on my rounds, I got to talking with Tom, and he told me about the crossed fingers being Richard's name sign, I guess that's what you call it. He's Sally's brother, I believe."

"Yes, he is. I know I may be making something out of nothing, but I still can't help but think that the crossed fingers mean something. I'm also worried that Sally's father might show up in Grabney, intending to take her back with him. She says she's going to stay, but I don't know what kind of a man he is. He might cause trouble."

"I've met the man a few times," Jim said, "and from what I've seen I don't think he'll do anything rash, so I wouldn't worry about it. Let's see if this crossed fingers means something. I've worked this case over and over again, and I can't come up with anything. Usually if someone around here steals money, then it's pretty obvious, because they can't help but spend it. And this was a sizable amount of money, next to robbing a bank, I would say. The only thing I can come up with is that it was taken by someone who made a hasty exit. Let's see what this crossed fingers means, so tell me what you told Tom."

Anna repeated the story of when Sally got the postcard from her father and thought it was from her brother.

Jim thought a while, then asked, "Didn't Richard visit Sally a couple of months ago?"

"Yes, but he stayed only one night. He left the day before we went down to watch Peter and Floyd get ice for the icehouses."

"You're sure it was that day?"

"Oh, yes. We wanted him to stay to watch them get the ice on Saturday morning, but he said he had to get back. He was going to meet a friend named Frank. I think his name was Frank. Anyway, they had plans to go to California and get jobs. I saw him walking toward the train. And the money wasn't taken until Wednesday, when Sally and Charley and Bill were at the funeral or over at the Parker's for the gathering afterward."

"What makes you so sure the money was taken on Wednesday?"

"But it had to be taken then, because that's the only time all three of them were away from the house."

"All right. Let's go back a little," Jim suggested. "I'm just trying to jiggle pieces together that may not fit, but let's try to look at it from all angles. Now, you saw the crossed fingers on Mrs. Wheeler when you found her dead. Isn't that right?" Anna nodded. "As I remember it, you, Charley and Sally had just come in from the river."

"Sally and I went into the house first, and then we heard Jonah coming in with Charley," Anna added.

"Let's see, Bill had been out in the yard chasing his hogs back into the pens, and from the sounds of it, it took him quite a while to get them in. Is that right?"

"Yes. He blamed Charley for leaving the gate open. He said he had a terrible time getting the pigs in. He came in after the rest of us. He was pretty mad."

"I can imagine. So actually, there was no one in the house for over an hour that day," the sheriff continued.

"Maybe longer than that, because Bill had other chores to do. But the money wasn't taken until Wednesday," Anna stated.

"How do you know it was taken Wednesday? Did you check under the mattress to make sure the money was there when Mrs. Wheeler was put into the casket?"

"I wasn't there when this happened. Sally and Inger took care of that."

"And I understand now that there is a gold watch missing, too."

Anna thought before she answered. "They didn't notice the gold watch being gone until later, when Charley and Sally cleaned out the room."

The reason I'm pressing you on this Anna is that it's the only lead I have. So bear with me, won't you? Sally mentioned that her brother had been there and slept in the bunkhouse. So he was fairly independent."

"But they didn't have room for him to sleep in the house."

Yes, I'm aware of that. Now did you see Richard get on the train?"

"No, I couldn't. I was just coming home from school. He stopped by the schoolhouse after school."

"Why'd he stop by the schoolhouse?"

Anna felt herself blush. "He said he wanted to say good-bye to me and asked if he could send me a postcard. I remember he was surprised that I didn't lock the schoolhouse door. Oh, speaking about locking the schoolhouse door, I just remembered it was that weekend that Anders said someone had stayed in the schoolhouse, because on Monday morning all the coal and cobs were gone."

"That's probably not too unusual," Jim commented, "although no one has mentioned anyone staying in any other schoolhouse. Usually these fellas go the rounds from one to another, often in pairs. Matt did mention to me that there were two men around, about a day or so before she died. He said he didn't know where they went, and he hasn't seen them since. It does raise some suspicion though, since they were here around the same time. Some of these men have been around so long that they know all the comings and goings of every farm. Edna Wheeler was pretty much the laughingstock among them, and most of them probably knew where she kept her money and also hoped that there'd be plenty of it. Yes, I'll check some more. That's a hard one to trace, though. If they did get the money, they'd hightail it for—well, as far away as possible. Anyway, to get back to Richard, what happened? Did he leave the schoolhouse with you?"

"Oh, yes. He never came in. He was just walking up to the schoolhouse when I was leaving. It was late, too, after four o'clock. I kept telling him he'd have to hurry to make the 5:10."

"When did you last see him?"

"When he was walking down the road between the Wheeler's and the Larsons'. I asked him if he knew the train didn't always stop in Grabney, and he said the conductor told him it would. It was snowing, and I wanted to hurry home, so I didn't see him go very far."

Jim thought a moment. "He had a couple of miles to go before he'd get to the depot, but plenty of time to make the train. Anyway, I think I'd like to ask Richard a few questions. Here we have a person who was in the vicinity. No one saw him get on the train. I checked with Matt, and he doesn't remember him leaving and Matt is usually up on most everything. He said Jonah got off the train, but no one got on, and they only use one door."

"I forgot about Jonah getting off that train," Anna said.

"Matt does remember seeing him arrive, though. Now, do you have any idea where I can find this Richard?"

"Some place in California is all I know."

The sheriff shook his head. California's a big state. And what's more, he could be anywhere. But if he sends you that postcard, be sure to let me know. He may even have seen something that would help us find the thief."

"Oh, I will. But you don't think it could be Richard, do you?" she asked. "When I saw the crossed fingers that Sally made for his sign, I got chills. But I keep thinking, how could he have taken the money? And did she die of a heart attack because she saw someone steal it?"

"That's possible," he answered. "With her penchant for saving money it could happen. However, I'm thinking of a worse scenario than that. It's possible that Mrs. Wheeler was alive when the robber, whoever he was, came in to steal the money, and that the robber didn't want any witnesses."

Chapter Twenty-five

"Come in," said Jim Wilson, as Matt opened the door to the sheriff's office. "How's the new car?"

"It's just great," Matt proudly exclaimed. "Have you'n Anna finished?"

"We're sort of up a dead end now," the sheriff stated. "I'm not sure where we stand, but anyway, each bit of information, no matter how small, may help us solve the case. And Anna's been a great help."

Anna was still stunned by the sheriff's last pronouncement about the robber not wanting any witnesses. She knew also that he was not counting Richard out as one of the suspects. This was as great a shock as when she saw Sally make the crossed fingers sign. She found it difficult to think about anything else.

"Ready to go, Anna?" Matt asked. "Anna?"

"Oh...yes," she said, quite preoccupied as she put on her coat. "Where's Ed?"

"He's in the car," Matt answered. "I thought it best to let him drive out of town. I can practice, once we get on the road."

Anna had a sinking feeling. Here was Matt planning to drive a new car when he didn't even know how to drive a car. Would Ed really let him drive?

"Watch out for him, Anna," said the sheriff. "I don't know if I'd trust his driving or not."

"Now Jim," Matt answered, his pride slightly ruffled. "This drivin's gonna be no problem at all. I've got Ed ta help me, and what's more, we passed only one car on the way here."

"Just look out for the occasional horse and buggy. Why, with you coming down the road you're likely to have a stampede. Anna, I have a couple of nice beds in private rooms just around the corner. No one to bother you, either."

At last this brought a smile to Anna's face. "Thanks, Mr. Wilson, but I think I'll take my chances with a wild ride in a new Ford. A night in the jail doesn't appeal to me."

"All right then, let's get going. Ed's out there with the engine runnin'. He says it's ta get the thing warmed up but I suspect he wants ta use up the gas so he can sell me some more." Matt had the door open and ushered Anna out into the cold, followed by Jim, who was interested in seeing the new vehicle.

"I went back and got the blanket for you, Anna!" Ed shouted over the din from the engine. "Can you manage to get in by yourself?"

Jim had the door open for her and helped her into the back seat. As she tucked the blanket around her, she noticed that the side curtains were up. Matt climbed into the front seat next to Ed, both doors were slammed and they were off. "Hang on while I make a U-turn here," Ed called out, and after they were tossed around a bit, they headed in the direction of Grabney.

"I think it's my turn ta drive now," Matt said as they approached a fairly even stretch in the road.

"Sorry Matt," Ed said as he concentrated on the ruts and ridges left from the winter's storms. "This isn't a very good place to let you practice. It may be fairly smooth here, but we're about to come on that stretch of washboard."

"All right then, but let me know when it's my turn."

"I sure will," Ed answered, and a few more miles rolled by.

"Now, this place looks pretty good to me," Matt declared.

"Not good enough," Ed surmised. "Just wait, you'll get your turn."

Each time Ed insisted on driving, Anna gave a sigh of relief. Mile after mile passed with Matt coaxing Ed to let him drive. At last they were approaching Grabney.

They pulled up to the post office. Liza ran out to meet them. "Why Matt! I thought you'd be drivin'. How come you're not?"

"Ed kept sayin' that the road was too rough, or ta wait until we'd come ta the next good spot, an' here we are. I haven't learned ta drive yet."

"Well, if you haven't learned ta drive, how're you gonna teach me?" Liza complained.

"Beats me," he said. "But I kep' lookin' to see what Ed was doin', and maybe I can get the hang of it myself."

"Don't worry," Ed consoled him. "I think it's best to practice around here. First you'll have to learn to start it, and then comes the driving. But I'll help you, and in another week or so you'll be sailin' along the roads."

"What about me?" Liza asked. "Maybe you could teach me first?"

"I think it's best to teach Matt first," Ed answered, hoping she wouldn't press the point. As an excuse he added, "Matt knows a lot about mechanical things. He'd be a good one to teach you."

The next week, Anna was getting ready for her mother's arrival on Saturday. She wanted her room to look especially neat, and she also wanted to help Milly, who was doing double duty with the spring cleaning added to the usual chores. Every rug was taken outside, hung up on the clothesline and had the dust beaten out of it. Floors and woodwork were scrubbed. Curtains were washed. Every day after school, Anna hurried home to start on the next chore. She felt obligated to do as much as possible, as it was her mother who was causing all this work.

"I think you two are working too hard," Peter commented while Milly and Anna were finishing with the supper dishes. "Milly, you cleaned everything just before Christmas."

"That was a long time ago," she answered. "And anyhow, it's time to do spring cleaning. This is almost the end of March."

"I know my mother will appreciate all your hard work, Milly. I hope you can get a little rest tomorrow. I think everything's finished, isn't it?"

"Well, tomorrow we'll yust have the regular work, and we'll have a nice quiet little supper," Milly answered. "Your mother will be tired from traveling, and so we'll have a restful evening."

"I don't think you know how to rest, Milly," Peter said.

"Oh, listen to you," she remarked. "Why nobody works harder than you do, Peter. And in all kinds of weather, too. I'll sit down now and show you I can rest." She dried her hands, took off her apron and sat in her favorite rocking chair. "See! Here I am, resting." She rocked back and forth a few times with a smile of satisfaction on her face, then her expression changed. "Oh! I forgot, it's time for the children to get to bed," and she was quickly on her feet.

"No! You sit back down, Milly. I'll put Lucy to bed," Peter said.

"And I'll get the other two to bed," Anna added.

"All right," Milly agreed. "Then I'll yust sit here and rock." And for once she did just that.

Peter drove Anna to the station to meet her mother Saturday afternoon. The weather was nippy but not freezing. "I sure wish I had a fancy car to meet your mother, Anna," he said to her as they drove toward town.

"My mother doesn't expect you to have a car. She knows what farm life is like."

"Everyone around here will be getting cars soon, and I know Milly would like one, but I just don't see how we can afford it. I don't want to borrow any more money than what I owe on the place. I've been lucky so far with good crops so I could make the mortgage payments in the fall and still have some left over."

"I think you manage very well," Anna said.

"Well, maybe, but I was probably crazy to breed six sows. That might mean sixty or seventy pigs to feed, and pigs quickly become hogs. They can eat a person out of house and home. I'll have to buy feed for them. But I don't know why I'm telling you all this."

"You'll get a good price for them in the fall, so you'll really be ahead."

"Yeah. Well, let's hope the prices are good. Farmers can lose their shirts when prices fall. Well, here we are." He pulled the buggy up to the station and tied the reins around the hitching post. "Let's hurry and get inside out of this cold."

Matt and Liza were there. It was obvious that they had been waiting for them. "Thought I'd just do a little cleanin'," Liza commented as she swept the floor. "My land! You'd never think this place would get so dirty."

"Train'll be on time," Matt stated. He looked at the clock on the wall. "It's five after now, so we got about five minutes to go."

Anna glanced at the clock to confirm his report as Liza pushed the broom toward her and then stopped to lean on the handle.

"I'm sure you'll be glad ta see yer ma."

"Yes, I will," Anna replied as she gave the woman a weak smile.

"S'pose you last saw her at Christmas."

"That's right." Anna looked at the broom and the sweepings from the floor. "I guess you're almost through. Here, I'll move out of the way and you can finish this side." She quickly crossed the small room and stood next to the wooden bench that was just inside the door. She was anxious about meeting her mother and didn't want to get involved in a meaningless conversation.

"You don't need ta do that," Liza said. "I got plenty a' time. How're things out at yer place? S'pose Milly's been cleanin' ta git the place ready fer yer ma."

"Yes, we've been quite busy, spring cleaning you know." She paused to listen. "Oh Peter, I thought I heard the train whistle, did you?"

"Not sure I did," he replied. "But on second thought, maybe it is coming in."

"It's comin' in fer sure," Matt said as he walked toward the door and looked out through the window. "Yup! About a mile away. I can see the smoke. Come on, Anna. Come 'n see fer yerself."

Anna walked over to the door and peeked out of the window. Yes, there was the train rounding the curve to the east. In a moment the whistle sounded, and Matt opened the door, holding it for Anna and Peter, who followed him onto the platform. The train roared up next to them and screeched to a stop, letting out a hiss of steam. "She'll be on the car down here," Matt called to them as he ambled toward the third car.

The coach door was opened by the conductor, who jumped down and put out the step stool so passengers could alight with ease. Anna was excited as she waited to see her mother. She guessed that there would be no other passengers getting off at Grabney.

Her mother appeared in the doorway and exited the train looking like an elegant lady, dressed in her brown wool coat to which she had added a fur collar. She wore a matching fur hat. A porter placed her suitcase on the platform and was tipped with a coin held in a beautifully gloved hand. Anna quickly thought back to last fall when she took the train to Grabney and her mother had given strict instructions that she was under no circumstances to tip anyone. She recognized the suitcase as belonging to her Aunt Hazel, Uncle Lars' wife. Instantly she was aware that her mother wanted to make a good impression, perhaps too good of an impression.

She ran to meet her. "Oh Mother! I'm so glad to see you." She enthusiastically took hold of her mother's hand. "I hope you had a nice trip."

"Yes, it was quite pleasant," her mother replied, taking her hand from Anna's and looking at Matt and Peter who were now approaching.

Bang! The conductor slammed shut the door. They turned to look at the train. There was the first chug as the connecting rods on the wheels began their first push. Then the chugs became faster and the wheels turned faster and faster, and soon the train disappeared into the distance leaving them alone on a deserted station platform.

Anna realized Matt and Peter were standing next to them. "Oh Mother, this is Peter Jensen. Peter, this is my mother, Lydia Swenson. And Mother, this is Matt Crawford. He's the stationmaster."

"How do you do, gentlemen," Mrs. Swenson said at the same time as Peter and Matt mumbled their greetings.

"Lemme getcher grip," Matt said as he reached over and grabbed the handle of the suitcase.

"Oh, I can do that," Peter offered.

"No," Matt replied. "You get the ladies tucked into the buggy."

Nothing more was said as they walked quickly toward the carriage. As they passed the station door, Anna noticed Liza peering out of the window. No doubt she would soon be on the phone.

"Here, Mrs. Swenson, take my hand and I'll help you up," Peter offered.

"Thank you, Mr. Jensen," she replied as she took his hand and gracefully stepped up into the buggy.

"Here, Anna," he said as he helped her. "You get your mother situated in the middle between us. And be sure to get the lap robe over you. Don't want her to freeze to death on the way home." Matt put the suitcase behind the seat. Peter unhitched Ginger and jumped in on his side. "So long, Matt," he called as he pulled the reins to the left and called, "Come on Ginger! Let's go home." As they passed the store he inquired, "I hope you're comfortable, Mrs. Swenson. I'm sorry all we have is an open one-seater. When Milly and I first started, we thought it was all we would need for a while, and we couldn't afford anything fancier. But it gets us there. Some day I'll be able to buy us a car."

"I'm perfectly fine," she replied in dulcet tones. "I haven't ridden in one of these for a long time. It's certainly different."

"Oh, Mother," Anna said as she pointed to the post office. "That's the post office, just on the other side of the depot. And there's the store over there." She pointed it out, also. "We can even walk to the store on a path by the river. And there's the church on the other side of this bridge, and the parsonage."

"Anna, please don't point," Mrs. Swenson uttered in a muted tone of reprimand. "I can see what these places are."

"Oh, and you'll be going to church tomorrow. Reverend and Mrs. Blakeley are so nice. I'm so glad that you came so you could see everyone here."

"And please don't chatter so." She paused, then turned to Peter. "You must be glad that the snow is gone, Mr. Jensen."

"Oh, call me Peter," he said warmly. "Well, yes, we're all glad that the snow's gone. The ground's warmed up enough so that I've started plowing. The work really begins now."

"Yes, I can see that," she said as she looked at the freshly plowed soil on the Larson farm as they turned the corner. "Just where is your place?"

"Oh, we're another mile down the road," he answered. "At the next corner we make a right turn, and then we're halfway down on the left hand side."

They rode along in silence until they approached the turn, and Peter spoke up again. "Look down the road on the left side. That's the schoolhouse."

"Oh yes, I see," she commented. "And that's where Anna teaches."

"She can tell you all about that herself," Peter acknowledged. "She's a mighty fine teacher, too, from what everybody says."

"Yes, I'm sure she is. She's had a good education, and she never was afraid of hard work."

"Oh we're coming up to our place," Anna said. "In the summer, Milly has flowers planted all around the house. It looks so different then."

"Well, nothing looks too good in the winter," her mother added.

"Well, here we are," Peter said as he pulled up next to the back porch. "Whoa, Ginger!" He jumped down from the buggy and quickly came to the other side. "Here, I'll help you two ladies out, and then I'll take Ginger to the barn."

"We'll go up the back steps, Mother," Anna advised. "Almost no one around here comes to the front door. Besides," she giggled, 'the front door leads to the parlor, and it's ice cold in there because they don't heat it."

To this her mother didn't reply but cautiously climbed the steps to the porch. Anna opened the door. "Come on through the back porch, Mother. I'll take you into the kitchen where you can meet Milly, and then I'll come back and take off my hat and coat. We hang ours up out here, but you can put yours in my bedroom."

As she opened the kitchen door, the heat flowed out to envelop them. Milly was standing in front of the stove, her hands clasped in front of her. She had heard them enter the yard and no doubt was waiting for them to come into the kitchen. "Oh, come in! Come in!" she called out as she hurried to meet them. "Oh, I know you are Mrs. Swenson. It is so good to have you here."

"Mother, this is Milly Jensen," Anna said.

"Yes, I was sure you must be Mrs. Jensen," her mother replied.

"Oh, you must call me Milly. Everyone does."

"I'm going to take off my hat and coat," Anna said as she went back on the porch. "I'll be right back." She closed the door behind her but could still hear the conversation in the kitchen.

"Oh, what a beautiful coat and with a fur collar, too," Milly exclaimed as her eyes sparkled. "And such a lovely hat. Anna tells me that you are a wonderful seamstress. I can believe that from the dresses you have sewn for her."

Anna quickly took off her coat, hat and scarf and hung them on her hook. She straightened out her hair, then came back into the kitchen. As she did so, her mother turned to her and stopped still. She stared at Anna as if she couldn't believe her eyes. "Anna! What have you done with your hair? It looks terrible."

Chapter Twenty-six

"Mother!" Anna cried out, quite surprised at her mother's outburst.

Milly quickly rescued the situation. "Oh, Mrs. Swenson. We think Anna's hair is quite beautiful. Why, she looks yust like the cover on a magazine."

"But your beautiful long hair," her mother moaned. "Oh I know that it's the fashion now, but I think it's so ridiculous."

"I'm going to have my hair cut," Milly firmly announced. "I think it's the best idea. I'm tired of long hair to comb every night, and to wash, and to pin up every morning."

"But it's so—so ladylike to have long hair," Mrs. Swenson continued as she gave a slight shudder. "I can't believe it, Anna. You didn't even tell me you were going to do it. Oh! I hope you didn't let them throw your hair away. And who cut it, anyway?"

Milly eased herself away from them and walked over to the stove. Anna was anxious to get off the subject. "Come up to my room, Mother, and take off your coat. I saved my hair, and it's in two long braids. I'll show them to you." She directed her mother to the steps.

"Don't hurry," Milly called after them. "Peter hasn't done the milking yet. Take your time, Anna. Give your mother a little rest."

"My room is right at the top of the steps," Anna said as she opened the door. Sarah and Davey have the rooms down there."

Mrs. Swenson hesitated at the bedroom door, then entered the room. Her eyes slowly swept from one corner to another. "Well, I think it is quite nice," she remarked with a patronizing tone. "I can see that Mrs. Jensen has done her best to make this a comfortable place for you." Then she turned quickly to Anna. "But what

I want to know is, what gave you the ridiculous idea of cutting your hair? And imagine Mrs. Jensen saying that she was intending to cut hers, too. Well, I suppose farm wives do try to imitate the fashion magazines, but I— "

"Just a minute, Mother," Anna interrupted. She quickly went to the floor register and closed it. "This is what heats my room, but it's an opening to the kitchen, and Milly can hear everything we say."

"Oh! Well, I didn't know that. I'm sure I wouldn't say anything that would be out of place."

Anna walked to the dresser, opened the bottom drawer and removed a parcel wrapped in soft white paper. "Here's the hair I had cut off, if you want to see it." She set it on the bed and unfolded the paper.

"Well, I can see that it looks very nice. At least you had the sense to keep it, although I can see that you won't need that beautiful hair receiver any more. I can't imagine what the world is coming to when girls don't need hair receivers."

"It's still on my dresser, mother, and I have lots of hair in it from when it was long and I combed it every night. Now I can put other things in it."

"Oh yes," and Mrs. Swenson shook her head. "So let's sit down, and you can tell me what else you've been doing here." She looked at the register to make sure it was still closed.

At the supper table Milly seated Anna and her mother on the wall side of the table with the three children opposite them. After grace was said, the food was passed, with Milly helping Sarah and Lucy, who sat next to her. The children kept their eyes on Anna's mother and had to be told to start eating.

Mrs. Swenson seemed eager to make a good impression. She smiled at the children and looked around the table, breaking the silence by saying, "I see you have prepared a lovely supper, Mrs. Jensen. So much work for you when you have three little ones to take care of."

"I'm not so little," Davey interrupted.

"Hush, Davey," Milly admonished him, then turned to Anna's mother. "Oh please call me, Milly. No one calls me Mrs. Yenson," she said in as cheerful a tone as she could muster, considering that she felt very nervous with this guest. She glanced at the children to make sure they were minding their manners.

"Oh, yes then, Milly," Mrs. Swenson replied hesitantly.

"Well, it's no more than I do every day," Milly insisted. "But I did want things to be nice for you. It's not every day that we have company, and I like to keep a good house."

"Milly's a hard worker, Mother," Anna added.

"Yes, I can see that." She turned to Peter. "And what about you, Mr. Jensen?"

Peter had his hand halfway up to his mouth with a fork full of potatoes. He lowered it to his plate, looked straight at Mrs. Swenson and spoke slowly. "I like living on a farm. The work isn't easy, but it's a good life. I couldn't do without Milly, though. She's not afraid of anything. When I'm short-handed, she even comes out in the field. Sometimes I think farm wives work harder than the men."

"Oh that's not true, Peter," Milly responded quickly. "No one works harder than Peter. He even milks the cows, and at home, well, I mean in Sweden, milking cows was women's work. So you see, I have a nice life." She stiffened a little, then looked at the children again to make sure they were still minding their manners. "Now children, finish up quickly so we can have dessert." At this suggestion, everyone resumed eating. As they finished the meal, Milly sat up very straight as if she were making an announcement. She smiled as she said, "We'll have dessert here, and when we're through we can have coffee in the parlor. I lit the stove in there."

"That was nice of you, Milly," Anna said gratefully as she got up to help Milly clear the table. "You see Mother, because you came, this is a special occasion."

"That's very thoughtful of you," Mrs. Swenson replied. "I will enjoy having coffee in your parlor."

Dessert finished, Peter suggested, "Anna, you take your mother in the parlor. I'll help Milly clear the table."

"Oh, that's a good idea," Milly quickly added. "And when we're through, I'll bring in the coffee, and we can all sit and visit."

Anna also thought this was a very good idea. She was going to volunteer to clear but felt that Milly would be quite uncomfortable trying to make conversation with her mother on her own. She also knew that she would have quite enough time alone with her mother after they went up to bed. "Why don't the children come in with us?" she suggested. "Come on, Davey and Sarah. I'll bring Lucy."

"Oh, Anna, you don't want them in with you," Milly said.

"Oh, yes I do," Anna answered. "Come on, children." She picked up Lucy, who was dressed in blue chambray coveralls with red trim at the square neck. The knees were worn and slightly soiled, as the youngster spent half her time crawling around on the floor playing with her toys.

"Oh Anna!" Milly called. "I had no idea Lucy had gotten so dirty." She rushed over to take Lucy out of Anna's arms. "Let me change her clothes."

"She's just fine," Anna said as she held on to Lucy. "You have enough work, Milly, and Lucy's not dirty at all. Come on, Mother. Bring some of your toys, Davey and Sarah." Together they entered the parlor, with Milly rushing ahead to light the lamp on the table, and then making a quick exit to get the coffee ready.

"I suppose Mrs. Jensen…er…Milly made this braided rug," commented Anna's mother, as she examined each item in the room.

"Yes," Anna replied. "And she made the curtains. I don't know the story behind the little walnut table, but I know that she and Peter bought the davenport after they were married. It makes into a bed, and Milly said that she and Peter slept on it for the first year or so. She said she would rather have that than a bed since they could afford only one piece of furniture. This way they could use it in their parlor for company."

"Yes, I've seen others like it, " Mrs. Swenson commented as she looked at the heavy square-sided piece of furniture. It had a wood frame with the cushions and padded areas done in a gold-brown upholstery velvet. " I know it folds out to make a bed. They used this room for their bedroom, then."

"Yes," Anna explained. "You see, when they were married, Peter was remodeling the house, so the bedroom wasn't finished until later. The kitchen and this room were the first two finished."

"Aunt Inger gave us this chair," Davey announced as he climbed up to sit on it.

"Davey, why don't you get a couple of chairs from the kitchen?" Anna suggested. "That way when your parents come in, they will have a place to sit."

"But don't let Sarah sit in this chair," he complained as he got down to do as he was told.

"I'm going to play with my doll and Lucy, so I don't want your chair," Sarah answered.

As Davey finished bringing in the second chair, Milly came in carrying a tray with cups and saucers, a cream pitcher and sugar bowl. "We poured the coffee in the kitchen," Milly apologized. "I don't have a fancy coffeepot." She set it on the table.

"You sit down, Milly," Anna said. "I'll serve the coffee." She poured cream into a cup for her mother and gave it to her.

"Oh, my!" Mrs. Swenson exclaimed. "You do have such wonderful thick cream. It floats on top of the coffee. I haven't had cream like this for ages."

"That's one of the advantages of living on a farm," Peter said as he entered the room with a plate of cookies. "Of course, you have to milk the cows to get the cream."

"Well, it's all very nice," Mrs. Swenson added. "And cookies, too, when we've just had apple pie."

"You'll never go hungry around here, Mother," Anna said. "Oh Milly, why don't you sit down."

"Yust long enough to drink my coffee," she answered. "I have to bathe the children to get ready for church tomorrow. Now, you folks stay and visit. I'll take Lucy first and get her scrubbed up. When I'm through with her, Sarah, it'll be your turn, and then Davey."

"I'll pour the water into the tub for you, Milly," Peter offered as he got up.

"That'll be fine," Milly replied as she picked up Lucy. "Now, Davey, why don't you tell Mrs. Swenson about your school? Maybe tomorrow on the way home from church she can visit it."

"Well, I'm sure I don't know if I'll have time to do all that," Anna's mother remarked.

"Oh, of course you will, Mother." Anna was almost pleading. This was going to be a long evening and maybe a longer day tomorrow. She gave a sigh and then turned to Davey and said, "Now, Davey, can you tell her about school?"

"Anna, I'll let you take Ginger to church," Peter announced at the end of breakfast. "Milly's going to stay home and get the dinner ready. I think you and your mother and Davey and Sarah can fit in the buggy just fine."

"Will we be leaving for church so early?" Mrs. Swenson asked.

"Church isn't until eleven, but we have Sunday School at ten, Mother."

"Well, I don't need to go to Sunday School," she stated. "I could stay here and perhaps help Milly with the dinner."

"No, no!" Milly answered, and fluttered her hands in front of her chest, the usual sign that she meant what she said. "I can get the dinner myself. Part of it is practically done. I had Peter get one of our hams, and it's been simmering all night and soaking up water, so it should be nice and tender. I soaked it yesterday, too, to get rid of some of the salt."

"Yes, I'm sure you can manage just fine," Mrs. Swenson commented. "But I don't know why I should be going to Sunday School."

"Miss Swenson plays the piano, and she's my Sunday School teacher," Sarah exclaimed proudly.

"And Mother, we make just one trip to church, so it's best if you come with me and the children. Davey, you can help me clear the table now, then I think it's best if we go upstairs and get ready."

Anna knew that she could count on Reverend Blakeley to give a warm welcome to her mother. She followed her mother and the children as they went downstairs to the basement. "We're so lucky to have a minister like Reverend Blakeley, Mother. Isn't he wonderful?"

As they reached the bottom of the steps her mother replied, "He seems nice enough for a country minister. Oh, I see you have tables set up back here."

"Yes, those are for the classes," Anna explained. "My class meets at this second table. We sit on the benches for the worship service. I'll have to go up front to play the piano, but first let me introduce you to some of the others."

"Oh, don't bother, Anna. You have other things to do. I'll just sit back here. Don't worry about me. You go ahead and do what you have to do."

"Oh there's Inger, Milly's sister," Anna exclaimed as Inger came out of the church kitchen. "She's the head of the Sunday

School and the school board. You must meet her." She waved at Inger who walked toward them. "Inger, this is my mother Lydia Swenson. Mother, this is Inger Parker."

"I'm very happy to meet you, Mrs. Swenson," Inger said. "It's so nice of you to come out here and visit Anna."

"I'm pleased to come," was the rather stiff reply. "I understand that you and your family will be coming over for dinner."

"Yes, we'll be quite a crowd. If you will excuse me, I have to hurry off and get things started. We're not a big Sunday School, but there are still things to do," and she walked back to the front of the room.

"Why, she didn't even have an accent," Mrs. Swenson remarked to Anna.

"Yes, Mother," Anna replied as she took a deep breath and pushed her shoulders back. She felt as if she were slumping, and the next thing her mother would do was to tell her to stand up straight. "Is it all right if you sit here? I have to go up front and play the piano."

"Yes, of course. Don't bother about me. I'll just sit here by myself."

While the Sunday School classes were in session, Reverend Blakeley was most courteous and spent every spare minute visiting with Mrs. Swenson. She appeared to enjoy the attention. This was a relief to Anna, who had wondered what her mother would do while she was teaching her class.

During church, they sat toward the back of the room. They were late as usual, as Anna had to clean up after her class. A few people found an excuse to turn around and look at them, but no one really gawked. Bertha and Ed were seated closest to them, and at the end of the service Bertha dashed across the aisle with Ed in tow. "Oh, you must be Anna's mother. I'm Bertha Clemson, and this is my fiance Ed Marson. Ed's folks run the store."

"How nice to meet you, Bertha, and you, too, Ed," Anna's mother replied with her consistently formal tone.

Bertha turned to Anna. "Oh, Anna! I'm so excited about the dance on Saturday. Have you heard from Jonah?"

"Yes," Anna answered. She felt excited thinking about the dance, going with Jonah and Bertha and Ed. "I got a letter this week. He's coming in on the afternoon train, and he'll be staying the week to help with the planting."

"I'll phone you on Saturday when I get in, and we can talk about what to wear. Guess we'd better go now. Come on, Ed."

As people filed out of the church, Anna introduced them to her mother. She could see they were impressed, and it was obvious that her mother was pleased to have created quite a stir among the local folk.

Davey and George had walked home, so it was with Sarah that they rode back from church.

"Who is this Jonah that your friend mentioned?" her mother inquired. "I don't think I've heard of him."

"I met him last fall," Anna answered. "You remember when I wrote and told you about finding the old man Bill Evans frozen to death?"

"Oh yes! That was horrible. I could hardly believe it," her mother answered.

"Jonah was the one who found me and carried me into the barn. I guess I had fainted."

"Well, no wonder. And now because of that, you're going to a dance with him?"

"I've seen him since. His mother even invited me to dinner one evening. I'm sure I wrote you about it."

"I guess you did. But I thought that when you went to the dances, you went with a family?"

"Yes, I did for the last one. But this time Jonah and I are going with Bertha and Ed," Anna explained.

"I hope you're not serious about him."

"No, Mother. We're just friends, and we're going together to the dance. It should be lots of fun."

"And do you have to dance with, well all the riffraff around here, I mean all the hired men?"

This was getting to be too much for Anna. "Yes! I dance with anyone who will ask me. It's a big community affair. I even danced with Reverend Blakeley."

"You mean your minister goes to the dances?"

"Yes, he and Mrs. Blakeley both come. And their son Michael came up from Des Moines with his girlfriend, and they went, too."

Anna was glad they approached the next intersection where she could have turned off to the Jensens'. She tried to brighten up when she said, "The schoolhouse is just up the road a little. See! You can see it from here. I'm going to go there now, so you can see where I teach."

"I've seen plenty of schoolhouses before," answered her mother. "Don't do it on my account."

"But I thought you would like to see it, and see my desk and the bell that you sent me."

"I wanna go to the school," Sarah said. 'I don't get to see it very much."

"All right then, Sarah, we'll go," and Anna continued down the road.

There were twelve at dinner. Milly had set the table with her good linen cloth. The food was delicious, and everyone seemed cheerful. Walter, Floyd and Peter sat together and talked about spring planting. Mabel sat with Sarah and Lucy. George and Davey were opposite them. This left the four women together at one end of the table. Conversation was going quite amicably when George looked up at Anna and asked, "Miss Swenson, Sally wanted to know if you've heard from her brother."

"Oh no, I haven't, George. If I do, I'll be right up to tell her."

"Is this something I should know about?" asked Mrs. Swenson.

"Oh no, Mother. It's just that Sally's brother visited her and said he would send me a postcard when he got to California. That's all."

"Do you think he really stole the Wheeler's money?" Mabel asked.

"Little pitchers have big ears," Inger said, looking at Floyd.

"Now, Mother! What'd I do?" he said, looking the picture of innocence.

"You mean someone around here has had money stolen?" Mrs. Swenson asked.

"Not only that," George added. "Mrs. Wheeler may have been killed, too."

"That's enough!" Inger commanded. "This isn't dinner table conversation. Let's talk about something more pleasant. What about telling Anna's mother what a good teacher Miss Swenson is. George, Mabel, what can you tell her?"

"I think she's the best teacher I've ever had, and I'm sorry I won't be here next year to have her," Mabel said.

"Oh Mabel, that's very nice." Anna was thrilled.

"I'll be here," George remarked. "And I'm going to study so hard that I'll be able to pass the eighth grade tests to get into high school. That way, Lars and I can go to high school together."

"Jus' see what your daughter has done," Floyd joked as he looked over at Anna's mother. "Why, she even has the kids likin' school."

"That's very nice, I'm sure," Mrs. Swenson remarked. "But of course Anna will be teaching in the city next year. This was only a beginning for her."

Everyone was stunned. Anna most of all. "But Mother," she said.

Mrs. Swenson turned to her and said quietly. "We'll discuss this later, Anna."

Floyd broke the silence. "That sure is a darn shame. Here we was all set to git her fixed up with Charley 'r Bill. Now you go and tell us that she's not even gonna be around."

Sarah started to cry and was comforted by Mabel. Davey and George looked shocked.

Anna looked at all her friends seated around the table. "Yes, I will be here next year, that is, if you want me. I love teaching here, and I can't think of a better place." Her mother started to interrupt, but Anna said, "I'll be going to summer school, so I won't be here during the summer, but I'll be back in the fall. And Floyd, if it's all right with Milly, I won't even bring my trunk home, so you won't have to carry it again."

Chapter Twenty-seven

Anna said good-bye to her mother before she left for school on Monday. Anna was reluctant to leave, as Milly would now have the responsibility of entertaining her mother all morning.

She slowly went out the door, looking back at Milly, who gave her a cheerful good-bye. "Now don't you worry about a thing, Anna. This is wash day, and your mother and I can have a good visit while I do the work." On Monday during the cold months, Peter moved the washing machine from the back porch into the kitchen. She recalled last fall when she found Peter on the back porch pushing the washing handle back and forth, which turned the agitator on the square-shaped machine. She also remembered using the big wooden spoon to lift the clothes out of the hot soapy water up to the first tub of rinse water and then to the second one. Peter wouldn't be helping with the washing today. He had to keep on with the plowing, and Milly wouldn't have to worry about talking to her mother. She would be too busy to become engaged in much conversation.

All week, Anna kept thinking about Saturday night. This was the first time that she had been invited by a young man to attend a dance. She thought of so many different scenarios. What would happen when? She could hardly believe it when Saturday morning arrived.

They were finishing breakfast when they heard three long rings on the phone, Inger's ring. Immediately, Milly jumped up and dashed to the phone on the wall between the kitchen and the parlor. She put her hand over the black mouthpiece and then carefully lifted the earpiece from its hook on the large wooden instrument.

"Guess things are hopping early today," Peter mused. "First we hear Liza's ring, and now Inger's. Just look at Milly's face. It must be something pretty important."

Milly was completely engrossed in the conversation and paid no attention to remarks from the family. At last she hung up the phone and came over to the table shaking her head. "Guess what? Esther Pearson's gone into labor, and Mrs. Bailey said that the doctor is out on another delivery, so Joe called Inger to get her over there. Esther isn't due 'til April, so it's a little early. You know she's lost some before, so they're awfully worried. Anyway, Inger said she'd go right away." With that much said, Milly sat down to catch her breath.

"I wouldn't worry too much," Peter remarked. "A week or so too early isn't that bad. Anyway, Inger's delivered babies before."

"But with Esther," Milly continued. "They are so anxious that things go all right."

"Do you know if Mrs. Bailey thought the doctor could get out here in time?" asked Anna.

"No, I don't," Milly answered. "Oh! And Inger! There's the dance tonight. She's planning to bring potato salad. I'll call them and see what's happening." She dashed to the phone and rang three long rings. "Mabel.———This is Aunt Milly. I yust heard that your mother is going over to the Pearsons'.———Ya———Ya———All right. You let us know then.———Goodbye."

"Can't Aunt Inger go to the dance?" asked Davey.

"Oh no," answered his mother. "This is much more important than a dance. Victoria is about to get a little baby sister or brother."

"Can we still go to the dance?" Sarah wanted to know.

"Yes, yes. We'll go. Now hurry up and finish your breakfast. This is Saturday, and there's plenty of work to do. Come on, now. Hurry up! Mabel will phone us when something happens." Milly quickly started to clear the table. Anna got up and helped. Saturday morning chores had begun.

The phone continued to ring off and on during the day. No doubt the entire countryside was aware of the pending event. However, Mabel did not phone again until after dinner. By that time, the doctor had arrived and they were now waiting for the arrival of the baby. Inger was asked to stay and help, so it was arranged that Milly and Peter would take Mabel and George to the dance with their family in Floyd's two-seater buggy. Floyd and Walter had not the slightest desire to go.

In the middle of the afternoon, Ed and Bertha pulled into the driveway. "I've got a couple of strangers here," said Peter as he escorted them into the house. "I think they've lost their way."

"Come right in," Milly welcomed them. "You're yust in time for a cup of coffee. I think Peter was looking for a good excuse to come in. Here, take off your things and take a seat. I'm sure Anna saw you, so she'll be right down. Have you heard anything more about Esther?"

"No, we haven't," Bertha said. "We didn't want to phone, because that way we'd tie up the line in case there was something important."

"I wish more people were that considerate," Peter added. "I've known times when people have talked on for hours, and they get huffy when you try to get them to hang up." He looked up to see Anna coming down the stairs. "Come on, Anna. Get some coffee now before these strangers drink it all."

"I don't think you've been to our house before, Bertha," Milly said. "Well, after you get your place built, we'll almost be neighbors."

"As far as it goes around here," Ed added, "you will be neighbors. After all, it's just down the path by the river to our house."

"When'll you get the place finished?" Peter asked.

"It better be by June," Bertha said, as she poked Ed playfully. "And if it's not finished, we'll move in, anyway. I guess we won't be the first couple to do that. Anyway, one reason we came is so I can talk to Anna about the dance. I thought I'd wear my cotton dress. It gets so hot dancing. What about you?"

"If you're going to talk about clothes, Ed an' I'll go out and look at the stock. You're sure you want to buy one of my sows? I've way too many, and I'll be more than glad to have you take one of them off my hands."

"I sure do."

"Well then, if you've finished your coffee, let's go." The two left the women to discuss all the things that women have to talk about before an event such as this.

"I found another stranger coming into the yard," announced Peter as he came into the kitchen carrying two pails full of milk, followed by Jonah. "Well, Jonah, you came too late to do the milking, but you can do the separating."

"I don't want you to get out of practice," Jonah answered him. "I'll stay here in the kitchen and talk to the ladies."

"You must have yust gotten off the train," Milly remarked.

"That's about right," he said. "Will met me, and I jumped off at our place. Thought I'd talk to Anna about arrangements for tonight." He turned to Anna. "Have you talked to Ed and Bertha?"

"They stopped by this afternoon," Anna explained. "They said they'd be here about 7:30. Is that all right with you?"

"Sounds fine," Jonah replied. "Say! Will told me about Esther Pearson. He said the last he heard, she hadn't delivered yet. Have you heard anything more?"

"Not a word," Milly told him. "Mabel said she'd phone if anything happened."

"We can only hope for the best, then. I'd better be running along. Haven't even stopped in to say hello to the folks. I'll come by before 7:30."

"That'll be fine," Anna answered. She felt excitement well up in her as he got up to leave. How could she be so lucky as to be going to the dance with him?

"Okay, then. See you about 7:15 or so," and he was out the door and on his way home.

Anna enjoyed the drive to the dance. She and Jonah were in the back seat with car robes tucked around them. She had dressed warmly as she remembered the cold breeze that came in, in spite of the mica windows being put up. Ed hollered back at them. "Hope you'll be warm enough."

"We're fine," Jonah called back. "Just try to keep one hand on the steering wheel, Ed."

"Don't want Bertha to get a chill. I gotta keep her shoulders warm. What about you, Jonah?"

"Never you mind!" he laughed. "Just keep your eyes on the road."

Anna wondered if Jonah would put his arm around her. Oh, if her mother could see her now.

They pulled up at the dance hall a little before nine o'clock. Anna noticed that there were more cars here than last fall. She surmised that more people were taking advantage of the easy payment plan. Bertha carried the hot dish that Vi had prepared, and they walked up the steps that led to the door. Anna recognized the same lean, tall farmer who collected a dollar from each man. Ladies and children were admitted free. They had passed Milly and Peter and the children on the road, so they knew it would be only a short time before they arrived, too. The room was large, with a stage at one end. Wooden chairs were lined up on three sides. As people entered, they put their coats on chairs. "Let's save places for Milly and Peter," Anna said.

"How many do we need to save?" asked Bertha.

"There's Milly, Peter, and their three children and then there's Mabel and George. I suppose that's seven seats. Milly brought the clothes basket for Lucy to sleep in. At least we're a little early."

"Look!" said Jonah. "There's a bunch of seats right next to the basement door. Let's go over there."

"That looks fine," Bertha commented. "I'm going to bring this hot dish of Vi's down to the kitchen, and I'll be right back. Save a seat for me," she called back at them as she started down the stairs.

The members of the band were on the stage warming up and visiting with the audience. There was someone at the piano, a man with an accordion, two more with fiddles and another with a saxophone. Anna was anxious to have Milly come soon, as she felt awkward saving so many seats, but she needn't have worried, as everyone seemed to be saving seats for family members who hadn't arrived.

Bertha reappeared from the kitchen. "Oh Anna, you look so nice in that dress. With the full skirt, it's just right for dancing."

"Thanks, Bertha. I really like your dress. Is it new?"

"Yes it is," she admitted. She came closer for a confidential remark. "Don't you think we look the best with our new hairdos? I told you we'd take the place by storm."

Anna laughed at this remark, but she looked around and felt that she and Bertha did look just a little bit of all right, even if she was a bit chilly until the room got warmed up.

"I suppose this is our corner!" Peter proclaimed in a loud

voice. He was carrying the clothes basket piled high with blankets.

"Oh there you are," Anna said with some relief in her voice. "I'm so glad you got here a little early."

"Oh yes, we made it in fine time," Milly told them. She was carrying Lucy, who was wide-eyed. "And there's still no word from the Pearsons. Mabel, you and George take the food to the kitchen. Peter, let's fold a couple of the blankets on the chairs for when Davey and Sarah get sleepy. The rest can stay in the basket for Lucy. I yust hope she's not too big for it, but she can double up her knees if she is. Anyway we can't put her in it until she falls asleep."

"I'm not gonna fall asleep," Davey asserted.

"Oh, the music has started," Milly exclaimed. "Let's get everyone settled so we can dance. Here Sarah, you keep an eye on Lucy. Oh, I do want to get in this first dance. Here come Mabel and George."

"I'll watch Lucy and Sarah for you, Aunt Milly," Mabel volunteered. "I know George and Davey will want to be off to talk to some of their friends. Anyway, I'll wait until Erica comes. Maybe she can sit with us."

"Oh yes, there's plenty of room," Milly said. "Yonah, I didn't know your family was coming."

"Oh yes," he smiled. "Mother said she's come to almost every dance, and she wasn't about to miss this one. Dad's a good dancer, too, so they'll have a good time. Everyone's coming, even Will and Kirsten. But I don't want to miss this dance, either, and it's half over now, so come on, Anna." He took her by the hand and led her out onto the floor. Soon they were swinging to a fast foxtrot. Anna quickly realized that he was a good dancer. He had probably had more practice that she had. She had learned to dance mainly by practicing with Elsa singing the tunes. Occasionally her mother would play the piano for them. Her first real dance was the one last fall.

Bertha smiled with delight at Anna as they danced past each other. Then the music stopped. "Let's stay out on the floor," Jonah suggested. "No point in going back after just half a dance."

Anna agreed completely. She glanced at the door and saw the Blakeley family arriving, and behind them was Grace Kloster with Jack Jarvis, the shoe salesman. Anna had danced with Jack last fall. "There's Grace with Jack Jarvis," she told Jonah. She remembered when Grace's husband was killed and then she and the children moved to the county seat to live with her aunt. It was Jonah who bought her farm, across the road from the Jensens'.

"It's good to see Grace again," he said. "Let's go over and talk to them." They darted between couples, and Jonah hailed Jack to get his attention. "Well, Jack, guess the county seat can't hold a candle to our dances."

"You're right, Jonah. Good to see you, and you, too, Anna," he said, smiling warmly.

"I'm glad to see you, Grace," Anna said. "How's Joshua doing? I miss him. He was a good student."

"He's doin' jus' fine," she answered, "but he misses you, too."

"Josh is a nice kid," Jack added. "You know, I board at Grace's aunt's place, too, so the kid an' I spend lotsa time together. We're puttin' up a swing in the back yard."

The music started again. "Tell him hello from me," Anna called back at them as Jonah steered her out onto the floor.

"I'm glad she's found someone to have a good time with," Jonah said. "She certainly had a rough enough time in Grabney."

"Yes," Anna added. "It looks as if her life is turning around. At least, I hope so."

After several dances, they met Milly and Peter and together walked back to their chairs. "I'm going to insist that you have one dance with me, Anna," Peter claimed. "I'm not going to let Jonah have you all evening."

"I'd love to," she said. "Just give me a chance to catch my breath."

"All right then, fair is fair," Jonah said to Milly. "It's my turn to dance with you. I remember you as the liveliest dancer here. And you always danced every dance, so let's go."

"Come on then, Anna," Peter insisted. "We can't let them get ahead of us."

As the evening progressed, they also exchanged a dance with Ed and Bertha. Anna noticed that Erica and Mabel and several other girls were occasionally dancing together. Peter danced with Sarah, carrying her in his arms. Other fathers did the same. The boys stayed at the far end of the room talking and looking over the crowd. Children were beginning to fall asleep, lying on coats or blankets on the chairs. Lucy was still awake, but her eyes were drooping.

The band stopped for an intermission. Jonah, Peter and Ed bought a glass of lemonade for everyone. They sat down for a change and enjoyed the cold liquid. The temperature in the room had increased considerably. Anna looked around and remembered that last fall she had spent part of the evening watching Lucy and Sarah. She had worried that she wouldn't be asked to dance, but everyone was so friendly that she danced many times, even with Reverend Blakeley.

"If you're finished with your lemonade, let's go over and visit with my folks," Jonah suggested. "I'd like to have a chance to dance with my mother, and I'm sure my dad would love to dance with you."

"That would be nice," Anna said hoping that it would be. It turned out to be a great success. Jonah's mother was pleased to dance with him, and Mr. Larson was as good a dancer as Jonah had claimed. He brought her back to her chair next to Sarah and thanked her. Before Jonah could get back to her, Reverend Blakeley intervened, and she danced a slow waltz with him. They also exchanged with Grace and Jack Jarvis, and before they knew it the song *Good Night Ladies* was being played. It was midnight, and this was the last dance. Peter insisted on dancing this with Milly, so Mabel, Erica and George went down to the kitchen to help with the supper. Many of the Brewster ladies had spent a good part of the evening setting the tables and getting the food ready.

By this time Lucy, Sarah and many other youngsters were asleep on chairs, baskets or baby buggies. Everyone else filed down the stairs to sit at long tables where fried chicken, potato salad, sandwiches, cake and hot coffee were served for an additional fifty cents.

Davey kept nodding off and soon was asleep with his head resting on Milly's lap. Peter went upstairs a couple of times to check on Sarah and Lucy.

As people finished, they left to go home. "Don't stay to help clean up, Milly," Jonah said. "You and Peter get on home with the children. We can help with the clean-up."

"If that's all right with you, I'm much obliged," Peter said. "Here Milly, I'll carry Davey. Mabel, can you get your mother's potato salad bowl and Milly's plate? You ready to go, George?"

Both George and Mabel nodded as they followed Peter and Milly up the steps.

There were quite a few people helping clear the tables. The dishwashing crew was ready, so it went like clockwork. Once the tables were cleared the Brewster ladies told everyone else they could go home. As they reached the upstairs they saw the Brewster men setting up chairs for the church service in the afternoon. Reverend Blakeley would be preaching.

Anna was feeling tired. It was not only after one o'clock in the morning, but she had danced almost every dance. "Here, let me help you with your coat," Jonah offered. "Bundle up good, now. It's going to be freezing outside."

"If I'd only thought," Ed remarked, "I'd have brought the car robes inside. Now they'll be freezing cold, and it'll take us forever to get warmed up."

"We'll manage," Jonah said.

They all shuddered as the blast of cold air hit them as they opened the door to the outside. "Hurry up now!" Ed called. "Let's get into the car and get it started, and let's hope it starts on the first try."

After a few false starts the engine roared a welcome sound. The car was freezing cold. Jonah tucked both blankets around them, but it would take a while before they warmed up. "How're you doing, Anna?" Jonah asked.

"I'd be all right if I weren't so cold," she answered, her teeth chattering.

"How about this, then," he said as he put his arm around her and gave her a tight squeeze.

"That's fine," she said and looked at him and smiled.

Chapter Twenty-eight

"Did you hear the phone ring this morning, Anna?" Milly asked as Anna came down the stairs.

"Yes, it woke me up. Was that Inger?"

"It was. And she said that the Pearsons are the proud parents of a fine baby boy. He was born a little before midnight, so he missed being an April Fool baby. Thank goodness for that."

"Thank goodness he's all right," Peter added, as he poured cream in his coffee.

"You are right, Peter," Milly acknowledged.

"How is Esther?" Anna asked. "I hope she's all right, too."

"Ya, she is fine. I'm so glad of that, too. Now Peter, Anna and I have to hurry. It's late. Yust let the children sleep, and you see if you can get in a few extra winks yourself. When you got up to do the milking, I couldn't help it but I fell back to sleep."

"I noticed that," he joked. "I thought you were playing an April Fool's joke on me. Anyway, since it's April 1st, why don't you and Anna stay home and play an April Fool's joke on the Sunday School?"

"Now Peter, we couldn't do that. What would people say?"

"You stay home, Milly," Anna advised. "There won't be many in Sunday School this morning. I'll walk down. I need the fresh air to wake up."

They all looked up to see Davey and Sarah slowly coming down the stairs. "I want perfect attendance," Davey mumbled.

"Me, too," echoed Sarah.

"All right then," Milly said. "Daddy'll get Ginger hitched up while you grab some breakfast. Hurry up now, so you won't be late."

Crossed Fingers

"Happy birthday," Milly greeted Anna as she came down the stairs on Tuesday.

"How did you know it was my birthday?" Anna asked.

"Inger told me, April 3rd. You had to write it down on your application, and she has the application."

"Thank you, Milly. It's nice to be remembered so early in the morning."

"And after school," Milly continued. "I'll have a coffee cake, and we can invite Inger and Sally and maybe some more."

"Oh Milly, that's too much work for you," Anna remarked. "You are too nice."

"What do you mean too nice and too much work?" Milly asked rhetorically. "Why, we yust have to have some fun sometimes, and how often are you twenty-one years old?"

"Only once, I think," Anna replied. "When is your birthday, Milly?"

"Now, that's a secret," she said.

"No it's not," Davey called out as he came down the stairs. "It's April 21st. Daddy told me so. How old are you, Miss Swenson?"

"Davey! You never ask people their age," said Peter as he came up the stairs from separating the milk.

"That's all right. This year is a big year for me. I am now twenty-one."

"Can I tell the kids at school?" he asked.

"Let's keep my birthday a secret at school," Anna stated rather firmly.

However, this was not to be. When Anna and Davey arrived at school, they found Mabel and Erica had already come, and on the blackboard they had written "Happy Birthday, Miss Swenson."

Anna hardly knew what to say, she was so surprised. "Oh, you girls," she exclaimed as she shook her head.

"And we have another surprise for you," Mabel announced. "After school yesterday, I went over to the Larsons', and Erica and I baked you a coffee cake."

"And we'll have it during lunch time," Erica added.

Anna hurried home from school and felt a warm glow as she thought about the students wishing her a happy birthday and enjoying the coffee cake. And now Milly had planned a little party. She didn't want to be late, as anyone coming for coffee couldn't stay long because there was supper to get.

As she hung her coat up in the entryway, she heard voices and laughter in the kitchen. She tried to guess who might be there. There definitely were three or four people. She could hear Inger, but expected her. And Sally, that definitely was Sally. They were talking about the Pearsons' baby. This morning Victoria told Anna that the baby had been named Gustav Erik, after the two grandfathers. Anna knew that this blessed event was going to be the main topic of conversation for some time. Entering the kitchen she saw Inger, Sally, Sylvia Larson, Thelma Blakeley and Vi seated around the table. "Happy birthday!" they called out as she entered.

"Oh, thank you," she said rather self-consciously. "I didn't know there would be so many of you. This is a real party."

"A real party in the country for a city girl," Vi added, smiling and nodding.

"Well, sit down now, so we can start on the cake and coffee," Milly directed.

"This is the first time I have been to a birthday party," Sally remarked. "And I'm so glad I could come to your party, Anna."

"I'm glad you could come, too," she replied. She looked up as Milly brought the cake to the table. "Oh Milly, the cake looks wonderful."

"It's fodelsekaka, yust like our mother made in Sweden, isn't it, Inger?" Inger nodded. "Yust bread dough with strips made into this design. I tried to get it to be a '21'. Can you see it?" They all peered at the cake and nodded in agreement. "You let it raise and brush with milk. Then sprinkle with sugar and cinnamon." She cut it carefully, put each piece on a plate and passed it around. "Now you have your coffee, so I'll sit down."

"This day has been so special," Anna told them. "All of you probably don't know that Elsa and Mabel baked a coffee cake for school."

"Oh yes, even I know that," Vi remarked. "You can't keep a secret around here."

"How nice of you to come, Vi," Anna said. "I hope you didn't have to walk over."

"Oh no! Elmer wouldn't pass up an excuse to drive that car," she answered. "He brought both of us," she said nodding toward Thelma Blakeley.

"Tom offered to pick us up," Mrs. Blakeley put in, "but Elmer refused to take him up on it."

"Who's minding the store, then?" Anna asked.

"Oh, Ed's doing that," Vi answered." He said he needed a break from working on the house. And that reminds me, I brought something for you, but it's not from me, it's from Sylvia."

"Mrs. Larson?" Anna asked.

"You must call me Sylvia, Anna. And the gift is from our family."

"It was this way," Vi explained. "You see, Anna, they wanted to get you somethin', an' didn't know what to get, so Jonah talked to Ed. Well, Jonah and Ed were gettin' together anyway to talk about each buyin' a sow from Peter. An' they started talkin' about your birthday, an' to make a long story short, Ed told him what he thought you would like."

"That's the way it happened, Anna," Sylvia said. "So here it is, and we hope you like it." She gave Anna a neat parcel wrapped in brown paper and tied with string.

"Be careful!" Vi warned. "It's breakable."

Anna felt the package and guessed what it might be, so she opened it carefully. "Oh, it's beautiful. I love these plates. This is one that Bertha's mother painted, isn't it?"

"Yes it is," Vi stated proudly, as it had been painted by the future mother-in-law of her son. "I had only a couple left, and we thought you'd like the one with pink roses."

"I love it." Anna glowed with excitement and pleasure. "Thank you, Sylvia. Tell the others in your family 'thanks' from me."

"I'm sure Jonah will come down sometime this evening. As Vi said, he wants to buy one of Peter's sows and is going to use that as an excuse." She smiled a knowing mother's smile. "But I know he wants to wish you a happy birthday. And of course, he was the one who talked to Ed about the present."

Vi added, "Ed remembered the china plates you liked so much and bought for Christmas presents, so he thought you would like one, too."

"He was right," Anna said. She held up the plate to examine

the beautiful hand-painted roses. "Here, I'll pass it around so you can all look at it."

"I have one, too," Milly reminded them. "Anna gave it to me for Christmas, and I save it for special occasions. I keep it high up on the shelf where the children can't reach it."

A little after four o'clock they heard a horse and buggy enter the yard. "I suppose that's Floyd," Inger said. "He can probably smell the coffee cake from our place."

"There's plenty of cake, and he's welcome to some," Milly added. "I'm sure Peter will come in with him. He has a good nose for cake, too."

They listened to the heavy footsteps coming into the entryway. Floyd was the first to come into the kitchen. "Well, will you look at you ladies. Why aren't you home gettin' supper for the men folks?"

"Why aren't you home doing the plowing?" Inger asked.

"Well now, I can't do the plowin' when I have two husky young lads around. I no sooner got to the end of the row when there was George. I couldn't let the boy stand around idle, so I told him to take my place. Walter was doin' the plowin', so I let George follow him with the harrow."

"Sounds like a good idea to me," remarked Peter. "I'll be mighty glad when Davey gets old enough to do a little real work."

Davey spoke up, "But you don't have two teams of work-horses like Uncle Floyd has."

"You have a point there, son," his father answered.

"So what have you been doin' since George took over?" Vi asked as she looked him in the eye.

"Well now, that's a good question. I don't believe in idleness, so I did everyone a favor and went to town for the mail," he answered.

"You probably went to get a ride with Liza in her new car," Milly said, laughing.

"Now, Milly!" Floyd shook his head in mock disbelief. "In the first place, I ain't gettin' into no car. An' the day I get into a car with that woman will mean I should have my head examined."

"Then I think you went in to hear all the gossip," Milly asserted.

"Nope! I simply went in and got the mail. O' course, knowin'

Liza, it did take me a mite longer than I had intended, but here I am, and here's the mail. Let's see. Here's for Larsons." He handed a couple of letters to Sylvia. "Hope those ain't bills, Sylvia."

"If they are, they go right to Olle," she answered jovially as she took them from him.

"Nothin' fer you, Sally, an' nothin' fer you, either, Vi. Guess Elmer beat me to it." He shuffled through the mail quite slowly. "Now let's see, oh, these are for our place, an' here's a paper an' a coupla things fer you, Milly."

"Thank you, Floyd, so nice to have home delivery. I guess you can have a piece of cake now."

"Just a darn minute. I'm not through yet."

"Well, take your time," Inger said with a tinge of sarcasm. "We've already eaten our cake."

"I've been lookin' through this, an' here's a coupla more things. Here's a pretty birthday postcard. Since it's your birthday, it must be for you, Anna. That right, it says Miss Anna Swenson," he read as he turned over the card. He handed it to her. "Liza said it's been sittin' there since yesterday, but nobody bothered to get the mail then. So you see, I was doin' you a great favor."

"Thanks, Floyd. Oh! Elsa always buys the cutest cards. You should have seen the one she sent me for Valentine's Day." Anna glanced over the written part and continued smiling.

"Now here's another one for Miss Anna Swenson. Gol durn, but you do have more than your share of mail. This one's a letter, so I can't tell you ladies what it says. Oh, I do see that it's from your mother. Well, here you are, Anna."

Anna was a bit apprehensive about this letter. Her mother had been annoyed with Anna's attitude about staying on in Grabney for another year. She could almost feel her mother's animosity through the envelope. "Thanks, Floyd."

"Well, aintcha gonna read it?"

"Not now, it's probably too long. I'll read it later."

"I guess you've been waitin' fer this one. I mighta' known." He held out a postcard that had a photo on one side. "Lemme see if I can read it. Oh yes, it's a postcard for our little school teacher, and will ya look at the pitchur on the front. My, but here's a fella with a fancy new car. I think you've been holdin' out on us, Anna. Le'see what it says. 'Dear Teacher Anna Swenson.'"

"Floyd!" Inger said rather vehemently and gave him a look that would have wilted a cornstalk at fifty paces. "Give that to Anna!"

"Now Mother," Floyd pleaded. "Can't a guy have a little fun?" Sally rushed over to Floyd and took the card before he could give it to Anna.

"Oh Anna!" she yelled excitedly. "It's from Richard. Oh, look at the picture. It's Richard, an' he's standin' by a new car. Oh, it must be his. Ain't he handsome though. Can I read it?"

Anna was startled. This was the card she and Jim Wilson had been waiting for. She hesitated and then looked up to see how proud Sally was. "Oh, sure Sally. Go ahead and read it."

Sally read:

Dear Teacher Anna Swenson,

We're doing fine out here. Sunshine every day. We sure hit pay dirt. Look at my new Ford Model T Coupe. And your still stuck in the country.

Richard

"Oh Anna, jus' look at this picture." Sally held it up for everyone to see. "Here Anna, you take it." She passed the card across the table to Anna. "I think he really likes you."

Floyd looked over Anna's shoulder at the card. "Well, I don't see no X's on it. That stands for kisses, I been told."

Anna didn't know what to say. Thoughts raced through her mind. She wanted to be very casual about it. While Richard didn't mean anything to her, he might definitely mean something to Jim Wilson. And what would Sylvia think? The last thing Anna wanted was for Jonah to feel that she was interested in Richard. And here was his mother sitting next to her and who had given her this lovely plate. "Oh, here Sally, pass it around. He must be joking," she said.

"Oh, I don't think so," Sally answered. "He always did have an eye out for pretty girls."

Everyone was more interested in the picture than what was written on the front of the card. "That's a pretty fancy car," Peter said with admiration. "That must have set him back some."

"Matt said Fords cost six hundred dollars," Vi informed them. "Our Chev cost more." She glanced at the photo again. "This one has just one seat, not really a family car. But look, it's all enclosed with a hard top and real glass windows. That'd sure help in the winter time."

"C'mon, Floyd, let's us get on home," Inger said as she rose from the table.

"What's yer hurry? I didn't even get a piece of cake."

"Here you are," Milly said as she handed him a piece on a plate. "Peter, you sit down too. Here's your cake. Inger, can you get them some coffee?"

"For a man who was complaining that I wasn't home to get dinner, he seems mighty slow about leaving."

"Oh Anna," Sally said. "Can I take the card home and show Charley 'n Bill?"

Anna hadn't counted on this. She hoped that when she got the card she could put it in a safe place until she could get it to the sheriff. She saw how anxious Sally was to show the men the photo of her brother and how successful he had been. "I guess so, Sally, as long as you don't lose it. Here, let me look at it first." The card was passed to her. She turned it over to look at the postmark, Burbank California.

Sally noticed this. "Oh, you wanna read it yerself. Well, I thought so."

"Oh no, Sally. That's all right. Here you take it. I'll get it back later." Then Anna had another thought. "If Jonah's coming over tonight to talk to Peter, maybe he'll walk me to your place and I can get it back then."

"He'd be happy to do that," Sylvia turned to her and added rather quietly, "And I know he's anxious to get over here tonight, and not just for the sow, either."

"Sally, we'll give you a ride home," Inger said as she put on her coat. "C'mon, Dad. Let's get a move on." With Floyd still complaining about not getting enough cake, the three of them left.

As they went down the back steps, Elmer was heard to drive into the yard. He offered Sylvia a ride home, and she took him up on it. "I've yet to ride in a Chev," she said. "And what with so many folks getting cars, William is fit to be tied. Just wait until I tell him I've ridden with you."

"Is Olle planning to buy a car?" Peter asked.

"That'll be the day," Sylvia exclaimed. "He and Floyd were cut out of the same piece of cloth."

Peter shut the door after them. “Did you hear that, Mother? Jonah wants to buy one of my sows, too. That’ll leave me with only four, and that’s about right. With the money I make on the sales, I can probably pay for a lot of the feed.”

“That’s good, Peter,” Milly sighed. “I’ve been a little worried about it.”

“Now don’t you worry. And I’ve been thinking that if a Ford costs six hundred dollars, we could probably swing it if I get good prices this fall. It all depends.”

“Oh, Peter! But as you say, it all depends. Oh, I’ll keep my fingers crossed. And I’m still saving the money Anna pays me. That’s twenty-five dollars a month.”

“That’s your money, Milly, and we won’t touch that,” he replied. “It’s for you to spend as you want.”

“Well, if I want to spend it on pig feed, then I will.” She was most emphatic about this as she cleared the table. “Or maybe I’ll choose to spend it on a car.”

Chapter Twenty-nine

"You're sure you want to buy this sow?" Peter asked Jonah as they sat at the kitchen table. It was after supper, and Milly and Anna were doing the dishes.

"Never more sure," Jonah confirmed.

"Well, that really helps me out," Peter continued. "And you can have your choice. I was foolish to breed so many. Somehow six hogs didn't look like too many last fall. Then when I got to thinking about six sows each having a litter of ten to twelve, well," and he shook his head, "I knew that I had bitten off more than I could chew. But with you and Ed each taking one off my hands, that leaves me with four, and that's about right."

"I'm sorry I can't take it now, and neither can Ed," Jonah replied. "I know Ed's building his pen as fast as he can, plus fixing up the house."

"That's no problem. Let them farrow first and get a start, and then we can move them. Little pigs don't take up too much room."

"As soon as the planting's done, Will and Dad will build the pens. We thought we would set mine up on old Bill Evans' place. I guess it's my place now, or it's really Dad's place until I get him paid back. Anyway, Bill sold off much of his stock. The rest Dad bought from Grace and took them over to our place, because his pens really needed working over. Anyway, it's right across the road from you, so it shouldn't be a problem to move them."

I expect the sows to farrow any day now, so maybe you can see them before you leave."

"Sounds good to me," Jonah said as he pushed his chair back and stood up. "Let's see. Anna, are you ready to go up to the Wheeler's?"

"I think so," she answered as she took off her apron. "Milly and I have about finished."

"You go on now, Anna," Milly told her. "There's nothing left but a few pots and pans."

"Thanks, Milly. I am anxious to get that postcard. I don't know why I let Sally take it, except she was so proud of Richard, seeing him all dressed up and with his new car."

"Of course," Milly said. "And I'm sure she won't lose it. You can get it and show it to Jim Wilson. Oh, dear! What have I said?"

"That's all right, Milly. I'll explain everything to Jonah as we walk up there."

It was a pleasant spring evening with just enough light to enable them to see where they were going. "Oh, Jonah! There is so much to explain to you."

"I guess a lot has happened since I went back to school."

"I hardly know where to begin," she continued.

"Just start from what I know. I know the money was taken."

"It's even before that. Remember when we found Mrs. Wheeler, we saw that the fingers on her right hand were crossed."

"Yes."

"I kept worrying about that. I talked to Reverend Blakeley about it and even went into town and talked to Jim Wilson. One day, Sally got a postcard from her father."

"That's interesting," he commented.

Anna continued to explain the postcard from Sally's father and Richard's name sign of crossed fingers. "Then I went to talk to Jim Wilson and explained it to him. He said we should at least talk to Richard. He asked me if I knew where Richard was, and I said I knew that he was planning to go to California. I looked at the postcard and saw that it was mailed from Burbank, California."

"California's a big state, and Burbank's probably a big city," Jonah commented. "It's interesting that he sent the card to you instead of Sally." He looked at her and smiled. " But then I can see he knows a good thing when he sees it."

Anna blushed slightly. "Oh, it was nothing like that. I had met him at the Wheeler's when Sally invited me over. Then the next day, that was Friday, he walked over to the schoolhouse when he was on his way to the train."

"That was a bit of a detour," Jonah joked.

"Oh, he was only being friendly. I had just gotten out of school, and he asked if he could walk with me. I think he was so filled up with his plans that he wanted someone to talk to. He was bragging how he and his friend Frank were going to go out to California and make a lot of money. He asked if he could send me a postcard, and of course I told him he could. Jim said that if I got one, I should bring it to him. And this card even has a picture of him on it. Jim said he didn't know Richard very well, so this will let him see what he looks like."

"Were you planning to take the card to him yourself?" Jonah asked. "How were you going to do it? Today's Tuesday, and you have school until Friday."

I know," she answered. "I have been so flustered with this today that I haven't thought it through. If Reverend Blakeley is going to the county seat, he could take it."

"Well, we'll figure that out later. It looks like Richard did make a lot of money. Mother said he had some flashy new clothes and a new car."

"Oh yes, I was so embarrassed about that. Floyd made such a big thing of it, handing me the mail from my mother and sister for my birthday and saving this one until last."

"That sounds just like Floyd." Jonah paused and smiled to himself. "When did Richard take the train back? I remember he didn't stay for Saturday when we got the ice."

"He said he was going to get the 5:10, but I'm not sure he did. You see, I saw him heading for the train a little after four on Friday. But it was snowing, and I went right home. I really never saw him go beyond the crossroads by your place."

"But I came in on the 5:10," Jonah remarked. "And I don't remember anyone getting on the train."

"It was snowing hard," Anna added. "And you were probably looking for William and wouldn't have noticed someone waiting to get on."

"Oh, no. I can say for sure that he didn't get on that train, because they only open one door, and anyone wanting to get on is waiting for people to get off. The train hardly stopped at all."

"Jim Wilson thinks he didn't get on the train," Anna continued. "But I keep thinking he must have gotten the train. If he didn't, then where did he stay Friday night, and why didn't we see him on Saturday? It doesn't make sense to me. Anyway, Jim wants to question him because he was around here about the time Mrs. Wheeler died. He may have seen somebody we missed."

"And he thinks he may know something about the money?" Jonah asked.

"Maybe. I don't know. But there are other things, too."

"Like what?" Jonah asked.

"Well, Anders told me that someone stayed in the schoolhouse sometime that weekend. Jim said it could have been someone passing through, or it could have been someone who took the money and was hiding out. Matt said he saw two men sometime the week before she died. He didn't know where they went to but never saw them again. He guessed they rode in on the train and probably had something lined up. It could have been the Wheeler money that they had in mind. Anyway, this is just speculation. Jim has tried to trace them down, but no luck there. You remember on that Saturday Bill had spent a long time chasing his pigs back into the pens because the gate was left open."

"I remember Bill was madder'n all get out."

"Jim thinks it's possible that someone could have been watching the house. That person would see Sally and Charley leave and Bill chasing the pigs, so he would have had time to get in and take the money."

"Or it's possible that whoever it was could have seen Charley and Sally leave and realized that if the gate were left open, Bill would have to chase the pigs, and there would be no one in the house except Mrs. Wheeler," Jonah continued.

"And if it were the two that Matt saw, they could have stayed in the schoolhouse until the coast was clear."

"Now he needs to figure out who it was," Jonah added.

"And since Richard was around here the day before, at least, he'd like to talk to him."

"And you think that the crossed fingers means that Mrs. Wheeler was giving a clue before she died," Jonah said thoughtfully.

"Or worse than that. Oh, how can I say it? Jim thinks she may have not died a natural death."

Jonah stopped and took her gloved hand in his. "Oh Anna, you have had so much on your mind. Why didn't you tell me about this sooner?"

She looked up at him. "I didn't want to tell you before the dance. That would have spoiled our fun. Anyway, as I said before, it's just speculation."

"A very alarming speculation," Jonah said thoughtfully. "And it's been a big worry to you. And now it looks as if Richard has come into a lot of money."

"But he could have gotten a really good job in California," Anna protested.

"That's possible. If that's the case, maybe I'll go there myself!" He laughed.

"Oh Jonah, how can you say that?"

"It might beat milking cows at 5:30 in the morning and chasing pigs. Anyway, this sounds very interesting. What a dull life I have at school, compared to that of a country school teacher!" They both laughed as they turned in to the Wheeler place.

They went into the back porch entry and knocked on the kitchen door. Charley opened it. "Oh, Jonah and Anna. Come on in."

Sally was finishing the supper dishes. The postcard was on the table. "I'll be through in a minute. Just let me get my hands dry and my apron off. Anna, show Jonah the card from Richard. Ain't it somethin'?"

Anna picked up the card from the table and handed it to Jonah. "Looks like your brother is doing all right for himself," Jonah commented. "That's a pretty snazzy car he has. And look at the new clothes. You can sure be proud of him."

"I knew he'd do all right for hisself," Sally said. "He's always done okay."

"He sure has some fancy clothes," Charley said as he examined the card with Jonah. "Look a' that new hat. He sure looks like some city guy. He's got a suit on, an' a vest. An' look! He's got a watch chain. He must have a pocket watch."

"Oh Anna, he looks like some of the pictures in that magazine you had. An' to think he could even buy a pocket watch. Won't Pa be proud of him? Ma always said that Richard would make good."

"It looks like he has," Anna said half-heartedly, as she wondered about the gold watch. Then she thought that of course any well-dressed young man would have a pocket watch.

"An' Jonah, I'll bet yer jealous with Richard writin' to Anna,"

Sally teased.

"Anna's pretty popular," Jonah said. "He knows a pretty girl when he sees one." He smiled at Anna and put his arm around her, then noticed her worried expression.

"Oh Jonah, I think we better go." Anna put the card in her coat pocket. "I still have schoolwork to do for tomorrow."

"Oh sure, Anna," he replied. "I'd better get home myself. Tomorrow's another workday for me, too, and what about you, Charley and Bill? Don't suppose you'll be sleeping in."

"Nope!" Bill answered. "Me'n Charley gotta get the plowin' done. Plenty a work."

Jonah opened the back door and ushered Anna through it. "So long, then."

"I wish you coulda stayed longer, but we all gotta get up early," Sally called after them. "Be sure an' save the postcard, Anna."

"I will," she called back.

They were quiet as they walked to the road. Jonah looked at Anna. "Something else is bothering you, isn't it, Anna? I could tell you were bothered about something. What is it?"

"It was the mention of the pocket watch. You see, when Charley and Sally cleaned up Mrs. Wheeler's room, they noticed that Mr. Wheeler's gold pocket watch was missing. It had always sat on her dresser. They looked everywhere for it. We hadn't noticed that it was gone when Mrs. Wheeler had her stroke or when the money was taken. We were too upset about those things.

"Yes, I can understand that," he said. "I also think you'll worry all week about getting the postcard to Jim, so here's what I suggest. I know that Elmer's going into the county seat tomorrow. Give me the card, and I'll ride over to the store tonight and give it to him. He can take it to Jim in the morning."

"Oh that would be so nice of you," Anna sighed. "And the card may mean nothing, but I promised it to him."

"And maybe now you can get it off your mind and leave the worrying to him."

"I hope so," she answered. "Anyway, let's talk about something pleasant. Maybe tomorrow your sow will have a litter of little piglets." She laughed at the thought. "Peter says they're all ready to farrow, so it could be any time. Just imagine dozens of little squeaking pigs. That's what he'll have on his hands. I'm dying to see them. I've never seen anything like that before."

"I just hope I don't get some cantankerous old sow, one that decides that motherhood isn't for her. I've known of some that kill their pigs as soon as they're born."

"That's why it's good that Peter'll keep them until they farrow. That way, mother and children should be settled down by that time." They both laughed at the thought.

When they arrived at the Jensen back steps, Anna reached into her pocket and gave the card to Jonah. "I won't come in, Anna," he said. "I'd better get on home so I can get this to Elmer before they go to bed."

"Oh, Jonah. I didn't thank you for that beautiful plate. It's the nicest present I could have gotten."

"I'm glad you like it," he replied. "I wanted something special, because Anna, you are special to me." They realized they were both special to each other. It was several minutes before she went into the entryway to take off her coat.

On Saturday the first sow had her litter, followed by the second sow. George came down to continue with the harrowing while Peter kept an eye on his livestock.

"I can't believe that George is old enough to take a team out and do a man's work," Anna remarked. "It must take some skill to get the rows even and make sure he doesn't miss a part."

"Oh, George is very bright and dependable," Milly proudly explained. "And when you're born on a farm, you learn from an early age. I'm glad he doesn't have to do the plowing. That's the tough part, digging up the ground from last year. When you look at it, it's a real mess with the cornstalk roots and weeds, but he could do that, too, if he had to. With the disk harrow, you sort of smooth it out. He'll probably be down here helping Peter all next week during the spring planting vacation. Inger and Floyd are very good about helping us out. Peter's a little behind, but he'll get it all done. He always does."

"It's good the days are longer now," Anna remarked. "I've noticed that the men work until the last bit of daylight is gone."

"Yes, we often have supper after seven o'clock. I'll be glad when Davey can do the milking. I try to do it now. If I do the morning milking, then Peter can get out working at daylight, and in the evening Davey can watch Lucy. But if we lived in Sweden, that's where the women do all the milking. I think I told you that before. Oh my, but I'm glad to be in America."

"Milly!" Anna exclaimed. "I had no idea you were planning to get up to milk. I'll get up early, too. I can at least do the separating and get breakfast on."

"Now, Anna. I don't have you here to work. This is what I usually do this time of year. I must admit that my hands get a little out of shape, and the first few times I do it, my fingers really ache."

"Of course I will help," Anna insisted. "And I can help with the supper while you do the evening milking. I can also separate the milk then. Just don't ask me to milk the cows." She laughed. "I know I would be terrible at that, but I can at least turn a separator, and I'll wash and scald it, too."

"You make me laugh, Anna. Oh dear! What would your mother think?"

"She probably knows by now that I am going to do what I want, anyway."

Milly smiled. "Well, you now know what life on a farm is like. And I don't think Peter will be through with the planting next week. It's a big yob."

"Does the week off from school really help get the corn planted?" Anna asked.

"Oh yes, it does help," Milly answered. "But it's not yust the planting done then. People are still getting the soil ready to be planted, and that's a bigger yob than planting. This time of year there's always too much work. And don't forget all the sows and their litters, and then there are always calves coming. We'll have a lot more milk when we have two more fresh cows. Many fathers would like their boys to stay home a month or so. And then some of them yust keep them home to work. And if the boys don't want to go on to high school, then there's an extra hand to help on the farm."

"When I'm bigger, I'm going to stay home and work," announced Davey.

"Oh you!" scolded his mother. "You will do no such thing."

"Davey, I think it's time that you took Sarah and me out to look at the pigs," Anna suggested. "How about that?"

"That's a good idea," Milly admitted. "Now, bundle up good.

It's not too warm outside."

"Wait for me!" yelled Sarah. "I wanna come, too."

"We won't leave until you're ready to go," Anna told her. "And maybe you can even name some of the pigs. That should be fun."

Saturday evening, Anna had supper at the Larsons'. It wasn't the grand affair that the first supper had been, because everyone had spent the day working, Erica helping the men and Sylvia preparing meals.

After church on Sunday, Anna hurried to the station to see Jonah off for school. William had driven him in and tactfully returned home so they were alone on the platform. It was a sad good-bye. As the train pulled out, Anna continued waving to him until he was out of sight. He hung out of the open door and waved back at her. She could see his figure grow smaller and smaller until he and the waving arm disappeared. They had promised to write each other. Anna felt lost and lonely and decided to walk home. She had no desire to go back where people were still bustling into cars and buggies, talking and talking and talking. She wondered when she would receive her first letter from him. Now she had two things on her mind: hearing from the sheriff and receiving a letter from Jonah.

Chapter Thirty

"One more day with the harrow, and I'll be ready to start planting tomorrow," Peter announced at breakfast Monday morning. "And before the end of the day I'll have your garden all ready for you, Milly."

"Oh Peter, that will be so good. I was hoping I could get the peas planted this week. With Davey home, I can do that tomorrow. Today is wash day, but at least now that the weather is nice I can hang the clothes out without their becoming stiff as a board."

"I always wondered why you went out in the cold to hang out your clothes when you could hang them up in the basement," Anna asked.

"Well, even though they freeze they come in smelling so sweet," Milly answered. "Of course I have to put them over a rack in the kitchen to thaw them out and get them really dry. But then the whole kitchen has the sweet smell of the outdoors. I hang them in the basement only when it snows."

"Do I have to still wear long underwear?" asked Davey. "I think it's warm enough now."

"If you think you'll be warm enough, then you can take it off," his mother told him. "But I don't want you catching cold. It may be spring, but Easter is late this year, so it's a little colder now than other years. Finish your breakfast before you go up to change. And Davey, I have another yob for you. Since you're staying home, I need potatoes peeled and grated for starch. I'm almost out of it."

"Oh no!" he groaned. "I thought I could help Daddy on the planter."

"The mechanical planter doesn't need two people, so you can stay home and help me. Once we get the potatoes on the stove, you can watch Lucy while I do the wash."

"I can't believe how much machinery you need to run a farm," Anna said to Peter as he buttered a stack of pancakes. "I was looking out the window the other day and I realized your machine shed was quite big."

"Yes, it costs a lot of money to buy equipment, and I still owe on some of it, especially the disk harrow and the planter, which are the newest pieces. But let's hope for a good crop."

"Yes, that's always the worry," Milly said. "Worry and worry about having a good crop, and prices being good for the hogs and having enough to feed them. Oh, my goodness!"

"Well, we haven't done so bad here," Peter spoke up.

"Oh, I know we've done very good. I yust keep remembering all the hard times in Sweden. Oh, I hope that it never happens here."

"We'll take it a year at a time, Milly. And with this new planter I've saved a lot of time."

"How does the planter work?" Anna asked.

"Well, you can come and watch some time after school once I get going, but it's pretty simple. It plants two rows at a time. There's a box full of kernels on each side of the planter. As the wheels go around, they turn a shaft, which goes from each box. There are plates that have notches in them, and with the turning a kernel is dropped through a tube into the ground. The wheels also cover the kernels that drop into the ground. It has to be done carefully to make sure the rows are cross-cultivated. That way they can be weeded by going in either direction. But remember, I don't plant all the land in corn. I leave a good part of it for hay. Cattle also need hay, and you can't make ends meet it you don't have enough hay."

"Things grow so well here. I can see the fruit trees are ready to bloom," Anna mentioned.

"Yes, and I'm thinking of starting a hive of honeybees," Peter said.

"Oi, yoi, yoi!" Milly exclaimed waving her hands in front of her. "I don't want anything to do with bees. If we get them, Peter, you'll have to take care of them, and I think you have too much already."

"Is it time to go to school?" Sarah asked.

Anna looked at her wristwatch. "Yes, Sarah, it is. We've been talking too much, I can see. So let's get going. We want to be a little early today, because it's the first day of vacation school. Don't forget your lunch pail, Sarah."

Anna could have taken the week off and gone to Fort Dodge, but she knew she would only be under her mother's thumb. Besides she enjoyed having the younger brothers and sisters come to school, and she wanted to be of some help to the families if she could. Most of the women wanted to get their gardens started. Anna also realized that she really liked farm life. She enjoyed being a part of the community. She felt needed and respected, and she liked the people here. Perhaps this was the main reason she stayed.

As they walked up the road, they met Mabel. Her mother thought that she was needed more at school than at home, since all the children would be young ones. Mabel also liked working with children. Inger hoped that Anna's good influence would rub off on her daughter so that some day she would be a teacher. "Erica's coming a little later. She's going to help her mother with the washing so Mrs. Larson can have time to get started on her garden."

"I'll be glad to have her," Anna said. "And I see you brought a bag full of toys just like you did last fall."

Walter had lit the fire in the room, so it was pleasantly warm. Anna expected the same children that she had in the fall during harvest. Soon Lars brought his sisters Elsa and Birgit, their lovely straw-colored hair braided and tied with ribbons. Anna knew most of them from Sunday School, although they were not all in her class. Some were still in the nursery. She had a total of five girls and four boys. She began the day by playing the organ and teaching them songs. Erica arrived mid-morning, and the girls played games with them. The children loved the lunch hour, eating lunch out of a lunch pail just like regular students. At the end of the day, someone came for each child. It was to be the procedure for the rest of the week.

On Thursday William had ridden to town and brought Anna a letter from Jonah. It was laying on the table when she came home. She felt her heart jump. She had written him on Monday telling him about the spring vacation school, but this was too soon to get a reply from that letter.

"Aren't you going to read it?" Davey asked.

"Davey! That's her letter," his mother told him. "You don't ask people to read their mail to you."

"Why?"

"Never mind. You yust don't." With this, Milly signaled to him that he was to be quiet.

"Oh Davey," Anna said. "Jonah says that school is going fine. He wishes he were home here with us when there is so much to do, but he will come back as soon as school is out. That will be in about six weeks."

"How come he didn't write to me?" he asked.

"Well," Anna answered. "I wrote him a letter. Perhaps if you were to write to him, then he'd write you a letter back."

"Oh, is that the way it works? Anyway, I'm gonna go and look at the pigs. We got lots more now," and he dashed out the kitchen door.

"William also brought my order from Sears for Easter clothes," Milly said. "I made a new dress for Sarah and a shirt for Davey, and of course Lucy can wear Sarah's hand-me-down good dress, but I got shoes for Sarah and a cute new straw hat."

"Can I try them on?" Sarah asked eagerly.

"Of course," Milly replied. "Yust take off your coat and hang it up and come back, and we'll see if the things fit."

"I know that we had a Palm Sunday service last Sunday, but Easter seems to have crept up on me," Anna said. "I'll have to think of something to wear. Do the ladies all dress up for Easter?"

"Oh my, yes," Milly replied. "It's quite a big occasion. You see new hats and dresses. Of course it's too cold to go without a coat, but those who have new dresses usually manage to have their coats unbuttoned so everyone can see what they are wearing."

"I guess I can manage with what I have," Anna remarked. "But I'll have to see if my summer hat fits with my hair cut short. I guess I'll go upstairs and take a look at my wardrobe." She gathered her things together and was happy to get to her room and read Jonah's letter over and over. As she put it down, she thought about Richard's postcard. She knew that Elmer had delivered it to Jim Wilson, and she wondered when she would hear from him. It had been over a week now. Perhaps he couldn't reach anyone in California who would have seen Richard. Well, it was just as well to forget about it for now. Perhaps this was a wild goose chase, as

Peter had said. Best to think about tomorrow. That was when Sally was bringing over the cookies she had baked.

The last day of the week was a huge success. Anna had boiled a dozen eggs and after lunch let the children draw on them with colored crayons. After this, Sally came and they had their party. The children entertained Sally with songs and very short recitations.

Before they left for home, Sarah carefully put her egg in her lunch pail. Then as they walked Sarah swung her pail back and forth and heard the egg bouncing around. "Oh Sarah! Be careful," Anna warmed. "You could break your egg."

"No I can't," she answered. "It's hard boiled." Nevertheless when she took it out to show her mother, to her surprise she found that the shell was cracked and broken. She couldn't believe it. Her lips quivered with disappointment.

"Never mind," Milly consoled her. "We'll have lots of eggs to color tomorrow. You can eat this one now, and tomorrow you can make one just like it to show us." Fortunately the child was pacified and slowly nibbled away at the egg.

"I have a favor to ask of you, Anna," Milly said. Then she turned to Sarah. "Sarah, leave the rest of your egg on the table, and go up and change your clothes." They waited while Sarah did as she was told. "I have a little shopping to do, so could you watch the children?"

"Of course, Milly. Are you going to walk to town?"

"Yes, of course. I don't want to bother to hitch up Ginger or Belle. It's a nice enough day, and I love to walk when the weather is like this." She looked around to see that the children were not within earshot. "You see, I have to pick up some Easter things. Vi gets a lot of things in and well, you know, things for the Easter bunny to leave for the children."

"Of course," Anna nodded. "You go right ahead. I'll be happy to play with them. And, oh, I just had a thought. Could you buy some white paper for me? I thought I could weave some Easter baskets. It ought to be fun, and I'll need some candy to go in them."

"Any special kind of candy?"

"Just Easter candy," Anna replied. "You get what you think is best."

"This is one time I like to go and have no children around to bother me," Milly said. "Sometimes I have Mabel come down and play with the children, but I know she's busy at home."

"Off you go then, Milly. And will you check to see if there is any mail for me?"

After supper on Saturday, Milly put on a couple of dozen eggs to boil. She had selected the whitest eggs she could find. With Rhode Island Reds, the colors ranged from light tan to almost brown. She had also bought a package of dye. The children were very excited and were most anxious for the egg coloring to begin. Milly had put an old oilcloth on the table in case the dye spilled over. Cups held the different colors.

"Why are you putting vinegar in the cups?" Davey asked.

"If you don't put vinegar in, the dye doesn't stick to the egg. Now let me show you that you can take a little candle and with it draw a design on the egg, and when you color it, the egg will still have that design." She demonstrated this and was rewarded with excited remarks.

"I want to do a design with a colored crayon like I did at school," Sarah told them as she reached for the crayons.

"Lucy's going to spill the blue dye!" Davey yelled out as Anna grabbed the cup and put it out of her way.

"We'll put Lucy in her high chair and give her an egg," Milly decided. Then she can do what she wants with it."

"Don't eat all the eggs tonight!" Peter called over to them from where he was sitting at the far end of the table reading his paper.

"You're not supposed to eat them tonight. You're supposed to save them for tomorrow," Davey announced.

Milly stopped what she was doing and listened. "That's a car I hear coming into the yard. Who could be coming to visit tonight?"

"If you hear a car, it's sure not Floyd," Peter replied as he got up from the table and went to the door. "I'll go see who it is."

Soon they could hear two male voices out in the yard, then footsteps up to the porch. "Look who I found," Peter said as he ushered Jim Wilson into the kitchen.

"I see I'm just in time to color Easter eggs," Jim remarked. "Looks like you have a going concern here."

"Oh Yim," Milly said. "Come in and sit down. Let me get

you some coffee." She bustled over to the stove to pour him a cup.

"I'd appreciate that," he answered.

"Let me give you some supper, too. You probably haven't had anything to eat."

"Well, I haven't, but I know supper will be waiting for me at home. This'll hold me over 'till then."

"Here's the coffee. Cream and sugar are on the counter. Help yourself. I'll get the cookies."

"This is just fine," he said as he stood at the counter, stirring a spoonful of sugar into his coffee. He then poured the cream, stirred again and went to the far end of the table to sit near Peter. Milly put out the tin of cookies, and he hungrily helped himself.

Anna felt her heart thump when she first heard his name. Could he be bringing news of Richard? If not, why would he have come? She watched his casual demeanor and became less agitated.

"I hope I'm not intruding on your Easter preparations," he said. "Gosh, but it's been a long time since I had little ones around the table coloring eggs. The wife still likes to do it, so I suppose when I get back she'll have the table set up much like this. We've just one at home: Elsie. She's a senior in high school. The two others have grown and gone." He drained his cup of coffee and was munching on a cookie when he looked up. "Oh, Anna! It's you I really came to see."

She looked at him with apprehension.

"Oh, nothing to worry about," he explained. "You'll be interested in what I found out. Milly and Peter, you can hear this too. It's nothing confidential. I knew Anna was worried about this whole matter, so I thought since I was out not far from here, I'd stop in." He reached into his pocket and pulled out a telegram. "As you know, Elmer brought me the picture of Richard, and the postmark was Burbank, California. I knew I had to get right on it, because these young fellows often move around from job to job. So I sent a wire to the sheriff in that county that very day. Let's see, that was a week ago Wednesday, wasn't it."

"Yes," Anna said. She felt somewhat relieved as he continued.

"Well I was expecting to hear from him, but no word came until today. Here's the telegram I received. It says:

LOCATED RICHARD GRISWOLD AND PARTNER STOP DEPUTY WILL INTERVIEW THEM MONDAY STOP WILL WIRE RESULTS STOP

"So, you see," Jim continued, "the postcard did do some good, and on Monday the deputy can find out what Richard knows. He may have seen these two other guys that Matt saw, or he may have some other information. Anyway, that's as much as I know, and I knew that you, Anna, would be anxious to hear. Thanks so much for getting the card to me when you did. So now I guess I'd better get going. It'll be another half hour before I'm home." He got up from the table and walked to the door. Peter went with him. "So Anna, I'll let you know what the sheriff in Burbank says. Maybe we can get this settled sooner that we thought."

Chapter Thirty-one

The children were up early on Easter Sunday to hunt for the baskets that the Easter bunny had left them. Anna heard them in the kitchen and peeked through the register to see Sarah still in her nightgown. She quickly splashed cold water on her face, put on some clothes and brushed through her hair, grateful that it was short. Then she hurried downstairs. She didn't want to miss out on all the excitement.

"I can read what the Easter bunny wrote this year," Davey declared.

"I can't," Sarah whined. "Can somebody help me?"

"I'll help you, Sarah," Anna volunteered. "Now, how do we start?"

"There are little papers on the table with our name on them," Davey informed her. "You read what is on the paper and then do what it says."

"All right," Anna said. "Now Sarah, where is your paper?"

"Here it is. And I can read my name. It says S-A-R-A-H, that's my name. Now what do I do?"

By this time Davey was off on his first clue.

Anna read the instructions. "It says, 'Look in the icebox.'" In an instant Sarah was out on the porch.

"I don't know where in the icebox."

"Keep looking," said her mother. "There must be another note somewhere. The Easter bunny always knows what he is doing."

"Oh, I found it." She ran back to Anna. "Now what does this one say?"

Anna read, "It says, 'Look under your bed.'"

Quickly Sarah ran upstairs and soon came down with another note. "What does this note say, Miss Swenson?"

By this time Davey had found his Easter basket. He came into the kitchen carrying it. It was a pretty basket woven out of reeds, with dried grass made into a little nest in the bottom. On top of the grass were many candy Easter eggs. "Oh, look what I got!"

"Oh hurry, Miss Swenson, what does this note say?" Sarah handed Anna the third note.

Anna told her, "It says, 'Look on the table in the parlor.'"

Sarah ran to the parlor door, opened it and hurried into the room to claim her basket. She came running out, proudly showing it to everyone.

"Now, don't eat too many of the eggs," cautioned their mother. "Hurry upstairs now and get dressed. We have to have breakfast, and then we're all going to Sunday School and church."

"Didn't the Easter bunny leave Lucy a basket?" Sarah asked.

"Why yes, of course," Milly answered. "It's on the table. Oh dear! Lucy, let's not eat all the candy now." Milly was quick to retrieve the basket and the remaining contents.

Easter breakfast was a special meal with various Swedish coffee cakes and plenty of hard boiled eggs. "In the old country we always ate so many eggs on Easter," Milly declared. "So you may eat as many as you like, but yust don't eat so many that you get sick." Afterwards, everyone dressed in their Easter best. Milly, Anna, Davey and Sarah took the buggy to Sunday School. Peter said he would walk to church carrying Lucy, since the weather was pleasant and sunny.

"I see everyone is wearing Easter bonnets," Reverend Blakeley said as he greeted them at the door. "Well, it's a lovely morning and just right for spring finery."

"I have a new hat and new shoes," Sarah said as she proudly displayed them.

"So you do," he answered. "And they are very nice, too."

"Come on, Sarah," Milly said. "Let's get down to Sunday School. Don't hold up everyone."

Anna had made a small woven basket filled with candy Easter eggs for each student. She looked around her as she put her class materials on the table. Seeing all the children in spring clothes seemed to push the winter out of sight. Even the room felt warmer. Perhaps she could play the piano without her gloves.

Peter came downstairs with Lucy at the end of Sunday School.

Mabel and Erica had put heavy quilts on the floor so the children could sit and listen to a story. It was a crowded nursery as the entire community had come to church. Inger had brought Victoria Pearson, and she stayed to help along with Annie Lindquist and Edna Reed. Next year, Anna thought, these girls might have to take over the nursery as Mabel and Erica will be staying in the county seat for high school.

Every seat was filled in church. Benches had been brought up from downstairs for the overflow crowd. As usual, Anna was seated in the back of the room. As she looked at the congregation she could see the heads of women in their Easter hats alternating with those of hatless men. This was a day when nearly everyone attended church. She wished Jonah could have been there. Winter and the cold were behind them. This was spring and a fresh beginning to a new season. Everything seemed all right with the world. There was Floyd sitting a few rows in front of her.

She got a glimpse of Sally and Charley. Hopefully this would be the beginning of better times for them. The sheriff in California had located Richard, and if anything were amiss he should have known about it, but she couldn't allow herself to think of problems like this when the day was so beautiful and she was sitting in church surrounded by friends.

Easter dinner was at the Parkers'. The kitchen was crowded to overflowing as Inger had invited Sally and the boys. Floyd and Walter had made an extra table out of planks on sawhorses. They didn't have enough chairs to go around, so they improvised by putting a plank on a couple of heavy wooden crates. The atmosphere was jovial, with Floyd leading the conversation and not letting anyone upstage him.

All the younger generation sat at the extra table, with Walter, Davey and George sitting on the plank. For each person, Mabel had decorated an egg, which acted as a place card, as their names were on the eggs. Anna was fascinated by some of the eggs that had a design in light brown. "How did you do these, Mabel?" she asked. "The design is like the color of brown eggs."

"Oh those," she answered. "It's best to use white eggs. Before I boiled them I cut out designs from onion skins and then tied them around the egg. When they were boiled, they looked like this. Mother taught me how to do it. We've always done it that way, but you can see we dye some, too."

"I ate three eggs for breakfast," Davey bragged.

"I ate five," George said, "but Walter always eats the most eggs. How many did you eat, Walter?"

"Eight," was his firm answer.

"You just make a pig of yourself, Walter," Mabel admonished him. "At least you didn't eat all the colored eggs. If you had, I would really have been mad."

"What would you have done?" he teased her. "Spanked me, I suppose?" and he roared with laughter.

"Would you really have spanked Walter?" a curious Sarah asked.

"Yes I would, Sarah. And I would have asked you to help me," Mabel replied with mock seriousness.

"I'm too little," she answered, looking across the table at Walter. "And Walter's too big."

"We'll just wait until next year, Sarah," Mabel nodded as she sat next to her. "We'll cook goose eggs, and then we'll see how many he can eat."

"You don't have any goose eggs," Walter shot back at her.

"But next year we might, 'cause Daddy said I could have a couple of geese. So there!"

"Let's quiet down for grace," Inger commanded. "Walter, settle down now and say the grace."

Walter held back the additional comments he was about to make and said grace.

At the adult's table Floyd carved the huge ham, first fixing a platter full for the children and then serving everyone else a generous portion. "Help yourselves to potatoes," Inger said as she stood up to get the vegetables from the counter, "and turnips and carrots too. I'll be so glad when we can start the garden and have fresh vegetables. We still have quite a few things in the root cellar, but it's tiresome eating almost the same thing every day."

"Don't you have any canned goods left?" Milly asked.

"Yes, but not too many. Mostly corned beef and tomatoes. We have a few quarts of peas and beans and some fruit, but that's about all. As soon as the planting's done, Walter's going to start the vegetable garden."

"Why me?" he asked. "What about George?"

"Because George is in school and you aren't," his mother reminded him. "You want to be a farmer? Well, this is farming. You like to eat? Well, a garden is for growing things to eat," and she sat down and filled her plate. "Anyway, George can go over and help Aunt Milly work on her garden after school."

"Oh good!" George exclaimed. "Aunt Milly had filled cookies last week."

"In that case," Floyd remarked, picking up the conversation. "I think I'll go over to Aunt Milly's."

Inger spoke up. "All Milly needs is to have you over. You'd never get out to the garden, but you would eat all her cookies."

"But I wouldn't eat them all up," George reminded her.

"Here's what I had planned," Anna spoke up. "Anders said that he could use Lars some more, so I thought that if George and Lars finished their work by noon, they could leave school and go home to work."

"Oh, good!" George exclaimed.

"Now, this just ain't fair," Floyd remarked. "How come I never got to have Walter home early to help with the work?"

"Because Walter never finished his schoolwork on time!" Mabel declared with great authority, then covered her mouth with her right hand to hide a smirk.

"Oh, Mabel! How can you say such things?" Walter said, pretending to get his feelings hurt. George and Mabel roared with laughter.

"How come you're laughing?" Davey asked.

"'Cause they're makin' fun of me," Walter answered, continuing with the charade.

"Didn't you finish your work on time?" Davey continued. By this time the adults were joining in with the hilarity.

"Don't you let them kids fool you, Davey," Floyd said. "Walter always got his work done on time. Why, he was home from school every day by at least five o'clock."

"That's too late!" Davey replied.

"Well, I'll tell ya," Floyd confided. "Walter was so anxious to get ahead of everybody else that he forgot about what time it was and just stayed in school an' worked."

"Imagination seems to be running wild around here," Inger said. "Finish up your dinner now, so we can have dessert."

Everyone was having such a good time. Anna looked around the table. She was glad that Sally, Charley and Bill had been invited. They seemed to be enjoying every minute. Maybe things would get better for them this spring.

On Monday morning, regular school started again. All through the day Anna kept thinking of the deputy in California talking to Richard. It might be some time before Jim heard from them, but still, every day she wondered when that would be. When she arrived home, she anxiously asked Milly if there had been any word. Milly was getting as concerned as Anna. The days went by, but still there was no word. George dutifully finished his work early, so he came and started on Milly's garden. The sun was out but the weather stayed cool.

At last it was Friday. Davey dashed up the steps ahead of Anna and opened the door for her. "Thanks, Davey."

"I'll open the kitchen door for you, too. You have so many books and things."

"You're right. I guess I have a lot of homework this weekend." She smelled the coffee as soon as she stepped into the kitchen. "Oh Milly, I'm so tired. Let me get my coat hung up. I can hardly wait for a cup of coffee." She put her books on the table and went into the entryway.

"Well, I haven't heard anything," Milly called after her. "Maybe the deputy couldn't find Sally's brother. Davey, go out and get George. Tell him to come in for a glass of milk and some cookies. Oh, and if you see Daddy, tell him the pot is on."

"I see you made some more filled cookies," Anna said as she returned to the kitchen.

"If George is good enough to come and help me with my garden, it's the least I can do. He's such a nice boy and so willing to work. Oh, Walter's a good worker, too. He'll tackle anything, yust as strong as a man."

"Inger has a nice family," Anna agreed. "I think Mabel will take after her mother. From what I've seen of her, she'll make a good teacher. She's a good student, but of course there's no one in school who can come up to George. He's very bright."

Soon Davey was coming through the door and slammed it shut. "I told George to come in, and I saw Dad and yelled at him.

I want to go out and help George."

"Fine," said his mother. "Go upstairs now, and change your clothes. Oh, let me sit down. I don't know what I've done today, but I sure am tired. Oh, I hear Lucy waking up. Sarah, go in and play with her while I rest my weary bones. Yust leave her in her crib, give her something to play with and stand by it and talk to her."

George and Peter could be heard coming up the steps. "Uncle Peter, I think I've got the whole garden raked and ready to plant. I'm glad you plowed it up. The disk helped a lot, too. It's just that it needed to be evened up."

They stopped on the porch. "You first, George. Get all the mud off your shoes." George carefully scraped first one boot and then the other on the metal boot scraper. Peter gave a nod of approval, then quickly cleaned his boots. "Yes, I guess we'll pass your Aunt Milly's inspection. Come on in. Let's see if we can find some more of those filled cookies, but we'd better wash up first." George pumped a basin of water from the cistern while Peter glanced out of the window above the sink.

"I see a car coming down the road. Yes, it's Jim's car, and he's turning in here."

Anna felt a chill go up her spine. She glanced over at Milly, who looked very sober. They all waited. Everyone was quiet while George and Peter washed up. They heard the car engine, then it was turned off. Milly stood up and went to the door. "Come in! Come in! You're yust in time for coffee."

Jim Wilson entered and smiled at everyone. "Thanks, Milly. Don't mind if I do."

"Come over here and sit down," Peter said. "Well, you're a little too early to do the milking, so don't s'pose that's the reason you came."

Jim looked at him and shook his head. "It's been a tough day. A cup of coffee will sure be good. Hello, Anna."

"Hello," Anna slowly replied. She glanced at Jim and then looked down at her cup of coffee. She could feel her heart beating, and she was almost afraid of what he would say. No one else said anything.

Milly thoughtfully broke the silence as Davey came down the stairs. "Oh George, you and Davey can go work in the garden now." They both grabbed a couple of cookies and went out. "Have some cookies, Yim, before they all get eaten."

"Thanks, Milly." He took a cookie and held it in his hand. Then he spoke slowly. "I guess you want to know what happened." He heaved a sigh and took another swallow of coffee. "Well, I heard from the sheriff in California, and I've just come from talking to Sally. I left the Reverend there. Richard will never be able to tell us anything. You see, he was killed Tuesday morning in an accident."

Chapter Thirty-two

For a moment everyone sat in stunned silence. Milly was the first to speak. "He was? Are you sure? This is too terrible." Her shoulders shook as she shuddered.

"Yes, I'm sure, all right." Jim took a swallow of his coffee and slowly put down the cup. "His friend Frank identified him, and he had his billfold on him. His name was on a card in the billfold."

"I don't understand," Anna said. "How did it happen? Oh, poor Sally."

"Yes, Sally's having rather a rough time of it. She's beside herself. I told Tom about it before I went to Sally's and asked him to come with me. As soon as Sally saw us, she knew that something terrible had happened."

"But what happened to Richard?" Anna asked.

"I'm not sure of all the details, but I'll tell you what I know," Jim continued. "You remember that I told you the deputy was going to talk to Richard on Monday. I talked to the sheriff on the telephone, so I learned more than sending telegrams. It was lucky he could get through to me, and there was so much noise on the line that a couple of times I had to ask him to repeat himself. When the deputy located Richard, he was still in bed. He was staying in a small hotel, and the sheriff said both boys had spent most of the night playing poker."

"Is this how he earned so much money?" Anna asked.

"From what the sheriff said, they weren't too good at it. The deputy asked around and learned that they usually lost more than they made."

"That's yust throwing away money," Milly said indignantly.

"You're right, Milly. And to make matters worse, the fellows they played with would let them win a little and get them all excited, then clean up on them."

"Did the accident have anything to do with the poker games?" Peter asked.

"I don't know," Jim answered. "I guess the two of them hadn't been getting along too good, because they'd been overheard arguing. The men in the room next door said it always seemed to be about money. Anyway, all I know is that Tuesday morning about eight o'clock, Richard was crossing the street in front of the hotel. According to those who saw the accident, they said he came out the front door and started to cross the street. He must have seen the two teams of horses coming his way that were pulling a load of lumber, because I was told he glanced in that direction and made a dash for it. His car was right across the street, and it's a good guess that he was headed for it. He would have had time to make it, but he didn't see a car coming in the opposite direction. That car hit him straight on. The driver tried to swerve to miss him, and instead of missing him, he shoved him right in the path of the horses. Of course, the freight driver couldn't stop his teams, and there you have it."

"I can't believe it," Anna gasped.

"It is pretty awful," Jim acknowledged.

"What happened next?" Milly asked. "Did someone try to help him?"

"There was nothing anyone could do. Of course the driver finally stopped the horses. He even had trouble trying to control them. What was left in the street was Richard who had been trampled by the hooves and run over by the wagon wheels. The driver of the car got out and knew there was nothing he could do, either. There was so much commotion that a crowd soon gathered. Someone, I don't know who, maybe some official, asked if anyone knew him. Nobody seemed to. A search of his clothes turned up his wallet, which in spite of the horror of the accident, seemed in good shape. The name Richard Griswold was called out. Frank was just coming out of the hotel. He heard Richard's name and walked over to where the body lay. They said he walked as if in a trance. He acknowledged that this was his friend and immediately threw up. He probably wasn't the only one who lost his breakfast that morning."

"That was a pretty bad shock," Peter commented. "I know I couldn't have done any better."

"Oh, it's yust too terrible," Milly shuddered. "Oh, I must go tend to Lucy." She got up and walked toward the bedroom. "I don't even want to think of it."

"Poor Sally," Anna said. "First her mother dies, and then Richard. She idolized him."

"Yes it's a sad situation," Jim agreed. "Would it be asking too much, Anna, for you to go up and stay with her this evening?"

Anna thought a moment before she answered. "Of course I will. When do you think I should go?"

"If you could leave now, I'd drive you up there. I have to go back and pick up Tom, anyway. Think you could do that?"

"Yes," she said, slowly nodding her head. "Let me put my books and things in my room, and then I'll be ready."

"Good! I don't want to rush you, but I do have to get back home."

"I'll hurry." She gathered her things and quickly went up the stairs.

"Guess it's time I better get out and tend to the milking," Peter said as he pushed himself away from the table and stood up. "This has really been a day for you. There are a lot of parts about your job that I don't envy, and this is definitely one of them."

"I wouldn't have chosen a day like today if I'd had my druthers, but I have to take what comes." He looked up as he rose from his chair. "Oh, here's Anna. You're sure you're willing to do this? It may not be easy. I don't want to impose on you, but I think you'd be the right person to have at a time like this."

"I want to help Sally if I can," Anna replied. "This is a terrible time for her."

Peter got the milk pails from the counter, and the three of them walked out together.

As they drove up in Jim's car, Anna wondered what she would do when she got to the Wheeler's. She had never before been in a situation like this. What could she say or do that would help Sally?

"By the way," Jim said as he glanced over at her. "As I was leaving, Charley dashed over to get Inger, so I imagine that she'll be there. She was probably right in the middle of getting supper ready, but she'll drop everything and come. You can always count on her."

"Yes," Anna replied. "Inger's certainly dependable. No matter what, she's ready to help out. I'm glad she's there."

"It should make things easier for you," Jim continued. "I know this is a heck of a thing to ask of you, to come over at such a time as this, but I also know that Sally considers you a good friend. You've gone out of your way to make her feel welcome, and you've also given her back some of the gaiety that she missed when she was your age."

"I like Sally," Anna said as they turned into the Wheeler yard. "She's such a nice person. There's not a mean bone in her body. I just hope that I can be of some help to her."

"I'm sure you can if anybody can. Well, here we are. I'll go in with you and see how things are going, then I'll have to be running along." They slowly climbed the back steps. Jim opened the door and they went into the entryway. Inger heard them coming and opened the kitchen door to let them in.

Sally was sitting at the table, her shoulders hunched over and her face swollen and red from crying. She looked up as they entered the room. "Oh, Anna!" She burst out crying and continued sobbing.

Anna rushed over to her and embraced her, at the same time seating herself in the next chair. "Oh Sally, I'm so sorry. I don't know what to say."

"Oh, Anna. What'm I gonna do?" she gasped between sobs.

"Let her get her crying over with," Inger advised. "That's all right, Sally. Best you get it over with now. There'll be more to deal with later."

Sally looked up at them, glancing from one to another. In her grief she hadn't thought about "more to deal with later." Charley and Bill were standing by the parlor door, completely stunned. Reverend Blakeley was seated on the other side of Sally, his hands folded on the table. He glanced first at Sally and then at his hands as if he willed them to make things all right. Inger stood by the stove taking the lid off the coffeepot, as if this action would make it boil faster. Jim had his hand on the doorknob, looking as if he couldn't make up his mind whether to go or stay.

"Oh! I forgot," Sally said somberly. "Where's Richard now? I mean, you know what I mean."

Jim started to say something, then hesitated. He looked at

her, took a deep breath and spoke. "You mean where is Richard's body."

"Yes," was her forlorn reply. She looked up at him as if she were hoping he would say Richard was alive.

He hesitated again. "I don't know if we should go into all this today."

"But I want to know," Sally pleaded.

"I think it's best to get all our cards laid on the table right now," Inger added. "The more we know the better we can deal with it."

"All right," Jim answered, giving another sigh and sinking into the closest chair. "And Inger, when that coffee's boiled I guess I could do with a cup."

"It'll be another few minutes," she remarked as she lifted the lid and checked the pot again.

"Well, where to begin," Jim sighed and nodded his head. "I guess the first thing is that Richard was buried the next day in California." Sally gasped. "It's best that way, Sally. No one would have recognized him, and it's not possible to ship a body that distance when it's in that condition."

She was quiet for a few moments while she got a full grasp of that bit of news, and then suddenly uttered a moaning cry. "But we can't even have a funeral."

"We can have a memorial service," Inger chimed in. "Just like they had for some of the soldiers that were killed in the war. And we can put up a stone for him in the graveyard in the county seat. It can be right next to your mother's grave."

"Yes, that would be nice," Sally said. "Ma would of liked that too. I wanna have a service for him. I can't believe this happened. Oh, what about Pa? Does he know?"

"I couldn't locate him," Jim replied. "But I'll be on the lookout for him when I get back. I'll have Bert, he's my deputy, get onto it."

"What about Richard's things?" Sally asked. "He had such nice things. Remember the postcard he sent you, Anna? You should show it to the sheriff." She looked up at Jim. "Oh you should of seen the postcard that he sent Anna. He looked so great. Anna, can you show the sheriff the postcard?"

Feeling uncomfortable, Anna answered, "Sure, Sally. I'll be

glad to show it to him."

"An' do ya think I could have it, I mean to keep?" Sally asked.

"Why doesn't Anna show it to me first and then I'll let you have it, Sally," Jim remarked. "That is, if it's okay with you, Anna."

"Oh yes, that's fine with me," Anna said with relief.

Charley could be heard shuffling his feet. "Well, what about his car? Where's that?"

"Oh yes, when can we get his things?" Sally quickly added. With the new topics of conversation she quit sobbing and sat up. "Oh, let's get some coffee. Is the coffee done, Inger?"

"Coming right up," was the reply as Inger got down mugs, filled them and started passing them around. "Sally's got a good point, and Charley, too. Richard had a lot of nice things, from the looks of it. Clothes and that sort of stuff could be shipped, but what about the car? Does the sheriff in California have all this?"

"That's another problem," Jim replied. "You see, they took his body away Tuesday. Everyone was so excited and upset over what happened that they forgot about Richard's things or even about his friend."

"Frank," Sally added. "Frank Wiggins."

"Well, they weren't even sure of his name. But when the deputy went back later on that day to talk to Frank, he'd taken off. The hotel manager said that he'd left. They looked through the room the boys had, and it was combed clean. Nothing there."

"What happened to his car?" Charley asked.

"It was gone, too. Guess Frank stuffed everything in the car and took off. After what happened, I'm sure he didn't feel much like hanging around that place. Can't say as I blame him. The car could be half his as he might have paid something on it."

"Can't we find him?" Sally lamented. "Oh, I want to get Richard's things. It's not fair if I don't get them."

"You said they found his billfold," Anna remarked. "Does the sheriff have that?"

"Yes, he does. And he said he'd send it to me."

"Did he have any money in it?" Inger asked.

"I'm not sure about that, but I'll find out sooner or later." Jim took a long swallow of coffee. "What I need to know now is, do you know anything about his friend Frank? Where'd he come from? I don't recall that he's a local boy."

Sally looked puzzled. "I never knowed him. Richard met him some place when he was workin', an' he worked in lotsa places."

"I remember Richard saying that Frank had an uncle in, I think it was South Dakota," Anna added. "He said if the weather got bad, they could get off the train and stop at Frank's uncle's place."

"That's something, but not too much help," Jim surmised. "Did Frank know where Richard lived?"

"Oh yes," Sally commented. "Richard said he brought Frank home with him, but that was after I came here, so I never knew him. Did you know him, Reverend Blakeley?"

The minister thought a little and shook his head. "No. Can't say as I've even heard of him. I've never even heard of the name Wiggins around here. I don't think I'll be much help, but I'll keep a lookout for someone in the family. Never can tell. If I ask around enough, I might come up with a winner."

"I'll do the same," Jim added. "But there's no telling where he's headed. He could be anywhere in any one of the states."

"And I'll ask Walter. He can ask some of the fellas around here," Inger said. "If enough of us keep trying, we're bound to come up with something."

Reverend Blakeley looked at his pocket watch and stood up. "I don't know about you folks, but I think my missus will wonder what happened to me. And my stomach's telling me that it's supper time."

"I'd better be running along, too," Inger said. "Mabel's down at the Larsons', or she'd get supper. I'd just as soon not leave it up to Floyd." Charley handed her her coat. "Thanks, Charley."

"How're you doing now, Sally?" Jim asked. "Do you think you'll be all right if we leave you?"

Sally looked down at the table. "Yes, I'll be all right. I've got the boys here, an' I have to get supper."

"I'll help with the supper. An' we'll take good care of her," Charley added. "I think it's awful what happened. But Bill an' I'll see that she's okay." Bill nodded his head in agreement.

"I'll stay and help with the supper," Anna volunteered.

"You don't need to do that, Anna," Sally said. "The boys are a good help."

"Well, if you say so," Anna replied. "Just the same, I'll come back after supper."

"That sounds good. Maybe you could read us a story. Then I'd think about somethin' else, instead of..." Sally tried hard to blink back the tears.

"I'll do that. I'll be back about seven o'clock."

"Well Anna, guess I get to take you home, too," Jim said as he got up from the table. "And Sally, I'll let you know if I hear anything else."

"Come on then, let's get going," Reverend Blakeley remarked as he herded them toward the door.

"You don't have to drive me home," Anna said as they walked up to Jim's car.

"Oh, get in. You can sit in the middle. There's room for three in the front seat, that is, if Tom doesn't take up too much room."

"Now Jim, how can you say that?" the minister joked as he slid in beside Anna. Then his tone became more serious. "I suppose that you want to tell Anna the rest of the story, and that's why you're sandwiching her between us."

"There is more to tell, Anna, and I guess this is an good a time as any. I'm telling you because I think it's only fair to tell you. And what's more, you could be of more help. You seem pretty good at coming up with ideas, so keep your eyes and ears open."

Anna looked surprised. "Well, if you think I can help, I'll try."

"To get back to the story. Yes, there was money in Richard's billfold, quite a lot of money. It was all in big bills. He could have won it playing poker, or it could be money taken from the Wheeler's. And he could have exchanged small bills for big ones at a bank. One interesting circumstance is that a wad of twenty dollar bills was found in his jacket pocket."

"Mrs. Wheeler's money was mostly in twenty dollar bills, wasn't it?" she asked.

"That's right. I have a theory about Richard," Jim continued. "Remember the deputy came on Monday. He undoubtedly had to explain why he was questioning them, so he probably mentioned something about the Wheelers."

"But that would get them suspicious, and maybe they would take off," the minister said.

"Precisely," Jim added. "Of course the deputy didn't have a search warrant and was just sort of asking around. He intended to come back later that evening but didn't make it. Now we know that the men in the room next to theirs said the boys were arguing. They might have been having arguments for some time, but for them to remember that the boys were arguing, to me it means that it was pretty strong on Monday night. It could be that Frank knew very little about the robbery, and with the deputy coming, he became alarmed. This would give Richard good enough reason to take off alone."

"And he probably got up early enough before Frank was awake to clear out," the minister surmised. "It could be that he had packed his things in the car earlier that morning."

Jim continued. "My guess is that Monday night Richard waited until Frank was asleep, and while waiting fell asleep himself; otherwise, he would have left earlier than eight a.m. Maybe he kept most of his things in the car anyway and didn't have to load them before he left. When he did wake up, he realized he better get the heck out of there—and fast. That may be one reason he didn't see the car coming. He was still half asleep. Anyway, right now I'd sure like to get ahold of Frank Wiggins. We'll never get to question Richard about that fateful day when Mrs. Wheeler died, but I think his friend Frank could give us a few answers.

Chapter Thirty-three

That evening Anna was very quiet at supper. She knew that the money in Richard's billfold could have come from the Wheeler's, but she didn't want to believe it. When she lent the postcard to the sheriff, she realized it was possible that Richard had something to do with it, but she had never really convinced herself that it was true. She thought she shouldn't mention this to Milly or Peter, as it was confidential information. Her visit with Sally after supper was even more trying. She excused herself early, on the pretext of having too much homework and could hardly wait until she got up to her room and write to Jonah. She could tell him everything because it would go no further, and he would reply with comforting advice. Once the letter was written, she would feel much better, and she could walk to town and mail it in the morning.

She wasn't surprised when Sally and Charley didn't show up for church on Sunday. Very few people in the community knew that Sally had a brother named Richard, much less that he was killed. Sally would have been placed in a very uncomfortable situation, where she might have to try to make small talk and end up bursting into tears.

During the next week, Anna tried to convince herself that this event wasn't really her problem. She could accomplish this fairly satisfactorily while school was in session, but each afternoon while walking home she would glance up at the Wheelers and know that she was caught up in the middle of the affair. So Jonah hadn't seen Richard get on the train, but she had watched him walk off in that direction. Anyway, Richard was dead, Mrs. Wheeler was dead, the money was gone, and no one knew where Frank Wiggins was. No one even knew if Frank could shed some light on this mystery.

Crossed Fingers

It was now Friday, one week after Jim Wilson had brought Sally the bad news. As Anna left the schoolhouse, she felt guilty about not stopping to see Sally during the week, so when she arrived at the corner she turned and slowly plodded toward the Wheeler's. The house looked even more gray and gloomy than usual. Going up the back steps, she listened but couldn't hear any of the usual household sounds. Sally was always at home. She stood on the porch, frowning and biting her lower lip. She knocked on the entryway door. Nothing. Perhaps Sally was busy in one of the bedrooms. She turned the doorknob, put her shoulder to the door and shoved it open. She went into the back entryway, then opened the kitchen door and called, "Sally! Are you home?" All was quiet.

"Hey! Anna! Is that you?" It was Charley's voice, coming from the yard.

Relieved, she went back outside. "Yes! It's me! Where is everyone?"

"Oh, Sally's out spadin' up her garden again. She wants to get the peas in. I'll tell her you're here," and he disappeared around the barn to where her garden was.

Soon Sally came running toward the house. "Oh, Anna! I'm so glad to see you."

"Don't let me stop you from getting your garden ready."

"I'm glad to have a rest, and I've been wantin' to talk to you. Here, lemme get the mud off my boots an' let's go inside. Gosh, this mud is awful. It sticks to boots something terrible. An' I better put some more coal in the stove. I've been out almost all day, an' I forgot I'll need to have the stove hot to cook supper. Here, sit down. I can't even give you a cuppa coffee. This stove is stone cold, but it won't take much to get it goin' again."

"I'm glad to see that you've been out in the garden," Anna said.

"Well, I'm a little late, but now I can make up for lost time."

Anna put her books on the table and sat down on one of the well-worn wooden chairs. She couldn't believe that this was the same woman who one week ago had been so distraught. "I'm glad to see you looking so good, Sally."

"Well, it was a terrible shock when the sheriff came last week, but Inger's been comin' over, and she's helped me a lot. She said that now was the time to get on with things, and that the first thing I better do is get the garden going. She said workin' would make me feel better, and you know Anna, it has. I'm still really sad, but there's nothin' I can do about it. But I'm glad you come, 'cause I wanted to talk to you about somethin'."

"I'm glad I came, too. I've been wanting to get over to see you but was afraid I would intrude."

"Oh Anna, you would never intrude. You an' Inger are the two best friends I ever had. But I've got to tell you somethin'. It was Inger gave me the idea. An' I've talked it over with Charley and Bill, an' they agree. Guess what?"

"I'm sure I couldn't guess. You'll have to tell me."

"I'm gonna go back home." Anna was startled at the thought. "You look so surprised, well I'm not gonna stay there. I'm gonna get the rest of my things... an' bring 'em here."

"Oh!" said Anna with relief. "It sounds like a good idea. When're you going to do that?"

"I dunno yet, but real soon, maybe in a week. I don't wanna wait too long. You see, with Richard gone, there's nothin' to come home to. My pa ain't home much, an' he don't need me, anyway. An' as Inger said, the boys do need me."

"Yes, that's true."

"An' then Anna, there's things that my mother had, real nice things that she kept in a cedar chest. She got them when she an' Pa were married. If they get left at home, they'll just disappear. My pa will prob'ly try to sell 'em. That's why I think I've gotta hurry, 'cause he might take a notion to get rid of 'em any time. An' I want you to go with me."

"Me!" Anna exclaimed.

"Oh, Anna," Sally continued. "You act like you're surprised. Didn't I tell you before that I'd like you to see my home, well, I mean the place I grew up in?"

"Yes, we did talk about it," Anna recalled. "I guess this seemed so sudden. Inger's right, though. It would be good for you to get your things now. I keep thinking of that postcard that your father sent you."

"Yeah, I know. He can be real bossy, an' mean, too. I think I tol' ya that he gets drunk. Well with Prohibition, or whatever you call it, he can't buy it in stores, but travelin' on the railway like he does, he knows folks that make it, an' he brings it home, or goes into town an' drinks with some of his friends. Ma never let him drink at home, but now he can do anythin' he likes. An' Richard, too. After Ma died, he had a party. Pa was there, too. An' they left a real mess for me to clean up."

"That's terrible, Sally. That's against the law. What if the sheriff caught them?"

"We didn't live on the main road, an' we lived out far enough that nobody much ever come out our way. I remember Ma sayin she was so glad with this Prohibition, 'cause she thought it would stop Pa from drinkin'. But it didn't."

"Well, it's only been the law for a couple of years or so. Maybe people will eventually quit drinking. My mother never allowed any liquor in the house."

"My ma didn't either. Pa could do all the drinkin' he wanted when he was workin'. An' anyway, that's why I wanna get the stuff now, 'cause this is my home now. Once I get the things here, Dad can't take them away from me. Oh here! Lemme put some more coal in the stove. The cobs is hot now, an' the coal is startin' to burn." She shoveled the last of the coal out of the scuttle into the stove. "I should go out and get more coal now, but shucks, Charley'll do it for me when he comes in. I'm gonna sit down an' have a real visit. You know, Anna, I never had real visits before I come here." She pulled out a chair and sat across from Anna, with her hands folded in her lap. "Sorry I don't have coffee, but I do have some cookies." She pushed herself away from the table and jumped up.

"Oh Sally, sit down again. Forget about the coffee and cookies. I just want to visit, too. I'm so glad you came to Grabney. I'm sorry that it had to take Mrs. Wheeler falling to get you here and—." She stopped mid-sentence as she thought about what had happened after Sally arrived. But then she continued, "—and Charley and Bill have never had it so good."

"Well, we do get along okay. An' I really like it here. I'm sorta the boss of the house. I've never been the boss of anything before. Oh, but I wanna tell you about my ma's things. She showed them to me a coupla times when Dad an' Richard weren't around. She had a picture of her ma an' pa, an' a picture of when she n' my pa were married."

"I'd like to see them," Anna replied enthusiastically.

"Oh, you will. An' then she had embroidered pillowcases an' crocheted one edge of the sheets, an' there were other things that her ma gave her, too. While she was away at the state school, her ma sewed things for her an' saved them as a surprise when she came home in the summer."

"Your mother went away from home to school?"

"Oh yeah. She went to the state school, down south somewhere. Lemme think. It was in a state that begins with A. Oh well, I can't remember and it don't matter. That's where she met my dad."

"Then your mother's folks weren't deaf?" Anna asked.

"No. My mom was the only one in the family who was deaf. My ma had two sisters an' a brother, but I don't even know their names. Ma didn't talk about her folks."

"So your mother couldn't go to the public school."

"No, an' her folks, well, they didn't know what to do with her. They tried to start her in a reg'lar school but it didn't work out, so they sent her to the state school."

"I didn't think your dad was deaf."

"No. He just can't hear too good, hard of hearing I guess, but when he was young he could hear a lot better. He went to a reg'lar school. He lived in the same town that the school was in, an' he got to know the kids."

"So your mother learned sign language at the school, and your father learned it from the other kids."

"Ma said no one was allowed to sign at school. They were all s'posed to learn to talk an' read lips. But when the teachers wasn't around, like after class an' when they were in the dorm or out playin', they signed. But if the teachers caught them, they really got it."

"Who taught them the signs, then?" Anna asked.

"Oh, all the older kids taught them. My pa was a coupla years older'n my ma. Since he could talk real good, they'd go into town an' if they wanted to buy candy or somethin' he would do the talkin' for them."

"And that's how he got to know your mother."

"That's right. I have a picture of my ma's house, I mean where my gramma and grampa live. It's a real nice house. They had lotsa money, I think. My ma always had spendin' money, an' I think that's how my pa got to know her so good. You see my pa's family was sorta poor. My gramma an' grampa met him lotsa times when they would come to get Ma, like at Christmas, or bring her back to school. Ma said that Grampa called him a no good ruffian."

"They must have changed their minds to let your mother marry him."

"Well—" and Sally hesitated. "Ma was only seventeen when they was married."

"But then your mother didn't finish high school?" Anna asked.

"No, she didn't." Sally lowered here eyes. "Well, it was like this. She an' my pa got to runnin' around together, an' then Ma tol' them that she had to get married. You seem she was expectin' me."

"Oh, that does make a difference," Anna nodded. "Where did your father work? I thought you were born here. Did your father have a job on the railway and get transferred here?"

"Well, my pa thought that they could live near my folks and that grampa would give him a job, but my grampa was so mad at him, he said nothin' doin'. My gramma felt sorry for my ma, 'cause she knew that Ma had a hard time bein' deaf an' all. An' she was the one to get all the nice things packed up for Ma. She even gave her money for a sewin' machine."

"But how did they get to Iowa?" Anna asked.

"Pa knew somebody who'd come here, an' so they jus' got on the train an' came, an' this friend got him his job. He's a fireman on the engine, or a coal stoker's what most folks call 'em. An' he's been workin' the same job ever since."

"Do you ever hear from your ma's folks?"

"Ma used to get letters when I was little, but when she wrote a letter back she asked Pa to mail it, an' maybe he didn't, 'cause the letters quit comin'. My ma had a coupla sisters an' a brother too, but I don't know nothin' about them. She never ever got a letter from them."

They were so engrossed in the conversation that they didn't hear Charley coming up the back steps and into the kitchen. He looked from one to the other.

"Hey! You don't even have any coffee. Whatsa matter? Is somethin' wrong?"

Sally jumped up. "Oh Charley, I lost track of the time. Anna an' I were jus' visitin'. Can you fill up the coal scuttle for me? Oh my! Where has the time gone? I have to get supper."

"And I have to get on home, too," Anna said as she stood up. "Here I haven't even taken off my coat." She grabbed her books and headed for the door. "We've had a wonderful visit, Sally. Let me know when we're to go to get your things."

Chapter Thirty-four

It was May Day, the first of May. On the way to school Anna paid particular attention to the flowers that were just beginning to bloom. There weren't any cultivated flowers, but there were some wildflowers and lovely forget-me-nots. She picked a few that grew along the edge of the road.

She recalled fondly her first grade teacher getting out all the colored paper and showing them how to make May baskets. She had asked if she could make two baskets, one for her mother and the other for her Aunt Hazel. She was nearly finished with them when she started to worry, and what a worry it was. She didn't know where she could get any flowers. Living on the second floor of the store, they didn't have a garden. Other children were talking excitedly of how they were going to sneak a few flowers from their yard and put them into their basket, then hang the basket on the front doorknob, knock on the door and hide, waiting for their mothers to answer the door. What fun it would be, and they would keep hiding and not let their mothers know where the basket had come from. After a few minutes they would enter the house and feign great surprise on seeing this lovely flower basket. There were great giggles of laughter as they anticipated this.

She remembered being very quiet as the teacher walked over to her desk. She looked down at the two nearly finished baskets, not wanting to meet the teacher's eyes and have to explain her problem. She hoped the teacher would walk on by, but she stopped. "I think these flowers I found this morning would fit nicely in your baskets, Anna." She picked up the baskets and carefully arranged a few flowers in each. "Look, children! See how nice the baskets look with flowers. When you go home, see if you can find a few little ones like this and tuck them in your baskets."

Anna hurried on to school, recalling how Elsa and her mother had been so pleased with her May basket. She wondered how the older boys would respond to this activity, but with George in the lead they all made baskets, and during the lunch hour they wandered around finding small bunches of little flowers. She laughed to herself at their plans to surprise their mothers.

She told Davey that she would go into the house first, and she had not been in but a few minutes when there was a loud knock on the kitchen door and the sound of feet scrambling down the steps. "It sounds like someone knocked on the door and ran away," Sarah said. "Who would do a thing like that?"

"Never you mind, I'll go," Milly replied. "Yust sit still now." She slowly opened the door, peering all around but seeing no one. Then she let herself see the basket. "Oh my! Sarah, look what some good fairy brought to our house, a lovely May basket full of flowers. Oh, who could have done that? Oh what a lovely surprise." At that moment, Davey walked in, pretending to be unaware of the "surprise," and the project was a great success.

At school the next morning, Mabel brought a note from Inger. The note said that the sheriff in California planned to send Richard's billfold by registered mail to Jim Wilson, as soon as they had cleared up all the legalities involved. He thought it would arrive in about a week or two. This meant that Sally would probably plan her trip home at the same time that she could get the billfold. Whenever it was, Anna would go with her.

She stopped by Sally's on the way home from school that day, finding her in the garden. "Hi, Sally! Just thought I would stop by, because Inger wrote me a note this morning saying that the sheriff in California was sending Richard's billfold some time in the next two weeks."

"Oh Anna!" she said as she put down the hoe. "Let's go inside. I'm tired, and I do have coffee on the stove. Oh, I see Inger coming. Hi, Inger!"

"I saw Anna, and I thought I'd come and join the party," she remarked as they climbed up the back steps. "It's a beautiful day. I've been out gardening myself, but with George home from school now, I've given the chore to him. It's almost time to start supper, anyway."

"I got your note, Inger," Anna said.

"That's what I want to talk about."

"Has he gotten the billfold already?" Sally asked.

"Oh, no. Not yet. It'll take a little while before that happens. Anyway, what I came over for was to talk about the situation. Now sit down. I don't have much time, but here's what I think you can do. Now Anna, I know that Sally has asked you to go to town with her and pick up her belongings."

"But I don't know how we're gonna get there," Sally interrupted.

"That's what I'm coming to. Jim will let me know when the billfold comes in. Then I suggest that the next Saturday morning you go into town."

"But how?"

"Hold yer horses, Sally, and let me explain. Now, Elmer goes into town almost every Saturday. You can go in with him. He leaves about eight o'clock, so that should give you plenty of time to pack up your things and meet Jim about noon or so."

"But how can we get my things into town? Who will take us back here?"

"Now, just wait." The two sat still, giving Inger their rapt attention. "I think I've taken care of it all. Elmer said that once a month he spends a lot of time getting shoes from Jack Jarvis, and checking with other places. He likes to have dinner with some of his friends and said this would be a good excuse to stay longer. So you see, he'll come back and pick you up after a couple of hours, bring you into Jim's office, and while he's out having dinner you can be talking to Jim. Now, how does that sound?"

Anna was the first to respond. "It sounds as though you've thought of everything, but then you always do plan things well, Inger."

"Well, I wouldn't say that, but anyway, this sounds like it will work out. Now we'll just have to wait and see when Jim lets me know he has the billfold."

"Doesn't Sally's father have to be there, too?" asked Anna.

"That's another point," Inger said, "and I don't know how that will work out. Anyway, that's not my problem. Jim just asked me to see if I could get you two into town, and I said that I would."

Sally hesitated. "Inger."

"Speak up, Sally. What's on your mind?"

"I think my pa would think he should have Richard's billfold. An' he may cause trouble."

"Well, from what I've learned about your pa, Sally," Inger continued, "you can bet yer boots that he'll put up some kind of a racket. But Anna'll be with you, and Jim is no fool. He won't let your pa put one over on him. Well, I've got to be going, so I'll let you two sort out this one, and it'll be some Saturday, but right now we don't know which one."

On Saturday morning, May 19th, Anna was about to leave the house when she heard a car in the yard. She peeked out the window above the sink and saw Elmer heading toward the back door. "It's Elmer!" she called out. "I was going to walk down there. I didn't want to trouble him to come here to get me."

"Well, you know Elmer," Peter said as he looked up from yesterday's paper with a grin on his face. "He just can't miss an extra mile riding with a pretty girl. Here, I'll go let him in." He put down the paper and shoved himself from the table as he heard the entryway door open. "Come on in, Elmer," he said as he opened the kitchen door. "Anna said she and Sally planned to walk to the store to meet you. Could've saved you an extra mile or so of gas."

"Don't listen to him, Elmer," Milly scolded. "It's nice of you to pick up the girls."

"Well, I thought we better get goin', an' the earlier the better. An' no point in havin' them walk to the store when I've got a car. You 'bout ready, Anna?"

"Yes. I'll run up to my room for a minute but be right down."

"I sure am worried about Sally goin' inta town," Elmer said, shaking his head.

"Why's that?" Peter asked.

"Well, I'm glad Anna's with her. But I think her ol' man'll be there, too, an' no tellin' what he'll do. After all, if there's money, he's gonna want it."

"I think there's a lot we don't know," Peter replied. "But I'd appreciate it if you didn't say anything to worry the girls. I'm sure Jim can handle any situation, and there's no point in getting Sally and Anna all worked up."

"Oh sure, you're right, Peter. Well, here comes Anna. Guess we'll be goin' now."

They picked up Sally, and the girls piled into the front seat next to Elmer. Sally was so excited that on the way to town she kept up a steady stream of conversation. She could hardly wait to get to her old home, get her things packed and bring them back to the farm. Seeing the sheriff was of secondary consideration, even though he had Richard's billfold. "You turn right at the next corner, Elmer," she directed as they approached the town. Then you go down that road until you come to another one. I'll tell you when to turn left."

"I think we're runnin' out of houses, Sally," Elmer observed. "Don't tell me you live way out here?"

"That's right. Now turn left here, an' go down this road until you come to a house with two trees in front."

"If you say so." He made the left turn. "Which side of the road is it on?"

"On the right side. See it? Down there," she pointed. "That's it. Just turn in the yard."

He followed her directions, and turned into the yard. It was like driving between hedgerows, the weeds were so high. "Is this it?" Elmer asked.

"That's right. This is it," Sally said as she jumped out of the car. "I can see that pa ain't done nothin' with the yard."

Anna slowly climbed out of the car. The house was almost derelict. It definitely had an abandoned look. The porch was sagging, and steps leading to it were rotting out. If there had once been paint on the place, one would never know it now. Some of the shingles on the roof had blown off and littered the yard.

"Come on, Anna," Sally called as she made her way to the front door.

"I'm coming, Sally," she answered. "Oh Elmer, what time will you be back for us?"

Elmer took out his pocket watch. "Well it's near nine o'clock now. Will a coupla hours be enough? What ya think? I s'pose I'll be back sometime around eleven, maybe before that. That all right? You should get to Jim's office by eleven o'clock, at least."

"That will be fine, Elmer. Thanks for taking us. I know Sally will be glad to get her things, and we'll try to hurry."

Elmer shook his head. "Well, from the looks a' things, I think she'll be mighty glad to get her stuff and get outta there." He waved at Anna as he backed out of the yard. Anna returned the wave and headed for the house.

"Help me, Anna," Sally called. "I can't get this door to budge. It always gets stuck."

"Is it locked?" Anna asked.

"No one ever locked this door. We don't even have a key." She gave an extra strong push with her shoulder, and the door slowly ground open. Another shove and she was inside.

Anna walked cautiously up the steps, being careful not to step on a rotting board. The porch floor was in sad shape, also, leaving Anna to wonder what the rest of the place was like. She didn't need to wonder any longer, because her next step brought her inside the front door. She could smell mildew. The place was a mess. There were telltale signs of rats. Even on this sunny May morning, it was cold and damp. The parlor, where she was standing, was small. Furniture consisted of a dilapidated sofa—with worn upholstery where the stuffing poked out in several places—and a chair, which at one time had matched the sofa.

Sally stood in the middle of the room. "Ain't this a terrible mess, Anna? I can't believe my pa let it get so bad. It wasn't this way when Ma was alive. No sir! Even when she was sick she got Pa to take care a' things, an' then I was here, too. I had this place pretty nice. Well, things was wore out, but it was clean. Come on. Let's go to Ma's room. That's where my stuff is. I'm so happy to think that I can bring my things outta here.

"Where was your room, Sally?" Anna asked.

"I had the front room over there." She pointed to a small room off the parlor. "After Ma got sick, Pa took the front bedroom, so I moved all my things in Ma's room."

"Where did you sleep, then?" Anna asked.

"At first I slept with Ma, but when she got really sick, Pa put an old mattress for me on the floor next to Ma's bed. Richard's room is a little lean-to off the kitchen. Pa wanted him to have my room, but he liked it out there. It's like a room really, because it has four walls and a floor, but it's still a lean-to. I could've slept there when Richard was gone, 'cause it's close to Ma's room, an' I could hear her if she wanted somethin', but I didn't want to, and I know Richard would've been mad if I had." She looked around at the mess and heaved a sigh. "I never thought that this place could get so bad, Anna."

"Well," Anna replied, "you weren't here to keep it clean, that's what's the matter. And the sooner we get your things packed up and out of here, the better."

"When's Elmer comin' back?" Sally asked.

"In two hours or less. He didn't know how long it would take him. If we finish early, we can bring your things out on the porch and wait outside in the sunshine for him."

"Come on, Anna. I'm so excited to see the cedar chest again an' get my things." Sally hurried into the kitchen.

Anna followed, being careful where she stepped. The congoleum was cracked and broken, showing rough floorboards underneath. Wallpaper was peeling off the wall in back of the sofa where the rain had seeped in. As she entered the kitchen, she saw it was filthy. She was glad no one in Grabney could see this. If they did, some of them would have even more to criticize Sally about. She hoped it wouldn't take too long to collect Sally's things, and she reminded herself that Elmer would not return for perhaps two hours. Two hours in this place would be a long time.

She glanced at the table, which held a dirty plate and a cup that had once held coffee. As she walked by the stove she could feel a slight warmth, as though someone had been here recently. "Sally!" Anna called. Sally was in the small bedroom off the kitchen.

"Hurry up, Anna. I want to show you Ma's things."

"I know Sally, but listen to me. The stove is warm. And there are dishes on the table that have been used recently. I think someone has been here. Do you think your pa could be in town?"

Sally came to the bedroom door and looked at the table. "I didn't even see those, 'cause Pa would leave the table a mess, anyway. You said the stove was warm?" She walked over and felt the stove. "Yeah. You're right. I guess Pa was in town, an' now he's off to work again. He always left the place in a mess like this, an' I had to clean up after him. That's why he sent me that postcard."

"Do you know anyone else who would have stayed here?"

"No. It would be Pa. No one else ever came here, 'cept Richard, an' he can't never come here again."

"Are you sure he's gone off to work?" Anna asked.

"Yeah. This would be about the time he would catch the freight going to Dakota. Anyway, let's not talk about that. Let's get into Ma's room and open up the cedar chest." She entered the bedroom again, followed by Anna. "That's Ma's cedar chest over there against the wall under that quilt. Ma said my grandma made it. She always kept that quilt over it so it would stay nice. If the quilt is still there, Pa didn't get into it yet. But I don't see Ma's sewin' machine. It just ain't here. What could have happened to it?"

Anna looked around the tiny room. "I don't know, Sally, but let's not worry about that. You don't need a sewing machine now, anyway. Let's get the chest out, and you can show me what's in it."

Sally carefully lifted the dusty, old quilt; underneath it was the chest in its faded glory. They pulled it out from the wall. The front and sides were still in reasonably good shape, but Anna noticed that the back was covered with a layer of black and green mildew. "I know where the key is kept, Anna. Ma never let Pa know about that." She went back into the kitchen and quickly returned with a tarnished brass key that she inserted into the lock. It turned easily. She took it out of the lock and carefully put it in her pocketbook, then slowly raised the lid and peered inside. It was about half full.

"Maybe we should pull it out into the kitchen," Anna suggested. "There's more light out there, and we'll have more room." Sally was still staring at the contents. "Do you think everything is there?"

"Yes, I think so," she answered solemnly. "Look at the picture on top. That's Ma an' Pa when they was married. Don't she look pretty?" She picked up the picture and handed it to Anna.

"Yes, it's a lovely wedding picture. Here, let's put it back for now and move the chest to the kitchen." She gave the photo to Sally, who looked longingly at it once more, then put it back and closed the lid. They dragged the chest into the kitchen.

"Let's look at all these things, Anna," said Sally. "I'll take them out and put them on the table."

"You'll have plenty of time to do that when you get back to the Wheeler's. I think the best plan is for you to hunt up all the things that you want to take with you, put them in the chest until it's full, and then we can carry what's left over."

"You're right, Anna. Oh, but I'm so glad it's here. I was so worried." She walked around examining each side and smiling, then stopped suddenly. "Oh! Look at all the mildew on the back.

Oh, this is awful. Ma never would have let this happen."

"You can clean it up later," Anna suggested. "For now, just go around and get your things and bring them here." Anna looked at her watch. "We still have plenty of time, but I don't know how much you have to get. Is there anything I can do to help you?"

"I don't think so. Oh yes! Could you fold up my gramma's quilt and put it in the chest? Maybe you could shake it out first. Here! We can put our pocketbooks on the table. I'll clear away some room for them." She pushed the dirty dishes aside. "This still ain't clean, but it'll hafta do." Anna reluctantly put her pocketbook next to Sally's. "After you get the quilt folded, I'll bring you some things, and maybe you can put them in the chest for me." She opened the lid again and left Anna with the quilt. She returned with another quilt. "My Ma started this one an' never finished it. It makes me sad to see it, but now I'll finish it for her." Anna carefully put it into the chest.

Gradually the chest was filling up: her mother's apron that had seen better days, handkerchiefs, a box of buttons, sewing that Sally had left behind. Anna dutifully placed each item in the chest. As she did so, she realized that she was helping this woman draw the curtain on an old life and open it up on a new one. After the chest was filled, Sally bundled a few items to go on top.

"I think that's all, Anna," she said. "There's more here, but nothin' that I want. Let's haul this out to the front porch. What time is it?"

"It's about 10:30. We still have a little time before Elmer comes."

"After we put this on the porch, we can sit on it," Sally suggested. "An' we can visit, like folks do on front porches."

Together they pushed it into the parlor. As Anna gave a big heave, she laughed. "I don't think Elmer will be too happy about this. It's pretty heavy."

"You're right, Anna. Let's stop a minute."

"Listen Sally. I think I hear someone coming through the grass toward the house."

Heavy stomps on the steps and porch answered her. The front door was shoved fully open, and standing just inside the room was Sally's father, his face red with a drunken rage.

Chapter Thirty-five

"What're you doin' here?" Mr. Griswold screamed at Sally. "Come to steal my stuff, have ya? An' who's Miss Hoity-Toity over there?" he snarled at Anna.

Anna had never seen a drunk before. She instinctively took a few steps back.

"You *better* back up. Yeah, an' get outta here, or I'll make you wish you had," he bellowed. "What you got there? Heh, your ma's chest. Well, you think that's yours, do you—not on yer life. That's mine. You can't take that."

"It is not," said Sally. "Ma gave it to me. You weren't here all those days that I stayed with her, an' she said I could have the chest."

"Well, you left here," he bawled at her. "An' you wouldn't come back. So this here stuff's all mine. An' I sold the sewin' machine, so you'll never get that, so there." He took several unsteady steps and stood on the other side of the chest, opposite Sally.

She refused to give any ground. Her voice became louder as she cried out defiantly, "This ain't yours, an' I'm gonna have it, 'cause Ma promised it to me."

His right hand swung up and slapped her face so hard that she lost her balance for a moment. "We'll see who's boss around here. An' if you don't do as I say, you'll have more'n that comin'."

"Pa! You're drunk!" Sally yelled at him as she put her hand to her face to soothe it from the stinging blow.

"Drunk, am I?" he yelled as he came around the chest to get closer to her. "I'll show you what drunk means." Sally turned to get away from him, and as she did so he hit her hard on her upper left arm, throwing her down to the floor.

Suddenly, there was Bert, the sheriff's deputy, grabbing Mr. Griswold, throwing him down and handcuffing him almost in one motion. "That's enough out of you," he said firmly. "Didn't your ma teach you not to hit women?"

"That's no woman," Mr. Griswold yelled. "That's my daughter, an' I have a right ta hit her." Bert pulled him to his feet. "She's tryin' ta steal from me. You oughta cuff her an' not me. She's the crook. I was just doin' what's right. Gotta teach them kids a lesson."

"You're the one who needs to be taught a lesson!" Bert yelled at him. "And what's more, it's against the law to drink, much less to get drunk."

"I ain't drunk!" Mr. Griswold yelled. "I'm sober as a judge."

"And we'll let the judge decide how sober you are. I'll take him in, Jim. Soon as I get him locked up, I'll be back for you folks."

Anna was so absorbed in this that she hadn't realized Jim Wilson had come in and was helping Sally to her feet.

"You all right, Sally?" he asked. "That was a mighty mean blow. I got here just in time to see you go down. Sorry we didn't make it before. Here, let me help you to a chair."

"That's all right," she slowly answered in a half daze. "It's not the first time. I'll think I'll sit on the sofa." She reached out to grab the arm of the sofa, and Jim quickly reacted to help her get seated.

"You stay there now, and take it easy," he told her. "We'll take care of your pa." He looked up. "Oh, Anna. I saw you when I came in. We weren't sure where the trouble was, so Bert came in the front door and I came by way of the back. I got here just in time to see Sally hit the floor. Pretty awful, I must say. Why don't you sit down next to Sally, and see if you can help her."

Anna was so bewildered by this entire experience that she was in a daze herself and was happy to sit next to Sally and try to offer her some comfort. This didn't seem real. There was Bert. She had never given him much credit for great intellectual capacity, but he certainly made up for it in strength. Mr. Griswold wasn't a big man, but Bert handled him as though he were a kitten. Finally she regained her senses enough to ask, "You said you knew there was trouble here. How did you know? Sally and I only came to get her mother's chest and a few things that she had here."

"Well, it's this way," Jim answered. "You see, I had to contact

Sally's father when it came time to hand over the billfold. He arranged to be home this Saturday when he knew that Sally would be in town. I had already talked with Inger and knew that she would have you girls here."

"But how did you know there might be trouble?" Anna asked.

"We always keep an eye out for trouble, Anna, and we knew that Griswold would probably be drinking, and there was a good chance that he would get drunk."

"But that's against the law," Anna stated. "Can't you stop people from drinking?"

"Well, it may be against the law, but it's pretty hard to go around everywhere checking on who's drinking and who's not. Anyway, Bert saw him come into town last night. We were sure he wouldn't be home when you two would be arriving. We knew where he went and about a half hour ago, Bert went to see if he was still there. His friend, that's a lady friend he has in town, said he had left."

"I s'pose it's that same one that he had when Ma was still alive," Sally mumbled.

"Yes, I think it's fair to say he's known her for some time," Jim remarked. "But when we realized he had left, we headed here. I'm sorry that we didn't arrive sooner. Yes, I'm really sorry, Sally. If we'd been just a minute earlier, you wouldn't have had to go through this."

"Oh, that's all right," Sally said somberly.

"Well, as far as I'm concerned, it's not all right," Jim emphasized. "The only good thing that can come of it is we can lock him up for being drunk and disorderly. It'll be much easier talking to him about the billfold when he's locked up in a cell. But come to think of it, we could have locked him up if we had found him staggering home drunk."

"I think I hear a car coming," Anna said as she listened intently.

"I don't think it'll be Bert coming back this soon," Jim remarked. "Don't know who else would be coming here." He went to the door and looked out. "Well, sure enough. It's Elmer. Hello there, Elmer. You're a little late to get in on the excitement. Come on in. I suppose you came to get the girls."

Elmer's footsteps could be heard coming onto the porch. "I saw Bert bring in Griswold, an' he told me what happened. I thought it best to hightail it out here and see if I could be any help."

"You could have been about twenty minutes ago, but then I don't think you'd want to tangle with a drunk," Jim observed as he looked at Elmer's slight frame.

"You betcha! You're right there," Elmer declared. "I'm happy to leave all those guys to Bert. I can't compete with a six-footer who prob'ly weighs as much as one a' my hogs." They all laughed. It was a relief to have some amusement. "I just thought I'd take what gear Sally had and put it in my car now."

"This is it," said Jim pointing to the chest with the bundle on top. "Think you're up to carrying that out?"

"On second thought, I think I'll wait for Bert," Elmer joked. "He can prob'ly manage that with one hand tied behind his back. Well now, I guess that would be a bit awkward. You can't lift a chest with one hand."

"We'll wait for Bert anyway," Jim said. "He should be coming back shortly. If you take the chest, then we'll take the girls. You haven't had dinner yet, have you?"

"No siree. The boys 'n me get down to the Café about noon sharp, but then I was goin' to meet Jack Jarvis about eleven. That's another reason I wanted to get out here an' get back. An' I have some real good news. Jack and Grace are gettin' married next month, about the same time that Ed an' Bertha are."

"That wonderful news," Anna was elated. "Now Joshua and Elaine will have a father. Oh, I'm so glad. He is such a nice man."

"He's a real gentleman," Jim agreed. "Everyone likes him. He's a good, upright, honest businessman. And what he's done for that little boy is a wonder. When's the date?"

"I think I heard the first Saturday in June, but I'll find out more when I see him. I just heard this at the hardware store."

"Here comes Bert," Jim said as the deputy pulled in behind Elmer's car. "Well now, we'll get this loaded in your car, and then Bert and I'll take the girls. After we discuss the billfold situation, and I hope it won't take too long, we'll probably take the girls in to get a bite to eat, so we'll see you later. Can't let them go home starving."

Anna and Sally walked with Bert and Jim into the sheriff's office. Occasionally Sally would put her hand to her face. It was still very sore. Then she would gently rub her arm where her father had struck her.

"You girls sit out here a minute," Jim suggested. "I want to go back and see how Mr. Griswold is." Bert went with him, and Sally and Anna each took a seat in one of the wooden chairs that lined one side of the office.

"I've never been here before," Sally said quietly. She glanced at the opening next to the inside wall. Through it, one of the cells was visible. "Have you, Anna?"

"Yes," she answered. "A couple of times."

"Have you really? What about?"

"Nothing to worry about," Anna answered. She didn't want to tell Sally the reason for her last visit was to discuss Richard and the crossed fingers sign and the stolen money. Then she brightened as she thought of a plausible explanation. "Don't you remember my telling you that that was the day that Matt got his new car, and I had to ride in back with Ed driving us home, and Matt kept wanting to drive but Ed managed to keep him from it?"

"Oh!" Sally laughed. "I remember that. An' then Liza wanted to learn how to drive. I guess she must be drivin' by now."

"If you can call it driving." Anna looked up to see Jim coming back into the main room.

"Well Sally, I think this is a good time to settle this matter. Why don't you come with me to the back room."

"I want Anna to come too," Sally pleaded. "I don't want to go alone."

"Sally, it might not be fitting for me to be in on a private family matter," Anna reminded her.

"Oh please, Mr. Wilson. Please let Anna come."

"I guess it'll be all right," Jim answered her. "If you want her, there's nothing to say she can't come. So let's go. Now remember, this place isn't fancy. Bert!" he called out. "Bring in some chairs, will you."

Bert came from the jail area and took two chairs from the office. He disappeared again behind the wall in front of the cells. As Sally and Anna followed Jim Wilson, Sally held onto Anna's arm. Anna could feel her trembling.

Mr. Griswold was sitting on the bunk in the center cell. The two chairs had been placed opposite it. When the girls entered, he staggered up and grabbed the bars of the cell. "Whatya mean bringin' them in here. I got my rights. Lemme outta here."

"We'll let you out when you are ready to come out," Jim stated firmly. "And that means when you're sober. But we're here to discuss an entirely different matter. I have here Richard's bill-fold." He reached in his pocket and pulled it out.

"I don't see no money in it," the man yelled. "You musta stole the money. I know Richard had a lotta money. Wait'll I tell a judge that you stole Richard's money."

"You can do that after you explain why you were drunk and hit your daughter," Bert added. "This judge doesn't take too well to people who break the law and get drunk."

"I'm not drunk, and I didn't break no law."

"Let's calm down now," suggested the sheriff. "First of all I want to explain what there was in the wallet. There was some money."

"I knew it! I knew it!"

"Calm down, Griswold," Jim advised. "You're not doing yourself any good by yelling at everything I say. Now there was money, but part of it may belong to Richard's friend, Frank Wiggins. We have to locate him first to find this out, and we haven't been able to do that."

Anna looked at Jim and realized that he thought that this was not the time to mention the possibility of the money belonging to the Wheelers. Neither Sally nor her father knew of Jim's suspicions.

"Yer jus' a bunch of stupid dopes," Mr. Griswold yelled at them. "I know where Frank Wiggins is. I saw him this week, drivin' Richard's car. An' he was on his way here. Ya think ya know so much. Well, you don't know as much as I do."

"Where did you see him?" Jim asked.

"He was drivin' on the road outta Rapid City."

"How did you know it was him?"

"A' course I knowed it was him. He was drivin' a Ford Model T coupe with California plates. Now just how many people have a Model T with California plates? Besides, I seen him. He was bringin' it to me."

"What day was this?" Jim asked.

"Lemme see. This is Saturday, an' it was the run before the

last one, so I dunno." He sat down on the bunk. "It musta been Monday or Tuesday. It had ta be Tuesday. Well then, why hasn't he brought it to me? He's had plenty a' time." He got up shaking his fist. "Now I know. You folks got ta him first, an' you got the car. Well, where is it?" he screamed. "What have you done with my car?"

"We don't have your car, but we'll try to find it as fast as we can. If you saw him at the beginning of the week, then he should have been here by now, that is if he intended to come here."

"A' course he intended to come here. Richard wanted me ta have that car."

Jim interrupted him. "If you saw him, and I'll assume that you did, and if he intended to come here, it's strange that Frank hasn't shown up by this time. I guess there are at least two reasons that he isn't here. The first is that he never intended to come."

"You're wrong there, sheriff!" Mr. Griswold yelled.

"If you don't shut up, I'll have you in for a month or so for disturbing our peace!" Bert yelled back.

"Now everyone, let's think," Jim continued. "The second reason could be that the car broke down along the way, and he had to stop and have it fixed. Have any of you heard from Frank Wiggins?"

Anna and Sally shook their heads while Mr. Griswold thundered, "A' course I haven't heard from him. We don't have no phone, an' writin' would take too long. I saw him, an' he was drivin' along the road headed straight for here."

"Since you think you saw Frank and the car—" Jim began.

"I don't just think," came the drunken bellow. "I know! I saw him driving the car. Lemme outta here, an' I'll find him."

"Take it easy, Griswold," Jim advised. "We can't let you out of here, and I think that if I make a few phone calls we might be able to find an answer to this problem. At least, I hope so." He turned to face Anna and Sally. " Well ladies, I guess this has to be all for now. There's nothing more I can do until we find out a few more answers. If Frank were a thousand miles away or so without a chance of finding him, the situation would be different. But as it is, he may be somewhere a great deal closer, and if that's the case we'll just have to wait until we see if we can locate him."

"Can't I have the billfold?" Sally asked.

"Don't let her have it, sheriff," Mr. Griswold said as he again grabbed the bars of the cell with both hands. "That belongs ta me. All Richard's stuff belongs ta me."

"I can't let anyone have the billfold," Jim answered. "It will go back in the safe along with the other contents. Come on, Anna and Sally. Let's go out into the office." They followed him, leaving a furious Griswold ranting and raving. "Bert, when you have time will you pick up some dinner for our boarder?"

"I'll do that," Bert answered as he brought out the two wooden chairs and set them back in place.

"Oh, and it just occurred to me," Jim continued. "Anna, you and Sally might stop by Jarvis' shoe store. Grace is often in there waiting on customers, especially on Saturday when they're likely to be fairly busy. Do you know where it is?"

"I'm not sure," Anna replied, "but I think we can find it."

"Bert, why don't you escort them there on your way to the Café."

"Be glad to. Not often that I get to escort two pretty ladies."

Sally looked at the floor and blushed with self-consciousness at his remark, but Anna paid no attention. "I'd like to see Grace," she said. "It's been a long time since I've seen her, and I'm so happy at how things are working out."

"In the meantime, I'll do a little checking on my own, and I'll meet the two of you at the Café at noon. I'm sure you can find it. That's what it's called, "the Café," and it's just a couple of doors down from Jarvis' store."

Bert left them at the door of the store. Only the front part of the left side was for shoes; the rest of the front and the back part of the store was for general merchandise and was run by someone else. "That's Grace in there," said Anna. "I've told you about her. She used to live across from us, and her husband was killed. You remember, don't you?"

"Oh yes," Sally answered. "And she had a little boy who was in first grade with Davey. He told me he was so sad when, what's the name of the little boy?"

"Joshua."

"Yes, now I remember," Sally continued. "And Davey was so sad when Joshua had to leave. Didn't his grandpa die, too?"

"Yes. It was such a sad story, and it was certainly the best thing for Grace to take the children and move here to town. They live with her aunt who takes in boarders. That's how she and Jack Jarvis got together."

"Here I'm feelin' sorry for myself 'cause I lost my mother n' brother, an' here's these children who're so young an' lost more'n I did."

"In spite of it all, I think this story will have a happy ending. Let's go on in." Anna pushed open the heavy door, and they walked over to the shoe section. Grace turned around, thinking it might be a customer.

"Hello, Grace," Anna said.

"Oh, Anna!" Grace rushed over to her. "I'm so glad to see you. It's been so long. What brought you to town? You don't need a pair of shoes, I imagine." She looked from Anna to Sally.

"This is Sally Griswold. She's been living at the Wheeler's ever since Mrs. Wheeler fell."

"Oh, I heard about that. That was really sad. But what brings you to town? You almost never get here."

"I came along to be company for Sally. She used to live here, and we were collecting her things. But what's the good news I hear about you and Jack?"

"Oh, isn't it wonderful. Jack is so nice, and he's so good with the children, especially Joshua. I'm so lucky to have found a man like that."

"When is the wedding, Grace? I have to find out some of the details, because everyone will be asking me. Now that Jack doesn't come around selling shoes any more, we hardly ever have any news."

"We're getting married June 2nd. That's a Saturday, and it's gonna be in the afternoon. Do you think you can come? But, oh let's sit down, and I'll tell you about the house we're going to buy and everything else."

It was around noon when Sally and Anna left Grace and walked the short distance to the Café. "I've never been in here before, Anna. I think mostly men eat in here, don't they?"

"I don't know Sally, but let's go in. I see they have some booths, so we can sit in one of them."

"Hello, ladies," the woman behind the counter said. "Make yourselves at home. Sit where you like. I'll bring you a menu soon's

I get finished here."

"I see Elmer and Jack are in a booth at the back," Anna nodded her head in that direction. "Let's sit in one toward the front. We should be where we can see Jim Wheeler or Bert come in." The first booth was unoccupied, so they chose that. "You sit on that side, Sally, and I'll sit over here."

"Shouldn't we sit on the same side, Anna, 'cause when Bert or Jim come in, they'll wanna sit together. An' I mean I'd feel a little strange sittin' next to one of them."

"Fine, Sally. Let's take our coats off. We can hang them on this coat hook at the end of the booth." Anna hung up her coat and then slid over on the seat to make room for Sally.

"This is the first time I've been to a place like this." Sally continued to gaze around the room as she hung up her coat and then sat down next to Anna. "The back of this seat sure is high. Ya can't see over the top unless ya stand up." She strained to see over the top of the seat opposite. "I guess they did that on purpose. What do we do next?"

"Here's the menu," the waitress said as she handed them a piece of paper that listed a few items written in pen and ink. "You must be new around here. Never seen you before. Jus' goin' through town?"

"We're from Grabney," Anna said. "Just here for the day."

"Doin' shoppin', I s'pose. Well if you're lookin' for somethin' good for dinner, I'd say choose the roast beef and mashed potatoes. Comes with biscuits, gravy and canned peas. We also got meatballs, but the roast beef's better. That's what I think, anyway. Well, do ya think ya'll have that?"

"That's fine with me," Anna answered. "What about you, Sally?"

"Yes, that's fine."

"Two roast beef!" she yelled to the man behind the counter, and then walked the few steps to that area herself.

"Oh, Anna. This is real nice. She asked if we were shoppin'. I've saved some money, and maybe we can come shoppin' sometime."

"I'd like that, too, Sally. With two weddings next month, I should come into town to look around and see what I can get for presents. I can't really buy something from Elmer's store to give to Ed and Bertha. Elmer comes into town every Saturday, so maybe we can come in next week. I'd like to give Grace something, too."

She looked up to see the sheriff come in the door, followed by Bert. They saw the girls and came over to join them in the booth. "Things are happening faster than I expected," Jim explained to them. "We've located Frank Wiggins."

Chapter Thirty-six

"How could you have found him already?" Anna asked. "You mean he's here in town?"

"Oh no, it's not quite that simple," Jim replied, "but it is interesting how it all went together rather quickly. By the way, ladies, did you order dinner?"

"Yes," Anna answered, "the roast beef."

"Sounds good to me. Roast beef okay with you, Bert?"

"Fine with me."

"Two more roast beef!" he called to the waitress. "Here, you go in first Bert." He motioned for the deputy to sit opposite the ladies. "Slide over, Bert. I have to get in, too." He lowered his big frame into the seat and rested his arms on the table. "Now to tell you what's happened."

"I want to hear about it, too," Bert interrupted, "'cause I didn't get to hear the whole story."

"All right. The first thing I did was to phone the sheriff in Rapid City. He wasn't in, but his deputy was. The sheriff was out hunting up a robbery suspect, who just happened to be driving a California-licensed Ford Model T."

"Frank Wiggins?" Anna asked.

"I guess so, because it seems that the man who was robbed is Frank's uncle. Last Tuesday when he got home from work he noticed that someone had broken into his house, because the back door was smashed. He looked around and saw nothing much out of order. Then he had a sinking feeling. He kept a fairly large wad of bills behind a brick in the chimney. He had fixed it so that no one would notice that the brick could be removed, and the only one he had told about this was his nephew Frank."

"Huh!" Bert said. "So he was robbed by his own kin."

"It looks that way," Jim continued. "A neighbor told him that a Ford Model T was parked outside the house that day."

"And Pa saw Frank drivin' on the road on Tuesday."

"That's right. But the problem was, how to find Frank? Where had he gone? Well, right after the uncle reported the robbery, the sheriff notified people to be on the lookout for his car, but it seems no one remembered seeing it. He knew that Frank couldn't have disappeared, so he made phone calls to the towns on the roads leading out of Rapid City and came up with a winner. After all, he surmised that Frank would have to get gas, so someone would have seen him."

"An' Pa saw him."

"That's right Sally, and that's the road he took, the one that goes along by the train track. I don't know why he didn't take the road that he came on that goes through Wyoming, but that doesn't matter. We learned later that he was heading for the main road south. That's about twenty-five miles past Kadoka."

"Is that where he stopped to buy gas?" Bert asked.

"It's a little more complicated than that," the sheriff continued. "Several miles outside of Kadoka, he had car trouble. From what I was told, the car just plain wouldn't go. Anyway, he was stalled right in the road."

"Prob'ly didn't keep enough oil in it or keep it lubricated," Bert surmised, anxious to show the women that he knew a little about cars.

"Whatever it was, he wasn't going anywhere until a farmer came along with a team and said he could pull him to Kadoka, but he couldn't do it until the next day. The farmer lived a half mile away, so he pulled the car into his place, and Frank spent the night there."

"That's a stroke of luck," Bert added.

"Yes it was, and from what the sheriff told me, the family was fascinated with the car, especially the kids. They hadn't been so close to one before, and Frank let them crawl all over it. He was almost like an honored guest."

"That means he wouldn't get towed in to Kadoka 'til Wednesday," Bert added.

"That's right! Only the story slows down from there. On Wednesday the farmer pulled Frank into town and left him at a gas station, where they did mechanical work. He was told that the car wouldn't be ready until Friday at least."

"That's yesterday," Sally said. "Where did Frank stay the rest of the time?"

"The farmer's family liked him so much that they invited him back to the farm to stay a couple more days. In the meantime, the sheriff from Rapid City had called all these towns, and not a bit of luck until several people in Kadoka remembered seeing a Ford Model T coupe with California plates being towed behind a wagon pulled by a team of horses. It was quite a sight and something they would remember. By this time it was Thursday morning, and the sheriff headed for Kadoka."

"But Frank wasn't in Kadoka," Sally said with concern.

"No, that's right. He was out on this farm having the time of his life, eating three square meals a day and being treated like royalty. I'm told that he also offered to pay the farmer for his trouble, and when he pulled out his billfold they were astounded at how much money he had. He fed them a line about being out in California and striking it rich, and they bought it."

"I s'pose that was his uncle's money," Bert added.

"Could very well be," the sheriff nodded as he spoke.

"What happened next?" Anna asked.

"What happened is that the man at the gas station told the sheriff where Frank could be found, the sheriff and a deputy drove to the farm, and in front of the family of worshipping farm folk, they arrested Frank."

"Don't that beat all!" Bert roared with laughter, along with Anna and Sally who expressed their amusement in a more restrained manner. "But didn't he put up a fuss?" Bert asked.

"You bet he did. He really raised Cain, and the farm family was pretty angry, too. They couldn't imagine why their friend should go to jail. Believe me, I was told they really put up a ruckus."

"I s'pose the sheriff found the money on him, an' that would prove it," Sally said.

"It's not quite so simple as that," Jim continued. "He had money on him, but who was to know but that it was his own money? The thing they got him on was that they had checked up on the car at the gas station. Richard had left the registration in the car, and according to it, Richard owned the car. Frank's name wasn't on it at all. So you see, they could arrest him on that charge. Now since Frank is in the Rapid City jail, we don't have to worry about losing him again. First thing Monday morning, I'm going over there and see what the situation is."

"Where's the car?" Sally asked.

"Oh, it's still at the station in Kadoka, and it'll stay there until someone with some legal authority goes and gets it. The sheriff made sure of that."

"What'll happen to Frank?" Sally asked.

"I just don't know," Jim answered. "If his uncle presses charges and if it's proved that he did the robbery, he could be spending the next year or so in jail."

"If he had so much money to show the farm family, it must have been his uncle's money," Anna added.

"Anyway, we won't know a thing until next week. I'll be able to get an idea of what's happening when I go there." He looked up as the waitress came with two large plates filled with roast beef, potatoes and gravy and the canned peas.

"These'r fer the ladies," she said as she set them down on the table in front of Anna and Sally.

"You mean no grub for us?" Bert joked.

"Just you behave yourself, Bert Olsen," she quipped, "or I'll tell yer ma on ya. You gents'll have ta wait 'till I get back." She quickly turned and headed behind the counter.

"I guess she told you, all right," laughed Jim.

"An' ta think that she used ta be my Sunday School teacher," Bert said as he smiled and shook his head. "Don't that just beat all."

"Think you two can get around all that food?" Jim asked as he looked from one plate to another.

"It's sure a big meal," Sally replied.

"Well, what you can't eat, Bert'll take off your hands," Jim continued. "He's still a growing boy, you know."

The waitress returned with the plates for the men. "Here ya' are, now," and she set them on the table. Anybody fer coffee?" All four answered in the affirmative. "All right then, I'll be back with the coffee."

"Well, eat up folks, while it's hot," Jim advised.

Anna was still thinking about Frank as she picked up her fork. "So if you go there Monday, will you let us know what's happening?"

"Sure will," he answered. "And that'll be the next chapter in this saga."

On the drive home Elmer could hardly keep his mind on the road as Anna and Sally kept up a constant stream of conversation. This was the most exciting thing that either of them had come across, and they couldn't wait to let him know all the details. Even though Elmer was used to Vi's constant chatter, he was relieved when they reached the Wheeler home, and even more relieved to see Charley and Bill come out to carry the chest from the car to the house.

Anna couldn't wait to tell Milly what had happened. "I'm going to hurry on home now, Sally," she said as she got out of the car.

"Wait a bit, an' I'll drop you off," Elmer suggested.

"Thanks," she replied, "but there's no need for you to do that. I'm used to walking home." With that she waved to the boys and was off down the road.

As she climbed the back steps, she heard Inger's voice and knew that she would have rapt attention for her story. She barely had her coat off when Milly opened the kitchen door for her. "Liza had a phone call from that woman who works in the Café," Milly explained. "She said that someone was arrested, and that Jim had to go to Rapid City to get him."

"It's not quite like that," Anna laughed, remembering how the woman seemed very attentive to their needs while they were eating. It took her some time to set the story straight. Her remarks were often punctuated with comments like "Well I'll be darned," from Peter and "I yust can't believe it" from Milly.

The phone rang. It was Vi, who had heard one story from Liza and another from Elmer, and since the accounts differed, she wanted to talk to Anna, who could tell her what really happened. Anna knew that by evening half the community would know about it, and after church the next day, the story would have made the rounds of everyone. She avoided talking about Sally's father and hoped that the story of his incarceration would not go the rounds. Sally had enough to deal with, without having to be embarrassed about her dad. No doubt when the gossips heard that she had moved bag and baggage into the Wheeler home, tongues would be wagging from morning until night.

During the week, Anna kept wondering if she would hear from Jim Wilson, but there was no word. She was anxious to find out what he had learned when he found Frank Wiggins. It was strange that he hadn't called. Perhaps he didn't go to Rapid City on Monday. Perhaps the uncle hadn't pressed charges against his nephew, and maybe there was no way of proving that he had any stolen money from the Wheelers. Perhaps Frank could prove the car belonged to him as much as to Richard. It was hard waiting to hear, but she and Sally were going to town on Saturday, and they could talk to the sheriff then. With this being the last week of school, she couldn't let herself dwell on that and be distracted from work that had to be accomplished.

By Friday, everyone was ready for the end of the school year and the annual picnic. The boys cleaned up the yard while the girls worked in the schoolroom, helping Anna tidy up. The mothers brought enough food to feed twice their number. They also brought dishes and tablecloths and blankets to sit on. They spread it all out on the grass, and at noon everyone was ready to eat. Sally came with a big basket of cookies and sat by Anna. This was her first school picnic, and she was delighted. Milly came with Sarah and Lucy. Hilma Anderson came with Elsa and Birgit. Elsa would be in first grade next fall. Joe Pearson brought Esther and their baby boy Erik. Everyone marveled at how much the infant had grown and how healthy he was. Esther put him in the clothes basket she brought. It had been lined with blankets and was a perfect place for a sleeping baby.

Anna relaxed as Inger saw to it that everyone got enough to eat and also kept an eye on the boys who might tend to get rowdy. After greeting everyone, she sat next to Sally, but it wasn't until everyone had gone home and the two were picking up from the picnic that their thoughts went to Rapid City and Frank Wiggins.

"Have you had any news from the sheriff yet?" Sally asked Anna.

"No, not a word," was the reply. "I thought we certainly would have heard from him by now, but maybe there's no news."

"Maybe Frank really owns the car an' the sheriff don't wanna tell us, like maybe Frank didn't even steal the money from his uncle.

An' what about the billfold an' all that money that Richard had?"

"Don't worry about it, Sally," Anna said. "I would guess that the sheriff wasn't able to bring him back, or we would have heard. Jim Wilson knows what he's doing. Tomorrow when we go into town, we can stop by his office and find out."

Elmer dropped the girls off in front of the courthouse. "When you git yer shoppin' done, come on over to the Café. I'll prob'ly be there. An' don't take forever doin' it, neither. I know it always takes Vi an age to buy justa cupla things. Jus' gits to talkin', that's the problem."

The girls laughed. "We'll hurry, Elmer," Anna called to him as she slammed the car door.

"Besides, we don't know enough people to visit with," Sally added.

"Jus' remember now, I'm leavin' right after lunch," he called back to them as he pulled out into the road.

"I hope it don't take too long to shop," Sally said as they walked up toward the sheriff's office.

"I think we can be on time," Anna added. "Anyway, Elmer shouldn't talk about Vi talking a lot. He's worse that she is when it comes to that. When we get back to the Café he'll be so busy talking, he won't even know we've arrived. Here we are." Anna opened the door and they entered the sheriff's office. Bert was sitting behind the desk.

With a touch of disappointment Anna asked. "Is the sheriff in?"

Bert rose quickly to his feet. "No, sorry, ladies. He should be comin' in real soon, but he's not here now."

"But I thought he was gonna be here," Sally insisted.

"Was he expectin' you?" Bert asked.

"No, he wasn't," Anna replied. "But we thought that since we were in town we'd like to find out what happened in Rapid City. Can you tell us anything?"

"Well I s'pose I can tell you a little. What is it that you want ta know? I jus' got here a few minutes ago."

"Well," Sally began, "did he bring back Frank Wiggins from Rapid City?"

Bert hesitated, "I guess you could say that he did."

"Well, I wanna see him an' talk to him about my brother," Sally explained.

"Sorry, ladies. I can't let no one go to see a prisoner without the sheriff's permission."

"But that's not fair," Sally insisted. "I wanna find out what he did to my brother."

"Sorry, you can't go back there. Sheriff's orders."

"We can come back later, Sally," Anna tried to console her, and then turned to Bert. "When do you think the sheriff will be in?"

Bert turned to answer Anna.

With a determined look on her face Sally darted around Bert and ran to the cell area.

"Hey! Come back here!" he shouted. "You can't go back there!"

But Sally was already in front of the cells.

Bert stood helplessly, shaking his head.

For a moment everything was quiet, and then Sally gave a piercing shriek, "Richard!"

Chapter Thirty-seven

"What in the Sam Hill's going on!" Jim Wilson said as he entered the room. "Anna! You look like you've seen a ghost. Wait a minute! Where's Sally?"

"She's in there," Bert mumbled as he pointed to the jail area.

"What do you mean she's in there? I don't hear anyone in there. Oh, no!" He darted past Anna and Bert behind the partition separating the cells from the office.

Anna felt a little sick. She sat down in the nearest chair and tried to make sense of what was happening while she and Bert waited for the next development, listening to what was happening on the other side of the wall.

"Sally! Are you all right?" Jim asked her. "Did you hurt yourself when you fell? You must have fainted."

A dazed Sally answered slowly. "Oh, Sheriff. It's you."

"Yes, it's me. Are you all right, Sally?"

"Well, what happened? I musta fell."

"Yes. You had a terrible shock, and it was enough to make you faint. Now if you feel all right, let me help you up."

"Oh, I can get up by myself, Sheriff."

"I'll help you just the same."

"Oh! Now I remember." Sally sounded more like herself. "Sheriff, you've got the wrong man in jail. That's my brother. The one who should be in jail is Frank Wiggins."

"Let's go out into the other room, and I'll try to explain it to you Sally. Come on now," the sheriff pleaded.

"But that's my brother," she insisted. "That's not Frank Wiggins. You've gotta find Frank and put him in jail. Isn't that right, Richard?"

"Shut up, Sally!" Richard growled.

"Don't talk to me like that," she blurted out. "Let's get Anna to come back here. She knows Richard. She'll tell you you've got the wrong person."

Jim now spoke with more authority. "Here we go, Sally, into the other room."

Anna looked anxiously at the entrance to the jail area and soon saw Jim with his arm around Sally's shoulders pushing her into the office.

"Oh Anna!" Sally cried. "You've gotta tell the sheriff that he's got the wrong person. That's not Frank back there at all. That's Richard. An' he's not dead. He's alive."

"Here, Sally, you sit in the chair next to Anna," Jim said as he ushered her into the chair.

"But Sheriff," Sally argued. "You don't understand. That's my brother you've got in there."

"I know it is, Sally. Yes, I know it's Richard," he explained kindly. "But what I want to know is how Bert let you get back there in the first place." He turned and stared straight at the deputy.

"I don't know how it happened," Bert feebly explained. "I was talkin' to both of them, an' then before I knew it, she was in by the cells. I jus' don't know how it happened. Anna can tell you."

Jim took a deep breath. "How did she know we had a prisoner? What did you tell them?"

"I don't remember," Bert mumbled. "It all happened so fast."

"But that's Richard," Sally kept repeating. "You've got the wrong person."

Anna turned to the sheriff. "I don't think it was Bert's fault. As he said, it all happened so fast."

"Well, what's done is done," Jim shook his head. "Now you just sit here, Sally, and I'll pull up a chair and see if I can explain it to you."

"What's there to explain?" she asked. "You don't believe me. Didn't he tell you he's Richard?"

"Yes, I know he's Richard," Jim calmly stated. "And this may be a little hard for you to understand. I think we better go back to April 20th. That was the day that Frank was killed."

"Frank?" Sally questioned. "But everyone said it was Richard. An' now Richard ain't killed. He's in that other room, in jail."

Jim paused and looked at her as he was trying to carefully

choose his words. "Sally, we all thought it was Richard who was killed because the jacket Frank was wearing belonged to Richard. We couldn't identify the body because no one knew him, and also it was not, well let me say, the accident was so bad that you couldn't tell who it was."

"Oh," she muttered. "But why did you think Richard was Frank?"

"That's what he wanted everyone to believe. You see, Richard had done some things that he thought he could get away with if people thought he was Frank."

Sally looked up at him. "Richard never did nothin' that bad."

"Do you remember the gold watch and the watch fob that belonged to Mr. Wheeler?"

"Yeah."

"In the picture that was on the card that he sent to Anna, he was wearing it. That made us wonder if he could have taken it."

"But he coulda bought one jus' like it," she surmised.

"He was wearing it when the sheriff from Rapid City arrested him. We know it was the one that had belonged to Mr. Wheeler, because it had Mr. Wheeler's initials on it, RBW. Those aren't Richard's initials. Of course I'll have to let Charley and Bill see it. They can tell us for sure if it's the one that belonged to their father."

"You mean Richard stole it from Mrs. Wheeler's dresser?"

"Yes, that's what I'm saying. And there are some other things that we've learned. You see, when people do things that are wrong, and get away with it, or think they've gotten away with it, they start bragging. That's what Richard did. It appears that when he and Frank first came to stay with Frank's uncle, he told him about what he did at the Wheeler's."

"Why didn't the uncle tell the sheriff over there about it?" Anna asked.

Jim continued. "I guess he didn't feel he wanted to. Maybe felt rather proud that someone his nephew knew had gotten away with something. Maybe he had broken the law himself and didn't want anything to do with a sheriff. And if he had turned Richard in, it would be Richard's word against his. Of course Richard would deny it."

Anna thought about that. "What made him tell now?"

"I think he got so mad that Richard had stolen the money from him that he spilled the beans on everything he knew."

"He didn't know everything!" Richard shouted from his cell.

"You be quiet back there," Bert yelled.

"Now let's calm down," Jim suggested. "Sally, I know this has been a terrible shock to you, and to Anna too. Isn't that right, Anna?"

"Yes," she answered, hoping that the sheriff would not divulge that he learned much of the information he needed from her.

"I think it's best that the two of you get out of this room and into the fresh air. Let's go outside and sit on the bench under that tree over there. We can talk a little, and then you can go about doing the errands you had planned to do in town."

"We were going to buy wedding presents, and Sally wanted to get a new dress," Anna offered.

"I don't feel like buyin' nothin'," Sally said. "An' anyway, we don't have that much time. Elmer said we had to be ready to leave when he was through with dinner at the Café."

Jim picked up on that remark. "I think I can solve that problem for you. I have an idea that Reverend Blakeley is coming into town this afternoon. You could get a ride home with him. Bert, when you get dinner for our prisoner from the Café, tell Elmer that the girls will be getting a ride to come back later."

"Sure thing," Bert answered, hoping he was out of the doghouse. "I'll do that."

"All right, ladies, you go out and sit down on that bench and rest a little. I have a couple of things to take care of in here, and then I'll join you. It'll do us all good to get out in the fresh air."

"Come on Sally," Anna coaxed. "It's getting rather stuffy in here anyway."

"But I wanna talk more to Richard."

"You'll have plenty of time to talk to him later," Jim advised. "Now you go on, the two of you." As an afterthought he tried to add some levity to the situation. "Be sure to leave some space for me on the bench."

Anna led a reluctant Sally out across the grass to the tree. "Sit down here Sally, next to me."

"But I don't understand, Anna. How come Richard is in there? And why does the sheriff have him in jail?"

"You remember that we were told that Richard was killed."

"Oh yeah. That was awful." Sally was close to tears. "But who was it that got killed then?"

"It was Frank Wiggins," Anna explained. "They thought it was Richard because Frank was wearing Richard's jacket."

"Yeah, I remember that's what the sheriff said." Sally paused. "But how come he was wearin' Richard's jacket?"

They looked up to see Jim striding across the lawn. "I think I can answer that for you, Sally. Here, I'll sit in this space on the end. At first we were just guessing why Frank was wearing Richard's jacket, but Richard confirmed our guess."

"He did?" Sally asked. "How would Richard know?"

"Well, you remember that beautiful leather jacket of Richard's."

"Yeah. It musta been really expensive."

"When Richard woke up and realized that Frank had taken off with his jacket and the money he had stashed inside it, and also was planning to steal his car, he got really mad. He dashed out of the hotel just in time to see Frank killed. You see, they had been arguing the night before, probably about money. Richard told me that part of the story."

"But sheriff," Sally interrupted, "why did Richard say he was Frank?"

"Let's put it this way," the sheriff continued. "The boys had been gambling and had lost a lot of money. Also, I was concerned about a certain situation, so I asked the sheriff there to see if he could find Richard. A deputy did find them Monday, April 16th, but the boys were so sleepy he couldn't get anything out of them. He came back the next day, but by then Frank was dead and Richard was gone."

"That was right after Easter," Sally added.

"Yes it was," Jim continued. "And now comes the tough part. Sally, do you remember anything particularly interesting about Mrs. Wheeler's body, that is, when you came back from the river with Anna and Jonah?"

"She was lyin' there dead," Sally shuddered.

"Sally," Anna said. "When we first saw her body and realized she was dead, did you see anything unusual?"

"No. Just that she was dead and it was awful."

"Where were her arms?" Jim asked. "Were they at her side or across her chest or something like that?"

Sally looked dumbfounded and shook her head, then looked up at the sheriff. "I dunno. Oh yeah, her right arm was hangin' over the edge of the bed. Her fingers were crossed like an R, an' I thought that she was still rememberin' R for 'right'. You see it was her right hand, an' also the right side of the bed. She really learned a lotta signs."

"You saw that?" Anna asked in surprise.

"Oh yeah, but I didn't want to tell no one, an' I was glad that Inger straightened out the fingers. You never want someone to go to the grave with their fingers in a sign. An' Inger made her look real nice in the coffin."

Jim gave a big sigh. "Well Sally, can you think of another meaning that crossed fingers has?"

Sally looked at him and smiled. "I didn't know you were int'rested in sign language, Sheriff."

"I'm afraid I don't have the time to learn it, but I am interested in whether you know of another meaning for R besides 'right'."

"Oh, well, that's easy. It's the sign for Richard. Mrs. Wheeler learned that real well, too."

"So then Sally, think about it. If Richard stole the watch and fob that belonged to Mr. Wheeler, couldn't Mrs. Wheeler be trying to give us a sign that told us who also stole the money?"

"But she was dead?"

"Exactly. And he didn't stop to notice that her fingers told us who the thief and the murderer was."

Sally shuddered and looked up helplessly at Jim. "Then you mean that Richard was the one who made her die?"

"You could put it that way."

"Oh no!" she wailed. " I can't believe it. How could he do that?"

"I don't know, either," Jim admitted. "But Richard told the whole story about stealing the watch and fob and the money, and putting a pillow over Mrs. Wheeler's face to smother her to death, then putting the pillow under her head to make it look like she was sleeping. He thought he was very clever, and that's why he told Frank and Frank's uncle and that's exactly the story Frank's uncle told us."

Sally looked horror-stricken. She didn't say anything more. Then she turned to Anna, and Anna put her arms around her. Sally let herself be comforted and was so shocked that she couldn't even cry.

Jim eased himself off the bench. "I think I'm going to let you two stay here, Anna. I'll bring back a couple cups of coffee. That's about all I can think of to do now. So sorry all this had to come out, but it's best that she found out with us, instead of having Richard shout it out to her, or to hear about it in the courtroom. In a few minutes Reverend Blakeley should be here. That's what I was doing when you girls walked out here. I think he's the best one to handle a situation like this." So saying, he turned and slowly walked back to his office.

Chapter Thirty-eight

Half an hour later, there were two empty coffee cups sitting on the bench. Anna and Sally sat quietly. They would look at the grass, or the trees or anything else that came within their field of vision. Everything that needed saying had been said. Occasionally a sob would shake Sally.

Two figures strode up the walk. Anna saw them first. One was Reverend Blakeley, and the other was Jonah. She hastily rose to greet them. "Oh, Reverend Blakeley. I'm so glad to see you."

"I'm sure you're really more glad to see this young man who accompanied me," he said with a twinkle in his eye.

"Oh yes. Jonah."

"Well, Sally, I understand this has been a tough morning for you," the minister said as he went to her and took her hand."

"Oh, Reverend Blakeley. It's been awful. I can't even talk about it. It's so terrible." Sally stayed seated as if she were glued to the bench.

"You don't have to talk about it, Sally," he said to console her as he sat down next to her. "I think I know all about it, so don't fret about telling me, or telling anyone else for that matter." He looked up. "Anna, why don't you and Jonah go into town and do your shopping, and I'll stay here with Sally. What about meeting you at the Café in about an hour?"

"I couldn't eat anything," Sally moaned.

"Well, maybe in an hour we can tempt you with something. I see you've already had some of Bert's coffee."

"I just wanna go home," Sally continued. Then she suddenly gasped and looked horror-stricken. "How can I go home to the boys after all this? They won't want me. Not after Richard...oh, I don't know what to do."

"You had nothing to do with what happened, Sally," he counseled. "Now we'll sit here and talk it all out, and you'll feel better about things after a while. By the way, weren't you going to buy a dress in town today?"

" I don't feel like that now. I.... "

Jonah interrupted her. "Well then, Reverend, we'll plan to meet you in an hour. The noon rush should be over by then, so I think the Café will be fairly quiet."

"All right, you two, be off with you now, and save a place for us if you get there first."

"We will," Jonah answered and then turned to Anna as they walked toward the street. "It's been a long time since I've seen you. I got in on the 5:10 yesterday like I wrote I would, but the evening was so busy with the family that I couldn't get away."

"Oh, don't worry. I knew you would be busy. I was rather busy myself. It was the last day of school, you know. I tried to get most things done and put away for next fall, but I'll have to do some of it on Monday."

"Thank goodness I'm through school," he sighed. "Of course, going to school isn't like teaching. By the way, when do you leave for summer school?"

"With these weddings, it makes life a little complicated. There's Decoration Day on Wednesday. I know my mother will want me to come home so I can go with her and Elsa to put flowers on my father's grave. I thought that I would leave Tuesday and come back on Friday."

"You mean you'll have the whole week here between the weddings?"

"That's right," she answered.

"Oh, I'm so glad." He grabbed her hand and squeezed it.

It was about 1:30 when Sally and Reverend Blakeley met them in the Café. Sally had calmed down by then, but it was obvious she was still struggling to get a grip on herself. No one could coax her to have more than a cup of coffee. Anna thought she could liven her spirits by showing her the gifts she had bought for the two weddings, but Sally was despondent.

The ride home was even less cheerful. Sally sat in the front seat with Reverend Blakeley and kept wiping her eyes, which by this time were red and swollen.

"I'm going to drop Sally off first, if that's all right with you folks," Reverend Blakeley announced as he drove up the road to the Wheeler's.

By this time Sally was sobbing. She cried out, "I can't go in there. It's just too awful what Richard did. I just can't face them."

The car came to a stop around by the back door. Anna had been sitting behind Sally, so she got out and opened Sally's door. Jonah and Reverend Blakeley were soon beside her. "Come on, Sally. Things will be all right," Anna coaxed. "Here come the boys. Remember, nothing was your fault."

"I should never a come here in the first place," she sobbed. "If I hadn't a' come, then nothing like this woulda happened."

"If you hadn't come, then Mrs. Wheeler wouldn't have lived as long as she did," the Reverend said. "And think of the pleasure you gave her in her last days."

"Who's makin' Sally cry?" Charley shouted as he hurried to the car. "I don't want no one to make Sally cry. Whatsa matter, Sally? Is someone bein' mean ta ya?"

"No," she wailed.

"Whatsa matter with her?" Bill asked. "Who's been makin' her cry?" Both men looked at the Reverend.

"No one's making her cry. At least, it's not one of us. Let's go in the house, boys. We have something to discuss. It's something that's made Sally very unhappy, as you can see."

Anna and Jonah started to turn away and head for their homes. "You two stay, also," Reverend Blakeley called to them, and it was more of an order than a request. "And Charley, put on the coffeepot. And get some of those cookies out that Sally always makes. Come on everyone, into the house."

Anna looked at Jonah and said quietly. "I suppose we better go in."

"Yes," he answered, as they hung behind the others. "I think the Reverend needs all the help he can get." The others were in the house when Anna and Jonah slowly climbed the back steps. They could hear Charley's voice.

"You jus' tell us who made you cry, an' me n' Bill'll take care of 'em." Anna had never heard Charley sound so determined.

"That's right," Bill added. "We sure will."

"Now Charley, get the coffee on," the minister cut in to change the subject.

"It's already on," Charley said. "We done kept it on all morning so's Sally could have a cup when she come back. Ain't that right, Bill?"

"Sure is," he replied.

"Good!" the Reverend exclaimed. "Let's all sit down at the table." As they seated themselves he continued. "Now get out the cups and some cookies. I'm sure Sally has some cookies around somewhere."

Sally looked up, showing her tear-stained face. She fumbled with her over-used handkerchief, sniffing as she tried to find a place to blow her nose. She shook her head looking at it, as if the situation were hopeless.

"Here, I have a clean handkerchief, Sally," said Reverend Blakeley as he reached into his pocket to bring one out that was neatly ironed and folded. He gave it a shake to open it up and handed it to Sally.

"Thanks," she mumbled as she quickly made use of it.

In the meantime, Anna had gotten out the cups and was pouring coffee. Charley put the cookie jar on the table. It was very quiet, as if no one knew where to begin. All that could be heard were Sally's sobs.

"Whatsa matter with Sally?" Charley asked. "I wanna know."

Well," the minister started. "It's rather a long story, but let me start. To begin with, you remember your father's watch that was stolen?" The boys nodded. "Well, that's been found, and the sheriff will give it back to you one of these days."

Charley perked up at that news. "How'd he find it?"

"It seems that it was stolen when the money was taken."

"You mean he found the money, too?" Bill asked, suddenly aware of the implications of what had been said.

The minister continued. "Well, we guess part of the money has been found, but we're not sure how much. The sheriff will have to figure that one out." He looked at Sally and saw that she was more composed before he continued. "And of course, there will be a trial for the person who stole these things."

"That's good news," Charley brightened up. "You mean we'll get the money and the watch back?"

"I said just part of the money," Reverend Blakeley replied. "We don't know how much yet, and it may not be much. But there's more to it, and this is something you'll have to know."

Sally cried out, "Oh no!" and burst into near hysterical crying.

Anna was sitting next to Sally and put her arm around her, trying to comfort the unhappy woman.

"Why's Sally cryin', if we're gonna get the money back, an' the watch too?" Bill asked.

There was a silence until Jonah spoke up. "You remember the day we went down to the river to see the men get the ice?"

"I sure remember," Bill answered. "That was the day that Charley left the pigpen gate open, an' I had to chase all around to catch them hogs."

"Yeah. I remember too, "Charley said thoughtfully. "An I don't remember not shutting the gate on the pen."

"Well, you did!" Bill said accusingly.

"Now let's stop this," Reverend Blakeley cautioned. "I'm pretty sure that Charley didn't leave the gate open. I have an idea it happened this way. The person who stole the money opened the gate so Bill would have to be outside chasing the pigs while he was inside stealing the money."

"See! I told ya I didn't leave that gate open."

"Who was it, then?" Bill asked. "I didn't see no one around."

"He made sure you wouldn't see him. Charley and Sally were off to the river, and you were stuck outside catching the hogs. So he crept into the house without anyone knowing it." Reverend Blakeley looked at Sally and realized that hearing this again would be too much. In an effort to spare her he said, "Anna why don't you take Sally into her room and let her lie down."

"That's a good idea," Anna said as she got up from the table. "Come on, Sally."

"Yeah, Sally," Charley said. "You go lie down in yer room."

"But I don't know if I should," she wailed.

"Yes, you should," Reverend Blakeley added, as Anna helped her to push her chair away from the table. Slowly she was coaxed into the bedroom where Anna made her lie down. She covered her with the quilt that came from her mother, then sat on the edge of the bed trying to be of some comfort. But she still listened to the conversation coming from the kitchen.

"But what I wanna know is, whatsa matter with Sally?" Charley asked again.

"All right, I'm going to tell you, but take it easy now. I don't want you to get upset, so let me finish first." The minister paused and looked at them. "The person who stole the money and your father's watch and fob was Richard."

"Who's Richard?" Charley asked. "The only Richard I know of is Sally's brother, an' it couldn't be him, 'cause he was nice an was wearin' those fancy duds. An' he wasn't even here."

"You thought he left here, but he didn't. He wanted you to believe that he left, but he only went far enough so he could come back the next morning."

"How'd he do that?"

"I'm not sure about all the details, but anyway we can learn all about that later. Right now I can tell you he's in the county jail."

"You mean he stole the watch an' the money? So that's why Sally was cryin'," Charley declared. "She must feel awful havin' a brother in jail. Wait 'til I git him. He has no right to make Sally cry."

"I think the sheriff will take care of him," Reverend Blakeley added. "You don't have to worry about that."

"If he don't, Bill an' I'll do it. Right, Bill?"

"Yup. We shore will."

Reverend Blakeley slouched back in his chair and looked exhausted. In an attempt to take some of the burden off him, Jonah decided to speak. "That's not all, Charley and Bill. You remember how sick your mother was?"

They nodded, wondering what was going to come next.

"Well, it seems that the person who stole these things decided that your mother saw him, and so he decided to make sure that she never told anyone. But what he didn't know was that your mother gave us a clue, so that after she died we would know who did it."

Bill suddenly was interested. "Good fer Ma. We never knowed about it. How'd she do it?"

Jonah looked at Reverend Blakeley, who gratefully nodded for him to continue. "I remember coming into the house, and we found that your mother had died. I saw that her right arm was hanging over the side of the bed. Anna and I talked about it later, because we had noticed that her fingers were crossed. Anna thought that your mother was making an R sign, the sign for 'Richard.' And that's just what she did. She signed Richard's name so we would know."

"Our Ma was really smart," Charley added. "We always knowed that, didn't we, Bill?"

"Yup, we shore did," Bill answered and paused. "Is that why Ma died? Did she die 'cause she was so scared or somethin'? Did he do somethin' that made her die?"

Reverend Blakeley took over the conversation. "Yes, it looks like he did. And that's why Sally is so upset. You see, she figures if she never came here your mother would still be alive."

"No, she wouldn't," Bill shook his head. "She almost died when she fell, an' if it hadn't been for Sally, she never woulda made it. It's sorta like when one of the stock falls an' breaks somethin'. Like if a horse has a broken leg, then you hafta shoot it, or else it'd jus' die by itself an' suffer so much."

"That's right, Bill," Jonah said, surprised at Bill's reasoning.

"Well, Charley an' I couldna taken care a' Ma. She jus' woulda died. When Sally came, she thought Ma was gettin' better. Well, she was a little, but not enough so's she'd be really okay. I knowed Ma woulda never wanted to be like that, so's one day I went in to talk to her. I asked her would she wanna live an' be like this. She shook her head. Yup, she knowed what I was sayin', an' she jus' shook her head like 'no'. Then I asked her if she was ready to die. She nodded her head like 'yes'. I knowed you don't shoot people like you do animals, so's when she died I jus' thought it was the way it was s'posed to be. I didn't know Richard did somethin' to make her die, an' I know he shoulda never done nothing like that, but Ma didn't want to live like she was, in bed all the time n' everything."

"Well, I'll be darned," the minister said, realizing that this was probably the longest speech Bill had ever made.

Charley looked puzzled. "You didn't tell me you did that."

"I didn't tell no one. It was jus' between Ma an' me. An' I sure didn't want Sally to know, 'cause she thought Ma would get back on her feet again. She woulda felt awful if she knowed Ma was never gonna get better. She was tryin' so hard, an' workin' so hard."

"That's very interesting, Bill," Reverend Blakeley said, shaking his head as if he couldn't believe what he'd heard. "So you feel that even if Richard did have something to do with your Ma dying, that she was ready to die, anyway."

"Yup. An' I asked her about Sally. Did she like Sally stayin' here an' takin' care of us. She nodded 'yes'. So's when she died I knowed that Ma wanted Sally to stay here. Anyway, Ma knowed that Sally could keep house an' cook real good."

"Sally's a real good cook," Charley added. "Look at all them cookies. We never had cookies like this before."

Reverend Blakeley pushed back his chair and got up. "Well, I think it's time that you boys told Sally you want her to stay here. And don't forget to tell her that it's what your mother wanted, too." He took out his watch to check on the time. "Goodness me! It's time I was getting home." He walked toward the door, then turned around. "Jonah, I'm sure you and Anna can stay while all this gets sorted out. You can do a better job of it than I can."

Chapter Thirty-nine

Jonah walked Anna to the station on Tuesday, May 29th. He carried her grip as they made their way on the path next to the riverbank. What a wonderful feeling to be alone, just the two of them. It was as though they were the only two people in the world. They arrived at the station a little before five o'clock. The train was on time, and saying goodbye was not painful, as they both knew that Anna would return in a few days.

Her mother met her at the station in Fort Dodge. "We'll wait here until your trunk is unloaded."

"I didn't bring my trunk, Mother. I thought I mentioned that in my letter."

"Well, I guess you did, but when are you going to bring your things home?"

"I'm going to leave my trunk there," Anna answered. "I don't need such a big one for the things I'll be bringing to school. I can use the steamer trunk that I used last year. That's smaller and about the right size."

"But you mean you aren't leaving Grabney? Don't you know that you'll never get anywhere teaching in that little rural school? That was fine to get started, and we can thank your Uncle Lars for getting it for you, but it's not good enough. This fall you should be teaching in a school closer to Fort Dodge. It's what I've planned for you. I've already asked Lars to see about this. You might even be able to live at home, and that would save some money. You will just have to change your plans."

"No, Mother," she answered as firmly as she could without being rude. "I'm going back to Grabney next year." With this introduction, Anna welcomed the thought that her time at home would be short.

Crossed Fingers

On Wednesday, Decoration Day, Anna, Elsa and Mrs. Swenson brought flowers to Mr. Swenson's grave in the late morning. The cemetery looked beautiful. Almost all the graves had flowers or were being decorated. They met friends they saw only from year to year. Her father was so young when he died. Anna wondered what life would have been like had he lived. She saw how wonderful it was for the Jensen children to have a father like Peter, and from what she could remember of her father, he had been a kind man. Perhaps the reason her mother was such a strong person was that she had to be. Her mother might also have been very different had Anna's father lived.

Early Thursday morning Anna took the bus to Cedar Falls so she could register at the Cedar Falls Normal College. Normally she would register the following week, but she had made arrangements to register early so that she could attend Ed's and Bertha's wedding. She spent the night at Mrs. Phipps' boarding house and got the same room on the third floor that she had had the year before. Friday, without going back home, she left on the train for Grabney, arriving at 5:10. Jonah was there to meet her. As he grabbed her grip he commented, "This must be empty. It's so light."

"It is empty," she replied. "When I return this time it will be filled with clothes I'll need for summer school. That way I don't have to lug that big trunk around. We have a smaller steamer trunk at home. I took it last year to school, and it works out just fine."

Few people from Grabney were attending the wedding of Grace Kloster and Jack Jarvis. Anna and the Blakeleys were about the only ones who had kept up with Grace since she moved to the county seat. The Blakeleys invited Anna and Jonah to ride with them. Jonah had known Grace from the time he was little as he had lived next door to their farm, and thus was going to represent his family.

The ceremony was held in the First Methodist Church, and there were far more people than Anna had imagined. Jack had lived in the county seat for many years and had many friends as he was so outgoing. Anna was delighted to see Joshua, who had grown since she had him as a pupil in Grabney. Elaine was now three years old and no longer seemed such a mama's baby. Anna and

Jonah sat on the left side of the church next to the Blakeleys as they were friends of the bride, although they could also claim to be friends of the groom. The reception was held in the church basement. Since they sat toward the back of the church, and the people in the front rows left first, they had to wait in a long line that led down the steps.

"I am so happy for Grace," Anna remarked. "Jack is such a nice person, and he seems to have taken quite an interest in Joshua."

"Yes, she's lucky," Jonah added. "It doesn't seem possible that she could go from her horrible life in Grabney to a decent one in town."

"We're both very happy for her," Reverend Blakeley remarked.

"I think her aunt had something to do with it," Anna said. "You remember that Jack boarded with the aunt, and when Grace and the children moved in with her, they became friends."

"As if it were ordained," the minister added.

"I think so, too," Anna continued. "Well, he wasn't a complete stranger. I know he went to her house when he went around the county selling shoes."

"Those days are over now," Mrs. Blakeley said. "And lucky for Grace, too. I understand she's helping out in the store."

"That's how I saw her again, when we were in town a couple of weeks ago."

"Anna said they've bought a house," Jonah remarked. " I think that the money we're paying her for the farm has helped out on that score."

"And Jack has a good business going," said the Reverend. "Yes, I think that things should go along quite well for that little family. It's a story with a happy ending."

After a busy week of closing school and packing, it was Saturday June 9th when almost the entire community would be attending Ed's and Bertha's wedding in the county seat. The church was filled to overflowing. During the ceremony Jonah gave Anna's hand a squeeze, and this set Anna to wondering about her future, especially where a wedding was concerned. It took much longer to go down the steps to the basement for the reception than it had the week before, but neither Anna nor Jonah seemed to mind. At last they reached the bottom.

Their reverie was interrupted when a familiar voice called

out to Anna. "I hear yer gonna take the late train to Fort Dodge." It was Liza Crawford.

"Yes," Anna replied as she looked over her shoulder to see where the voice was coming from.

"Lemme know when yer coming back. I'll be drivin' by then. Glad ta give ya a ride."

"Thanks, Liza. It's nice of you to offer." She didn't know what else to say.

"Oh, that's all right. Glad we've got a car ta help out," she shouted from the top of the steps.

"That's one ride I've got to see," Peter quietly joked as he turned to Anna who was standing near him. "By the way, I hear that Floyd'll be giving her driving lessons."

"Oh you," Milly remonstrated and then stifled a giggle.

"If anyone comes to get Anna, it'll be me," Jonah added. "I may not have a car, but at least we won't end up in a ditch."

"Now, here I was going to be first in line to give her a ride," Reverend Blakely said. "Doesn't that beat all. There's no chance for us older fellows."

"Hey, Mom! Look at that big cake!" Davey yelled. "Can I have a piece?"

"Hush," scolded Milly. "You'll get a piece after we go through the reception line."

"But we've waited so long," he continued. "This line takes forever. Did you have a line like this when you were married?"

"Oh, no. We had a very small wedding," she answered. "Now settle down."

It was early evening when Jonah waited with Anna at the depot. "This bag's a lot heavier than when you got off the train."

"Yes," she agreed.

"I wish you didn't have to go today," he continued.

"Yes."

"I'll write you as often as I can."

"Oh, I'll write you, too."

He looked at her and hesitated as he said, "I just hope that you don't meet too many good-looking fellows. I don't want to lose out to one of them."

"Oh Jonah," she laughed. "I was there last year, and I don't remember anyone like that."

"That's good to hear."

The whistle blew, and they both looked down the track as the earth shook with the vibrations of the train.

He grabbed her gloved hand with both of his. "Oh, here it comes. I'm sure sorry to see you go."

They stared silently as the oncoming behemoth screeched to a stop. Jonah grabbed her valise, and they walked to the door that opened a couple of cars away. The conductor put out the steps.

Their reverie was interrupted by the call, "Miss Swenson! Miss Swenson!" It was Davey, running pell-mell down the platform.

They turned and saw the Jensen family coming toward them.

"You don't think we'd let you leave without saying goodbye, do you?" Milly said as she rushed toward them.

Anna was genuinely happy to see them. "Oh, I'm so glad you came."

"We knew Jonah'd be here," Peter said as he scurried along carrying Lucy. "But we had to come, too. And the kids, well, they wouldn't hear of you leaving without seeing you off."

"Board!" the conductor called.

They quickly hurried to the door. Jonah helped her up the steps and shoved her valise in past the top step. The conductor shut the door, and Anna stood at its open window. "Goodbye! Goodbye!" everyone called and waved.

Slowly they disappeared out of sight, still waving and still calling out to her. It had been a wonderful year with this warm-hearted family. And then to meet Jonah. She was genuinely sad to be leaving, but she could be happy knowing that she would return in a few months.

Now to settle down and get prepared to meet her mother.